Gaby Hauptmann was born in Trossingen, Germany in 1957. She has worked as a TV producer, film script writer and has run her own press office. This is her first book.

In Search
of an
Impotent
Man

GABY HAUPTMANN

Translated by Shaun Whiteside

A *Virago* Book

Published by Virago Press 1998

First published by Piper Verlag GmbH, München 1995

Copyright © Piper Verlag GmbH, München 1995
Translation copyright © Shaun Whiteside 1998

The moral right of the author has been asserted

'Autumn' (pp. 95–6), translated by C.F. MacIntyre, in *Rilke: Selected Poems*. Berkeley, University of California Press, 1956.

'Love-Song' (pp. 298–99), translated by J.B. Leishman, in *Rilke: New Poems*, London, Hogarth Press, 1964.

A CIP catalogue record for this book is
available from the British Library

ISBN 1 86049 508 7

Typeset in Berkeley by M Rules
Printed and bound in Great Britain by
Clays Ltd, St Ives plc

Virago Press
A Division of
Little, Brown and Company (UK)
Brettenham House
Lancaster Place
London WC2E 7EN

For Mum

Thanks to Maria Hof-Glatz,
the 'herbal witch'

His eyes are fixed dully on her legs. It's a while before Carmen Legg notices. At first she thinks it's a coincidence: he's thinking about something else, staring blankly at her legs at the same time. Then she notices that he isn't thinking about something else, he's thinking about her legs. Carmen is sitting opposite him in the horseshoe-shaped arrangement of the seminar chairs. The leader of the seminar is explaining a strategy to achieve higher sales figures, and sitting opposite is someone who clearly hasn't the slightest interest in the subject. He has booked and paid for the course, certainly, but he isn't taking in a word of it. Carmen puts him to the test. She moves her legs together, then leans them slightly to one side, and rubs her nylons against each other to make a quiet, erotic sound. The man opposite blushes right down to the roots of his hair. She shifts position, rocking on her high heels, then stretching her feet forward out from under the table towards him. He kneads his hands, loosens his tie. Fool, thinks Carmen, as saliva drools out of the corners of his mouth. She focuses her attention back on the leader of the seminar. Training isn't cheap. If that guy isn't taking any of it in, then that's his lookout. She wants to get on in her profession.

That evening Carmen drives home feeling riled. She could be flattered by someone paying so much attention to her legs. But she isn't. On the contrary, she's annoyed. Like being stared at in the zoo, and by a disagreeably horny bloke like that. She sticks a Genesis tape into her car radio, and her mood slowly changes. It's weird really. This guy drives God knows how many miles to take part in a seminar, forking out a fair amount for the privilege, and by the time he drives back home all he has in his head is a few half-baked lusts, and he's struggling to remember anything about the seminar he's just attended.

Carmen Legg has always enjoyed getting ahead. She's tall and slim, with long legs and long red hair – at the age of thirty-five she's the prototype of the confident, independent woman. She drives a fast BMW with leather fixtures and air-conditioning, she has her own small insurance business and lives in a parquet-floored apartment in a listed building. She goes abroad on holiday twice a year, she's good at sports and she never lets a goal slip through. But guys like that get on her nerves. More than ever lately. Sometimes she takes a man's admiring gaze as an affront. Let him and his stupid hunting instinct leave her alone. A good hunter always finds his prey, as a new client said to her recently on the phone when she asked who had recommended her. If you take out insurance with me, you're the prey, she answered. The man on the other end of the line didn't think that was very funny at all.

Carmen has arrived home. She has to get out of the car. One of her neighbours has been kind enough to close the garage door early again. She's never been one for communal projects of any kind, let alone communal garages, but that's just the way it is in the old part of town where she lives. A light autumn rain has started to fall, and Carmen, in her thin linen suit, shivers. She gets quickly back into the car, drives into her narrow parking-space, then takes her briefcase, bag and coat and dashes over the cobbles to her building on the other side of the street, which practically merges into the other old buildings. She's glad when she finally reaches the third floor. The architects hadn't thought of high heels when they'd built those endless wooden stairs. Carmen kicks off her shoes, throws her coat, briefcase and bag on to the nearest chair and walks over to the answering-machine. She switches it on and walks into the kitchen, a room away. Aha, Marlene wanted me to go out for a meal. But that was last night, so it's well past its sell-by date. Fritzi wants to tell me a tale of love and heartbreak. Old hat as well. Fritzi's always telling tales of love and heartbreak. And what was that last one? She swings around from the fridge, walks over and plays back the tape. Herr Who? She presses rewind again. Who could that be? Herr Schrade? Never heard of him. What does he want?

'I'd like to introduce you to a friend of mine, Herr Hermann, who owns a big factory and would like to take out better insurance for his company. But Herr Hermann's only around for today. Do you think we could meet up tonight, for dinner perhaps? I'd be delighted if we could. Please call us back on 0171 255 79 00. It's six o'clock on Sunday evening. Thanks.'

Carmen pensively sits down on the arm of the chair where she had left her briefcase. What's this all about? She's never heard of either of them. And she's tired, she's exhausted, she wants a bath, a glass of wine and a good film on TV to send her off to sleep. She certainly doesn't feel like seeing Herrs Schrade and Hermann, whoever they might be. Carmen gets up again, walks to the kitchen, and listens to the other calls in the background. Her mother would like her to call back, Frau Leisner's become a mother and wants some insurance for the baby. That's nice. But this Herr Schrade is playing on her mind. It's odd that a stranger should want to bring her new business. And with a customer she doesn't know either. How did he get her home number? On the other hand the prospect of a good deal is always enticing. Especially for a company that might be under-insured. It doesn't sound so bad. Carmen picks up the telephone.

Three rings, then, 'Schrade speaking.'

'Good evening, this is Carmen Legg. You asked me to call you back?'

'You're in luck. We were just about to get out of the car!'

So what, thinks Carmen, like it would have mattered? Pompous creep.

'But it's nice of you to call anyway.'

That's better, thinks Carmen.

'Have you just got home?'

What's that got to do with him? 'Yes, I was at a seminar.'

'Great, you'll be able to give Mr Hermann some pretty good advice then, ha, ha, ha!'

Ha, ha, ha! 'Course I can. But it is a bit inconvenient at the moment. All my documentation is in the office, so it might be better if he dropped by tomorrow morning instead.'

'Perhaps, but Mr Hermann's heading off again early tomorrow, so perhaps it would be a good idea if he could take a few of your ideas away with him. Just a rough outline or whatever. Then you could discuss the rest in detail later on.'

'Hmm . . . where are you now?'

'We're still in the car, so we can be flexible. We were about to go to the Farmers' Rest, but you might have a better idea. We can pick you up if you want.'

'No that's fine. But I don't feel like driving anywhere tonight. There's a good Italian restaurant around the corner from me called the Laguna. Would that be possible?'

She hears a whispered confab, then an okay.

'St Martin Strasse? Fine, see you there at nine.'

'Fine, I'll book a table in my name.'

Shortly after nine Carmen is sitting in the Laguna, her briefcase full of documents and contracts placed inconspicuously against the leg of her table. She is resisting the temptation to enjoy a glass of red wine. Keep a clear head, she says to herself. You never know!

Two men are standing in the doorway. Carmen knows immediately that it's them. Trying too hard to be chic, too many bold colours, too old for their outfits. Okay, but that's not what matters right now.

The waiter brings the two men to her table.

Their greeting is clearly supposed to be gallant, but it's a bit old-fashioned for Carmen's liking.

'You must forgive us.' Hans Hermann kisses her hand and then smiles at her with his head tilted to one side. 'But we saw no other way. Herr Schrade has told me so much about you that I simply had to meet you in person.'

'But I don't know Herr Schrade.' Carmen casts him a quick glance. 'Or do I?'

'No,' he confirms. 'Not personally.'

'So?' Carmen inquires. 'How?'

'Klaus Wiedemann at the Rotary Club has spoken of you very highly. That's reference enough for Herr Hermann.'

'Klaus Wiedemann's our district manager.'

'Yes, I know. Herr Meinrad was very touched as well!'

'Meinrad? I had a call from a Herr Meinrad recently, I remember. Is he in the Rotary Club as well?'

'Yes, he is!'

'He's a hunter, isn't he?'

'That's right,' laughs Herr Schrade, revealing a set of expensive crowns. 'How do you know that? Did you insure him against flying bullets?'

'Sort of. He's very . . . very frank.'

'Ah.' Herr Schrade looks at Carmen with mild irritation, and beckons the waiter over.

'So, what can I do for you now?' Carmen wants to get this over with as quickly as possible and get back home. She'd be much happier with her bed than the champagne that Herr Schrade is now loudly ordering. Nouveau riche, thinks Carmen, brushing back her long hair and wishing she could finally start talking business.

'You've got beautiful hair,' says Herr Hermann in a familiar tone, leaning towards Carmen.

In a flash Carmen understands. The men just want some pleasant company, nothing more. Christ knows what Klaus Wiedemann's been telling his Rotary Club. Her first impulse is to get up and leave. Then she thinks about it. If you think you're going to have a pleasant evening with me, I'm going to turn the tables. I am going to have a good evening. And you are going to have an expensive one!

'Thank you,' says Carmen, with a guarded but grateful smile.

5

Hans Hermann is ecstatic. 'Can we turn our attention to your company now?'

'But of course. Before we do, though, why don't we drink a glass of champagne to our future together?'

'Love to!' Carmen raises her glass. Hans Hermann looks deeply and meaningfully into her eyes as they clink glasses. Herr Schrade gives her a friendly smile but is rather more guarded.

So that's what it is, thinks Carmen. Schrade wants to do a deal with Hermann, and I'm the bait. She grins. There's one thing you men still haven't understood – we women think with our heads, and you do your thinking downstairs. Well, it's going to be a cosy evening. Let the battle begin.

Carmen hardly knows herself. She tries out various glances and smiles, playing erotically with her hair and making teasing gestures with her hands. Gradually she takes out her documents, offering explanations, asking questions, quite the serious businesswoman. The constant interruptions are too much for Hans Hermann.

'Give that to me, girl. It's okay, you don't have to take so much time explaining. I'm fine about it, just let me sign!'

'But we still need to perform an insurance analysis so that we don't insure you twice over, Herr Hermann.'

'Ha, ha, twice over is better than once, am I right, Erhardt?'

Erhardt Schrade, no longer quite in control of his senses after the champagne and the third bottle of chardonnay, nods knowingly. 'Too true, Hans, too true!'

By midnight they are the last people in the restaurant, and the proprietor wants to close up for the night. They have grappas. Carmen sips and, stone-cold sober, looks at the men beside her. I'm dying to see what happens next!

'Okay, I'll get the coats,' says Hans Hermann as he stands up on rather bandy legs. 'And don't run away on me, my pretty gazelle,' he whispers loudly, giving Carmen a slightly cockeyed glance.

'How could I – without a coat?' she answers.

Hans Hermann roars a loud and randy laugh and walks to the cloakroom.

'You are thinking of a little something in return for this favour, aren't you?' Everything about Erhardt Schrade suddenly appears quite clear to her.

'What sort of something?'

'Well, you should be grateful for what I've just done for you!'

'You mean you're expecting some kind of payment?'

'I'm not short of money. Think about it!'

Carmen tells herself to calm down. Hans Hermann is standing there with the coats.

'Let me help you,' he says, holding out her coat.

'That's very sweet, thank you! And, Herr Hermann, thanks so much for the invitation. It was a very interesting evening!'

'It's going to get a lot more interesting, ha, ha!'

You bet, thinks Carmen, nodding in Erhardt Schrade's direction, as she struts to the door.

Hans Hermann has trouble keeping up with her.

'Stop, stop, not so fast. Where do you think you're going?' And more quietly: 'Shall we go to your place, or shall I call us a cab?'

Carmen turns round and says loudly, partly for the benefit of Enzo Caballo, the restaurateur, who knows her as a regular customer, 'I'm afraid you've misunderstood something.'

'What? What do you mean? I thought . . . it was obvious.'

'I think, Herr Hermann, that you got things a bit mixed-up. I'm sorry. If there's anything else you're not sure about, could you please call me at the office tomorrow. During working hours. Thanks very much for a pleasant evening, and good night!'

With these words the door swings violently shut, and she walks home through the night.

She takes a deep breath in the stairwell. What a palaver! He'll cancel everything tomorrow. Then it really will have been a complete waste of time! But, then again, maybe it won't. In which case it might have been worth it. Who knows?

7

When she reaches the top of the stairs she turns the key in the door, goes inside, kicks off her shoes, throws her briefcase on the chair, calculates as she goes into the bathroom what she's earned if everything goes smoothly, jumps through the shower, brushes her teeth, throws on a flannel night-dress and is about to get into bed. But someone is there already.

'You!'

'You could sound a bit more enthusiastic! Aren't you pleased to see me?'

'Pleased . . .? No, right now I'm completely lost for words. I thought you weren't coming till Wednesday.'

'Ah, so that's why you're so late. You thought you had the all-clear. Where have you been until this time of night?'

'Come on, Peter. Don't start all that again!'

Carmen's boyfriend, hardly visible in the darkness, sits up in bed. He has nothing on. And it's quite clear why. He wants to have sex. And he'll have come over just for that. But she's not in the mood. She possesses not even the tiniest spark of lust, just the annoyance that he's sitting there naked and unannounced in her bed.

'Hmmm!' he groans irritably, sliding under the covers.

'Don't get pissy, now! You could have called!'

'I did. Three times. But Fräulein Legg is never at home!'

'That's right, I went out at nine!'

'I noticed. Who were you with? Or is that a secret too?'

She sits down next to him on the edge of the bed and blows a kiss on to his forehead. 'Hiya!' Then she lies down beside him. 'There's no secret, Peter. I just don't want to talk about it right now. It's completely harmless, funny in one way, but annoying too. I'll tell you about it tomorrow. I'm absolutely shattered now.'

'Right,' he says moving closer. 'I can imagine!'

'You know what? You're getting on my nerves. What are you getting at with all these stupid innuendoes?'

'I've been away for ten days. And instead of being pleased to see me you tell me you're tired. I want to give you a proper welcome!'

'Yes,' she says, as she slips under the covers, 'I can imagine. Let's catch up on our welcomes tomorrow.'

'You never used to be like this.'

'I see, we're playing that old tune.'

He lies down, hurt, and pulls the blanket up to the tip of his nose. She looks at the top of his curly head. Well, perhaps I might still be in the mood, she thinks to herself, listening out for any internal stirrings.

'I might as well go, then!' he says.

No internal stirrings. Not a quiver.

'Fine, great,' she says, propping herself up on her elbows. 'Why don't you stop banging on and leave then.'

He lies where he is and thinks. Naturally, he doesn't want to get up, get dressed and drive home in the middle of the night.

'You don't love me any more,' he says sulkily. She knows that little-boy tone. She sighs.

'For God's sake, Peter, you don't have to make such a drama out of everything. I'm tired. I've had a hard day. I've been at a seminar. I've just had dinner with some clients. And that's enough for one day. Is that so hard to understand? It has nothing to do with other men.' And as an afterthought, a bit more quietly, as she gets under the covers, 'Anyway, as far as I'm concerned you can stay.'

'Why won't you have sex with me, Carmen? Did I do something wrong? Say something wrong?'

This is unbearable, she thinks, rolling on to her side. 'If you keep this up you're going to drive me out of bed.'

'The light's on in the bathroom.' Peter has pulled the covers back. She sees his penis, stiffly upright in the darkness.

'Then turn it off!' she murmurs.

She feels him reaching for her hand, guiding it towards his member.

Ah, now he's trying to pull out all the stops. He probably thinks that touching his penis is the magic way of turning me on. The cheek! She jerks her hand away.

'Why can't you just accept that I don't feel like it?'

9

'Because I can't believe it! I've never been with a woman who just didn't feel like it! You never used to be like that!'

'Does this have to disintegrate into an in-depth discussion at one o'clock in the morning?'

'I'm still wide awake.'

'How nice.'

She furiously turns her back on him.

'Tomorrow I'm going to take out a personal ad. For a man with higher things on his mind.

'Typical.'

'We can still be friends.'

He has a short crewcut, and looks at her out of the corner of his eye.

'You're serious?'

'Of course! Do you think I'd pay for it otherwise?'

'I think it's great!'

Grinning, the athletic young man picks up the ad from the counter and carries it over to a pile. Then he comes back and prints out the bill. Carmen looks at him, lips pursed, 'That is, until looking at you – I might have to rethink . . .'

The man, about twenty-five, comes closer, grins cheekily so that his white teeth flash out from his tanned face, and half-whispers, 'Let's just leave it. I'm gay.'

Carmen laughs, pays, and still has a smile on her face when she leaves the newspaper office through the revolving door.

It's unbelievable, she says to herself. Everything's upside-down. I'm looking for an impotent man, Peter wants it four times a day, this guy's gay and every third marriage ends in divorce.

Coming towards her a man in his late forties catches her radiant expression and grins back at her. Carmen smiles even more. Hardly has he walked past when he turns around and runs after her.

'Excuse me, but would you like to join me for a cup of

coffee? I – perhaps it's strange, but somehow I have the feeling I have to talk to you.'

'Are you impotent?'

'Me? Impotent? No! Why do you ask?'

'Then there's nothing going on, I'm afraid. Sorry.'

She waves at him cheerfully, and he stands there completely flummoxed. Carmen has seldom felt so free. Caviar and champagne make her feel exactly as she does this evening, sitting cosily on the sofa in old leggings, a cucumber mask on her face and a weepie on television. Oh, life can be sweet.

The phone call and the newspaper come at the same time the next morning. She's already sitting in her office, she's put on the first pot of coffee of the day and she's looked through a few customer files. Time to add on a few premiums, she is thinking, but the moment her assistant brings in the paper she moves everything else to one side and opens it, her heart beating. There it is. At the top. Centred, outlined in bold, impossible to ignore.

Wanted: Clear-thinking male

Attractive, successful 35-year-old woman
seeks man for good times,
days out, nights in, companionship.
Must be intelligent and impotent.
Send photograph to: PO Box RZ3417

She lets the phone ring longer than usual. The advertisement draws her in. Unbelievable. It's hers. Does she really want an impotent man? Yes, she's going to stick with it. From tomorrow everything's going to change, her life will take a turn for the better. She'll finally have a man who worships her, not his penis, someone she can party, live and talk with, and who will not constantly oppress her with an erect member. If that's what she wants, well excuse me, there are enough of them walking about. She takes a deep breath, in and out, and then picks up the receiver.

'Hello, Legg Insurance.'

'Lessing Solicitors speaking.'

'Hello, what can I do for you?'

'We represent Herr Hermann.'

'Oh, fine. What does that mean exactly?'

'We take care of Herr Hermann's interests!'

'I know them well . . .'

'Do you? It's about the contract you signed with him the other day.'

Thought as much, Carmen thinks. Here comes the cancellation. 'And what can I do for you?'

'Herr Hermann has signed some contracts with you, and they need to be re-examined in the light of the pre-existing agreements.'

Nicely oblique, thinks Carmen waspishly. 'And what am I to understand by that?'

'We mean that we are going to be examining the procedure in close collaboration with company management.'

'You have every right to.'

'That's what we're assuming.'

Arrogant tosser, thinks Carmen, irritably, but adds in a friendly voice, 'You've got fourteen days to consider everything. After that it's non-negotiable.'

'But we could cancel preventatively if we realise that's not enough time.'

'It would be easier to talk things through again beforehand. I might be able to help you out.'

'The problem is that Herr Hermann often signs things that later turn out to be unnecessary. It causes lots of problems for his shareholders.'

Carmen has to bite back a smile. 'Yes,' she says, 'I can fully imagine. But maybe there's more point to these contracts than anyone realises.'

'We very much hope so.'

'I'd like to repeat my offer of assistance.'

'Thank you for your suggestion. We may come back to you on that. Goodbye.'

Before Carmen can reply, they've put the phone down. So, it seems not to be as bad as she'd feared. Her chances are still fifty-fifty.

Carmen goes and gets her cup of coffee and reads over her advertisement again. Will anyone call? Could an impotent man come face to face with a woman he doesn't know?

She stirs four sugar cubes into her coffee, and the phone rings.

'I'll get it,' she calls to her assistant who is sorting the mail. 'Good morning, Legg Insurance.'

'Congratulations on your fabulous ad. I can see our relationship is well and truly over.'

'You don't have to, Peter. I told you we can stay friends.'

'Friends – what utter rubbish! You're looking for another man, so it's over. That's how I see it.'

'I'm looking for – oh, let's leave it. I don't like talking about things like this in the office anyway, you know that. Just take it the way it is. We can still be friends, it'll just be on a different level.'

'Friendship without sex doesn't work.'

'You're more pathetic than I thought.'

'Thanks. So, is that your final word on the matter?'

'For this morning, yes. If you want to talk about it some more, we can meet at the Italian tonight.'

'No thanks, Carmen. I don't think my nerves could stand it. I'd rather go boxing.'

'You don't know how to box.'

'I will by this evening, don't you worry.'

'Well, Peter, if you think . . .' She takes a sip from the cup and burns her lips. 'Ow, that's hot!'

'You don't seem to be paying attention.'

'Peter, I'm sorry, I've got to work. We can see each other this evening, or whenever, but I've got no time right now. Have a good day, ciao!'

'Stop, stop – okay, bye then.'

Carmen puts down the receiver, looks up and meets the gaze of Britta Berger, who has been watching her.

'Problems?' she asks.

'No more than usual.'

'I wouldn't have thought a woman like you would have to put up with stuff like that.'

'Why not?' Carmen looks up in astonishment. 'You're very much mistaken. I'm a woman, and I have problems like any other woman.'

She closes the paper and finally gets down to work.

The first replies from the ad arrive in her mail-box three days later. Carmen carefully runs her fingers over an A5 envelope, cheap brown paper, quite innocuous-looking, tucked among two bills, a furniture catalogue and a flier from a financial adviser. How many letters might it contain? Two, three? She tucks her post under her arm, picks up her briefcase and runs up the wooden staircase.

'Goodness, Fräulein Legg, we are athletic today!'

The eighty-year-old lady from the first floor hobbles towards her, leaning on her stick.

'Not really, Frau Gohdes. I'm just in a terrible hurry, and anyway I'm wearing flat heels today.' She stops two steps up. 'Do you need any help, Frau Gohdes?'

'No, that's kind of you, but I'm almost there.'

'I mean if you ever want anything from the shops I'm happy to get it for you.'

The old lady turns towards her and Carmen is downcast to see that there are tears in her eyes.

'That's very nice. I'd be really grateful.'

'Fine.' Carmen walks back down the two steps. 'But it's too late now. Could I get you something tomorrow?'

'If I could write you a little list – and if it really isn't too much trouble?'

'No, of course not, I'd be more than happy. I'll pick up your list tomorrow morning. Is half past eight too early?'

'Oh, no, you know, at my age you don't need much sleep. It comes of its own accord.'

'But you've still got plenty of time left!'

Carmen looks into the woman's face and wonders what

she can have been through. Her features betray a former beauty, but her skin is creased now, and her bright eyes are slightly veiled. What might she have looked like? And why does everyone call her 'Fräulein'? At eighty? Doesn't she have a husband, was she never married? Or didn't she want a husband? Was this old lady once like Carmen is now?

'Ah, well,' says Elvira Gohdes and turns to go.

'No, wait, Frau Gohdes, why don't we sit down and have a nice glass of wine together? It would be lovely to talk to you.'

'Sweetheart, what would you want with an old woman like me?'

'I'd like to talk, hear how things used to be, how people lived, what they thought, what they felt.'

'Would you? I'd be delighted. If you want, why don't you come and see me in a little while? I have to go down to the mail-box.'

'But I could do that . . .'

'No, sweetheart, don't worry, my old bones need a bit of movement too.'

'Fine. Half an hour, then!'

'Lovely!'

Strangely inspired, Carmen runs up the stairs. At the top she remembers the envelope. How stupid to arrange something for this evening. What on earth had she been thinking? She had wanted to read her letters in peace over pasta and a glass of red wine. She opens the door.

Carmen takes off her shoes, takes her post from under her arm and leaves it on the table, puts her briefcase on the chair, and goes into the bedroom to change her blouse and trousers for leggings, thick socks and a lovely big woollen pullover. So that's the evening ushered in. And now? Read the letters immediately? Or save them for last thing at night?

As a child she had always saved her biggest Christmas presents till last, and she had carried her first love letter around with her under her pullover for three days before she finally read it. Can my curiosity stand it? A bit longer?

She's a perfectionist. She walks slowly over to the table. At least she can open the brown envelope. Then she will know how many letters are inside. She runs her index finger under the gummed edge and unseals it. Two long envelopes and a letter in a small, almost square format. The sender of one of the long envelopes seems to be very stylish. Or else he wants to make a big impression. The address is written in a great flourish of black ink, with big, extravagant letters, ending in a series of curlicues. No ordinary person at any rate, Carmen muses, putting the letter down. The address on the second long envelope is typed. How unimaginative. Carmen picks up the third. Tiny printed letters, written in biro. Doesn't really say much. Let's see the name. She turns the envelope over. Heinz-Peter Schulze. Okay, she doesn't like it. The typewritten envelope bears only the initials D.S., which doesn't give her much of a clue, and the third isn't giving his name away.

Oh, my God, she looks at the clock. Frau Gohdes will be waiting. She grabs a bottle of red wine, picks up a packet of biscuits (the old lady isn't going to be one for crisps), grabs her keys and dashes downstairs. *Elvira Gohdes* reads the artistically inscribed brass plate under the bell-push. Quite unlike her own, that scribbled temporary note she put up the day she moved in, and which will doubtless remain there, unchanged, for years to come. Carmen presses the button. Their doorbells are different too. This one is a quiet, bell-like sound, three notes. Her own, upstairs, rings loudly, pitilessly. Frau Gohdes opens the door. She beams, and her face folds into a thousand wrinkles.

'You have no idea how happy I am that you've come to see me. I have visitors so rarely. Sometimes I think I've been buried alive.' She hesitates. 'But what am I saying. Please come in. You must think . . .'

Carmen follows her into the apartment. It has the same layout as her own, but the effect is quite different, as if it belongs to another era. Dark, heavy oak furniture, well-worn runners along the corridors, bulky velvet armchairs, crystal glasses carefully arranged in rows. And from the ceiling hangs an old and skilfully wrought chandelier.

'Do sit down.' Frau Gohdes points to one of the heavy chairs.

'Thanks.' Carmen suddenly feels self-conscious. What on earth can she talk to this old lady about? She can't just ask her what she used to think about men, can she?

On the way to sitting down she sees several silver-framed black and white photographs on a wall. 'May I?' She walks over to them.

Frau Gohdes follows her and sighs. 'Those are my memories. At my age you live in your memories. But a young person like yourself wouldn't understand.'

'My mother always says the same thing, and she's only in her mid-sixties.'

'So young? In my mid-sixties I suppose I'd have only just got back from Africa.'

'You were in Africa?' Carmen is startled. 'What were you doing there?'

The old lady laughs. A short, genuine, cheerful laugh. 'I spent half my life in Africa!'

'Really,' Carmen says, astonished. 'As a missionary? Or what?'

'Yes,' Elvira Gohdes laughs, 'a bit of a missionary perhaps, but not for the Catholic Church. Maybe more for that universal cause of loving your neighbour.'

'I'm overwhelmed,' says Carmen, looking more closely at the photographs. 'Are these your parents?'

'Yes.' She points to a little white smudge with her index finger. 'And that's me. In a starched white dress, I must have been two years old. And those are my brothers, my sister, that's my aunt. They're all dead. Of course.'

'And that?' Carmen points to the faded picture of a big, farm-like building.

'That's my parents' house. My grandparents built it in 1887 in German South-West Africa. My mother married a German there, and I was born in the house. You probably know

Germany acquired the country as a colony in 1884. And my grandparents were among the first settlers. They called them "the colonial masters" back then. A terrible phrase. But of course it was unjust simply to acquire people and land like that. Later I tried to make up for it with my work.'

'So what is your work?'

'I'm a doctor. I was trained in Germany, which was very unusual and difficult for a woman in those days.'

'That's really interesting.'

Carmen studies the unassuming old woman from the first floor. Behind such an ordinary human façade, you can see what's hidden.

'I've brought some wine. Do you fancy a glass?'

'I'd love some. But I've got a bottle here. I'd be happy to offer you a glass myself.'

'Why don't we do that next time?' Carmen laughs and is about to turn away from the pictures when one photograph attracts her eye. Small, yellowish, hidden behind faded roses.

A man, his face barely discernible, stands beside an aeroplane, an open-topped propeller plane.

'Was he a family friend?'

'He was a very good friend – a wonderful person.'

'Oh, and what happened?'

'Hannes died in a plane crash, not long after that picture was taken. In that very plane. It was his own.'

'I'm sorry.' Carmen looks more closely at the photograph. It's hard to make out the face. Young, probably foolhardy, wearing a pilot's cap and a white scarf.

'But it's so long ago. Didn't you ever marry?'

'I wanted to marry. But fate had other ideas in store for me. It wasn't to be.'

'Hmm. But all those years? You must have met some extraordinary men.'

Elvira walks to a drawer, brings out a silver corkscrew and takes two long-stemmed glasses from the glass cabinet.

'Oh, you know, I was never really interested in men. I was

interested in people. I didn't care whether they were male or female. And animals. I operated on animals as well, brought calves into the world if they were in breech. I did everything in the hope of making the world a better place.'

'That's extremely admirable. I only ever do what makes me feel good.'

'Of course you do. You're still young.'

'I'm thirty-five. I take it that at thirty-five you were constantly surrounded by crowds of sick people and had a great deal of responsibility.'

'People are different nowadays.'

Elvira pours the wine, the two women look at each other and clink glasses.

'Your life is very interesting, Frau Gohdes.'

'It *was* very interesting, my dear Carmen. May I call you Carmen? You can call me Elvira. It's easier.'

'That would be great. You know, it's funny, I've been living in this building for five years, and this is the first time we've really talked to each other. Isn't that awful?'

'It's the times we're living in, my darling!'

'You know, the times really are strange. The idea that a woman couldn't even look at another man once the great love of her life had been and gone – I don't think people think that way any more.'

'That's not quite what it was like. I wasn't completely abstemious – and by the way, you don't have a man in your life either, do you?'

Carmen sips her wine, savours it. 'Hmm, this isn't bad. Do you like it? I bought it as an experiment in the off-licence around the corner. Shall I get you some as well? Yes?'

Elvira takes a long sip, lets it run slowly down her throat.

'It's a bit too dry for my liking. Pleasant enough for now, but I'd prefer something a little sweeter.'

'No problem. We could have a wine-tasting. No, you're right, Elvira, I'm not married, but that doesn't mean I don't have a man in my life.'

'Yes, yes, I know,' she smiles mischievously, 'that tall, slim man who often comes late in the evening and goes again in the morning . . .'

'You've noticed?'

'Well, as I said, at my age sleep isn't so important . . . Do you think you'll get married?'

'Yes . . .' Carmen thinks for a moment. 'I don't know how to tell you this – we've split up.'

'You have? That's a shame.' She hesitates and looks inquiringly at Carmen with her slightly cloudy eyes. 'Or is it?'

'No, I would really have to tell you honestly that for some time men really have been getting on my nerves. In the end I figure you're better off doing without.'

'Ah, I've never thought that way. I met Johannes fairly late in life. It wasn't that easy in Africa, I was in my late twenties. Johannes was quite simply the man I wanted, and after him there was no one I would have dreamed of marrying.'

'Does that mean . . .' Carmen wonders whether you can talk to an eighty-year-old woman like this, 'you've never slept with a man?'

Elvira laughs heartily. 'You think we were all completely narrow-minded and living in the Stone Age. Every generation thinks that about the one before!' She shakes her head. 'The only reason people held back was because they didn't have the pill back then. You can't imagine what people did to avoid getting pregnant. Of course we slept with each other. But what are your plans now? Are you staying single, or are you looking for a new boyfriend?'

'Do you have today's paper, Elvira?'

'Of course. Why?'

'Can I go and get it?'

'It's in the kitchen on the sideboard, that room over there.'

'Thanks, I know where the kitchen is. I'll be right back.'

Carmen comes back with the paper, opens it and holds the ad up under Elvira's nose.

'Here, this is what my next boyfriend's going to be like!'

'Sorry, I can't see a thing. My reading glasses are in the kitchen too, next to the paper – could you . . .?'

'Of course!' Carmen leaps to her feet, runs outside, feeling almost like a young girl owning up to a prank to her mother.

Elvira Gohdes puts on her glasses and attentively reads the ad. She takes her time. Carmen sits excitedly opposite her and sips her wine.

'You wrote this?'

'Yes! What do you think?'

'Incredible!'

Carmen hesitates. 'Incredibly bad?'

'Incredibly good. Fantastic. I'd never have thought of anything like it!' She laughs at the top of her voice.

Carmen joins in, quietly at first, then they both laugh loud and long.

'Oh, God, what a mad world. Have you had a reply?'

'Yes, but I haven't read them yet.'

'No? Why not?'

'I haven't got round to it – I'd just got the letters out of the box when I met you on the stairs.'

'And you've managed to come and see me and leave the letters behind?'

'I did. I thought you were more important.'

'That's nice, but don't you think it's time to open them?'

'You mean . . .?'

'If you're not embarrassed?'

'Me? Why would I be? It's a great idea, I'll be right back.'

'I'll make us some sandwiches.'

Elvira studies the handwriting and comes to the same conclusion as Carmen. They should open the letter with the typewritten address first.

There is a silver letter-opener in front of Carmen, and she smiles at Elvira's discreet style. To the manner born.

She opens the envelope and takes out a typewritten letter.

'My goodness, you don't write personal letters with a typewriter,' Elvira says, aghast. 'Is there a picture?'

Carmen's fingers reach about inside the envelope. There is. A man of about sixty kneeling with his boxer dog on the grass in front of a detached house.

'Hmm, there's a certain likeness there,' Elvira says, poker-faced, and Carmen bursts out laughing.

'I can't bear it. They say a dog and its master grow more alike over the years, just like married couples! Let's drink to that.'

They drink, Elvira fills their glasses, hands her a plate with four sandwiches on it. 'What does it say?'

Carmen takes a bite out of a ham sandwich, has another sip of wine, wipes her mouth with the napkin – starched white linen, of course – and starts to read:

Dearest Madam,

You are addressing a problem that I have never dared mention to anyone. My dog Amoritta is the only one I have ever talked to about my problem. It's not that a man is defined by whether he can or can't do it, as it were, but it is hard to deal with it if he can't. Particularly if you're on your own as I am, if you have an old circle of friends and you're always being asked why you're not living with a woman. But what woman could I ever satisfy? Who would want a eunuch like myself? I can't tell a woman I've just met that I can't get it up, as it were. And I've tried time and again. I've thought it might be the woman's fault. Now I know, a woman like yourself is the angel I've been waiting for. I beg you, write back to me, phone me, let's meet. I would be the happiest man alive.

With very best wishes
Dieter Suske.

Carmen glances up.

Elvira's head is tilted to one side and she sips her wine. 'Pathetic. Wouldn't have lasted a week in Africa!'

Carmen laughs. 'Maybe there's no impotence in Africa!'

'I can't say I've checked the matter that closely. The people who came to me had other problems. Carbuncles, severed veins, broken bones, septic wounds . . .'

'Thanks. Shall we read the next letter?'

'So, he's a No. Or am I being over-hasty? What do you think, Carmen?'

'He's a No. No!'

'Okay, let's proceed!'

Carmen opens the square envelope with the capital letters.

Hey girl,

I don't know why you want to save me, but don't waste your words: just get on with it. I've been having problems for two years. After I caught my partner in bed with my best friend I wanted to show her who was boss – and that was that. My therapist has told me I've never recovered from the shock. And it's true that it really was a shock – which I don't believe – but okay – then I'll never get over it on my own. So, my liberator, come to me. I'm the impotent man you're looking for, and with any luck with your help I'll soon be ready for bedtime action once again. Ring me, give me a call, I'm looking forward to hearing from you.

Yours

Heinz-Peter Schulze.

Elvira looks up, Carmen puts down the letter. 'Do I have to do that? He's missed the point somehow. He wants me to rescue him? So who am I? Have I just got rid of one man, only to start on reconstruction work with another? It would be crazy, Elvira!'

'Absolutely! Is there a picture?'

Carmen shakes the envelope.

'He's a coward too. His girlfriend will have slept with his friend for a reason. He probably drives a Manta and wears a silver ring in his nose.'

'What?'

'Just a joke, Elvira, but by their works shall ye know them . . . what do you think?'

'Absolutely not!'

'Okay, then here's the last one. Let's hope he's interesting, or the whole business will have been a complete waste of time!'

'You'll get other replies. And anyway – you can run ads like that again.'

'You really think so?'

'Of course, you're not the kind of person to give up easily, are you?'

'Not normally, you're right. So, now, Mr Unknown Person, our last hope.'

Carmen slowly and carefully opens the letter, takes another quick sip from her glass and then pulls out a letter handwritten on hand-made paper.

'The man's got style,' Elvira nods admiringly.

Dear Advertiser

For a long time I wondered whether your ad was serious or not. Then it occurred to me that you don't make a joke about something like that – what woman would be looking for an impotent man if she didn't want to have one?

So: I've been impotent for about five years, and I've come to terms with it. I compensate for it with sport, with evenings out with my friends, with visits to the theatre or the opera. I enjoy life and must admit that I live extravagantly. This may be my little quirk, but perhaps you should find that out for yourself. I liked your advertisement, I am a 'clear-thinking male', but I'm not just a thinker. I like to savour all the everyday things in life.

I would be delighted to meet you.

I enclose a photograph. I am slim, 6 ft 2 in., 13 stone, fifty years old, a non-smoker. I love wine and I am an animal-lover.

Please grant me the pleasure of asking you out for a glass of wine in the near future,

Yours,

Stefan Kaltenstein

'That sounds better!' Elvira leans forward. 'Particularly with that name. I once knew a Kaltenstein – but it was a long time ago. Can I see the photograph?' She pulls her glasses down the bridge of her nose and studies the picture that Carmen hands her. 'He's good-looking. Unfortunately he's a bit too young or I could fancy him myself.'

'Really? We could place an ad for you too!'

The strangest ideas come into Carmen's mind. She can see it already: Lively eighty-year-old seeks sprightly partner, or whatever. Carmen takes another look at the photograph.

A striking male face in large format, crisp-cut short hair, full mouth, blue eyes.

'That man can't be impotent. It's impossible,' says Elvira, shaking her head. 'That's not how I've ever imagined an impotent man!'

'So how have you then?' Carmen takes the picture back and looks at it closely. Does she fancy him, does he do anything for her? She doesn't feel anything. And she doesn't have to either, she says to herself, because that's not what it's about.

'Well really, I don't know. I've never really thought about it . . . just differently!'

'Aha,' laughs Carmen. 'What do you think? Should I meet him?'

'Straightaway! Don't waste a minute!'

'Okay, Elvira. I'll tell you all about it.'

'What do you mean, you'll tell me? Just bring him along!'

And Carmen has to laugh.

'That's a scream. I'd always thought you were this quiet little mouse, you'd probably been dumped by a man, then you'd been a teacher until you were sixty-five and then that was that, and tonight I learn that you were an old colonial, had worked as a bush doctor and probably had a pilot's licence – didn't you?'

'If you want to help people in Africa it's the only way!'

'See, and now you're trying to steal my impotent men. Enough already!'

'Fine. I'll write that shopping list for you. Then I won't

have to keep popping down to that flashy delicatessen down the road. The old man there's over sixty!'

'Tsk,' Carmen shakes her head. 'The delicatessen. Nothing surprises me any more. I'm immune to surprises tonight.'

'And are you immune to the fact that your boyfriend went upstairs half an hour ago, and that he's probably waiting for you in a far from impotent state?'

'What? How do you know?'

'I know his step. He always walks quietly and quickly – like a man with expectations.'

'Well, I'll satisfy them pretty smartish. He'll be out of that door in a flash. The cheek, showing up like that. He can give me back his key.'

Elvira writes a few things on the note-pad and pushes it over to Carmen. 'Don't be too hard on him – he's only a man, you know.'

Carmen picks up her three letters and the shopping list, and kisses Elvira Gohdes on both cheeks. 'Thanks for the advice – and it was nice to have met you. You've really enriched my life.'

'Glad to be of help. And many thanks for everything – and if your boyfriend needs a bed for the night, send him on down to me!'

'Ha,' laughs Carmen. 'I can see I'll have to keep an eye on you.'

By the time Carmen gets upstairs she has thought up a few choice phrases. She's in a good mood, exhilarated, she's enjoyed her evening with Elvira Gohdes. She really doesn't want to talk things over with Peter. She'd rather dream a while, reread Stefan Kaltenstein's letter, imagine what kind of man he might be. Peter no longer belongs to her new world. She opens the door and noisily enters the flat. The living-room is empty. Almost bursting with rage she walks into the bedroom. He wouldn't have the gall . . . but he isn't there either. She looks in the kitchen, in the bathroom, nothing. She even tries the handle of the toilet door. Elvira must have been mistaken, she thinks, and goes back into the living-room.

Then she sees a white envelope on the table. She hadn't noticed it before. She tears it open. In it is the key to her apartment and a postcard with a cartoon of two mice sitting on a bed, one with a condom pulled over its nose, saying to the other, 'Did it come with an instruction manual?' Carmen laughs. On the back Peter has written:

> If you ever need a man again, just call me. If I know you, it won't be long. I've always loved you very much, and still love you. But at least an impotent man won't take anything from me. That's a comfort. So do what you have to do, and call me once the spectre has passed.
> With kisses
>
>   Peter

Hmm, thinks Carmen. Peter has sent her thoughts spinning into complete confusion. She really wants to concentrate on Stefan, and here's Peter weaselling his way in again and praising sexuality to the skies.

Carmen sits excitedly on the pavement terrace of the little café. She has just been back to the paper and asked for more replies. They would be sent on to her anyway, she was told. But Carmen wanted to take them straightaway. Who knows how long the post would take? So the woman rose irritably to her feet. There were four letters.

'That many?' Carmen was delighted.

The woman shrugged her shoulders.

'You should be pleased I'm picking them up, I've saved you the postage,' Carmen said cheerfully.

'It's not my money,' the young woman replied bluntly.

'It's an opinion.' Carmen nodded approvingly. 'Good for you.' She turned around and left.

Carmen is studying the three envelopes in front of her on the café table. But not with as much interest as the first three

27

yesterday. And rather distractedly, because she has made a date with Stefan Kaltenstein. He sounded very pleasant on the phone. Sonorous voice, well-chosen language and yet spontaneously witty.

She was going to wear a red linen dress so that he would recognise her, she told him, giving him a brief description of herself.

'Why are you looking for an impotent man?' he finally wanted to know.

'Because I'm fed up with potent men,' she replied.

'Till Monday then. Look forward to it.'

'Yes, till Monday.'

A dark blue Jaguar drives slowly past the café. Inconspicuously Carmen tries to spot something inside, but she can't because the windows are heavily tinted.

Don't keep expecting the best to come along straightaway, she says, pulling herself together. But she gives him about five minutes to turn up, including time to find a parking place. And sure enough. Her Irish coffee is just being served when a man walks through the rows of tables. She recognises him immediately. Tall, slim, the striking face, a red polo shirt, light-coloured linen trousers.

Some women cast secret glances at him.

Carmen grins. If you knew . . . But she's excited now. He's good-looking. He looks like a man of the world. Experienced, successful, confident.

Carmen is almost sorry he's impotent.

It's a strange feeling, weighing a man up but taking that ulterior motive totally out of the equation.

Pull yourself together, Carmen Legg, she says to herself. This is someone who doesn't want to get you into bed. It's brilliant!

She raises her arm and waves.

He sees her, nods and smiles and makes for her table.

Carmen has butterflies in her stomach. What am I going to talk about?

'Good afternoon, I'm Stefan Kaltenstein.'

'Hi, Carmen Legg, please sit down, Herr Kaltenstein!'

They shake hands and Stefan Kaltenstein sits down opposite her.

'It's the first time I've met a woman in such circumstances,' he says, shaking his head slightly. 'I'm still amazed at myself!'

'Really?' laughs Carmen. 'I can imagine that. I admire your courage.'

'Now that I've seen you and know that you're a serious kind of person, I'm pleased.'

'Oh God – what did you expect?'

He hesitates briefly. 'I don't really know, maybe a toothless, doughy creature with a grey face and hairs on her chest!'

'Ha.' Carmen picks up her Irish coffee and sucks on the straw, giving him a mischievous smile. 'I think,' she says, as she slurps more coffee through her straw, 'I think almost any woman would emerge well from that comparison.'

'But you compare particularly well.'

'Thanks, I'll take that as a compliment.'

'It's the truth. And that makes me even more suspicious. With an ugly woman I'd have understood why she was looking for a solid relationship. But what about you?'

'Are you looking for the catch?'

'I probably am,' he says and beckons the waiter.

'There isn't one. I told you on the phone. I'm simply looking for a man who's imaginative, who likes good conversation, who enjoys life and doesn't have just one thing on his mind night and day. It can really get on your nerves.'

'Good afternoon, sir, what can I get you?' The waiter disturbs the flow of Carmen's thoughts. She was in full flight.

'The same as the lady, please. And a strawberry tart. Do you have strawberry tart?'

'Yes, but plums are in season, and I could offer you a wonderfully fresh plum tart.'

'No doubt, but thanks, I'll stick with the strawberries. Can I assume that they're fresh as well?'

'Of course, of course – certainly, sir. Of course. I'll bring it right away.'

Carmen studies Stefan. Not someone to be fobbed off. Not someone easily riled. His hands, long-fingered and well manicured, lie peacefully on the table. He gives the full impression of a man with everything under control. And then nature goes and plays a trick on him. Who knows, maybe that's why?

'Good.' He looks at her again, straight into her eyes, like a man who wants to seduce a woman quickly. 'You may be right about all that. But don't you think that people – even you – sometimes crave an equal partner? What would you do then? Be unfaithful?'

'Unfaithful?' Carmen thinks it's a strange word in the context.

'Yes,' he stresses. 'Would you want another partner for sex?'

'I hadn't thought about that,' she says evasively.

'Well, you see, you should. Then imagine that impotent people have feelings as well. If you were my girlfriend and you wanted to go with another man anyway, I'd be very hurt.'

Carmen starts feeling uncomfortable. She hasn't thought all this through. It's true, at some point she wouldn't entirely rule it out. Peter had been quite right to see that.

'So you don't know?' he asks, slightly screwing up his eyes. Because of the low autumn sun, or because he's rather critical by nature?

'Maybe we should get to know each other a little better,' she says, trying to remedy the situation.

'No, Carmen. First you have to be sure what you want. I wouldn't want to fall in love with you only for you to break my heart.' He looks at her. Carmen tries to find a suitable answer. 'And you're the kind of person someone could fall in love with,' he continues.

'Thanks. But so are you!'

'Nice of you to say so. But can I make a suggestion. Let's just talk a while, about God and the world, let's drink our Irish coffees and eat our tart – would you like one? You

wouldn't? No? Not even a fresh plum tart? – and then go our
separate ways. As soon as you're clear what you want, call me.
Simple as that.'

Carmen nods. With the best will in the world, she can't
think of a single thing to say. To assure him that she never
wants to sleep with another man again wouldn't be right.
Now and again, with one man or another – why not? But,
Stefan is right, she hasn't thought any of it through properly.
Either that or this guy is seeing things from too narrow a per-
spective. That'll be it. It's obvious, really, that a woman can't be
faithful to an impotent man for a lifetime.

They talk of trivia over Irish coffee and strawberry tart and
walk together to the car park.

She was right. The Jaguar is his. It suits him. They both
have something of the English landed gentry about them.

They say goodbye with a firm handshake.

In the car she puts the GENESIS cassette into the player.
That man is much too straight. He's so straight she's sure all
his books will be lined up neatly on shelves at home. He
probably lives in a castle, and his name isn't Stefan
Kaltenstein, but Stefan Graf Kaltenstein or something like
that. And I would always be dancing around nicely in my
little dress, playing the perfect hostess. No, I think I'll spare
myself the pleasure.

She drives into her garage, the garage door is open, what a
surprise, and walks slowly across the street. When she's wearing high heels, she always tries to step on the middle of the
cobbles and not get stuck in the cracks. For Carmen, cobbles
are the most obvious sign that men are in charge of urban
planning. If sports car drivers can take city authorities to
court because their low-slung cars get stuck on the sleeping
policemen in go-slow zones, how would Germany's mayors
feel if thousands of women turned up and threw their broken
heels down on their polished tables? The city authorities
would go bankrupt! They are already, anyway, thinks Carmen,
looking up and seeing Elvira at the window.

She waves, beckoning her to drop by.

Hardly has Elvira's door closed, and Carmen is standing in the living-room of a bygone age, then explodes, 'It was a total disaster! Elvira. I behaved like an idiot!'

'Goodness, my darling, what's the matter? Your meeting with Stefan Kaltenstein?'

Carmen drops down on to the sofa, close to tears. 'Can you imagine? A man out of an oil painting – and he's impotent? Isn't that terrible?'

Elvira puts two wine glasses on the table. 'But that's what you wanted, Carmen!'

Carmen sees the wine glasses and shakes her head. 'But not like that. I didn't want it like that – Elvira, I can't drink today. I don't suppose you've got any antacid?'

'Oh, it must have gone really badly. Do you want to talk about it?'

Carmen looks up and nods: 'That's why I came. I feel so, I don't know, I feel like half a person. As if this Stefan was a whole man and I was half a woman. He made me feel like a little schoolgirl talking about something she doesn't really understand. And the worst thing is, Elvira, he was right.'

'What sort of a man is he, this Herr Kaltenstein?'

'It's hard to explain, Elvira. He's most certainly the kind of man any woman would want. But I think he's damned difficult as well. Such a sensitive flower – I think he can hear the grass growing.'

'Maybe his impotence made him that way.'

'Goodness, I hope they don't all have problems like that. Things could get stressful.'

And then Carmen tells her the gory details of her meeting. Elvira nods and says, finally, that she can understand him.

'Yes,' Carmen agrees. 'But what can I do? I can't guarantee that I'm never going to have another sexual urge. I'm not impotent, after all.'

'That's true. But if you choose between potent and impotent and you come out in favour of impotent, you've got to stick with it!'

'Elvira, I think I'm going to go upstairs now. I'm going to

have a bath, lie down in bed, read the four new letters and think about myself.'

'You've got some more replies?'

'Yes, I'll leave them in your mail-box tomorrow morning, or even better – outside your door.'

'Under the mat. You never know.'

'Yes,' and Carmen's spirits pick up, 'that would be something, if Frau Domhan from next door read your post. Her world would be turned upside-down.'

'You're right. She would probably place an ad with just the opposite message – or do you think Herr Domhan's still up to it?'

'Sure,' answers Carmen as she leaves, 'the world is topsy-turvy. Whichever way you have it, it's never right.'

The second letter appeals to Carmen. The first was so overheated and suggestive that she couldn't even read it all. The second writer seems youthful and fresh. He writes with such euphoria that he gives the impression that impotence is the best thing that could ever happen to a man. Carmen has made some tea, and is sitting at an angle on the couch, her knees drawn up. She sips her tea and bites into a sandwich she bought that afternoon. I hope he can cook, she thinks. Frederic Donner, with a phone number underneath. She likes his name as well. On the spur of the moment she picks up the phone from the coffee table in front of her, and dials the number.

'Donner.'

A woman's voice. My good God, is he married? Instinctively, she hangs up. Her heart is leaping into her throat. And it isn't great etiquette to put the phone down without speaking, she chides herself. Her thoughts run hither and thither. Could an impotent man be married? Of course he could! And have replied to her advertisement? Why not? She had sometimes been tempted, despite her relationship with Peter, to reply to particularly appealing advertisements. She never did – but that's a different matter. Why does he give her his phone number? A box number would have made more sense in the circumstances.

33

She drinks some tea. What'll I do now? The sandwich has almost disappeared, automatically devoured. She bravely picks up the receiver again.

The same voice answers.

'Donner.'

'Hello, excuse me, could I speak to Herr Donner?'

'Frederic?'

'Yes, if it's possible?'

'Of course it's possible, if he happens to be in – hold on a second.'

Carmen hears the woman calling for Frederic, hears a faint male voice, then the woman is on the phone again, 'Here you are.'

'Thank you very much,' Carmen answers, but the woman has already put her phone down.

A male voice answers. 'Donner?'

'This is Carmen Legg, good evening, sorry for disturbing you so late . . .'

'If you could give me a clue who you are, you mightn't disturb me quite so much . . .'

'Okay, of course, my name means nothing to you – you replied to my ad!'

Short pause. 'Ah yes, now I know!'

Another short pause, and Carmen wonders what to say next. 'I thought I'd give you a call . . .' Stupid thing to say, she thinks, but nothing smarter comes to mind.

'That's kind of you.'

Another pause. Now Carmen is starting to get annoyed. Then an idea comes to her. 'Are you not alone? Is it hard for you to talk?'

'Pretty much, yes!' So he is married, she thinks, cursing the fact that she called him in the first place.

'But we can meet up,' he says.

Carmen is completely taken aback. 'Really? When?'

'Today if you want.'

'Today?' She looks down at herself. 'But I'm lying on the couch in my lazing-around-the-house clothes.'

'So you're the kind of person who has to look smart all the time . . .?'

Well yes, actually, she thinks. 'No, actually, I'm not.'

'So, what's the problem?'

She doesn't want to haggle over the time of day, given that she phoned him: 'So where would you like to meet?'

'The best thing would be for me to come over to your place, then you won't have to move.'

'Okay.' Does that suit me, or does it not suit me? It doesn't really! A strange man?

'What time?' she asks.

'Right now, just tell me the address . . .'

'Number 7 Zur Zinne.'

'That's in the middle of the old town, isn't it?'

'Yes, just around the corner from the Laguna, an Italian restaurant, if you know it.'

'Great, I'll be there in a tick.' Down goes the phone.

Carmen slowly replaces the receiver.

Then she jumps to her feet, dashes into the bathroom, puts on a bit of make-up, takes light-coloured woollen leggings and a big pullover the same colour from the cupboard and quickly pulls them on. The pullover has an overlapping V-neck, very sexy. She plucks at it for a moment, then shakes her head. An old habit. It's not important for him to think she's attractive. He should think she's nice. And she should think the same about him. That's all.

She runs into the kitchen and looks in the fridge.

What can she offer him?

There's champagne, wine, beer, mineral water, orange juice. Half a dozen eggs, some sausages for breakfast, a little bit of butter. Nothing too exciting. But he can eat somewhere else. She'll wait and see what he wants.

Carmen runs back to the phone. She dials 3 13 57. 'Elvira, guess what, I've got a visitor coming.'

'Really? Who is it?'

'I'm sorry, did I wake you? It's ten o'clock, and in the heat of the moment I never thought!'

'No, you know, old people like me . . .'

'Yes, yes, I know,' Carmen interrupts her impatiently, 'but just imagine, I called someone, and now he's coming over.'

'Who is it?'

'Frederic Donner. I was going to leave you his letter tomorrow, so you haven't read it yet.'

'Oh, that's exciting! Did he sound that good?'

'Yes, I think so.'

'And the others?'

'The first one was useless, and I haven't got to the others yet!'

'So it must have been exciting.'

'Yes, it was . . . Elvira?'

'Yes?'

'If I haven't called you by midnight, could you come round and take a look? Or at least ring?'

'You or the police?'

Carmen laughs.

'No, seriously, are you at all worried?'

'No, not really, but you never know . . . or is midnight too late for you?'

'No, you know . . .'

'Yes, thanks, I know,' Carmen laughs. 'You're an angel, Elvira. I'm really pleased to have met you.'

'The pleasure's all mine.'

They finish their call, Carmen runs off again, tidies something away here, puts something in a different place there.

No flowers. Why do I never buy myself flowers, she thinks, looking around.

From tomorrow things will be different!

She goes into the bathroom and quickly brushes her teeth, and then there's a ring at the door.

He can't live far away – she hastily rinses. One last look in the mirror. Stop, toothpaste in the corner of her mouth. She quickly damps the corner of a towel and wipes it. Now she has to do her lipstick. The doorbell rings again. She runs to the door and presses the buzzer.

Three floors, that takes some time.

Back to the bedroom, quick bit of lipstick.

He's knocking at the door.

Goodness, he's quick.

She walks evenly to the door. Just don't look hassled or made-up. That would be fatal.

She opens the door.

In front of her stands a young man in a drenched brown leather jacket. Short black hair points wetly in all directions, raindrops dangling in it. His jeans are wet too.

'My goodness,' Carmen can't help saying. 'Is it raining?'

'Raining's not the word. It's leading up to Judgement Day out there!'

'Really?' Slightly confused, Carmen takes a step back. What did he mean by that? Is he some kind of religious fanatic? Belongs to some dubious sect? Polygamy rather than impotence?

'What's up? Can I come in?'

'Sorry, of course, please do!'

She steps aside and takes his leather jacket. It's a dark brown, smooth leather blouson with a belt around the waist and broad, reinforced shoulders.

'Did you come on your bike?'

'In the old town it's quicker than the car. But I hadn't expected a downpour like that.'

'Your jeans are wet through.'

He looks down. 'I can always take them off!'

Help, Elvira, Carmen thinks, and points to the living-room. 'This way, please.'

She walks behind him.

His broad shoulders indicate that he works out. Despite the time of year, he wears a sleeveless T-shirt revealing an expanse of brown skin.

'Lovely,' he stands where he is and looks around, 'no, really lovely!' Then he walks over to the couch and drops into it.

Carmen is undecided. She can't work out what's going on.

'What can I offer you to drink?' she asks, using the formal word for 'you'.

'Can't we forget the formalities? You're a mere thirty-five, I'm a mature twenty-eight, so surely we don't need to bother with all that?'

Christ, he's so young, Carmen thinks, glancing at him again. And that body? What's that supposed to be? Impotent?

'So,' she says, adapting to his abrupt manner of speech. 'Beer, wine, champagne, fruit juice?'

'Mineral water, if you've got any. I've got to ride home.'

He looks at her. 'Or do I?'

'Sure,' she answers quickly. What's this all about? Was that a suggestion that he's not impotent at all, or can he be breezy about things like that because he is?

She reaches into the fridge for the bottle of mineral water and gets two glasses. She rarely serves guests like this. She puts them both down on the table and sits down facing him.

'So,' he begins questioningly.

'What?'

'What?' he copies her, raising his eyebrows. 'What's up with you that you need an impotent man?'

'Can I ask you a question first?'

'As long as you don't forget mine . . .'

'Are you married?'

Frederic runs all ten fingers through his short hair. Drops of water fall off and his hair stands up at even more perverse angles than before. 'What makes you think that?'

'A woman answered your phone just now.'

'Of course, Clara Donner – my sister. My parents were killed in a car crash, and the house was too big for one person on their own. So we divided it up between us. We get on okay – so why not?'

'I see, I'm sorry!' Carmen fills the glasses. Is his parents' death the cause of his impotence? A shock? Or perhaps he had a relationship with his sister after that, and his bad conscience deprived him of his potency?

'When did that thing with your parents happen?' she asks.

'Six years ago. But let's talk about something else. About

why you're looking for an impotent man. I mean, why don't you get a potent one and throw him out when it gets too much for you? You could manage that, surely.'

'I'm amazed to hear something like that coming from a man!'

'Equal rights for everyone. Men do things like that as well. Or at least so I dimly remember.'

Carmen has to laugh and, to hide it, takes a large gulp from her glass.

'I don't want a potent man any more. And when I look at you, I'm sorry, but I really don't believe you,' she says, looking at his body. 'You look so incredibly masculine. I simply can't imagine you being impotent!'

'I'll prove it.'

'How?' Carmen looks at him in astonishment. 'Prove it? How?'

'Take your clothes off!' he says curtly.

'Excuse me?'

'Take your clothes off!'

'I can't just take my clothes off in front of a man I don't know!'

'Why not? Nothing's going to happen!'

'How can I be sure of that?'

'You can't! That's why I want to prove it to you!'

Carmen picks up her glass again. 'I don't know, I'll feel funny just taking my clothes off.'

'You don't have to take them all off. Just down to your bra and panties. Any normal man would leap on you. You'll see – I won't!'

Elvira, help, Carmen pleads silently, what am I doing? 'But,' she says, automatically pulling the neck of her pullover closer together, 'don't you understand? I've only known you for half an hour. I don't know whether you're telling me the truth, and imagine if I were to take my clothes off and you . . .'

'Great! You think I'd pounce on you? If that happens I'll buy you a Ferrari. I'll put it in writing.'

Carmen can't help laughing again. She thinks about it. 'And if someone else was present? I've got a friend who lives only two floors below. She could come up straightaway.'

'I think a chaperone would make the situation really peculiar.' He shakes his head. 'In those conditions not even a highly potent man would get a hard-on!'

Carmen rubs her nose with her forefinger. 'You could be right there!' She imagines Elvira as a severe guardian of her morals, and laughs herself hoarse. Frederic raises one eyebrow and waits.

'Do you think up things like this very often?' she asks finally.

'No, this is the first time. But until now no one's ever demanded proof.' He pours himself some more water and puts the empty bottle on the table. 'Is there any more?'

'Water? Or do you mean flavoured water? Tea, for example? It would certainly do you good, you're soaked to the skin!'

'Can you do hunter's tea?'

'What's that, with rum, or what?'

'Rum and water, half and half, and loads of sugar.'

'Oh God, I just wanted to get through today.'

'I'm only doing it for you. You might relax a bit and stop being so incredibly uptight.'

'Me, uptight? You're off your head.' Carmen laughs again. She feels good, and she likes Frederic.

'I know what. Let's make the tea together, drink it, and then organise a fashion show. I'll put on something from my sexy drawer, and we'll see.'

They stand in the kitchen and fool around like children. Frederic is responsible for the hot water and the sugar, and Carmen pours in the rum. They walk back into the living-room with two steaming mugs.

'You're sweet, Carmen. I could fall in love with you, really! Why didn't you ring before? Six years ago everything would have been different!'

40　　The tone of his voice becomes threateningly serious.

Carmen doesn't feel like a serious conversation. Not tonight. She would like to keep the light, easy mood going.

'Six years ago you would have been much too young for me. What mature woman would go out with a twenty-two-year-old whipper-snapper?'

He laughs again, flashing his white teeth.

'Sit down, drink your tea, I'll be right back.'

Carmen pushes him into the chair, takes her tea with her and disappears into the bedroom. She doesn't want to overdo it, but she'd like to challenge him a bit. In her wardrobe she has a long black cat-suit that shows off her figure to good effect, but still leaves her covered up from throat to ankles. And with a wide belt and high heels – it would get any man going. And if it doesn't, then everything's fine!

She changes her clothes quickly, reflecting that she has never dressed up for Peter like this. But it wouldn't have been necessary, he'd have looked right through her outfit and seen nothing but her bum and her bosom. She puts on a bit of red lipstick and brushes her long hair. And what if he's gone when I get back, and with him my purse, cheque cards and cheques? The idea occurs to her as she walks out through the door. But she doesn't believe it. Somehow, for some unimaginable reason, she trusts him.

He has switched the chair for the couch, and is sitting comfortably in the corner with his legs up, his shoes beside him, and the fat mug of tea warming between his hands.

'Christ almighty!' he says, nodding appreciatively. 'A bit much for the man in the street. He'd have come before he even got a hard-on!'

Carmen laughs. The Genesis cassette is playing one of her favourite songs, and she dances to it.

'This is too much even for me,' he says, holding his hand dramatically in front of his face, but blinking through his fingers.

'You!' Carmen threatens him with her finger, hesitates for a moment and then asks curiously, 'Anything happening?'

'Take a look for yourself!'

Carmen comes closer, but stops a respectable distance away.

'You can't see it from there!' Frederic pulls down the corners of his mouth and shakes his head.

'I can't see it anyway!' Carmen points to his trousers. 'Or do you think I've got X-ray eyes?'

'Oh come on.' Frederic looks down at himself. 'What's the problem?'

'Take off your trousers!'

'Do what?'

'Oh yeah? So sensitive all of a sudden? A moment ago you were going to do that and you'd hardly got through the door.'

'That was spontaneous.'

Carmen laughs loudly. 'And now? What's the problem? I assume you're wearing something underneath.'

'Can I just check that my undies are decent today?'

Carmen totters towards him on her high heels.

'Don't be like that, I've played my part.'

'Only halfway,' he says sulkily.

'Anyway.' Carmen is really starting to enjoy this. 'It's your turn now!'

'Hmm.' Frederic undoes his belt, then the button and, before he reaches for his zip, he reaches an inch or so into his underpants with his thumb and forefinger.

'That was a piece of luck,' he says then and exhales noisily, 'I'm wearing a really elegant pair today!'

What he reveals is a pair of silk boxer shorts in light grey and claret stripes. Frederic strips his jeans down over his legs, then gets to his feet and holds the wet trousers far away from himself by their loops. 'Can I take the chance to hang these over a heater somewhere? They might dry out.'

'I see – and how long were we expecting to stay?' Carmen tilts her head to one side.

'Until I've convinced you,' he answers and walks over to one of the radiators with the trousers.

'I could chuck them in the drier if you like.' Carmen walks a few steps behind him.

'What a waste of energy. Over a pair of trousers – just think!'

She stops and looks at him. She likes what she sees: brown, hairy legs, the muscles of his calves standing out as he moves. A sexy bum, emphasised rather than concealed by his silk shorts. Frederic carefully hangs up the jeans and comes back to her. She examines him from the front. His thighs also betray signs of him working out. Only the bit just above them appears lifeless. Beneath the fine silk nothing, nothing at all, raises its head.

'Can you see now?' he asks, and she almost blushes.

'Sit down, and I'll see what I can do.'

'I'm happy to have a look, but you'll see – I'm absolutely the right man for you. We'll spend the next sixty years together, virginally side by side.'

'How awful!' says Carmen – it slips out. Horrified, she claps her hand over her mouth as if to unsay it. 'Sorry, but I'd already seen us lying together as dried-up mummies. Sex isn't everything. You can just like each other,' she adds. 'You can take each other in your arms, stroke each other, cuddle, love each other. You don't have to be constantly humping each other.' She sits next to him on the couch.

'Come on, help me out of my cat-suit.' He starts undoing the little buttons on her back. They're actually more for decoration, they're not really needed for putting it on and taking it off, but she likes this little game.

Frederic opens one button after another, kissing her on her bare shoulder, kissing her lower and lower until he reaches the last button at waist level. Carmen stretches. It's a pleasant, very erotic feeling. His hands, firm and dry, pull the top part forward, and he reaches for her breasts with both hands. Gooseflesh runs down her back. Ah, that's nice, that's good. Frederic brushes her long hair forward and gently kisses her neck, while his hands gently stroke her nipples. They become erect, her skin is firm and expectant. Carmen reaches for his penis. Frederic quivers slightly, but acquiesces. It isn't small, it's quite big, but it lies indifferently against his thigh. Carmen massages it for a while with her hands, then bends down and takes it in her mouth. She has never kissed a flaccid penis, but she no longer wants to believe that an athlete like this guy can't be excited. And then there's her pride to think of. This is impossible, he's got to react to her.

His right hand slides down between her legs. He finds her clitoris and strokes it so expertly that Carmen moans. She works him with her mouth, tongue and both hands, but it's all in vain. Nothing moves, absolutely nothing.

'You'd love it now!' he says finally, and Carmen feels as if she's been caught out.

She comes back up again and cuddles up against him. 'But only because the mood is right and I imagine it might be wonderful with you. It'll probably seem slightly schizophrenic to you, but in general I'm fed up to the back teeth with men who are randy all the time. I don't always want to be oppressed by an erect penis. It's so much better if I can choose.'

'Well.' His tone is sceptical, but he goes on stroking her lightly and precisely in the right place, sending shivers running hot and cold across her body, and leaving her almost tempted to ask whether he had ever been a woman in a previous life. But in view of the situation she thinks better of it. She enjoys it. Now he is running his left hand gently over her face and then bunching her heavy hair at the back of her neck.

'Well,' he repeats, 'are you sure?'

She nods. 'Absolutely. And you're showing me that it really does suit me.'

'And you're . . .'

Frederic is interrupted. There's a frantic ringing at the front door.

'Oh my God.' Carmen jumps up, and Frederic slowly draws back his hands. 'I completely forgot!'

'What? Your husband? Your boyfriend? Coming home at midnight?'

'No,' laughs Carmen, quickly pulling a sleeve back over her shoulder. 'My bodyguard. I've organised someone to free me from your clutches if I hadn't called by midnight! And here they are.'

'Should I arm myself?'

Carmen laughs heartily. 'You look as if you could deal with my knight in shining armour – as long as he's had a bad day. He's in pretty good shape, as you'll see.'

And she runs, half-naked, to the door.

'Coming,' she calls, and to Frederic, over her shoulder, 'You can leave your jeans off. They're still damp anyway.'

Frederic, who was getting up with just that purpose in mind, drops back on to the couch.

It's a still-life, Carmen thinks, and opens the door.

'Thank God, you're still alive, my dear!'

'Pleased to see you, Elvira, come in,' says Carmen, noticing that she's slipped seamlessly into the familiar form of address. 'Can I introduce Frederic?'

She points to the couch. Frederic sits bolt upright and then starts laughing.

'I'm sorry,' he says. He leaps to his feet, walks over to Elvira, takes her hand and kisses it with perfect elegance, 'I didn't mean to laugh, it's just so funny because Carmen had threatened me with you!'

'Quite right too, young man,' Elvira smiles, 'and not without reason. I brought my truncheon specially!' She raises her walking stick. Then she looks at Carmen, 'Did I disturb you?' and, with an accusatory glance at Frederic, 'Did you creep into Carmen's flat under false pretences?'

'No, no,' Carmen laughs. 'Come and sit down. I hope you don't mind me speaking to you informally, it seems so natural now.'

'But of course you can,' and, glancing at Carmen's outfit, 'What's been going on?'

'Nothing, my dear Elvira, nothing to worry about at all,' Frederic grins, showing Elvira to a chair as though he was head of the house. Carmen adjusts herself slowly back into her cat-suit, and Frederic asks Elvira, 'Does it worry you that I've got no trousers on? They're wet.' He points to the radiator. 45

Elvira nods, 'No, no, I understand.'

'I doubt it,' Carmen laughs. 'The whole thing's so crazy that no one could understand it.'

'Not bad, though?' Elvira inquires, and when Carmen, smiling, nods her head gently, Elvira closes her eyes for a moment, and then says, 'That's the most important thing.'

The three of them sit there chatting for a while, but they slowly tire, and after about half an hour, when Elvira is about to go, Frederic links arms with her.

'I'll walk you down – who knows, there are so many rogues about. They lurk everywhere.'

Elvira, looking at him. 'You're right, that's what we thought too!'

Carmen escorts them to the door.

'Are your trousers dry, Frederic, so that we can say the evening's been a success in one way at least?'

'That's good of you. Many thanks, Carmen – for everything. You'll be hearing from me, sweetie!' And, lips pursed, he plants a kiss on her mouth.

'Ciao,' Carmen nods. 'And many thanks for your intervention, Elvira. It's a good thing you didn't call the police at midnight.'

'Oh yeah?' Frederic wrinkles his forehead. 'So that's what might have happened? They'd have been delighted with a catch like me. Shame, it would have been quite amusing,' and, casting a little sideways glance to Elvira, 'though the advance guard was perfectly charming.'

'I hope so,' Carmen hears Elvira answer, and waves to them both as they walk downstairs side by side. Frederic, quite the cavalier, gently holds on to Elvira's arm and says, still within Carmen's hearing, to his companion, 'And what will we two get up to now? A nightcap at your place, or should we go to mine?'

Elvira laughs, 'Wasn't Carmen enough?'

'I prefer the more mature woman. I can't get enough of them!'

Carmen closes the door.

He's really cute, she thinks. In his tattered T-shirt and wet jeans. Like something out of a James Dean movie. But is he really for her? While she puts away the glasses and goes into the bathroom, she imagines Frederic in various situations. In a restaurant, five-course menu, someone has to choose the wine. He's sure to ask for a Coca-Cola. Or at the opera. Would he like that sort of thing? He'd probably rather be at an open-air concert. One open-air concert with Tina Turner in Munich had been enough for Carmen. On the way in she had got stuck in the mud, had lost a shoe, and couldn't get it back because she was being jostled from behind. She only managed to get within sight of the stage with considerable difficulty, and ended up standing next to the speakers, getting practically knocked out by the volume. She had to fight against crowds trying to get to the toilets, the refreshment stalls or wherever, then she saw a woman who'd collapsed being carried to the ambulance. Finally she'd had enough, and fought her way out but got a big dent in her car. And she had paid fifty-four marks for the privilege. Never again, she had sworn, and she would stick by it. With or without Frederic.

What are you getting so worked up about, she asks her reflection. You don't even know that he likes open-air concerts. You need to get to know him better. In fact, what just happened was pretty incredible anyway. She has to laugh at herself. If he'd been potent, you'd have given him a sharp rap on the knuckles, and you let this guy get close to you as if it was the most natural thing in the world. What came over me? It was just a quickie. A quickie with an impotent man, right at the very moment when you're about to give up sex. But it might be something to do with Frederic too. He doesn't seem the kind of person to take advantage of his contact with someone. Really, he was just doing me a service and expected nothing in return. Of course there are other conditions, and that's fun too. That's enough, she says to her reflection, and goes on removing her make-up. Frederic is witty, youthful, fresh – she stands still for a moment – but is he what I wanted? Wouldn't I rather have something a bit more mature? A bit more grown-up?

We'll see, she concludes as she removes the rest of her make-up. She nods to her reflection, taking off her clothes as she leaves the bathroom, draping the cat-suit over the nearest chair before she slips into bed.

Oh, it's wonderful to feel so contented. She plumps up her pillow and lies on her belly. How wonderful, when you're tired, to go to sleep and have no hand reaching between your legs and a voice whining on until you finally surrender. She rolls into a ball and goes to sleep with a relaxed smile on her lips.

Britta looks over Carmen's shoulder. What's up? Carmen turns around. Frederic is standing in the doorway. He is wearing tattered jeans and his tatty old leather jacket, and is holding an enormous bouquet of red roses. His face almost disappears behind it. It takes a second for Carmen to react.

'Frederic – what are you doing here?'

'It's Tuesday, and I always buy flowers on Tuesdays. Today they're for you.'

'That's nice.'

From the corner of her eye she sees an open-mouthed Britta Berger.

Of course, she says to herself grinning, she's never seen me with anyone like this.

She walks over to Frederic. He puckers up his lips and blows a kiss on her mouth, then presses the flowers into her arms.

'Where's the vase?' he asks.

'The vase?' Britta repeats, although he hadn't been speaking to her, and looks around. 'We haven't got one.'

'What kind of a place is this?' Frederic seems genuinely annoyed. He walks back to the main door and says over his shoulder, 'I'll be back in a minute,' and is gone.

Britta Berger looks mutely at Carmen, who grins. 'That was

Frederic Donner.' She says nothing else. What does her private life have to do with Britta Berger? Through the big window of the office on to the street she watches Frederic marching resolutely away. There is a light drizzle. Autumn rain. It always seems to be raining when Frederic comes. Carmen sits back down at her desk. That morning she has been trying to set up some meetings with prospective new customers. Britta Berger goes back to her typewriter to finish the letter she has just started. Then the phone rings.

'I'll get it,' Carmen says, gesturing to Britta who is about to pick up the receiver.

'Legg Insurance?'

'Kaltenstein!'

'Stefan? Pleased to hear from you!'

Britta Berger glances out from behind a sheet of paper.

'Sadly, Carmen, I can't get you out of my head. It irritates me. Can I see you again?'

'Yes.' Carmen hesitates slightly. 'Of course. Perhaps our meeting was too short . . .?'

Britta's ears are twitching again, she thinks.

'Exactly, that's just what I thought. I'm glad you see it that way too. Thank you. So, what about tomorrow evening, Carmen?'

'Tomorrow evening, tomorrow evening, no, wait, I'm busy. Thursday would be better.'

'Yes,' his voice sounds deep and worldly, 'all right, I've arranged something too, but I can postpone it. Fine, it's a date. Can I pick you up?'

Carmen thinks of Elvira and answers, 'That'll be fine.'

'Where do you live?'

'Number 7 Zur Zinne, in the middle of the old town!'

'I'll find it. Half seven okay?'

'Great.'

'I'll look forward to it, Carmen. Goodbye.'

Carmen slowly puts the receiver down. What am I getting myself into here? Now she has two men. One used to be too many.

Behind her the glass front door opens again. Frederic puts an enormous vase on her desk.

'That must have cost a fortune!' cries Carmen. 'Are you crazy?'

'No, just in love!' He grins, kisses her on the ear and says, more to Britta than to Carmen, 'All courtesy of the Minister for Education!'

'What a relief!' Carmen shakes her head, but laughs anyway. 'You're not quite how I would have imagined a *Rosenkavalier!*'

'It's time for you to rethink a few things, my dear, I didn't arrive on a horse either, I came on a Kawasaki. We live in the twentieth century, ladies don't wear crinolines and gentlemen don't wear wigs, please take note!' He runs his fingers quickly through his short hair.

'Yes, that's very sweet,' she embraces him. 'You sly old fox,' she whispers in his ear, 'what's my colleague going to think?'

'Do you think I'm up to no good?' he asks Britta loudly over Carmen's shoulder.

'Me? No, why?'

'There, you see,' says Frederic, holding Carmen away from him. Carmen flashes her eyes at him. She could have throttled him, the idiot, for laying her open like that!

'So, ladies, the caviar and champagne arrive tomorrow, but now I've got to go. Can you possibly forgive me?'

He nods to Britta, kisses Carmen briefly on the mouth, turns around and walks into the drizzling rain.

Carmen sits down. She doesn't know what to say to Britta Berger.

Britta saves the situation. 'Maybe we should put the roses in water,' she says. She gets to her feet, picks up the flowers and the vase and goes into the little side-room and toilet.

'I don't know, I hope I'm not getting out of my depth with all this.' That evening Carmen is at Elvira's. She has brought two take-away pizzas from the Laguna, and they are slowly and pleasurably devouring them. 'If I phone all the others, there'll be tons of them.'

'That's right. First you've got to meet them all.'

'But now I've got Kaltenstein phoning me again. I'd already crossed him off the list.'

'Maybe you like him?'

'Yes, perhaps I do, in a way. And what's more important, when he collects me you can see him for yourself!'

She smiles at Elvira and raises her glass.

'One thing I wanted to ask, Carmen – don't you have a girlfriend, a best friend, like all women have?'

'Yes – you!' Carmen nods, pouting her lips into a kiss.

'That's very nice of you, and I'm flattered – but I'm an old woman. I mean a confidante the same age as you, a bosom pal like my own Anna, whom I loved like a twin.'

'I do. My Anna's name is Laura, and she's in Brazil for two weeks, missing the most important developments in my life.'

'Two weeks in Brazil? Is she a tour guide?'

'Nearly,' Carmen laughs. 'She's a teacher and she's on holiday. But you're almost right – she is a bit of a tour guide. She likes being abroad more than anything else. And she usually is.'

'Married?'

'Boyfriend.'

'What's wrong with women today? Why don't they want to get married – or,' and she looks at Carmen with a crooked smile, 'have a real man?'

'I'm sorry Elvira, you have been living on your own for a good fifty years. And? Did you have a steady boyfriend at any point?'

'No – yes. Yes, in fact, I did. At home, in South-West Africa, I had a boyfriend I got on very well with, but he was black, so it was impossible for us to see each other in public. We could only meet in secret.'

'Really?' Carmen moves closer. 'Tell me more.'

'There isn't much to tell.' Elvira cuts herself another piece of pizza. 'We were about the same age as you are now. We were both doctors, but his background was quite different. He came from the Congo, I was German, his family was poor, 51

mine was rich, he was black, I was white. And he wasn't a
Christian – there was that too!'

'Did that bother you?'

'Not me. None of it would have bothered me. But everyone
else . . . Imagine, the white women would have seen me as a
white whore, and the white men would have lynched him.'

She looks into her wine glass and smiles quietly. Her fingers grasp the long stem and turn the glass slowly back and
forth. Carmen gives her time. The grandfather clock ticks.

'But it was nice,' she says. 'The time we spent together was
really nice. Completely unlike Johannes, but nice all the same.
We were that bit older!' Elvira pauses reflectively. 'He was
tall, and had a very athletic, muscular body. He was always in
a good mood, he didn't take things too seriously. He said that
in the great darkness there was always a light burning somewhere, and he could always prove it, even if it was only a
glow-worm. And he had a wonderful voice. Can you imagine,
those old songs that the Africans sing, that distinctive sound?
Sometimes when I listen to the wind, even today, I think I can
hear him.'

She falls silent again and then looks up.

Carmen is moved. After such a life, how lonely this woman
must feel here.

'You always speak in the past tense, Elvira. Is he dead?'

'A long time ago. He was shot. We had known each other
for a good six years. I'd come back to Europe for a few months
to continue my training, when his letters suddenly stopped.
And he was a fantastic letter-writer. His lines were always full
of poetry, the whole of life was there. Yes, at first I thought it
was the post, the mail wasn't particularly regular even from
Windhuk, and then I tried to find out by phone. But you can
imagine – forty-five years ago it wasn't very easy. I couldn't get
through. I flew back, worried. In the clinic where we had
both worked I was told he had been shot during a disturbance. He had no family in the country, so no one could show
me his grave. I didn't believe it. I did my own investigating.
My God what I would have given to find out the truth. Even

today I don't know what happened. And that hurts, especially because I don't know if I was the cause of his death.'

'Oh, Elvira, that's terrible.' Carmen impulsively reaches for the old lady's hand and squeezes it. 'All that you've been through. Two men who loved you, and now you're on your own.'

The two women sit silently together for a while. The pizzas in the middle of the table go cold. Neither of them has an appetite.

'It's all history,' Elvira says finally, looking up and forming her features into a smile, 'but we're living in the present and the future. To the future, Carmen,' and she raises her glass.

'You're very brave. I don't know if I would be. Things tend to rattle me much more.'

'You must never give up. Never give up. Go on, do things better. But after I broke my hip two years ago I suddenly lost my sense of purpose. It was a terrible experience, a really painful one. Up until that time I was still very active. I taught classes at the old people's club, I helped old people. But after my fall I really thought everything was over, I might as well give up. But see, hardly had I thought it, and there you were!'

'Much too late, I came much too late, Elvira. I'm ashamed to think that I've lived in this house and never noticed – that you suddenly weren't there, that you were all alone in the hospital, that all of a sudden you couldn't walk properly. I'm really ashamed of my blindness and the careless way I live.'

Carmen still hasn't read the last two letters. She plans to do it when she gets back from two customer meetings on Wednesday. It's about nine in the evening, she's carrying two shopping bags, one for Elvira, one for herself. Carmen is looking forward to a quiet night in. She's going to cook some calamari she got from the supermarket freezer section. There isn't much left to do, because after three hours in the car they've half-thawed already. The accompanying sauce has been recommended to her, and she has chosen the French red wine herself. And she will read the two letters that have been sitting upstairs since Monday. Maybe the Prince Charming she's waiting for will be among them? She puts everything down by the mail-box. A letter from the revenue, a nice surprise when you're just home from work, and another big brown envelope from the paper. My God, she thinks, so many replies to a single ad? Delighted, she tucks the letters under her arm, picks up the bags, closes the front door and goes up the stairs. At Elvira's door she puts one of the bags down and rings briefly. Not a sound. Maybe she's in the bathroom and can't hear. She'll go back down in a bit, or ring her. No one steals anything here, anyway. She leaves the bag where it is and climbs the stairs.

In thick leggings and a sweatshirt, Carmen stands in the kitchen and tries to negotiate her way through the instructions on the packet of calamari. Several languages, but where are the German ones? I see, fritters. She hasn't got a deep-fryer. She'll have to do something different. That's all it says in German, but deciphering the English she sees the rings of squid can be fried in a pan too. She's saved, and so is her dinner. Carmen gets a frying-pan and melts some butter in it, then tips in the calamari. Half-thawed as they are, they don't look too appetising. Don't worry, they'll soon get better. Carmen takes a wooden spoon and busily starts stirring the white rings. Some of them stick, some of them slowly turn black and the rest do nothing at all. Carmen keeps at it. This would be too much! She tries to save it with a bit of butter, but her calamari are a long way from Enzo's delicious brown crispiness. Never mind. When Carmen figures they must all be cooked through, she pours them on to a plate, squeezes a lemon over it, adds a spoonful of sauce, uncorks the wine, pours herself a glass and makes herself comfortable on the couch. The squid taste as bad as they look, and Carmen has a slight suspicion that they're going to upset her stomach. They have the consistency of rubber tyres, and are completely tasteless. Carmen chews carefully on four rings, and then leaves them. Maybe they'll do for Frau Neumann's cat on the ground floor.

She opens the envelope. It contains another four letters.

Among the names of the senders is that of a woman. That's interesting. She opens the envelope with her index finger. Sadly Elvira and her silver letter-opener are nowhere around. It's a very Christian lady who wants to explain the meaning of life. Christ's bequest to mankind is not that he should indulge in deviancy; rather that the duties of man and women lie, as decreed by His representative on earth, the Pope, in ensuring that they create descendants. And this calling could not be fulfilled with an impotent man and would therefore be a blasphemy. Carmen puts the letter down, her fingers twitching to phone the woman immediately and ask her various questions. About the Third World, for example, about children in dustbins, about children as living organ-donors, about the female babies left to die in India. This God-fearing person has simply signed herself Gerda H., with no further information. And directory inquiries can't do much with Gerda H. Carmen sips her wine. Why should she get annoyed? It's funny, really. She'll show the letter to Elvira. Elvira doesn't have children either, so she's living in sin too. What would Gerda H. have said if Elvira had obeyed her duty as a woman, and given birth to a mixed race child? Receive him into God's mercy? Or put him in a home?

She takes another sip. Next letter, no sender's name. It's a woman's signature again: Annemarie Weber, in small, curved handwriting. Not a ball-point, but a fountain pen. Carmen's astonished. She hadn't expected replies from women. Another narrow-minded do-gooder? No, this time a young woman congratulating her on her courage. 'You made me think of something indescribable. I'm someone who always chooses the wrong men, gets pestered and tormented, but I can never finish things off at the right time. I still say yes when the hairs of my neck are standing up with revulsion. My friend says I should see a psychiatrist, but now I know what I really need: an impotent man. Someone who'll leave me alone when I want to be left alone. Maybe you could simply send the replies of the men you turn down on to me. I must admit that placing an ad of my own would be far too expensive for me – and the

55

impotent man is your idea, after all. If you agree with my suggestion, it would work out to everyone's advantage. Take the one you want, and leave the rest to me!'

Interesting. Carmen puts her head on one side. A recycling service for impotent men. Not bad, and you don't have to worry about writing back.

Under her name Annemarie Weber has written her full address and telephone number. Carmen picks up the receiver and dials.

A very sleepy voice answers.

'Weber?'

Carmen glances at her watch. It isn't all that late, just after ten.

'Hello, this is Carmen Legg, is that Annemarie Weber?'

'No, it's her mother. Annemarie's gone to bed, she's on early shift tomorrow.'

'Oh, I'm sorry. Sorry to have bothered you. Could you just tell her that's fine about the ads. I'll collect the letters and send them on to her.'

'I don't quite get you,' comes the hesitant reply.

'It doesn't matter, Frau Weber. Your daughter will know what it's about. Say hi from me, she can call me back whenever she likes.'

'Has she got your number?'

'No, but Carmen Legg's in the phone book.'

'Just a moment, please . . .' Oh, no, off we go again! Carmen hears the receiver being put down and someone going away. Drawers open and close and finally the lady comes back.

'I'm sorry, but I don't really know my way around here, I'm just staying at my daughter's. So, once again, please.'

Carmen spells out her name three times until Frau Weber has written it all down properly, and then repeats, twice, slowly and clearly, her telephone number.

'I've got it now,' the voice at the other end finally says tensely.

'That's great,' Carmen answers. 'Say hi to your daughter, and good night, Frau Weber.'

This is one hell of an evening, Carmen thinks, curling back up on her couch. So on to the next letter. This is a guy who clearly wants her to be cured. He asks for measurements, height and weight, and if possible he'd like to see a photo of her in the nude. Why would an impotent man need wanking matter, she wonders as she throws the letter down. She should play a trick, and send him a dominatrix. Then he could have height, weight, measurements and a whip. Perhaps that's what he needs. She won't pass him on to Annemarie. Or maybe she should. So that she can see the kind of nutters you get with a harmless advertisement.

Number four. This seems quite reasonable, in clean, straight handwriting on smart paper.

Even today I can't explain what triggered it. I only know the effects. My marriage collapsed, my wife moved to Munich and took our daughter with her. My company – I work in computers – folded, I felt about a quarter of a person. I've pulled myself together now, life goes on. There are things more important than potency. I don't want to trouble you with my problems, but I'd be interested to know what sort of a woman came up with such a request, because it really is extraordinary. I would be delighted with even a short conversation. I very much hope you will call,

with many thanks
and best regards
Oliver Lehmann

Carmen is happy to call immediately. Unusual women are allowed to phone after ten o'clock. She picks up the receiver and dials.

'Yeah?' Carmen doesn't really like yeah people very much. Everyone has a name. You can say 'yeah?' when the tax people are on your back. But she's started the call and she's going to see it through.

'Am I speaking to Oliver Lehmann?'

'Yes?'

'This is Carmen Legg. You replied to my ad.'

'I'm sorry, it's late – what ad?'

Is this guy with it, or what, Carmen thinks. '*Wanted: clear-thinking male*,' she says bluntly.

Now the tone at the other end changes abruptly. It sounds as though he's had to inhale deeply.

'Are you still there?' she asks, to contain his surprise.

'Yes, yes, I certainly am! Nice of you to call!'

Now he sounds quite different. Alert, breathless. 'I've just read your letter, Herr Lehmann, and of course I'm happy to sit down and talk to you.'

'That's great, terrific. You have no idea how pleased I am.'

'Really?' Carmen can't help laughing at his enthusiasm. 'I was afraid I'd dragged you out of bed.'

'You did. Or rather, I'm still lying in bed. I had to fly to Hamburg for business this morning, and that's why I've gone to bed early.'

'Hamburg's a lovely city, a dream of a place. I wish I'd gone there.'

First there's a brief pause at the other end, then he laughs. 'Do you mean that?'

'I'd love to come out with you some other time!'

'Today's over, unfortunately. But next week I'm flying to New York. Why don't you come along?'

'Do you mean that?'

He laughs. 'Why not, there couldn't be a better opportunity for us to get to know each other.'

'You could be right. But maybe we should see each other briefly first.'

'You aren't up to taking a risk?'

'I'm not in computers – I'm in insurance.'

He laughs again. His voice is calmer, he seems to be genuinely amused. Well done you, thinks Carmen. You could have used that as an example in a marketing seminar.

'One nil to you. When would suit?'

'Tomorrow at midday?'

'I'd have to rush across – yes, I can do it if it's after one.'

'In the centre, in the Café Mohren?'

'Do they do something for the hungry man?'

'If you're after rump steak with salad, then yes!'

'Then that's fine. Okay, it's a date. You'll recognise me easily, I'm six foot five and bald, with a full beard.'

Oh my God, thinks Carmen. 'And I'm five eight with long hair and no beard!'

'Each to his own,' comes the amused reply.

'Fine, till tomorrow, then.'

Carmen puts the phone down. How about that then? He seems nice enough, and how important is hair after all?

She picks up the next letter but the phone rings.

'I never hear anything of you, I never see anything of you, you're always on the phone to someone else, just tell me you haven't forgotten me!'

'Frederic! This is a surprise.'

'Not the kind of surprise I was hoping for. I thought you'd have put out the candles, run a bath and made some ice-cubes.'

'What? Why?'

His voice sounds sulky, as if his mum has put spinach rather than pancakes on the table.

'I told you yesterday that the roses would be followed by champagne and caviar. Now it's all getting wet in my saddle-bag. It's raining you know.'

'Oh, come on!' Frederic on his way to her place? That doesn't fit in with her plans at all. 'Where are you?' Maybe it was just a joke.

'In a phone box around the corner. I can stay here, of course, until it's time for breakfast. Then I'll bring you champagne and croissants. We're flexible.'

Carmen laughs against her will. 'Come on, then. You can help me do the ironing!'

'Fantastic, a sensible job at last. I'll be right with you!'

Within five minutes there's a ring at the door. Carmen hasn't bothered to put on any make-up or lipstick; he's an old friend by now, and besides he's run up the three flights of stairs faster than you could twist a lipstick in and out. Frederic is standing in the doorway, with two bottles of champagne and a delicatessen shopping bag under his arm.

'You're off your head,' she says, and he gives her one of his pursed kisses.

'But in a nice way, I hope?' He walks past her and puts everything on one of the coffee tables by the sofa.

'What's that?' he asks, holding one of the calamari rings in the air with two pointed fingers.

'Food for Frau Neumann's pussy-cat, specially fried to go easy on its little tummy.'

'That's what it looks like, darling. Shall I chuck it?'

Carmen nods and looks at him. Then she sinks into the chair. Frederic doesn't need her anyway. He runs through the flat, finding a champagne cooler, champagne glasses, plates and knives. Then he unpacks. Two tins of caviar, a lemon, crème fraiche, sliced bread. He looks at her and snaps his fingers.

'Madame, all we are lacking is ice-cubes and a toaster!'

'Fine. The toaster's in the cupboard, ice-cubes I'm afraid I haven't got. Jack Frost and his pals have requisitioned my freezer compartment. I have no room for profane things like ice-cubes. But if you look very carefully, there's a perspex cooler on top of the fridge. It keeps things cold just as well.'

'Ugh, what sort of style do you call that? Perspex for such an excellent wine. I can't have heard right, I'm scandalised. Just concentrate your lovely little mind for a second – where can we get ice-cubes?'

'Look outside, it's probably snowing by now.'

Frederic shakes his head. 'Maybe Elvira will have some. Do you think we could ring her doorbell at this time of night?'

Carmen gives a start. 'I was going to drop by anyway because she didn't answer the door earlier. I completely forgot.'

'What would you do if you didn't have me? There's a

shopping bag outside her door, too, I noticed it when I was going upstairs.'

'Hmmm.' Carmen looks dubiously at Frederic. 'I left it there. She should have taken it in ages ago, that's what we'd agreed I'd do. I really don't like this. I'm going to call her.'

Carmen picks up the phone and dials, while Frederic fetches the toaster.

She watches him go. She can't place this man. Baccara roses, champagne and caviar, and then tattered jeans and a sweatshirt that flopped distressingly about him, and which had certainly seen better days. She'd have to find him something decent to wear.

'It's engaged.'

Funny, who could Elvira be phoning at midnight?

'All the better, it means she's still awake!' Frederic is standing in front of her with the toaster. 'Where's the socket?'

'Behind the couch.'

'The cable won't reach.'

'There's an extension cable in the cupboard in the hall, at the end on the right.'

He'll soon know his way around the flat better than I do, she thinks, pressing redial. Still engaged.

Frederic sets up the toaster, pops in two slices of bread, puts the butter on a little plate, the crème fraiche on another, slices the lemon and puts it next to it. Then he takes the two tins of caviar into the kitchen. Carmen hears cupboards opening and closing. Frederic comes back with two glass bowls, one inside the other, and the inner one filled to the brim with caviar.

'So,' he says. 'Now we really do need the ice-cubes. Chiefly for this caviar. And then a candle would be appropriate. Do you have such a thing?'

'In the bedroom.'

'How practical.'

He grins, and comes straight back with the candelabra and puts it on the table. He reaches into his trouser pocket, takes out a silver lighter and lights both candles.

61

'I'm impressed,' Carmen says to him and looks around. 'I must admit, you do surprise me!'

'Again?' he asks, and his white teeth flash. 'What about our ice-cubes?'

Carmen presses redial.

'Engaged!' She looks up. 'I don't believe it!'

Frederic looks at her thoughtfully. 'Perhaps we should go down and ring on her doorbell. Then we'll at least have an idea . . .'

Abruptly Carmen gets to her feet, 'Do you think something's happened?'

'You never know with old people, do you?'

Carmen picks up her flat key as Frederic extinguishes the candles with his thumb and forefinger. They dash down the two flights of stairs. Carmen rings the doorbell. First twice, one after the other, then, after a pause, three times, and finally a great long ring. Frederic pushes her hand away.

'Who in this building has keys to the flats?'

'Frau Neumann downstairs. She's the concierge.'

'Let's go there then!'

They thunder downstairs. Carmen gives three long rings.

At first nothing happens, then she hears noises inside.

Carmen presses her mouth to the glass pane, 'Frau Neumann, it's me, Carmen Legg from the third floor. We're worried something may have happened to Frau Gohdes!'

'What?' The door opens slowly. There's a chain on the door.

'Oh, it's you,' says Frau Neumann when she recognises Carmen. 'What's the matter? Wait a minute, I'll open up.'

It's all taking far too long for Carmen. By the time the door has opened and closed . . .

'Do you have the key to Frau Gohdes's flat?' she asks urgently.

'I've got the keys to all the flats. Why?'

'We're worried something's happened to Frau Gohdes. She didn't come out to collect a bag of shopping I left for her earlier this evening, and just now her telephone was constantly engaged and she didn't answer her doorbell . . .'

'Then she's on the phone. You don't need to wake me up
ringing doorbells at all hours.'

'On the phone? At this time of night? No, something's
wrong! Let's go up, quickly!'

Frau Neumann casts a suspicious look at Frederic who,
admittedly, doesn't look terribly trustworthy in his street-
sweeper's gear.

'This is Frederic Donner, an acquaintance of mine, there's
nothing to worry about.'

'All right then. Just one moment.'

Frau Neumann pulls the belt around her dressing-gown
tighter – no mean feat given her bulk – and goes back into her
hall. Carmen hears keys clattering, then nothing happens for
a brief eternity, until Frau Neumann finally appears. 'Let's go!'
Ideally, Carmen would run, but Frau Neumann, at sixty and
weighing a good eighteen stone, has difficulty keeping up
with her. With swollen legs she slowly stamps her way up the
stairs, and Carmen is tempted to take the keys off her. I hope
we won't be too late, she thinks to herself.

At the top of the stairs the breathless concierge rings once
again and then, at the urging of Carmen and Frederic, puts
the key into the lock. She turns and turns it, but can't open
the door.

'Let me have a go.' Frederic takes the key from her hand,
but he can't do it either.

'There's a key on the inside,' he says, 'that's why it won't go
in!'

Carmen tries to look through the rectangular glass window
in the wooden door. But it's opaque, and Carmen can't even
tell whether the light's on or not.

'What now?'

'Break it down!' says Frederic.

'We'll have to call a locksmith,' says Frau Neumann. She
groans, glancing at her watch, whose narrow gold band cuts
deep into her fleshy wrist.

'There's no time! Have you got tools downstairs, Frau
Neumann? A crowbar or anything?'

63

'No, no,' she stammers. 'And this week of all weeks my husband's away on a job. He's sure to have locked up his workshop. I never need to get anything out of it.'

Frederic has already taken off his sweatshirt and wrapped it around his right fist.

'Take a step back,' he says to Carmen and Frau Neumann. His chest muscles tense, and using his full weight he smashes his right arm through the bottom left-hand window-pane. He reaches in and opens the door from the inside.

'But you can't just . . .' Frau Neumann protests feebly, but Carmen interrupts her with a gesture.

'What's a pane of glass against a human life, Frau Neumann?'

Carmen is the first to go in. Frederic follows and presses the light switch. The corridor is lit now, but otherwise the flat is in darkness. Carmen dashes into the living-room. From the doorway she can see something dark lying on the telephone cupboard.

'Elvira!' She dashes over. Frederic looks for the light switch and finds it. Elvira is on the floor, her face as white as the wall, the telephone receiver clutched in her hand.

'Call an ambulance immediately!' cries Frederic, who rushes over to Elvira and bends over for her wrist to take her pulse.

Carmen takes the receiver out of her friend's lifeless hand. It isn't easy, Elvira has a firm grip on it.

'Oh God, she's dead, she's dead! A dead body in our lovely building!' wails Frau Neumann.

'Be quiet, will you!' Carmen yells.

On the display of the telephone there are three numbers: 452 – the last number, the 1, is missing. So she was trying to call me, Carmen thinks, as shivers run down her spine.

'She's alive!' says Frederic. Carmen heaves a sigh of relief. 'But her pulse is very faint.'

At that moment the emergency services pick up the call. Carmen explains, gives the address, the name and the floor.

'Can we help? What First Aid can we do?' she asks.

'Put her legs up, otherwise it's best to leave her as she is. We're on our way!'

Carmen slowly puts down the phone. She kneels by Elvira, lays her feet on some sofa cushions and dabs the cold sweat from her forehead. Tears run down her face. Frederic crouches down beside them.

'She'll be okay,' he reassures Carmen. 'She's unconscious, but that doesn't mean anything. It can be completely harmless. Maybe it's a lack of circulation!'

'But it can't go on too long it becomes dangerous.'

'We don't know what's happened before. She may not have been there long.'

'Oh, Frederic, she mustn't die!'

'She won't. She won't do that.'

Frau Neumann is still standing uncertainly in the middle of the room. Then they hear a siren and a vehicle stopping in front of the building, and blue and white lights flash on the high ceiling. It looks very strange.

'That didn't take long!' Frederic jumps to his feet and runs downstairs to show the ambulance men the way. In the meantime Carmen strokes Elvira's face. The old lady's eyes are closed, Carmen isn't sure she's still breathing. She's pale, very pale, and there are dark rings around her eyes. But her face looks relaxed, serene, the wrinkles aren't as deep as usual. Her mouth is slightly open. Dear God, don't let her die, Carmen prays quietly, adding, get them up here quickly so they can help her. She hears rapid footsteps, and Frederic and the emergency doctor come in.

'Good evening,' the doctor says quietly, putting his bag next to Elvira and kneeling beside her on the floor. He tests her blood pressure and then makes an infusion with an isotonic cooking salt solution. Carmen holds her breath. The doctor stands up. 'If she doesn't come round soon, we'll inject her with a cardiac stimulant. We'll only be able to tell you more once we've got her to the hospital, but everything indicates circulatory collapse. It's a good thing you acted so decisively,' he says, nodding to Frederic. 'It probably saved her

65

life. We'll take your neighbour in first, and then we'll come
back to collect you – you're going to need to get that arm
sewn up.'

'What?' Only now does Carmen see that blood is dripping
from Frederic's sweatshirt, which is still wrapped around his
arm.

'You've hurt yourself! Oh God, Frederic. Is it serious? Does
it hurt?'

Two young ambulance men, who came in just after the
emergency doctor, carefully lay Elvira on a stretcher and carry
her out of the room. Carmen points at Frederic's arm. 'Let me
see!' she demands.

'It isn't deep,' the emergency doctor reassures her. 'It's better
for him to keep his sweatshirt firmly wrapped around it and
we'll sew it up in a few minutes. There could be splinters of
glass in the wound. Have you had a tetanus injection? We can
sort that out later. Do you have some clothes he can bring?'

He clearly thinks we're a couple, Carmen thinks, and
Frederic grins. 'Get me my freshly ironed white linen shirt,
darling, would you?'

Carmen isn't in a mood for jokes. 'Should I pack something
for Frau Gohdes as well?' she asks.

The doctor nods. 'That would be a great help. Maybe the
concierge could help you.'

He'll be saying that so that no one could accuse me of steal-
ing anything later on, it occurs to Carmen, but she doesn't
care.

'Fine, are you going now?' she asks Frederic.

The doctor nods.

'Then wait a moment, I'll get you something.'

She runs past them, goes upstairs, gets her big sweatshirt
from her bedroom cupboard and runs back down. As she
passes the table, laid for a special dinner, she gives a tired
smile. A good thing that Frederic thought of something like
that this evening.

'But that thing's far too small for me,' Frederic complains,
'and I don't like the tiger on it, either.' And Carmen's biggest

item of clothing does look shrunken on Frederic. 'Just thank your lucky stars I didn't bring you a bustier too!' she says, and Frederic smiles.

The doctor glances from one to the other. 'Let's go, then,' he says. The ambulance men are downstairs, and Carmen goes with them to the front door. Other residents have woken up and are asking questions. Frau Neumann embellishes the story, telling it as though she was the heroine of the hour. Carmen hears her and pulls a face. All they need now is a television crew and an item on the local news. For cash, of course!

'Which hospital are you taking her to?'

'City Hospital.' The doctor is already sitting in the ambulance. 'When you get to Casualty, ask for me, Gerd Lindner.'

'I'll be there right after you.'

Carmen and Frederic sit by Elvira's bed all night. Elvira woke up in the ambulance, but after her examination she went straight back to sleep and a nurse wheeled her into an observation room where Carmen and Frederic were already waiting.

An attending physician came in shortly afterwards.

'She seemed to be fine, but we want to check whether she's done herself any damage in the fall. We're thinking of her hip, which may still be giving her problems after her previous fall. We'll keep her in for the time being, but if everything's okay she should be out by Saturday. After that she mustn't exert herself in any way.'

'Of course, I'll do what I can,' Carmen had nodded. 'Can you tell us what it was?'

'Circulatory collapse, as my colleague Dr Lindner correctly diagnosed.'

'Can we stay here?'

'Well, it's not strictly necessary, she's over the worst. But it would do her good if there was someone here when she woke up.'

He nodded to them and left the room.

Carmen and Frederic make themselves comfortable, in so 67

far as that is possible on two chairs, and talk quietly, philosophising about life, the universe, everything, about the beginning and possible end of humanity.

At about five in the morning Carmen takes his hand and says, 'You're a great mate, Frederic. I don't think many men would have done what you did.'

'But it was the only thing to do.'

'That's what you say. And I say to you that for most men, champagne, caviar and then the usual bit of hanky-panky would have been more important. Particularly the hanky-panky. And if some annoying incident disturbs the champagne preamble, everything else goes down the tube. It's true. And that's why they prefer not to be disturbed.'

'What an image of men you have.'

'Am I the woman or are you?'

He sighs. 'I don't really know. Actually I think you're the man and I'm the woman. If I think how I prepared dinner yesterday, and how you sat waiting – the distribution of roles looked pretty clear!'

'Oh, go on,' she laughs, and nudges him in the side with her elbow. 'Do you have to go to work tomorrow? Do you work?' it suddenly dawns on her.

'Good question,' he answers. 'What do you mean by work?'

'You know, work. Something you regularly do to earn money. Being a waiter, for example, or street-sweeping, sorting rubbish, cleaning windows . . .'

'It's interesting to see what you think of me! I have a shower every day, if that's what you mean. That's regular activity enough. Though I'll probably shower twice today because I want to go out with you tonight. I assume our little supper is no longer nice and cold, so we'll have to think of something else!'

Carmen suddenly feels cold. Only now does she remember that quite apart from her work she has arranged two dates. One at lunchtime with Oliver, and another in the evening with Stefan. Should she tell Frederic? Or should she call the other two off? She's really too tired to go to that kind of effort.

A whole night with no sleep, and then a circus like this of her own accord?

'What's up, did you have other plans?' He studies her sharply and then adds knowingly, 'You've got to try out all your impotent men, haven't you?'

'Yes,' she says, thinking honesty is the best policy. 'I've got a date at lunchtime and another this evening.'

'I thought we might be right for each other!'

'I think so too, Frederic, I think so too. It's just that . . .'

'You want to see if something better comes up.'

Carmen disconsolately pulls a scrap of skin from her fingernail. 'That's not it. You know that very well. I'm very fond of you.'

'Fine. I can't do anything about it. Can you find me a window in your busy diary? Easter Sunday, perhaps? Some time in April?'

'Oh don't be like that. I've started, so I'm going to see it through. So far you're the only one I'm seeing regularly.'

'Sure, because I never leave you alone.'

He puts his elbows on his knees and rests his head in the palms of both hands.

'Frederic, please.'

'It's fine. I'll wait for you to call me. You've got my number, and the woman who might come to the phone is my sister, not my girlfriend, just so you don't forget.'

'It hasn't even been a week. So how could I forget, Herr Donner?'

'Well, women are supposed to have extremely short memories.'

'What's that supposed to mean?'

'Prejudice. Nothing but stupid prejudice.' He looks up at Carmen from below. Carmen leans down to him and plants a kiss on the bridge of his nose.

'You're priceless. And if you didn't exist you'd have to be invented.'

'Psst!'

They both look at Elvira. She has moved. Carmen jumps to

her feet and walks over to her. She isn't as pale as she was, some colour has returned to her face. The supply of blood to her lips seems to have improved too. She looks peaceful, sleeping so quietly, almost like a child.

Carmen walks back to Frederic, sits astride his lap and wraps her arms around his neck.

'You know, I feel so stale next to you. Not old, no, not that, but so mature. Can you imagine that? I really love being with you. But I'm not sure it could be for the rest of my life.'

He presses her towards him.

'Ah, we're talking about life? You're looking for a man for the rest of your life? Do you know what you're saying?'

'Of course. That's what it's all about. I finally want to live in a harmonious, happy two-person relationship. Without spikiness, without compulsion, without coercion. That's exactly what I want, that's my goal.'

'Well, when you've done it all, you can come back to me.'

The door opens and a night nurse looks in. She clears her throat. 'Am I disturbing anything?'

'No,' laughs Carmen, 'it just looks that way. We're trying to stay awake.'

'I just wanted to see if you needed anything. Would you like a cup of coffee? I'm just putting some on.'

'That'd be lovely,' says Carmen.

'With fresh croissants?' asks Frederic, getting another pinch from Carmen.

'Let's see what we can do,' the nurse smiles and quietly closes the door behind her.

When Elvira wakes up at seven, Carmen and Frederic are still sitting at her bedside. Carmen jumps up and plants a big kiss on her cheek.

'Hi, Elvira. We thank all the angels in heaven that you've come back to us. How are you? Can you speak?'

'Yes . . . I feel a bit strange . . .'

It's a while before Elvira knows what's happened.

'It was . . . if I'd passed away I wouldn't have known a thing.'

'You dare say you're sorry we found you,' says Carmen, aghast. 'You can't just leave us. We still need you.'

'I just meant it would have been so easy. But now I'm back again, and I'm happy to see the sun, to hear the birds, to have you. No, really, I'm extremely grateful.'

Carmen places her forefinger on her mouth. 'Shh! Don't speak, you should rest. We're really happy that nothing serious happened to you.'

'What's that on Frederic's arm?' Elvira points weakly at Frederic's bandaged forearm.

'I simply couldn't wait to see you again, Elvira. You know how lovers are. Passion overtook me!'

Elvira manages a quiet smile, and Carmen runs her fingers through Frederic's hair. Then she presses Elvira's hand, 'I'm sorry, Elvira, but I think I'm going to have to go now. You've woken up now, we're pleased, the night nurse brought us a breakfast worthy of the Grand Hotel, but I've got some appointments to keep.'

'Don't worry, my dear girl, I'll have a good sleep, it'll do me good.'

Carmen sits in her office in a strangely good mood. She stopped off at home, showered and changed and then dashed off again. She doesn't feel tired at all, quite the opposite – boisterous, over-excited. Once again she's rejected her notion of postponing her meetings with Oliver and Stefan. What was she thinking about? She's set it up, and she'll see it through. It's Friday tomorrow, and she can sleep in at the weekend.

She spends the rest of the morning with clients who want to check up on minutiae, claim piffling damages and demand detailed information. It's really busy, and she only just manages to get out of the office before one o'clock.

The Café Mohren isn't far, but by the time she shakes the rain from her umbrella in the doorway and hangs her coat in the cloakroom she is shivering.

She goes in. The café is full, as always at lunchtime. But she's in luck, there's a table for two free by the window. She can't see a tall, bearded bald man anywhere. That's fine. It means she can have a hot cup of tea in peace, and collect her thoughts.

At the next table a young fair-haired man, a surfer type, keeps looking in her direction. Carmen brushes back her long hair. She glances at him briefly. Another one. From fifteen feet away she can tell from his eyes what he's thinking, what he wants. Her mood immediately plummets, and she has a curt 'Don't even think about it, sweetheart' on the tip of her tongue, when a giant appears before her. So her dream man certainly isn't Oliver Lehmann – she can tell that at first glance. He looks like an out-of-control garden gnome. But he holds out a big, warm hand and says, 'You must be Carmen Legg.'

'And what would you do if I wasn't?'

'I wouldn't look any further. You should always stick with the first thing that seems right. It seldom gets any better.'

Carmen laughs, the ice is broken. He isn't handsome, but he's nice. 'Well, have a seat,' Carmen points to the empty chair opposite, 'I'm she!'

Oliver Lehmann straightens his chair and puts the paper he was carrying under his arm on the table. It's the paper with her ad in it, and she nods to him with a smile. Seen close up, he's much improved. The beard covers half of his face, it's true, but it's very neatly trimmed. His eyes are greenish brown, his nose is large, his skin large-pored and slightly tanned. Maybe he has acne scars and he covers them up with his beard? Or else he's compensating for the lack of hair on his head. There's very little of it, nothing at all apart from a little ring around the back. But it's better than combing a few strands over the top, Carmen thinks. And bald men are supposed to be *very* potent. She grins.

'You must have noticed something,' he suggests with a shy smile.

'I'm sorry,' Carmen bursts out, 'but according to folk

wisdom you should be almost terrifyingly potent!' Now he'll make his excuses and go, she thinks. That really was forward.

'But if we were to follow folk wisdom, you would be completely sex-obsessed,' he counters.

'Why's that?' asks Carmen, although she knows exactly what he's going to say.

'Long red hair, big eyes, wide mouth, lipstick, the kind of figure that stops men dead in their tracks – you must have a different man every night of the week. Let alone during the day!'

'For God's sake!' Carmen shrieks, not quite sure how he meant it. Was that an insult? Or was it supposed to be funny?

'Okay,' she says, 'what you mean is I'm not the sort of woman who would go out in search of an impotent man.'

'Just as I'm not necessarily the prototype of an impotent man.'

'I see.'

The waitress comes. Carmen orders lentil soup with sausages, Oliver steak, salad and vegetables.

'Vegetables?' the woman asks. 'We've only got bread here.'

'That's what I guessed.' He casts a critical eye at Carmen. 'Nothing for real men. Two portions of bread, please. And a Pils.'

'The bread here's very good,' Carmen says encouragingly. 'It's wood-stove-baked, fresh from the bakery.'

He runs his hand over his shiny head. 'Very reassuring. Next time we'll go to the steakhouse. They have fresh bread there, too, and also baked potatoes, croquettes, mashed potatoes, chips, gratin, roast potatoes, rösti . . .'

'Thanks, thanks, got the message,' Carmen interrupts. And then, after a moment of hesitation, 'Were you always so decisive, or did it only start when your life began to go wrong?' She thinks of his wife who left him, his computer company that collapsed.

'I would place the woman I love on a pedestal!'

'Ah,' replies Carmen. 'Wrapped around with barbed wire? or can she jump down if she feels like it?'

He laughs, but it doesn't sound terribly sincere.

'She doesn't have to do that. The woman in my life wants for nothing,' he assures her with a nod. 'So let's assume we're going to New York together,' and Carmen thinks, over my dead body, 'then it's obvious that I, as a man, would make all the travel arrangements. I'd buy the tickets, book a good hotel, get tickets for a Broadway show and bring along a restaurant guide. What would be wrong with that?' He looks at her expectantly with his greenish brown eyes. The waitress comes and lunch is served.

'That didn't take long,' he says. Carmen isn't sure if his words were appreciative or accusatory. Maybe he thinks fast food means poor quality? She orders a glass of mineral water.

'*Bon appétit.*' Oliver nods to her and cuts himself a big chunk of meat. He looks at it critically, then nods 'okay' and shoves it into his mouth.

'I think,' she says in reply to his question, looking for the appropriate word, 'that all sounds a bit rigid. Do you work it all out yourself, or do you discuss it with your partner?'

'In the past I've always done everything on my own. My wife wanted no part in it. She wasn't interested.'

'But can't you imagine that some women might want a say?'

'Until I became impotent I always thought there was something else that women wanted, and that they wanted it all the time!'

Carmen sighs quietly. In a distinctly bored voice she says, 'And you obliged?'

'I'd have liked to. But sadly my wife was frigid.'

'She was what?' Carmen nearly bursts out laughing. 'Frigid?'

Looking past Oliver, her eye falls on Surfer Boy opposite. She must have spoken too loudly. He looks over at her, one corner of his mouth slightly twisted in mockery. He's listening, she thinks, annoyed. I don't care. I can't help a man with an attitude like this. Impotence chose a perfect target. 'How do you make that out?'

'Well, a woman who doesn't enjoy it and, if it happens, just lies there waiting for it to finish – well, she's got to be frigid, it's obvious.' His eyebrows meet, his expression darkens. There are two sides to this man, Carmen says to herself. One open and cheerful, one totally disagreeable and rigid in his attitudes – the typical male demigod.

Carmen puts her spoon to one side. 'There's no such thing as a frigid woman. They're a male invention. There are only the wrong men for those women.'

He looks up from his plate. 'Well, excuse me, but that's the most arrant nonsense. If a woman doesn't feel anything during sexual intercourse, what would you call that? A silent orgasm?'

'I don't think you learned anything at all in the years with your wife!' She wants to slap him for his stupid arrogance. She flashes her eyes furiously. 'I'd be more interested to hear your wife's opinion.'

'Well,' he chews, shaking his head, 'I don't see the point in that. And I don't know why you're getting so excited about my wife's frigidity. I thought we were going to talk about us. That's why we met up, isn't it? That and because we were going to fly to New York. We've strayed off the subject rather, haven't we?' And once again he has that nice, slightly amused tone that Carmen liked so much on the phone.

How can I change the subject now, she wonders, taking a drink from her glass.

'When are you flying?' she asks. 'And which hotel are you staying at?'

'I'm flying next Wednesday and staying the weekend. And the hotel?' He smiles at her and his eyes twinkle. Carmen inwardly shakes her head. Now he's completely likeable again. It's incredible. It's impossible to make this guy out!

'As far as I'm concerned there's only one hotel in New York. There's a tradition to it, that's how it has to be.'

Carmen thinks briefly. 'That would have to be the Plaza, or the Waldorf Astoria . . .'

'Correct!' He laughs, revealing a row of even teeth. They are slightly yellow at the edges, like the teeth of a heavy smoker. 'I love the Waldorf! Do you know it?'

'Sadly no. I must admit that I've been to America a number of times, to Florida, to LA, to San Francisco, to Washington, but I've never been to New York. Is that a gap in my education?'

He nods. 'But it's one you could easily fill. I'll repeat my proposition. If you have the time and the inclination, it would be lovely if you would come too.' He raises his Pils glass to her. 'I'll pay, of course.'

'Oh no,' she says. 'There's no question of that! If I come with you I'll pay my own way, thank you very much!'

'Are you off again?' he asks, threatening her playfully with his index finger.

'What? No, absolutely not, but I can't just let you take care of everything like that.'

'And as to whether you can just invite yourself along,' he says, looking up and beckoning the waitress. 'We'll see. Let's start now.'

Oh my God, thinks Carmen, an impotent macho man. What have I got myself involved in? 'Fine. But I've got to get through my meetings. Wednesday, Thursday, Friday – that's still three days. Let's see if I can get everything done in time.'

He holds her gaze and says, 'Let's see if you want to.'

He's seen through me, Carmen thinks. Well, fine. So he should. We'd just get on each other's nerves. Frigid women! Don't make me laugh!

Oliver pays, Carmen raises no objections. Why should she? Hardly worth the fuss for lentil soup and mineral water.

They say goodbye outside. It's stopped raining, but a leaden atmosphere has fallen over the town. New York would be nice, she says to herself. I'll do it, too. But with someone else. Let's see, what about Frederic? Then again there might be some more attractive replies in the post. There are still two unopened. Her good mood returns momentarily. Let's see what the day brings. She takes a few steps, and then remembers Stefan. With any luck the evening with him will be more agreeable. If he starts talking about frigid women too, that's me and men finished with. I'll go out and find myself a lesbian!

Now she really misses Elvira. Carmen feels completely abandoned. And she'd invited Stefan to the house especially to introduce him to Elvira. Well, she'll be back soon, thank God – but this evening, this evening! It's seven o'clock. Having just emerged from the shower, Carmen stands by her wardrobe. If she has read Stefan Kaltenstein correctly he'll ring the doorbell on the dot. That kind of punctuality drives her up the wall. Why is she going out with him? To get to know him. 'I'm a curious person,' she says out loud, 'and an irresolute one as well. What should I wear?' What would he prefer? Something elegant. Skirt, then? Skirt and pullover? No, skirt and jacket. She has one that looks like a smoking jacket and goes with everything – it peps up jeans, it makes skirts look fantastic. Dark stockings, black shoes. High heels again! She groans and walks barefoot to the window. It's raining. What a surprise. Never mind. Herr Kaltenstein will doubtless drive up at her door, and then pull up right in front of the restaurant. Carmen puts on a black lace body and black stockings. She walks up on tiptoes to the big wall mirror. Take a look at that! She's lost those damned four pounds. Her slim figure is clearly, evenly visible under the lace body. She runs her hand lightly over her hips and her belly. There they were, those nasty little rolls of flesh, resisting all her efforts to slim. And now, by some miracle, since she began her impotence campaign, they've completely disappeared. And she hasn't even been paying attention to cholesterol, fat or sugar. Maybe impotent men are more stressful than potent ones. She smiles at her reflection, lightly pats her flat belly and starts getting dressed.

At twenty-five past she's standing in the bathroom putting on fresh make-up. Not too much, but a little cream for her complexion, a good bit of mascara, no smudging, fine, black eyeliner and dark red lipstick. It goes well with her red hair,

77

which she brushes until it flows full and wavy down her back. She turns around quickly in front of the mirror. Oh no, there's a hair on her jacket again, pluck it off quickly, then put lipstick, keys and wallet in her little evening bag – and sure enough, there's a ring at the door. A glance at the clock, half-past seven on the dot. 'Pedant,' she says out loud. 'I can't bear pedants and conformists.' She presses the intercom. 'I'll be right down,' she pipes. If he'd been five minutes late she'd have liked him better somehow. She'd been planning on asking him to come up. And anyway, Elvira isn't there to check on her, and her flat needs that weekend clean. Who knows what a critical eye would find here? She grabs her black cape, slips into her shoes and steps outside. Not too quickly, she thinks, as she runs down the stairs. These old wooden stairs are terribly smooth, and if Frau Neumann has had another of her neurotic floor-polishing days then you're likely to take a tumble.

She pulls the front door open, and immediately finds herself under an umbrella. She knew it. Stefan Kaltenstein is the very epitome of the gentleman. His sharply etched face is slightly in the shade under the umbrella. It's barely discernible – and yet it carries a certain expression. Carmen can't see it, but she feels it. What is it? Carmen isn't sure, but he has an extraordinarily strong aura, she can sense that.

'Nice to meet you,' he says, taking her gently by the arm.

Carmen nods to him with a smile. 'Pleased to meet you too.'

He guides her to the waiting car, which he has – he really has – parked right in front of the front door. She would never have dared allow her car to be such a traffic obstacle. Stefan holds the door open and Carmen slides in feeling as if she's in another world. Dark blue leather and cedarwood, instruments surrounded by gleaming silver ornamental frames, it smells of leather and wood and somehow of security. It's funny, her car is comfortable too, and has leather fittings, but she's only ever seen it as a fast and reliable machine for getting from one place to another. This is different somehow.

78

Stefan has got in on the driver's side.

'This isn't weather for an English car like her.' He smiles and starts the engine.

'You talk of your car as though it was a person,' she says, looking at Stefan.

'Do I?' he smiles. 'Maybe it's because I know her so well. I know what she likes and what she doesn't like. It hates this weather. Although being English she should be used to it!'

'Funny,' says Carmen. 'I've never thought of my car as a Bavarian. But some things did occur to me when I was getting in. For example, our cars belong to completely different worlds. Looking at the fittings here. I drive a BMW. It's pure technology, functional, reliable, fast and practical. And here in your Jaguar you can imagine you can actually smell the English aristocracy. You see great broad meadows, dreamy stately homes, horses and hounds!'

'You have a romantic imagination,' says Stefan, glancing at her with amusement.

'So I'm discovering.' Carmen smooths her skirt and then looks out. The raindrops rattle against the windows, the Jaguar doesn't emit much light. At least not compared with her halogen headlights. And her windscreen-wipers work better. 'Where are we going, exactly?'

'Didn't I tell you? I'm sorry.' He reaches for her hand and kisses it lightly.

Of course you haven't told me, as you very well know! 'A surprise?' she asks.

'No, not immediately. Dinner'll be a surprise, but the place itself isn't a mystery. We're going to my house!'

Whoah, Carmen gives a start. What? To his house? That doesn't feel right at all. That's far too intimate? How can he have thought of such a thing?

'Well, I don't know,' she says carefully, 'isn't that a bit premature . . .?'

'Don't worry.' He laughs. 'We won't be alone. You don't need to be afraid of me.'

'So it's a party?'

'A party? No, in fact it isn't. Maybe it'll turn into one – but that's not the plan.'

'You're making it sound really exciting! We're eating at your house, we're not alone, but it isn't a party either, so you must have invited a number of people to dinner. And who's taking care of their needs while you're picking me up?'

He shakes his head and laughs heartily again. 'I'm not completely half-witted – inviting other people to dinner with you. I'd be punishing myself. No, no, the two of us will be completely alone.'

'Completely alone!' Carmen looks at him with irritation. 'You're contradicting yourself, Stefan. You were just saying . . .'

'Yes, yes,' he says dismissively and stops at a traffic light. The red light casts a ghastly glow across his face, and Carmen wonders, with a moment of panic, if he is mad.

'The people,' he goes on, shifting into first gear, 'are the staff. I'm not going to spend my time in the kitchen if you're there!'

'I think that's a charming idea,' she says, lying back relaxed. Brilliant. He's hired some kind of catering service plus waiting staff. She admires that. Almost as nice as that scene in *Giant*, where James Dean hires a whole restaurant and orchestra for dinner for two to surprise Elizabeth Taylor. Or was it Robert De Niro and Elizabeth McGovern in *Once Upon a Time in America*? Anyway, it's terrific. Carmen feels at ease. Somehow she has a good, familiar feeling with this man. The car radio is on, playing music from the seventies. Carmen's completely relaxed. The road sign welcoming visitors to the town slips past them.

'Do you live outside of town?' she asks, a little more tensely. Who knows, he might be driving her to a little hut somewhere in the forest. Elvira's hardly going to turn up at midnight all the way out here.

'Don't worry, we'll be there soon.'

On the left a tall hedge lines the road. The Jaguar stops in front of a big cast-iron gate that opens silently. Carmen sees cameras above the gate on both sides, red lights blinking to indicate that they are in operation.

'Good God!' she can't help exclaiming as Stefan puts his foot back on the accelerator and drives slowly through the gate. 'Where are we now?' The road ahead disappears into the darkness. There are poplars on either side. Right at the end, probably hidden behind clumps of trees, she sees a few lights. But the rattling rain obstructs any further view.

'Is that a house back there?'

She looks at him, and she can read it in his eyes. His face could have turned white, his canines could have grown, and she'd have thought it fitted perfectly with the situation – no way out. But his smile isn't demonic, it's more paternal. And she doesn't find it disturbing when he lays his hand gently on her thigh. He's hardly going to have descended from the Marquis de Sade!

'It's yours, isn't it?' she says.

He nods. 'Fourth generation. So it's no achievement of mine. I'm just the caretaker.'

Just, Carmen thinks. Just!

The avenue turns a corner and then runs straight towards the house. Carmen can't make out many details. The outlines disappear into the rain and the darkness. But it's either a very big villa or a castle. They drive by some outhouses, probably servants' quarters and stables, and then up a steep drive to a flight of steps.

'I don't know what to say. Either I'm dreaming or I'm in a film. I didn't know such things existed!'

'They certainly do, Castle Kaltenstein isn't completely unknown.'

Although he acts as though it doesn't matter, she feels like a schoolgirl who has failed a test. As though she couldn't answer a Trivial Pursuit question like, 'Was Napoleon Corsican or French?' Nonsense, she says to herself, there's nothing wrong with my IQ, my general knowledge is excellent, and if I don't know Castle Kaltenstein, Castle Kaltenstein isn't very well known.

Before Stefan has got out of the car, her door has been opened. A dark-clad man with an umbrella helps her out of the car. Why didn't we come in a coach, she wonders cheekily, but then she's impressed. Stefan comes to her side and together they climb the broad stone steps. In the middle is a thick carpet which, wet and squeaking, muffles their steps, and Carmen is afraid of getting her heels stuck in the mesh.

The wing doors are open. They walk inside, greeted at the portal by another man who takes their coats. Both – Carmen has never seen anything like it, but they must be butlers – are clearly older than Stefan. Carmen guesses they must be at least sixty. Then she is overwhelmed. The walls of the great vestibule are decorated with paintings. Not fantastic scenes or religious imagery, but scenes from life. But what a life! A gentleman with a wide-brimmed stetson sits high on horseback in some sort of quarry. Black people are working all around him. They all look up at him with smiling faces, all apparently enjoying the work . . . The man stares benignly into the distance, which, on the opposite wall, contains a baronial house in the colonial style. Big and white, with columns by the door. On the third wall stands the whole family in all its splendour. The same gentleman with a lady in a wide crinoline, wearing what is a clearly fashionable little sunhat and carrying a bright little parasol. Next to them are three boys and two girls, all in their Sunday best, and in the background is the nanny who looks after the children and who is responsible for the gleaming brilliance of their white dresses and suits.

'Africa?' asks Carmen, adding, to avoid seeming so ignorant again, 'West Africa, Togo? Or Cameroon?'

Stefan smiles, 'German South-West Africa!'

'Namibia,' Carmen nods, and then shakes her head. 'That's incredible. Namibia's been following me around for a fortnight!'

'Really? Come on, you must tell me!'

He guides her gently by the elbow into an adjoining high-ceilinged room with wood panels on the walls. A chandelier bearing real wax candles hangs from the ceiling, spreading a cosy, flickering light and an open fire burns on the long side of the room in a deep, head-high fireplace. The room is dominated by a massive wooden table with twelve high-backed chairs. Carmen glances quickly at the table settings. They are not at opposite ends, as the cliché would have it, but in the middle of its long sides. Stefan straightens her chair, then walks around the table and sits down facing her. Directly above them hangs the chandelier, the fire crackles behind Stefan's back. 'A lovely place you have here. Almost as if we've gone back in time. I can hardly believe there are cars, not coaches, in the garage.'

'Yes,' he laughs. 'Time really has stood still here. But we've modernised as well. Not too obviously, but we've done a lot of work over the past few years.'

The butler who carried the umbrella enters almost silently with a bottle of champagne. He carefully fills the long-stemmed glasses. He is followed by his colleague, who serves two little plates with an *amuse-gueule*. 'Warm lobster on a bed of cucumber, and *bon appétit*.'

'Thank you very much.' Carmen smiles at the butler and then raises her glass to Stefan. 'I'm sure we're going to have a very good appetite. It's wonderful here, Stefan!' He raises his glass as well, they clink glasses.

'Do, start.' Stefan makes a wide gesture with his hand over the plates.

Carmen picks up the little fork, and hesitates, 'Do you always carry on like this?' she asks. Somehow she can't imagine this extravagant lifestyle going on all the time.

'Sometimes more, sometimes less,' he smiles, and then leans forward a little: 'I admit that I also have a little flat in town, which isn't as big as the hall here. I retreat there when I have my slack days, my down time, if you like.'

'I can't imagine you having anything like that. You seem so . . .' she collects herself to find the right words, he waits in anticipation, '. . . so much in control, so much at ease.'

'More champagne, madam?'

The butler stands behind her with the bottle, and Carmen

looks questioningly at Stefan. 'As you wish, Carmen. The wine can wait if you prefer.'

'So what's our first course?' Carmen asks Stefan and Stefan looks inquiringly at the butler.

'As you agreed with the cook, Herr Baron, fresh wood mushrooms on radiccio romana.'

I can hardly believe this, Carmen thinks. And no one else is going to believe it either. Who could I tell? Elvira's in hospital, Laura's in Brazil, Frederic thinks I'm completely mad and my mother wouldn't know what I was talking about. Impotent baron found through lonely hearts ad? It's too daft.

'I'd rather have wine with that,' she says to Stefan, who nods to the butler, who in turn nods to Carmen, 'Certainly, madam. I could recommend a 1990 Chablis Grand Cru.'

'Excellent,' says Carmen, 'a very good wine,' and to Stefan, 'Thank you very much!'

'I'm delighted you like it. I chose the wine this morning. I thought it would go nicely with this.'

Carmen sits still for a moment and looks around her. 'It's like a fairy tale, Stefan. It's simply incredible! And all this extravagance – how can you afford it?

Stefan makes a dismissive gesture. 'I had clever ancestors. Hardly had Germany bought South-West Africa than my great-grandfather was out there looking for buried treasure. As you may know, they had copper, silver, lead, tungsten and diamonds out there. My great-grandfather was lucky and made a lot of money very quickly, then brought his family over, built offices here in Germany, and this house. His son, my grandfather, expanded the business, and my father also commuted between Germany and Africa until he died. Yes, and now I'm the typical exploiter of hard-working ancestors!'

'You're hardly an exploiter! I assume that some things here still belong to you, and perhaps you still have properties in Namibia, if that's possible there. I'm not too familiar with the history.'

'Well, by 1920 the magic was over. After Versailles, Germany lost all its colonies, mostly to France and England.

South Africa was given the mandate over South-West Africa. And in 1949 South Africa annexed South-West Africa, contrary to the resolution of the UN and the Court in The Hague. Ah, terrific, here comes our dinner!'

The first course tastes delicious. And the wine lives up to its name as well. But Carmen hangs fascinated on Stefan's every word. 'Please carry on,' she says, just before the first wood mushrooms disappear into her mouth.

'Well, little of interest has happened since then. My family was clever enough to adapt to changing conditions. I assume some kind of wage system was introduced and, according to the prevailing political situation, they gave the most generous support to different important people – civil servants, the military, politicians. The only system in the world, incidentally, that has so far survived all political upheavals – whether in the East or the West, whether in the present or a hundred years ago.'

'Pretty cynical, then,' says Carmen between bites.

'Isn't that always the case?'

'Of course.'

They eat in silence for a while.

'Does the name Elvira Gohdes mean anything to you?'

Stefan looks up briefly, thinks for a moment and shakes his head. 'Not that I know. Should it?'

'No, no,' says Carmen. 'She lived in South-West Africa too. In fact she was born there. Perhaps – sometimes chance plays the strangest tricks.'

'Where did she live exactly?'

'I'll have to pass there. I didn't ask that precisely. But I can ask her – unfortunately she's in hospital at the moment.'

'Essence of tomato with quark dumplings.' The butler makes a discreet bow.

Carmen eats slowly, and tells him of their adventure with Elvira the previous night. She plays down the intermezzo with Frederic somewhat, and leaves out the champagne and caviar. She doesn't want to hurt him. But the memory of Frederic makes her smile. Roses, champagne and caviar, and now Stefan and an evening beyond description – since she's been spending all her time with impotent men she's been really enjoying herself. Really enjoying herself. She's been more spoilt than ever before. Did Peter ever think about such things? He came in, looked in the fridge, took whatever he wanted, food or sex, and was off again. And his predecessors? No better. Carmen had dreamed of being spoilt, even once, but somehow it always went wrong. In the end she was always the one who paid – in emotions, patience, money. That must be it, she says to herself when the third course comes. Scampi with champagne mousse and wild rice.

'This is fantastic,' she says, suppressing the first little yawn. After all, she has just had a sleepless night, and now it's nearly ten.

Stefan has noticed. 'You must be tired after a day like that! Would you like something to perk you up? Or should we bring the evening to a close? Which would be a shame, of course – or can I offer you a bed for the night? There are enough guest rooms to choose from.'

'No, really,' says Carmen hastily, but the very mention of the word 'bed' reminds her: We've talked about everything but his impotence. And his past with women. At the age of fifty he must have been married at least once. Has he got any children? Should I ask him, or wait till he talks about it himself?

Finally she rouses herself, but first she checks that there isn't a butler in the vicinity. 'If we're to get to know each other better, perhaps we should talk about the reason we met in the first place,' she says, thinking, my God, you put that very politely.

'You mean my impotence,' Stefan says bluntly.

'Yes,' Carmen nods, but then waits because one of the butlers is offering her a cassis sorbet.

'Delicious, my favourite sorbet,' Carmen says, delighted, and waits until the coast is clear.

'Yes, precisely,' she repeats. 'Your impotence, after all, was the trigger behind our meeting. And I really have to admit that I'm thoroughly enjoying sitting here with you without

having to wonder about us going to bed together. I'm
delighted that I don't have to think about how to squirm out
of it if I decide I don't want to.'

'Have there been problems?' He enjoys his sorbet and leans
a little closer towards her.

'The question's in the air every time two people have
dinner. It comes with the bill, you might say. That's why I generally insist on paying for myself. That way I've demonstrated
from the very beginning that Carmen Legg isn't on the menu.'

Stefan laughs and sips some wine. 'Nonetheless, as a man
I'm struck that in my case you'd have to work out how to
escape my clutches. You could easily have expressed yourself
in more charming terms, given that nothing can happen.'

Carmen, who has also taken a sip of wine, looks at him
over the rim of her glass. Then she puts it down. 'Sorry, that
came out more harshly than I intended. But it hasn't got anything to do with you, even if it seems that way. It has to do
with the situation. And if I were now to tell you I'd like to go
to bed with you, you'd be sad again, because it wouldn't
work.'

'You're right,' he nods and, after a pause, 'Would you like
to?'

Oh no, she thinks, now the evening's going to get tricky,
just when everything had been sorted out.

'Herr Baron, would you like to try the wine? I would like to
decant it so that it has the right bouquet for the main course.'

'Certainly, of course,' says Stefan, and the butler holds a
bottle of red wine in front of him. 'A 1980 Chateau Lynch
Bages Grand Cru Classé Pauillac.'

'Excellent, excellent,' murmurs Stefan, taking another look
at the bottle.

'Can I?' asks Carmen. He hands her the bottle across the
table. Carmen studies the label. Then she regretfully shakes
her head.

'I like a good red wine, but I don't know this chateau.'

'Surprise yourself. If I have been right about your taste,
you'll like it, I'm – fairly – sure.'

'I'm glad.' Carmen hands the bottle back, the butler uncorks it, sniffs the cork and nods to Stefan.

'Excellent, excellent,' he exclaims.

Excellent, thinks Carmen, we've got away from the subject.

At first Stefan doesn't return to it. They talk about the colonial period, about Germany's role in the world back then and today. Stefan is very well read, and knows his history. He seems to have a particular gift for dates. Carmen doesn't. She can remember historical events in detail, but is rather vague about their position in time. Carmen laughs. 'Maybe that's a reflection of our personalities. I'm the coarse woman, everything has to happen quickly. You're the refined man, you have to get to the heart of everything to be satisfied.'

Stefan nods. 'That's a good definition. But I think things have improved. I used to be even more pedantic. The last five years have shown me not everything can be forced.'

Aha, thinks Carmen, now we're back on the subject.

The delicious red wine in the carafe has been drained to its dregs, and when Carmen is asked if she'd like some more she shakes her head. No, they mustn't open a new bottle for her. She's had more than enough. She had been unable to resist an ample second serving of the main course, medallions of lamb in tarragon *jus*, green beans and potato gratin. Now there's only room for coffee, if that.

'You can't disappoint my cook like that,' says Stefan sadly.

'Why?' asks Carmen, sensing what's to come.

'You can't turn down his avocado parfait with fresh figs. It would be a crushing blow to an artist!'

'Oh yes,' laughs Carmen. 'Maybe, but in that case I'm going to have to stretch my legs. At the moment I couldn't squeeze in so much as a fig seed.'

'Fine,' Stefan nods to her, putting his napkin to one side, 'then I'll show you the rest of the house if you like.'

'Fine.' And glancing at her watch she thinks, this all goes together, it's the witching hour in a moment or two.

They don't get far. They stop in the next room, a gallery of old paintings. It's a stylishly decorated gentleman's room.

Rows of books cover two walls, another is dominated by old masters, and old black and white photographs line a wall with an open fireplace.

'Can I have a look?' asks Carmen.

'Please do.' Stefan lets her walk ahead.

Old photographs have a magical power of attraction for Carmen. How people used to live, dress, cut their hair – she finds them all fascinating. The old cars, the big houses of the well-to-do, the very slightly dusty atmosphere. 'That's the house as it looked in 1903. Those are my great-grandfathers. The ones captured for eternity in the hall.'

'Lovely.' Carmen walks closer to them. Really, the same people. The children are a bit older, all grouped around an open car resembling a coach, with Castle Kaltenstein in the background.

'Which one was your grandfather?'

Stefan points straight to a boy of about twelve, tall and thin, standing beside his mother in his white suit. 'That's my grandfather with his own family, fifteen years later.'

The same motif, a family standing around an automobile, more modern, bigger, but still open, with spoked wheels and a big soft top.

Carmen compares the two photographs. The house looks friendlier, and there are flowers on the steps and the window-sills. The woman wears a long dress, cut straight, the children are wearing little sailor suits and sailor dresses, their father is wearing a knickerbocker suit in light-coloured linen. It all looks very dashing, much livelier than in the 1903 photograph.

Stefan points to a boy about a year old in the arms of the pretty young woman. 'And that's my father!'

'Great,' Carmen laughs. 'A brilliant idea, using the same motif to represent development and progress. Now all we need is your father's family photograph. I can't wait to see what you looked like as a little boy!'

'This is the last photograph ever taken of my father,' says Stefan, pointing to a photograph set slightly apart, which Carmen hasn't noticed before. She comes closer – and thinks her heart is going to stop. Shivers run up and down her spine. It can't be – is she dreaming? Is she about to wake up? No, she has both feet on the ground, and it's the very same photograph hanging in Elvira's flat. A young pilot of about twenty-eight beside his aeroplane.

Carmen is lost for words. She thinks Stefan must notice her excitement. How is she to react? Didn't Elvira say this man was the love of her life? The man she wanted to marry? A thousand thoughts swirl through her head before she can finally formulate a simple question.

'How come that's the last photograph of your father?'

'He and my mother crashed shortly after I was born. They were both killed. I grew up with my uncle, my father's brother, and his wife.'

'Oh!' Carmen is shocked. Gooseflesh covers her whole body, and her mouth is dry. His *parents* crashed? Elvira's boyfriend was married? And a father? 'Do you have brothers and sisters?' she asks.

'No, I was the only child. The honeymoon child, you might say,' he laughs.

Carmen is utterly confused. Should she tell him about Elvira? No, it's impossible. She must ask Elvira. As soon as she can. Stefan hasn't noticed anything. 'My father must have been a flying ace,' he says, 'but his brother, my foster-father, wasn't bad either. He was a very respectable man. Sadly he died two years ago. He was only seventy-six. Now, let's go and see to our avocados – shall we?' He smiles at her inquiringly. It takes Carmen a few seconds to relate the question to the food.

She smiles back. The photograph has so upset her stomach that she needs a cognac. Stefan agrees, they go to the *digestif* trolley in the dining room, and he pours her a generous glass.

'I've seen so many photographs of your ancestors now, but none of your mother,' she says, carefully returning to the theme.

'Unfortunately there aren't any, not even a wedding photograph. No one knows where they are. My father, forgive me, my foster-father, said they must have had the family album with them for some reason. The plane was burnt to a cinder, you see. Nothing was left.'

'A good thing you weren't there,' says Carmen, tears of emotion rising to her eyes. Incredible, she thinks, what part might Elvira have played in all this? Was she the lover? Could Stefan even be her son?

Stefan, standing on the other side of the trolley, sees that she's moved. He takes her spontaneously in his arms. 'You have a good heart, Carmen. That's nice. Of course it's bad, but since I was only a few days old I didn't even know my parents. I've never really missed them. I grew up very happily with my uncle. He and his wife couldn't have children, so that tragic accident might even have been a stroke of luck for them.'

The butler comes in with dessert, Carmen slowly frees herself from Stefan's embrace. How unemotional he is! Should she let it rest? But somehow the whole thing fails to fit together. Perhaps Stefan's foster-parents fed him a completely false story. Why were there no photographs of the woman who was supposed to be his mother? That's strange. Maybe Elvira is his mother and he just doesn't know. She calculates briefly. It could work, given their age difference. That would be something, if she could bring mother and son together.

Stefan takes her to her seat and straightens the chair. How pleasant it would be to live with this man, she thinks. In this wonderful house, and perhaps with Elvira?

'What are you thinking about?'

'I'm thinking about your life,' says Carmen. 'And the tricks that fate can play.'

Friday morning is hard for Carmen. When the alarm clock goes off at seven, she's tempted to switch it off and just go on sleeping. It was two o'clock by the time she got to bed, and then she couldn't get to sleep for ages. The young man with the silk scarf and the pilot's helmet kept haunting her dreams.

Tomorrow she will collect Elvira from the hospital. Should she mention it to her, or could it be dangerous for her health? But simply keeping the whole thing quiet – who knows what she might be doing? If she only had someone she could talk to about it. She thinks of Frederic. Or Laura. Isn't she coming back from Brazil this weekend? Doesn't school start again on Monday? That would be perfect!

It's a quarter past seven when she finally struggles out of bed. She tries to clear her head with a hot and cold shower, but after she's given herself a vigorous rubdown all that happens is that her teeth chatter violently. No wonder she's chilly. It's early November. She gets out a dark cashmere pullover, and puts on opaque black tights and a black woollen skirt. That should warm her up. But it doesn't. She turns the heating up full throughout the apartment, makes herself a cup of coffee and gets her big, elegant plush coat out of the wardrobe. It's definitely a winter coat, but Carmen doesn't care. She thinks enviously of Laura. She'll be sweating in the Brazilian summer until she hops on to the plane for Germany. Can't wait to hear what she'll say about my impotent men!

'We don't even have proper daylight today,' says her colleague Britta, and Carmen decides to make her escape from the office early. She isn't concentrating anyway, the work's too hard for her, she's off-hand, almost unfriendly, with her slower clients – all in all, it's time for her to go. Britta Berger is understanding: 'You don't look at all well! You might be getting the flu. Pop into the chemist on your way home!'

That's nice of her, thinks Carmen. Britta Berger is like a little grey mouse. She's always there, she's always dependable, always friendly, and no one notices her. The world is unjust!

'Thanks,' she says, gets her coat and goes. It's two o'clock, and the sky is lead-grey. Carmen wraps herself up in her warm coat, glad that she's wearing thick-soled winter shoes, and decides to take Britta's advice and buy herself something for a cold at the chemist's. Since the newspaper office is nearby, she drops in there too. She is served by the same

bored girl from a few days before. Their antipathy is notice-
ably mutual.

'I didn't want to disturb you, but I've just come to pick up
the post from my PO box. The name's Carmen Legg.'

'Too right. The envelope would have been a hard one to
forward.'

She dashes away, and Carmen waits. What could she have
meant? The young employee comes back with a monster of
an envelope. It must be about three feet long and over a foot
across.

'And you say that's for me?' asks Carmen, startled.

'It says it is!'

'Thanks, that's very kind of you.' Carmen nods, takes the
thing and goes. Who could have written her such a letter? It's
crazy! She hopes it doesn't start raining, or it'll go soggy. She
just manages to get to her car in time. Straight home and into
the bathtub and then to bed!

The hot water does her good. She has bought a special bath
oil for colds, and feels her limbs slowly relaxing. Ideally she
would have read her mammoth letter in the bedroom when
she was getting undressed, but she's put it to one side. First the
bath, and then to bed with some hot tea. Then the two other
letters and this unexpected bonus. Her answering-machine is
flashing excitedly, registering five calls, but Carmen hasn't the
patience to listen to them. She'll do that after the letters. Let's
see! She slides a bit deeper into the water. How wonderful to
close your eyes, listen to music, think about nothing. The
phone rings. Let it ring, she says to herself, it's call number six.
She hears her own message in the distance, but can't tell who
speaks after it. Beep, that's it, that's okay too. The phone rings
three more times, but Carmen is resolute. It's her day today.
Not Oliver's, not Frederic's, not Stefan's and certainly not
Peter's. Today she's devoting herself entirely to herself. But
what – the idea aches down to her toenails – if something is
wrong with Elvira? She gave her her telephone number for
emergencies. It's impossible, she reassures herself. I spoke to
her only this afternoon and she was fine. It'll be my mother,

wanting to see me for coffee on Sunday. And I'll deal with that cheery message later on as well.

When she gets out of the bath after the twenty minutes she allowed herself, she feels dizzy. She sits down on the edge of the bathtub. Oh dear, she thinks, something really is wrong. Her fingers are soft and wrinkled, and her skin is far too pale. I really need to get back into the sun, she thinks as she picks up her bathrobe. She thinks of New York, but it's November there too, and cold. She'd be better off flying to Florida or the Canaries.

Carmen puts on thick socks, swaps her bathrobe for a flannel nightie, and goes into the kitchen to boil the water for some medicinal tea. In passing, she switches on the answering-machine: Frederic, wanting to know if she's still alive. Stefan, wishing her good morning and wanting to know if she had a good night. Oliver, wanting to know whether she's still on for next Wednesday's flight to New York. Her mother, wanting to know if she can come for coffee on Sunday. A three-second call from Laura in Brazil wanting to know if she can fetch her from the airport at 5.30 on Sunday. And in the last three the phone was put down after a short, heavy breath. Either someone who didn't dare speak to an answering-machine, or someone trying to annoy her. But Carmen doesn't get annoyed. She pours the powder into her mug, pours steaming water over it, takes a packet of shortbread,(she always had that at her mother's when she was ill), tucks the phone under her arm, takes the letters and goes into the bedroom. Oh, how cosy. She puts everything the way she wants it, lays the letters on the bed and slips under the blankets. The lamp provides a homely atmosphere, Ray Charles is on the cassette-recorder, and the bright curtains shut out the rainy November day. Carmen plumps her pillow, takes a sip of tea and then opens the first of the two small letters.

It reads well. Short and to the point. Felix Hoffmann is thirty-five, he has had a lot of stress at work and from his girlfriend, so he unconsciously escaped into impotence. Since then he's nurtured it and would gladly share it with Carmen if they like each other at first sight. He doesn't believe in love at second sight.

Well, let's see. Carmen fishes around for a photograph in the envelope. And there is one, stuck to the gum. He's sitting astride a surfboard, wearing a brief pair of swimming trunks and beaming. The picture, speaking of leisure, fun and good times, looks very appealing. In the small photograph it's hard to make out his features, but they look regular and pleasant. Okay, thinks Carmen, put him on the yes pile. Then she opens the second, slightly fatter envelope. The man has made a list of all his woes, straight from the heart. Carmen has five A4 sheets in front of her, written in tiny biro handwriting on both sides. He must have spent hours on it, Carmen thinks. Oh dear. Does she have to? And if not now, when? She takes another sip, takes a biscuit from the packet, lies down comfortably on her side and starts reading. His handwriting isn't easy to decipher, which doesn't make things any easier. And the photograph she asked for is nowhere to be seen. Anyway! She battles her way through the first six sides and then gives up: she capitulates before the remaining four. He describes in minute detail how brilliantly everything worked before, how he was suddenly afflicted, how he tried to sort everything out, how he doubted himself, how he thought of suicide – at this point she puts the letter down. No, this isn't for her. Tomorrow she'll put together a parcel for this woman, what's her name, Annemarie Weber, maybe she'd enjoy a man like that. So, she takes another gulp of tea. It's getting slowly cooler – should she put it back in the microwave . . .? Later. First that thing that she's carted through half the town.

The envelope is blossom-white. Her PO box number is cleanly written in a thick, purple felt-tip, as well as, with exclamation marks, 'Do not bend!' On the back there is no name, no address but, in curved blue fountain pen, a poem:

> LORD, it is time. The summer was too long.
> Lay now thy shadow over the sundials,
> and on the meadows let the winds blow strong.

Bid the last fruit to ripen on the vine;
allow them still two friendly southern days
to bring them to perfection and to force
the final sweetness in the heavy wine.

Who has no house now will not build him one.
Who is alone now will be long alone,
will waken, read, and write long letters
and through the barren pathways up and down
restlessly wander when dead leaves are blown.

Rilke, thinks Carmen. That's lovely, really lovely. She turns
on to her back, pulls the blanket up to her chin and spends a
moment or two dreaming about what she has just read. How
lovely it sounds. 'Through the barren pathways up and down,
restlessly wander when dead leaves are blown.' Tears almost
well up, she's so touched. How lovely it would be to trudge
along a tree-lined avenue as a couple, kicking up the leaves
that lie like a thick carpet on the ground, to be wrapped up
warmly, to be happy? To return to an old inn, drink tea
pressed up warmly together by the stove, happy, secure, content? What's inside? She comes back out from under her
blanket. No, not with your finger, she reminds herself, that
would be a shame with such a lovely letter. She jumps out of
bed and runs to get a knife from the kitchen. Now her heart is
joining in. Maybe she was wrong, and it wasn't the symptoms
of a coming flu but complete fatigue, a coming exhaustion.
Whatever, now that she's herself again, she can allow herself a
glass of red wine with the letter. She quickly uncorks a bottle,
pours herself a glass, goes back to bed, leans her back against
the wall and pulls up the blanket. Right. Now the letter. She
slowly runs the knife along the fold. Open. She reaches gin-
gerly inside, and pulls out a piece of white card covered with
graphic designs. Carmen holds it at a distance. It looks like a
reinforced poster. Then she takes a closer look at the surface.
They are clearly computer-originated drawings that have been
coloured in with watercolours and a thick brush. In the top

left-hand corner is a big, red sun, two swans fly past, side by side, peacefully. Some way away, further down and to the right, two cats sit on a dark red gable, rubbing their heads together. In a window, further below, two canaries gently rub their beaks together. On the bottom edge of the picture two little mice sit in the tall grass, their tails entwined into a love-heart. And in the left-hand corner, two ladybirds go for a stroll together. One looks up at the sun, and says in a speech bubble, 'Look, darling, we're reflected in the sky!'

Carmen is fascinated. What kind of person would take so much time over such a thing? Some hand-written lines fit harmoniously around the drawings.

> Dear Stranger, I don't know you, of course, and of course I don't know whether we are soul mates. But I am drawn to you, I can't say why, and one should yield to intense emotions – who knows whether, if one ignores them, they will ever return?
>
> On one of the coming autumn evenings, I would like to go on a long walk with you and wade through the thick fallen leaves and somewhere, in some cosy inn, drink mulled wine by a stove.

At this point Carmen puts the letter down. That's exactly what she'd just been dreaming about. Was such a thing possible? She continues:

> I used to be the kind of super-potent man who could really get on a woman's nerves. I didn't see it that way, of course, I thought me and my excitable little friend were just fantastic. But recently I've realised that love and trust have nothing to do with sex.
>> Please don't call me, write to me,
>> Yours, David Franck.

Carmen leans slowly back. This is the one! She has a feeling, she's sure she's found the right man. She wants to pick up the phone immediately. What's his voice like? What does he look like?

She thoughtfully takes a sip of wine. He wants her to write? She hasn't written a letter for ages. She doesn't even have proper writing paper in the house. But what writing paper could compare with his? Paper with a printed pattern would look cheap in comparison. I'll buy some black sugar paper and a thin-lined silver metallic pen. That'll look good. Should she take a poem and . . . No, copying him would be soulless. She looks at the clock. She wants to dash off right away to the shops. Just before six. If she hurried . . .?

With one leap she is out of bed. She slips into her jeans and pullover, puts her bare feet into tennis shoes, grabs her purse and keys and runs down to the garage. If she hasn't got a cold right now, she thinks – she's certainly going to get one, because in her haste she hasn't put a coat on.

Half an hour later she's back. She's managed to get everything she needed. She's bought several different kinds of writing paper and a number of pens, including one with a nib, they make your handwriting look best. She sits at the table. Now all she needs is the initial spark. One sheet after the other flies up in the air, screwed into a ball. If only Elvira was here, she'd be able to help. Or Laura. Laura always has crazy ideas and an incredible imagination. But it's no use, she wants to send the letter off tomorrow at the latest. No time to lose! Finally it's all there, in silver script on a black background:

> Dear David, your mammoth card is overwhelming. It's going to get place of honour [in the toilet, although she doesn't tell him that], because the ladybird in particular appealed to me. I loved the innocent way it assumes the sun is its own reflection. There's something megalomaniac about it, but its innocence makes it funny. I'd love to accept your suggestion – like the poem by Rainer Maria Rilke it fits with my image of autumn. If I could I would draw a forest in autumn,

with two well-wrapped figures and a dog (I hope you
have one): you and me.

I look forward to hearing from you very soon.

Carmen Legg.

Should I send a photo too? And if I do, which one? He didn't.
Let it come as a surprise, she says to herself, carefully writing
the address on the envelope. Number 17 Rosenweg. Number
17 Rosenweg? Where might that be? Should she look on the
map of the town and drive past tomorrow? Of course, she
could go and pick up Elvira and take a little detour. But what
if he happens to be outside and she recognises him later?
That would be embarrassing. She could drive past in the
dark? How about now?

She's torn. If he delivered his letter to the newspaper in
person, she could do the same with hers. Or would he see that
as an invasion of his private space? Probably, because who
wants to be spied on? She'll ask Elvira tomorrow.

As she's going to bed her fingers brush Felix Hoffman's
letter. Oh, no, she'd completely forgotten about him. What
should she do with it now? Don't give in, Carmen says to herself. Meet him. Who knows, David might turn out to be a
wash-out, and you'd have missed your chance of happiness.
And tomorrow I'll put together a little package for Annemarie,
she says to herself as she's trying to find a comfortable position in bed, and then we'll all be happy! Shortly afterwards
she is fast asleep.

Elvira is sitting exhausted beside her little suitcase. Carmen
greets her tempestuously. She is bursting with unasked questions in the car, but manages to bite them back. She'll have to
wait for a better opportunity to talk about Stefan Kaltenstein.

'Where are we going?' Elvira asks after a while.

'Number 17 Rosenweg.'

'Number 17 Rosenweg? That's interesting. Are we collecting something there?'

'No, we're delivering something.' Carmen grins at her. 'Turn around!'

Elvira looks behind her. The giant card for David is on the back seat.

'What's that?' Elvira asks.

'The perfect man.'

'Be serious. And what about Frederic?'

'Frederic was never a serious possibility.'

'I see,' says Elvira, surprised, 'but things didn't look quite like that somehow.'

'You think so?' Carmen laughs heartily. 'No, things with David are quite different. And I'd just like you to drop off a letter quickly.'

'I see, so I'm Cupid's messenger now, am I?'

'If you like – ah, here we are, this is Rosenweg.'

'Romantic,' says Elvira dryly.

Romantic it isn't. Boring grey blocks stand side by side. Not a trace of Rainer Maria's autumn day, not a ladybird to be seen.

'Can you see the street numbers?' she asks.

'No, I haven't got my glasses.'

Carmen pulls up on the right and peers out of her window. 'There aren't any numbers. The sign has faded, like the whole building. Maybe the next one.' She drives on a block. 'Number 132. Thank God!'

'You think a few numbers are going to make that much difference?' Elvira peers sceptically along the uniform street.

'But Elvira, a bit more enthusiasm, please! His castle's bound to be hidden around the next corner!' She points vaguely ahead of them. 'Probably behind this high-rise.'

As she says the word 'castle', she thinks of Stefan Kaltenstein. She's going to have to mention it, or she'll explode.

After number 50 the neighbourhood becomes greener, the buildings smaller. Carmen drives slowly from street number to street number. Number 19 is a big, run-down villa, while set back from the road, in the shade of some tatty poplars, is number 17. It's built from glass and steel, ultra-modern, although even from this distance the fabric of the building reveals that it was built some time ago. The garden looks the same. Wildly overgrown, with no visible path.

'And you want me to go running up there?' asks Elvira, wrinkling her brow.

'Just to the mail-box. Please!'

'Why don't you do it yourself?'

'What if he saw me? That would be awful!'

Carmen presses the letter into her hand. Sighing, Elvira picks up her stick, gets out of the car and walks slowly up to the garden wall bearing the number 17. With tense excitement Carmen watches the house through Elvira's side window. Maybe she'll discover something. But everything is reflected in the glass box of the house, the sky, the house opposite, and she can't see inside at all. Nonetheless, Carmen is sure that nothing's moving inside. There's no one at home.

'Are you looking for me?' Carmen gives a start. There's a man standing by the open car window on her side. A bit fat, not particularly tall, about thirty-five years old, a black mane of curly hair, clutching a very full shopping bag.

'I don't really know,' Carmen finds herself stuttering. 'If you're David Franck, then yes.' My God, she thinks, if it really is him, how am I going to get out of this?

'If I was David Franck I'd be lying on a beach somewhere with at least three pretty girls running their fingers over my belly.'

'Aha,' Carmen answers, irritated.

'In fact I'm looking after our domestic requirements,' he continues, holding the plastic bag in the air. 'Do you want me to pass on a message?'

At that moment Elvira gets back in the car.

'No, thanks,' says Carmen. 'We've done so already.'

'Okay, then.' The man shakes his curly head and walks past the car to the garden gate.

'Everything all right?' Elvira looks quizzically at Carmen. 'Who was that?'

'You think that might have been him?' Carmen asks, horrified. 'You're seriously saying the perfect man would look like that?'

'Why not,' Elvira shrugs her shoulders. 'At least he's a good cook – I'd lay a bet on it.'

'Could be.' Carmen turns the car. 'But I'd rather rely on my own cooking – at least it won't make me fat.'

Elvira casts her a glance. 'While we're on the subject, maybe we should pick up something somewhere. I could cook us a nice big stew, just right for this time of year.'

'Oh, brilliant,' says Carmen enthusiastically. 'Let's go shopping. And to welcome you home I'll get you a bottle of champagne as an aperitif.'

Elvira puts her hand gently on Carmen's thigh, 'I'm just happy to be home again.'

Carmen is pleased by Elvira's gesture, but spontaneous affection always makes her feel tearful. She wipes her mood away, and suddenly finds herself thinking about Stefan Kaltenstein, and the fact that she still doesn't know what she should do about her discovery.

After lunch Carmen insists that Elvira go to bed. She takes Elvira's door-key, so that she doesn't have to get her out of bed, and goes back to her own apartment. There she picks up Felix Hoffmann's letter and dials his number. His answering-machine is on. She leaves him an innocuous message, just saying it's Carmen Legg, 'clear-thinking male', asking him to ring back and leaving her number. Then she looks at the photo of him and his surfboard. She really likes it. Since her meeting with the man with black curly hair she feels a bit different about David Franck. If he has such a peculiar friend, what kind of a person is he going to be himself – and she didn't much care for that business about the pretty girls, either.

She wraps up a parcel with the other letters for Annemarie Weber, writes a short, personal note to go with it, and addresses it. So, that's that done. The phone rings. She thinks of Felix Hoffmann – he might have come home by now – and picks up the receiver.

'Kaltenstein.' She hadn't been expecting Stefan.

'Stefan, how lovely!'

'It's Saturday, Carmen, and I thought you might be in need of a gentleman companion to invite you out to dinner this evening. I'd love to fill the gap.'

Carmen laughs. 'That's very sweet of you, Stefan, but my friend Elvira Gohdes, I told you about her, is just out of hospital, and I wanted to spend some time with her this evening.' She wonders for a moment whether she should ask him along as well. Maybe then things would work out of their own accord. But she rejects the idea. Who knows what harm she might cause. She must proceed more thoughtfully.

'That's a shame.' Stefan Kaltenstein's voice sounds gloomy. 'But of course I understand. Could I be of help in any way?'

'That's kind of you, thank you. But we've just eaten a huge lunch, and this evening we'll eat something light – nothing too heavy before bedtime. But of course I'll tell her about that divine dinner I had at your house!'

'Why don't you bring the lady with you. You don't get two people born in German South-West Africa meeting up every day!'

Carmen laughs awkwardly. 'You may be right. Can I make a suggestion, Stefan? Can we talk on Monday morning? Then we might be able to do something together next week.'

He sounds committed again. 'A good idea. We could go to a show, or a good play somewhere – do you fancy something like that?'

'I'd love to, that's a great idea. Okay, till Monday, Stefan!'

She puts the phone down and thinks about herself. What did she feel, if at all? At the moment she can't properly judge her feelings about Stefan, because she keeps thinking about that photograph and about Elvira. That floating suspicion is making her completely confused, so that she can hardly think clearly about Stefan. Could I live with him? she wonders, but she can't answer even that. In his presence she feels wonderfully secure, but so distinguished, so forced into this elegant role, that she can't imagine running about in the rain in her 103 jeans with him. With Frederic, on the other hand, that's all she can imagine. With him she's young, free, unburdened. Of course he isn't about to become her protector. He'd need one himself. While she's still mulling things over, the phone rings again. That might be Felix. No, it's Oliver. He wants to know what's happening about their flight to New York. Carmen doesn't like telling lies, and she really doesn't feel like talking to Oliver. But if she was honest, she would upset him, so she'll tell him her diary's full and on top of everything she's suddenly fallen ill. Yes, he already knew that, he'd phoned her office on Friday afternoon and her colleague had told him so. Well, thinks, Carmen, that's great, I've got an excuse. At the same time, though, she wonders what Britta's going to be thinking about all the men that have come into her life over the past couple of weeks.

It's not Felix Hoffmann on the phone, but Laura. She'll be catching her plane later, and she wants to check that everything's still okay. Of course, Carmen reassures her, tomorrow at half past five on the dot.

'It's time you came back!' she adds.

'I think so too,' Laura answers, before being cut off. Laura's money will have run out, Carmen thinks with a grin as she puts the phone down. She'd at least like to get another basket of clothes ironed before she goes back to Elvira's.

It's about seven o'clock when Carmen opens the door to Elvira's flat. Elvira has been snoozing on the couch, and is now reading a book. Carmen asks about her laundry. 'I could go on doing a bit of ironing down here, Elvira. I don't mind.'

'No question, darling. Let's not waste our valuable time together ironing. I can do it tomorrow morning!'

'No,' Carmen insists, 'I'll order us something from the Laguna and then I get on with the ironing.'

'Mary, Mary, Quite Contrary, I'm warning you,' Elvira threatens with a raised forefinger, 'I'm going to make us a ham and egg salad, and you will neither iron nor order us an expensive meal.'

She puts down her glasses and her book and is about to stand up when the doorbell rings.

'I wonder who that could be?' Elvira looks at Carmen in surprise.

'Frederic, perhaps? He was going to call the hospital, did he get you?' Carmen has run to the door, and presses the buzzer. 'We're about to find out!'

A big tray is floating up the dark staircase. 'Hold on, I'll turn the light on,' Carmen calls.

'Party catering,' a voice comes from below.

Has Elvira invited caterers in? What a sweet idea! The tray floats onwards.

'Are you Frau Gohdes?' Now the helpful soul is rounding the final corner. Carmen sees his face. 'Stefan!' she cries, almost crashing into him with fear and surprise. What do I do now?

'Who is it?' asks Elvira's voice from the living-room.

Stefan has heard her.

'Party catering!' he calls.

'Party catering?' Now Elvira comes to the front door.

Carmen has collected herself, and laughs.

'This is Stefan Kaltenstein,' she says, and Stefan is standing at the top, on the last step.

'Good evening, ladies.' He makes a slight bow. 'May I first deliver this? Just a little something, easy on the stomach, to aid your recovery. You look quite pale, my dear.'

'But this is a surprise, Herr Kaltenstein.' Elvira takes a step back and points into her flat. 'Won't you come in?'

Carmen walks ahead and shows him the way. He puts the silver tray down on the big oak table. Little snacks are laid out under the clingfilm. Various salads, smoked trout, fresh horseradish, trout caviar and crème fraiche.

'I don't know what to say!' Elvira looks at him, shaking her head. 'It's . . . I can't accept it!'

'Would you prefer to insult me?' asks Stefan, and Carmen shakes her head with a laugh, 'Stefan Kaltenstein, as he lives and breathes, Elvira. There's only one thing to do: let's open a bottle!'

'Great idea!' Stefan reaches into the big pocket of his loden coat and takes out two mini bottles of champagne.

'Too much alcohol wouldn't be good for you at the moment,' he smiles to Elvira, 'so I've chosen the smaller-scale version.'

Typical, thinks Carmen, a man who has all of life's situations under control, and likes to take charge of them himself. She feels slightly uneasy. Elvira is old enough to know whether or not she wants two glasses of champagne.

'Please, sit down.'

Elvira points to the table and then walks over to the big buffet. She stops and holds on to it. Carmen sees, and runs over. 'Leave it, Elvira, I'll do that!'

She leads the old lady back to the table and fetches plates, glasses, cutlery and napkins. Stefan takes his coat to the cloakroom, walking past the old black-and-white photographs of South-West Africa.

Just don't let him stop to look at them, Carmen prays, gritting her teeth as she tries to think quickly. Should she try to hide the picture while he's outside? But Stefan comes back. He looks at Carmen and not at the wall.

They join Elvira at the table, and Carmen takes the cling-film off the food.

'What a great idea,' Carmen smiles to Stefan. 'Really magnificent. You doubtless assumed our own kitchens wouldn't be up to it . . .'

Stefan shakes his head. 'No, I just wanted to help out. Particularly since Frau Gohdes is a compatriot of mine.'

'How long . . . have you lived here?'

Elvira's voice sounds croaky. Carmen looks up. She really doesn't seem to feel terribly well.

Stefan laughs. 'Not so long really – I've always preferred the city, and I had only ever lived in Hamburg. But for the past few years I found myself spending more and more time in the country, and then I moved down here completely. Now I live here all the time, and only go to Hamburg on business. I assume Carmen told you about our dinner?'

Carmen serves the salads and the fish, and shakes her head sadly. 'Unfortunately I hadn't got around to it. I only brought Elvira out of hospital this morning, and before then we'd only spoken on the phone.'

'I see. Well, I'd be very interested to know a little more about you, Frau Gohdes. But perhaps today isn't the right time for a detailed conversation, although of course I'm rather excited – how often does one come across another German born in South-West Africa?' He smiles at Elvira and fills the glasses, 'But let's wait until you're properly better. And I must rebuke myself – I really only wanted to drop this off then go, and now I'm piling my own plate high.'

Elvira reassures him, 'I beg you to stay, you've bought so much. There's more than enough, we could feed at least three more people.'

Stefan nods to her, 'Then eat up, restore your strength! Let's toast your health.' He raises his glass, and clinks glasses with Elvira and Carmen.

Carmen secretly studies them both. Are there similarities? Stefan is looking good. He's wearing a dazzling white, loosely cut shirt and elegant dark blue trousers. His slightly tanned skin spreads tightly over his chiselled features. He looks thoroughly aristocratic. Yes, she finds him attractive. Extremely attractive, in fact. And the way he spoils her – Carmen is fascinated by his behaviour. But she can't see any strong similarity to Elvira. Elvira is much softer, rounder. She has that same straight, sharp nose and bright eyes, but they don't look at all similar. Not at first glance, at least.

She listens with one ear as they talk together. Stefan asks about the doctor's diagnosis, and what she will have to be careful about in future, and then he returns to the subject of German South-West Africa.

'But I must come back to this. What an amazing coincidence, two South-Westerners coming together in a little town like this!' He toasts Elvira. 'I must admit that after Carmen told me I simply had to meet you. From that point of view the party catering was just a means to an end!'

Elvira nods. 'You could have come by at any time, I . . .' she breaks off and clutches her heart, 'I would have been delighted,' she continues slowly.

Carmen grips her hand. 'What is it, Elvira, are you feeling unwell?'

'I really should say goodbye and come back when you've fully recovered,' Stefan nods to her, and is about to rise to his feet.

'No, no,' Elvira says quickly. 'Please, stay!'

Stefan glances at Carmen, and Carmen nods.

'Have you been prescribed anything?' Stefan has risen slightly from his chair again.

Elvira nods. 'In the kitchen, ten drops in a glass of water. The bottle of mineral water is right next to it.'

Carmen is about to get up as well.

'No, you stay with her.' Stefan indicates with a nod of the head that it is more important to stay with Elvira.

Elvira is sitting with her back to the kitchen, but Carmen watches as Stefan goes out and comes back shortly afterwards with a glass of water. He walks purposefully past the wall of photographs, but suddenly stops with a jolt and takes three steps back. Carmen sits poker-stiff. Here it comes, she says to herself, he's seen it out of the corner of his eye.

'Frau Gohdes, there's a picture of my father . . . it's incredible! You knew my father?'

'Your father?' Elvira turns around to face him, and Carmen holds her breath.

'Yes, this is my father!' Stefan stands in front of the picture shaking his head.

'So I'm right!' Elvira rises to her feet.

'What do you mean by that?' Stefan looks at her questioningly.

'I wasn't sure, but I suspected as much!'

'Could you please explain?'

Carmen bites her lip. She's about to throw her arms around him and tell him she's his mother. Elvira stands beside him and takes the little photograph from its hook.

'I knew your parents very well, Herr Kaltenstein. Anna, your mother, was closer to me than my own sister. And Hannes, your father, was an extraordinary man. Strong, just. He took his own counsel.'

'What?' Carmen cries. His mother's best friend? Had she misunderstood everything?

'It's incredible! Simply incredible!'

Stefan takes the photograph out of Elvira's hand and looks at it thoughtfully. 'Hence the roses?'

'There were seven roses. Their favourite number. I shared them out. Three for Hannes, four for Anna!'

'You have a photograph of my mother?'

'Yes, in the bedroom, beside my bed. Can you get it for me, please, Carmen?'

Carmen has seen the picture on Elvira's bedside table. But she had always thought it showed Elvira in earlier years. And now she's struck by another photograph next to it. A gaunt male face with a clear, open gaze. She will ask Elvira about it later.

Elvira and Stefan are sitting at the table. Stefan is holding his father's photograph in his hand, but puts it aside when Carmen hands him the picture of his mother. He looks at it for a long time. 'So that's her!'

'Yes, that's her,' Elvira agrees slowly. 'She was a wonderful woman. Don't you have a photograph of her?'

'No, the family album was destroyed in the accident. There weren't many pictures of the two of them – they'd only been married a year.'

Carmen looks from one to the other and bursts out laughing. 'I'm sorry, but can I make a confession? I thought you were Stefan's mother!'

'What made you think that?'

'I must have misunderstood our conversation – you remember – that first day. I thought I was losing my mind when I discovered the same photograph at Stefan's.'

'Even better! Let's drink.' Stefan tops up their glasses: 'And you, Elvira, must tell me everything. I still can't believe it!'

He hands Elvira the photograph, but she pushes his hand back. 'I'd like to give it to you.'

'No, I can't accept it.'

'Of course you can. You must have a photograph of your mother. She was such a strong, honest woman. She fought for her ideals. As did your father.' She hesitates. 'They didn't really fit in as far as the Kaltenstein family were concerned.'

Stefan looks up. 'What does that mean?'

'In the eyes of your grandfather, your parents were impossible. Your grandfather was a patriarch, he couldn't tolerate disobedience, he wanted to keep the reins in his hands. But Hannes and Anna broke away from the Kaltenstein line. They were socially aware, and they wanted the family to change its politics. And the worst thing was, the family wouldn't leave them alone!'

'So the crash may not have been so inconvenient?' Stefan has turned pale.

Elvira says nothing.

'Tell me!'

'I couldn't say. The fact is that your father and your mother were flying to a Socialist Party election in Windhuk. There was a good chance Hannes would become chairman. Your grandfather did everything he could to make sure that wouldn't happen. He knew he wouldn't be able to hold his head up high with his friends. A Red in the Kaltenstein family! He didn't want to be a figure of fun at the club. He threatened Hannes and Anna. Finally he said he was going to cut them out of his will – but their feelings were too strong. They just laughed, and flew off.'

It is quiet. 'Strange,' says Stefan, tapping the palm of his hand gently on the table. 'I come into this house, and an hour later my world is turned upside-down. You know, if your suspicions are correct, that I grew up with my parents' murderers?'

'I am sorry,' says Elvira simply.

'So am I!' Stefan gets to his feet. 'This is confusing. I don't know what the truth is. There's no one left I could ask. I have to ask myself. I wouldn't put it past the family. But I'd rather not believe it!'

He takes his mother's photograph from the table and turns to Elvira. 'I'd like to take my mother's picture with me, I'll have a copy made. Beyond that, I don't know right now whether I should be happy to have met you. But you are my only connection with my parents – perhaps that's how it should be!'

He walks quickly to the door and halts there a moment. 'Please forgive my impoliteness. I need to be alone. Goodbye.'

Carmen has leaped to her feet to shake his hand goodbye, but he is gone.

'My goodness!' she turns around and picks up her champagne glass. 'I'm bowled over, Elvira. I don't understand anything any more. You told me Hannes was the love of your life. But Hannes was married – to your best friend.'

Elvira picks up her own glass. 'My darling,' she says, 'I think I've just made a mistake. I shouldn't have told him the truth. But it just came out, just like that – he had to find out somehow!'

'That was really hard. I wouldn't much care for a family like that. But I don't understand about Hannes. Did you share him, you and Anna?'

Elvira looks at her as if she was half-witted.

'What sort of nonsense are you talking now? You jump to conclusions too quickly! I never said anything about Hannes – Johannes was the man I loved. Johannes didn't crash his plane, Johannes left me. I was a doctor, I was doing well in my profession. And one day Johannes, the man I wanted to marry, met a girl who had lots of time for him. And yet he was the only man I wanted!'

'Is that his photograph beside your bed?'

'Yes, *that's* Johannes. Whenever I go to bed I look at him and wonder what he would have looked like at eighty.'

'You really do that?'

'Yes, and then I think that maybe I haven't missed a thing.'

Carmen nibbles at a canapé. 'Do you think Stefan will call you again?'

'I very much hope so. If I could discover a little of Anna in him I'd be happy. But I'm afraid the Kaltensteins have covered their tracks. Nonetheless, you must understand my feelings towards him, Carmen. I've found my best friend's child. You could only compare it with what would happen if you found Laura's baby. It makes me feel quite teary. I really think I'll go to bed now.'

Outside her door is an enormous bunch of flowers, wrapped in a huge sheet of decorative paper. At first Carmen gives a start, then she takes a step nearer. How did that get here? She carefully takes off the paper. There are asters, zinnias and dahlias, nestling in tendrils of bramble and vine leaves, and tied together with a big red bow. There is a little card too:

Dear Carmen,
I wanted to take my revenge for your spontaneous visit this afternoon. I was as unlucky, unfortunately, as you. Thank you for your letter. I think it's time for us to meet. I'll collect you tomorrow at ten o'clock.
　　　Best wishes, David.

Oh my God, thinks Carmen. David tomorrow morning, then coffee at my mother's and then collecting Laura from the airport, it's all getting much too hectic. She's looking forward to finally meeting David, but the time doesn't suit her at all. Should she call him? As she goes in she looks at the clock. Eleven, not that late. But somehow a phone call would ruin the mysterious game. So she would have to take him a message instead. Should she do that? She carries the flowers into the kitchen, finds a big vase and cuts the stems the same length. She notices that the answering-machine is blinking and places the flowers on the table. Wonderful, an autumn bouquet! Then she presses the button, 'Hoffmann here,

thanks for your call. I'm clearly out of luck, but perhaps you
could try tomorrow morning. We could meet for brunch
somewhere perhaps? Do let me know, I'm looking forward to
it. Ciao, Felix!' The second is Peter. He wants to know if she's
come back to the real world, and whether she'd like to spend
a long Sunday morning in bed with him. He'll wait to hear
from her. You can wait, Carmen thinks. The third is Oliver,
trying to salvage their flight to New York together. If need be
he could book a last-minute flight on Tuesday – why doesn't
she think about it? Then her mother, who wants to find out
whether Carmen will definitely be there at midday on the dot
because her dad has an appointment later on, and he'd like to
see his daughter too – Carmen raises her eyebrows, Dad will
want to play golf, that's his important appointment, and
finally Frederic, who wants to spend Sunday with her. All of
Sunday.

Carmen drops on to the couch. Well, she says thoughtfully.
David's coming tomorrow morning, so I'll have to turn all the
others down. David can always think about whether he wants
to come to my parents' – he won't – or go away again. Peter's
far too cocky, as ever. Brunch with Felix would probably be
fun, but no. So would Frederic, but no too. The same with
Oliver. She picks up the phone. First she rings Stefan. He's not
home yet, so she leaves a message. Then she informs the
others, it doesn't take long, because they all have their
answering-machines on. She's pleased. Of course, they're all
out on Saturday night. Apart from Frederic. She gathers that
he's very disappointed.

'Shall I come over now? We could spend the night
together.'

Some cosiness would do Carmen good too, and she's very
fond of Frederic, but then she thinks about David. It would be
a bit odd if he were to ring on the doorbell at ten in the morning and Frederic opened the door to him in his boxer shorts.
That would sort out the David question once and for all. And
she doesn't want to do that. 'Don't be annoyed, Frederic, but
so much has happened that I'd like to be alone for a while.

Shall we meet up on Tuesday? You could come and get me at the office at six if you like.'

'Why not Monday?'

'Because . . .' She doesn't know. Monday is simply too soon. 'Because Laura's coming back from Brazil tomorrow evening, and on Monday she'll want me to go out with her. As old girl-friends do!'

Frederic sighs. 'How times change. In the old days my rivals were men, now they're women!'

'Oh,' laughs Carmen, 'don't be like that. You'll like Laura, I'm sure. But let us have a girls' night out. On Tuesday you'll be the centre of attention again!'

'Yeah, yeah,' he says, 'I understand. No one wants me!'

'What's up with you? I barely know you when you're like this.'

'Time of the month.'

Carmen laughs. 'If that's all it is, then I know it well. It'll be over by Tuesday, you'll see, then you'll be on top form again, and we'll go out and do something wild and crazy.'

'Like what?'

'Collect some wisps of fog, gather some leaves, shoot some raindrops. I don't know, we'll find something to do.'

'On your word.'

'You've got it Frederic, and now good night.'

Hardly has she put the phone down when it rings again. It's Frederic. He had completely forgotten to ask about Elvira, he says. Is she okay? Can he do anything for her? Send her some flowers, Carmen advises. She'd like that. And she'll tell him the rest on Tuesday. Tuesday, Tuesday, always Tuesday, he moans, and puts the phone down.

Fine, says Carmen, when she goes to bed, Tuesday, dear Frederic. Tomorrow is a day for me. And David Franck!

At ten o'clock Carmen is already standing excitedly by the window. She has put on jeans and a light beige knitted pullover. She looks nice without being overdressed. Her hair has just been washed and flows silkily down her back. Carmen also avoids putting on too much jewellery; two little pearls shimmer in her earlobes, and around her slender wrist she wears the elegant gold watch her parents gave her when she graduated from high school.

Where is he? Okay, he isn't Stefan Kaltenstein, but she can't stand even someone like David Franck being twenty minutes late. She turns away from the window. Maybe she should go to the toilet quickly? The doorbell rings. Her heart beats faster. She presses the buzzer and opens the door to her flat at the same time. She takes a startled step backwards.

'The door was open,' says a young, fair-haired man, but she's not struck so much by him as by the enormous dog standing facing her.

'This is Cain. You said I should bring a dog along,' says her visitor, introducing the giant.

Carmen tries to find words.

'I'm David. Pleased to meet you.' David holds out a hand, and only now does Carmen look at him properly. An alarm bell immediately goes off in her head, but she can't think why.

'Fine, pleased to meet you. I'm Carmen. Come in!'

She stands aside to let the man and the dog come in, and watches them from behind. If the dog stood up on his hind legs he would be bigger than David. She's never seen a specimen like him. He looks like a shaggy, haggard wolf the size of a calf.

'We don't want to mess up your flat, we just wanted to pick you up,' says David, stopping indecisively in the middle of her living-room.

'Please,' Carmen gestures towards the couch, 'let's drink to our meeting. Does Cain drink champagne, or is he more one for lemonade?'

David laughs. 'You're not scared of him, are you? He's completely harmless. He belongs to a friend of mine. Unfortunately I don't have a dog of my own, but you mentioned a dog, so I wanted to show up with a worthy specimen.'

115

'Do you like to do everything to excess?' Carmen asks carefully, thinking about the enormous card and the massive bunch of flowers.

'No, it's just what's left over. I used to make love to excess, now I like to stage things to excess.'

Carmen doesn't know what to say.

Now that she thinks about it, she's never really talked about the topic. Certainly, Stefan Kaltenstein isn't the type to talk about his impotence just like that. After two meetings. Frederic has demonstrated his impotence to her, but they haven't talked about it either. And now here's David, starting in on the subject in his second sentence!

'Is it a problem?' she asks, fetching two glasses. David sits on her couch, Cain lies quietly beside him like a good dog. He looks like a worn-out Moroccan carpet.

'I used to love having sex. I loved caressing women, spoiling them and then coming inside them when we were both ready.' Carmen's mouth is dry. She isn't ready for this kind of intimate conversation on an empty stomach. But she did ask, and now she'll have to go through with it. She comes back with a bottle of Alsatian crémant, hands David the bottle and sits down opposite him.

'And how do you make up for that now?' she asks, determined to go with the flow.

'Oh, I can still love a woman. I just don't sleep with her any more. Necessarily. But if I love somebody there are other ways to show it!'

He has opened the bottle, and fills the two glasses. For the first time Carmen is able to look at him properly. He's good-looking, much too good-looking to be single. Though it's the wrong time of year, he's still sun-tanned, his hair is light blond, with the finger cut that athletes prefer – tidy but casual. His eyes are turquoise, or at least that's how it seems to Carmen because he's wearing a turquoise sweatshirt. Underneath she can make out a thoroughly fit physique, like Frederic's only lankier. He must be four inches taller, Carmen guesses about six foot one.

'Let's drink to life.' He hands her a glass. His green eyes move her strangely.

'Yes, and to our talents!' Carmen points to the little telephone table on the wall. Behind it is David's card. 'You're astonishingly talented! Or did your computer make that all by itself?'

David laughs, and his eyes flash. To die for, Carmen thinks. Quite a catch. I hope he likes me too.

'As far as my computer's concerned our roles are quite clear,' there are little laugh-lines around David's eyes, 'I'm master of the house.'

'Aha! And what about your friend?'

'Martin?'

'I don't know his name, the guy with the black hair.'

'The roles are quite clear there too. Didn't he tell you? It's usually the first thing he has to get off his chest. He takes care of the housework, and I take care of the girls!' David grins slightly crookedly, and Cain's big head moves on to the couch. David runs his hands over his bushy eyebrows and plays with his ears.

'Yes, yes,' Carmen nods. 'He did. But I must admit, I didn't like that much. I found it all – a bit weird!'

David laughs. His laugh is deep and hearty, not excited, not too shrill, not rushed. Right from his belly. Carmen likes that. She likes it a lot. David gives Cain a gentle tap on the nose. 'Come on, pal, we're off!' and, to Carmen: 'I promised him a long walk in the woods, and didn't tell him anything about a cosy chat in a nice old building. You should never break promises to dogs.'

'Okay,' says Carmen, 'so what are our plans for today?'

'Put on stout shoes and thick jackets, and leave your watch and your lipstick behind, you won't be needing them.'

Cain stands up and shakes himself. His long tail swishes expectantly, just missing the champagne glasses. Don't get agitated, Carmen tells herself, don't get nervous. What are expensive champagne glasses compared to a walk in the woods with David.

David stands up too. Broad torso, narrow hips. This man isn't impotent, Carmen thinks, he can't be.

'Hang on, I'll be back in a second,' she calls, runs into the bedroom, fetches a quilted jacket and looks in her shoe cupboard for a pair of watertight, ankle-high winter shoes.

'So,' she says. 'I'm ready!' Cain jumps up at her as though he is a little puppy, and almost knocks her down. She spins around and laughs out loud. 'Off we go, then!'

'Isn't it too cold for you?' Carmen asks, pointing to his sweatshirt.

'Don't worry, I've got everything in the car. Okay, my darlings.' As he opens the door to the flat, Cain dashes out and skids head over heels down the polished wooden stairs with boundless enthusiasm. Only halfway down does he steady himself, turning back to look at them and urge them, with two deep woofs, to follow him.

'Fine, pal, we're coming!'

David puts his arm around Carmen's shoulder, and she desperately wants to cuddle up against him. What's happening to her? She turns her head slightly towards David's neck. She can smell him now. He smells good. He smells sharp, of grass, of summer rain, of soap, of man. Not masked by aftershave. Not in the slightest. Just a light, fine, floating scent, something that you would hardly notice, but which definitely belongs to him, to his personality. They walk downstairs side by side. Carmen gives two quick rings at Elvira's front door, the sign that she's going now, and can be reached about two hours later at her parents' number if anything happens.

'A secret sign?' asks David.

'Yes. From this point on I'm scattering breadcrumbs so that I can be found if you make off with me.'

He laughs and presses her more firmly to him. She feels as if she's known him for ages. How can she feel something like this?

'Green-eye,' she says, tenderly.

'I'm sorry?' he asks, holding the front door open for her and

Cain.

'I've just christened you Green-eye!'

'That's very nice,' he says. 'I like that.'

In front of the door to the house, exactly where Stefan had parked a few days before, stands a black jeep.

'Come on, Cain, let's be having you.' David opens the back door of the car. Cain doesn't much like jumping into the unknown. He puts his front paws on the back bumpers and stays there. He looks over the roof of the car.

'Nonsense, Cain. You're supposed to get in – in!' David taps on the thick carpet that he's laid down for the dog in the back. Cain wags his tail but doesn't move an inch. Carmen joins them. 'How did you get him in before?'

'His master whispered some magic word in his ear, don't ask me what it was. Come on now, Cain, get in, come on!'

Cain gives a friendly wag of his tail, but doesn't move from the spot.

'Maybe he doesn't like your car.'

'Well, at such short notice it's the best I can do. I should have brought a horse-box.'

Carmen laughs. 'What breed is he, anyway?'

'An Irish wolfhound. I think it's the biggest breed of dog there is. They have the biggest heads, so they're the most intelligent and they know very well that cars were built for getting into and not for climbing over.'

Cain has laid his head on the roof, and really does look as though he's trying to climb on top of the car.

'Let me have a go.' Carmen knocks resolutely on the floor of the jeep. 'Come on, Cain, we're off, come on, into the car with you!' Cain looks down at her from where he is standing, a good head taller than she is. Carmen won't be intimidated. 'Come on, boy. We're going. Do you understand? Come on! Here, let me show you!' She clambers into the back of the jeep as Cain and David watch. Cain drops to his feet, and stands on his four paws by the car. 'Come on, now.' Carmen's already inside, clicking her fingers. Cain puts one paw inside the car, then another one. His long snout is close to Carmen now, and only his hind legs are still outside. David puts his shoulder into it, pushing his bottom and trying to lift his legs. With much moaning and groaning, Cain ends up in the jeep.

'Like an old granddad,' Carmen laughs. 'You did very well,' she says, praising Cain and clapping him on his strong neck. David closes the door from behind and comes over to the driver's side. He shakes his head. 'I haven't much time for Pekinese dogs, but sometimes they might be more practical!'

Carmen laughs and tickles Cain's nose, and David starts the car.

The world looks quite different from inside a jeep. So high up. Carmen feels like the queen of the country road.

'It feels nice.' She runs her finger over the black leather.

'And it's practical,' David agrees. 'I miss it when I do long journeys as I always swap with Martin then. He drives a BMW, nothing earth-shattering, but it's fast and reliable.'

Somehow a BMW doesn't seem like much of a car for an individualist, Carmen thinks to herself. Everybody drives them because they're fast and reliable. Not because they've fallen in love with them. Maybe I should get something different myself, like an Alfa Spider. If it doesn't feel like doing something it just stops. Like Cain. They would go well together.

She bursts out laughing because she can see the picture clearly in front of her eyes. That massive great dog on the back seat of a Spider!

'What's so funny?' David's driving quickly but safely. He takes a quick look at her and suddenly has to brake. Cain slips forward, and Carmen is just able to catch him with both arms before he lands on the front seat. They're at a crossing, and David lets another driver past before he sets off again. 'Sorry,' he says, 'I should really have some kind of a net for Cain, or put a seat-belt on him!'

'Does he belong to Martin?'

'Who? Cain? No, to my neighbour.'

'In the old villa?'

David smiles at her. 'You know your way around. Yes, him.'

'That makes sense.' Carmen grins. Of course, Tumbledown Villa would have to have a dog like that.

'Are we going far?' asks Carmen.

'Only to Raven Wood, twenty minutes away, why?'

'Because I've got to be at my parents' at midday, it's just occurred to me.'

He looks at her with an expression that openly shows what he is thinking.

'Don't be cross, David. It was arranged before I got your letter. You're free to come too.'

One raised eyebrow is joined by the other.

'Honestly, my parents are really nice!'

'Don't be cross with me, Carmen, but I want to spend time with you. It's nice that you want to take me to see your parents, but I think that would be a bit much for me today. I just wanted to talk, go for a walk, have tea in the Raven's Nest. If you want to see your parents I'm afraid we're not going to make it.'

'You're right.' Carmen pulls a face. 'I know, but there's nothing I can do about it. My mother likes cooking, and she's looking forward to seeing me. There's no way I can cancel.'

He sighs. Oh no, thinks Carmen, I've lost him now, just when I'd won him. And all because of my parents!

David snaps his fingers close to her cheek. 'Don't take it so badly. I've got the answer. I'll drive you to your parents and then pick you up again. At two, shall we say?'

That sounds much better. 'You'd do that? That's fantastic, you've taken a weight off my mind!' She blows him a kiss.

'Okay,' he grimaces. 'I'm not happy about it, I admit, because I've been looking forward to seeing you. But then you can keep the afternoon and evening free for me.'

Carmen beams. 'Sure, then we can . . .' She remembers Laura. Her beaming face darkens. 'We can . . .' she repeats, and breaks off. Things are really awkward today.

'What's up?'

He's guessed something, Carmen thinks. What'll I say now?   121

'My friend Laura arrives back from Rio at half past five. And I've promised to collect her from the airport.'

David shakes his head. 'That's just great. And when can you find time for me? Between two and five thirty, or would it be better between, let's see,' he looks quickly at his watch, 'twenty to eleven and twelve?'

'Oh, please,' says Carmen, close to tears. 'There's nothing I can do. I really wanted to meet you. You never asked me, you just rang up. And that's fine, but how was I supposed to know what you'd planned? And my other arrangements were made ages ago!'

'Peace, peace.' He brakes. Is he going to chuck me out? She turns back to face him. He is studying her with his green eyes and holds Carmen enraptured with his gaze. A funny feeling rises up inside her, a mixture of the fear of loss and of excited anticipation for the future.

'No problem,' he nods to her. The light changes to green and he drives on. 'You're right, I am completely selfish. Of course. I've painted you, in every colour in the rainbow, I've painted you into my pictures, into my words. Now I'm happy, do you understand, Carmen? I'm happy. You've put the spectre of my impotence in the dark. In other circumstances I'd have had to play hide and seek with you, always changing the subject when things got serious, not knowing how you'd react, not knowing how to tell you. Now it's all okay. You're looking for an impotent man, okay, here he is!'

Carmen leans impulsively towards him, puts her arm around his shoulders and kisses him on the cheek. He's slightly stubbly, and she inhales his odour.

'I'm delighted it's you,' she whispers, her face buried in the nape of his neck. He reaches out for her hair with his right hand and lets it slip through his fingers. 'Shall I tell you something? I knew it when I got your letter!'

'What did you know?'

'That it was you, David. That you were the one I was looking for.'

His fingers slip through her hair to the back of her head,

he presses Carmen to him and kisses her on the forehead.
'Okay, I wrote that something drew me to you. It's true, my
feelings didn't let me down – even if it's all going a bit too
quickly.'

'You're right.' Carmen feels wonderfully secure with his
arm around her. 'You're right, things are moving very quickly.
But emotions don't heed the rules!' They say nothing for a
while. The engine throbs evenly and Cain is lying down with
his head on his front paws, sleeping. Quiet music whispers
from the radio.

'Why are you impotent, David? How did it happen?'

Carmen has had to screw her courage together to ask about
it. She's never spoken to anyone as directly as that. Perhaps he
doesn't want to talk about it . . .

'It's organic, Carmen. It had nothing to do with some awful
woman, or a trauma involving my mother. I had a motorbike
accident three years ago. I wasn't castrated, but almost was.
My legs were pretty messed up, but a few nuts and bolts
sorted that out. But the rest. There you have it.'

'Are you . . . are you badly damaged there? I mean, is something missing?

He glances at her and laughs: 'No, it's not like the days of
Alexander the Great. All his servants were castrated.'

'Really?' Carmen is astonished. 'That would be simply . . .
how terrible! Then you were really lucky that nothing's missing. But how did you deal with your impotence after your
accident?'

'At first I didn't. I wrote to you. Before my accident I was
hyperactive. I thought I had to have new women all the time,
at least three times a day with three different women, three in
a row. Really, when I think about it I was pretty awful.'

He drives along a forest road. The jeep bumps from pothole
to pothole. Cain lifts his head and promptly bumps it against
the roof of the car.

'My impotence made a few things clear. Maybe it came
along at exactly the right time, so that I got my brain rather
than my little friend into gear. But I hope the learning

123

process will come to an end some day, and that I'll get my leaving certificate.

'You mean your impotence might be curable?'

'Would you like that?' He looks at her questioningly. She hates questions like that. If she says yes he'll feel undervalued because he'll assume she wants something that can't be. If she says no, he may feel rejected.

'Look, David, I'm going to tell you the truth.' The car stops and Carmen looks outside. They're standing in a lonely car-park in the forest. A little lake shimmers through the trees, and there's no one else for miles around.

He interrupts her silence. 'Come on, let's go. I've chosen a little roundabout walk, and you'll be with your parents in less than an hour – unless they live miles away, that is.'

Carmen is happy with that. Cain is crouched behind her, and David can only just stop him jumping over the driver's seat into the open air. 'Stop, Cain, get out the back!' Carmen pushes him backwards while David runs around the car and opens the rear door. With one bound Cain is out. Carmen gets out and wraps herself up in her quilted jacket, and David gets a jacket as well. It's claret-coloured and goes well with his light-coloured hair and green eyes.

'Should the dog be on a lead?' asks Carmen.

'He's far too clumsy to catch anything – a hedgehog, per-haps.' Carmen laughs and cuddles up against David. He puts his arm around her, and they slowly walk after Cain, who has bounded down the narrow path to the lake ahead of them.

'I didn't mean to interrupt you before,' says David, trying to get her to go on speaking.

'Yes,' Carmen muses, kicking little bits of gravel in front of her.

'You were going to be honest with me,' David helps her.

'Yes, what I want to say is that your impotence is the foun-dation of our encounter, David. Not just because you replied to my ad. Let me put it this way. If I'd met you somewhere by chance, I'd have thought of you as a good-looking surfer guy, if you'll excuse the expression, but in a rather negative way.

I'd have seen you as the macho man in constant search of new prey, running around with his penis permanently erect. I'm sorry if that sounds harsh.'

The forest path opens up, a cool wind rises, leaves blow away from them.

'No, no,' says David. 'Of course, you're right. But it hurts anyway. Do I really come across as so predatory?'

'I'd have thought so, yes.'

'We were talking about you.' David pulls her a little closer to him as they walk along. Carmen lets him, she wants to be close to him, it feels good.

'Yes, carry on, let's hear more!'

'What made you come up with the idea of trying to find an impotent man? I mean, I'm happy you did, but was there some kind of deep-seated shock?'

Cain is romping around. David picks up a stick, and throws it. Cain is delighted. Carmen ponders.

'No,' she says, 'no, there was no concrete trigger. It's the mounting-up of many details, many moments when I thought, what's the point, just let him, many moments when I should have cut somebody short and didn't, out of politeness, although a man never thinks about politeness when he's verbally groping in your knickers. It's all the things that have irritated me over the years, not just irritated but hurt me. And at some point I thought, why am I actually playing along with this? I'm just as crazy. I can free myself! And as I didn't want to turn into a lesbian I thought it was better just to drop the whole sex thing.'

He looks at her. 'Have you thought all this through?'

She hesitates briefly. 'Not at first, I admit. It was more emotional, it was perhaps an unconscious reaction to my ex-boyfriend. But meanwhile I've learned a few things and I feel better. It's right for me.'

They walk beside the shore of the little lake, arm in arm. Off to one side ahead of them, on a hillock, is a red-painted bench. From there the meadow slopes gently down to the water.

'Let's go up there,' says Carmen.

David nods, whistles to Cain, who comes quickly, and they climb the hillock. The autumn sun stands veiled in the sky. It can't quite break through the clouds, but the day is gradually brightening. At least it's not raining, which Carmen finds incredibly comforting.

They sit down. Cain bounces back down the hill to the water, and then to the right, back on to the path.

'Have you really thought this through?' David slides forward on the bench and stretches his face towards the rather brighter patch in the sky, the sun, as though he was in a deckchair. Carmen leans against him gently.

'Yes,' she says, 'it's what I want.'

'But what if you suddenly feel like sex again?'

'The two things have nothing to do with each other,' says Carmen. 'The contentment that comes from a harmonious relationship has nothing to do with pleasure.'

David remains silent for a moment, then looks at her. 'So you separate pleasure and relationship. You want to be happy in a relationship, but you don't want to be bothered by a man who's randy all the time. On the other hand, if you do feel like it you want to be free to go somewhere else to get what you need. Sorry. You can't have that, Carmen. That won't work. At least not with me.'

That was exactly what Stefan had said. But she couldn't imagine a tender relationship with Stefan. With David she could.

'You know, David, maybe I'm too inexperienced. In the end I want a relationship in which I'm not continually being bothered. And I'm only going to find that with an impotent man – that's what I've always thought. But who says an impotent man can't be tender? Couldn't we wake up next to one another and spoil each other tenderly if we felt like it? Where does it say that an impotent man can't do that?' She hesitates for a moment. 'Or can't he?'

'Ouch,' says David, 'I'd have to think about that.' And, after a brief pause, 'Oh, look, a deer!' He points to the other side of the lake. And sure enough, a deer has come out of the forest to the clearing. It walks cautiously to a shallow spot on the lakeside and drinks.

'I hope Cain doesn't see it,' Carmen whispers.

'I can't really whistle him, can I?' David whispers back.

'There, look!' Carmen excitedly pinches his jeans. A second deer emerges, and shortly afterwards a third one. And then two much smaller ones, their babies.

'Where's Cain?' Carmen asks urgently.

'Shh!' David puts his finger to his mouth.

It's a wonderful picture. All five stand by the water, two keeping a watchful eye around while the other three drink. The lake is a shimmer of silver, the forest rising darkly behind it. In the light-dappled meadow, bordered by reeds on either side, the deer are clearly visible.

What an idyll. Profoundly moved, Carmen takes a deep breath. David runs a cautious hand through her hair and strokes the nape of her neck. He avoids any rapid movements, so that he won't destroy the picture. The lake isn't big. The deer could see them or catch wind of them, and the harmony would be disrupted.

Suddenly Carmen leaps to her feet, clapping her hands and dashing down the slope. Before David can understand what's going on, a shot echoes over the clearing. He sits rooted to the spot. Carmen runs up to the lake shouting. The five deer flee into the forest. None of them seems to have been hit. David dashes down after Carmen.

'Did they get one?'

'I don't think so, they didn't seem to.'

She points to a hide up in a tree, well concealed at the edge of the forest, over to their right. It provides the ideal viewpoint, from the clearing where the deer were just standing, to the bench on the hill.

The barrel of a rifle flashes inside it.

Is David mistaken, or is it aimed at them?

'Watch out!' he shouts, pulling Carmen to the ground. A shot rings out. It isn't meant for them but for Cain, who is standing by the bench where Carmen and David were sitting a moment before.

'Put that filthy mutt of yours on a lead, or I'll blow his head off. This is hunting land,' a voice booms down from above.

'You shoot my dog and I'll wring your neck!' Carmen cries back. She marches belligerently towards the hide, up in its tree. 'Shooting defenceless deer, you monster. Who do you think you are? God?' Please let him have a heart attack and fall out, she prays.

'Leave my land immediately!' the voice booms down again.

The rifle barrel is still aimed in their direction. Carmen is enraged. David joins her, holding Cain by his collar, and together they walk towards the hide.

'I'm warning you, stay where you are!'

'What's going on, are you trying to shoot us? Like those deer back there?' David shouts. 'Do you know what that was, when you shot at us? Attempted murder.'

'Your dog was running around loose. I have the authorisation . . .'

By now David and Carmen are standing directly beneath the hide. The man up there still hasn't revealed himself. The rifle barrel follows each of the trio's movements.

'Go away.'

David wonders whether he should climb up into the tree.

Carmen pulls gently on his jacket, having sensed what he has in mind.

'Don't do it. He's trigger-happy. Who knows what he's capable of when he's cornered,' she whispers.

The hide is built high up in the fir tree. A long ladder, fastened with a few screws, leads up to it, and the wood has been rotted by exposure to the wind and the weather.

'Go away, I'm warning you,' the voice whines from above.

David gives Carmen the dog, walks to the ladder. He lifts it a little way off the ground and jerks it towards him. He easily manages to pull out the first two screws – higher up the bolts are more solid. David violently jerks on the ladder. It cracks and splinters, and the top third breaks away. David has a good fifteen feet of ladder in his hand, and now he lets it tip backwards. With a dull clatter it gets stuck in the nearest tree. David quickly pulls Carmen out of the line of fire – you never know – and then, in a friendly voice, calls up: 'Enjoy your Sunday afternoon. A hiker might walk by – you could shoot him. But it might be a better idea to ask him for help – November nights are cold. See you!'

At first not a sound comes from up above. David walks back towards the car with Carmen, still holding the dog by the collar and keeping under cover of the trees. Then they hear the voice coming from the hide. 'You can't do that! I'll tell the police! I'm on the council, and I won't have it. Come back.' When Carmen and David are nearly at the car they hear him calling for help. 'Please come back,' he calls.

'Funny how a piece of wood can change someone's tone,' grins David, shaking his head. Laughing, Carmen throws her arms around his neck. 'You were wonderful.'

'But you were faster.'

'Suddenly I just saw the rifle barrel flashing from the branches, and that was it!'

'I take it you saved a deer's life.'

'Fine, then I've done my good deed for the day.'

'Yes,' David stands still, Cain rubbing his wolf-grey head against his jacket, 'and what shall I do?'

'You can come to my parents.'

'Oh, no, please not that. Don't you have another good deed to do?'

'Then you could come to the airport to collect Laura.'

'Okay, fine. If she's your friend, and if you say she's nice – okay, I'll do it.'

She throws herself around his neck again. 'Thanks, David, I'm so pleased!'

With his one free arm he presses her to him tightly and then whispers in her ear, 'And don't let me forget to call the forestry office so that they find the old boy before he's mummified!'

'But don't let's call them too soon. Let him stew.'
'You bet,' and he gently bites her earlobe.

At quarter past five Carmen and David are already at the airport. Carmen loves the atmosphere of heartfelt farewells and
overjoyed greetings, of hustle and bustle and, over longer peri-
ods, of boredom. She likes the brightly coloured mixture of
different peoples, and Germans dressed up for abroad, proudly
strolling through customs bearing the insignia of foreign cul-
tures and then feeling peculiar the minute they've left the
cosmopolitan melting-pot and the first passer-by turns around
to gawp at them. All of a sudden the African plaits, the cowboy
hats, the Elton John glasses and the Ibiza party clothes disappear into the back of the wardrobe and wait for the next
holiday or for carnival. David and Carmen have a great time
watching everybody, and they nearly miss Laura's arrival.

'There she is!' calls Carmen suddenly, when Laura is
already standing in the arrivals area. 'Laura!' she cries. She
pulls David by the sleeve and runs over.

'Where did you come from? I didn't see you!'

'Back there,' she points vaguely over her shoulder. 'I didn't
feel like standing there for too long. But let's look at you,
sweetie, you look fantastic. You're in love, aren't you?' The
two women hold each other in a firm embrace, kissing one
another heartily on the mouth. David stands nearby, and
Laura gazes at him over Carmen's shoulder. Carmen breaks
away from Laura, and affectionately grabs David's arm, 'This is
David Franck and this, David, is Laura Rapp.'

David holds out his hand and Laura flashes her eyes at
him, 'Young love, eh? I'm very happy for you. In Brazil the
men are small and dark and most of them seem to be gay
anyway. Better off staying in Germany.'

Carmen casts a quick glance at David, but he doesn't seem
bothered by Laura's loose tongue.

'That's what Carmen thought – and that's where I was
lucky. Who knows whether I'd have met her otherwise!'

'Oh, that sounds good. Best of luck, Carmen, the boy's serious. So, shall we go for a drink, or would you rather grab something to eat later? I'd love a pizza.'

'Instead of sauerkraut and a nice big hunk of German pork?' David asks innocently.

Laura laughs. 'If you stayed there long enough you'd probably eat anything at all, but after only two weeks I'd be happy with a real German pizza.'

'Goodness,' says David, amazed. 'Where can you get such a thing?'

'You know, at Wagner, Iglo or Eismann.'

David grins. 'I'd love to take you out, but I'm afraid men would be surplus to requirements this evening.'

Carmen hesitates. She'd really rather have spent this evening with David than with Laura, but on the other hand she desperately needs to talk to someone, and it could only be Laura, who hasn't for a minute doubted that it was going to be a girls' night out.

'Could you drive me back home, Carmen? Then I'll drop off my bags and have a shower, and we can meet at the Laguna.'

'No, we'll wait for you, then you can pack what you need for tomorrow and stay over at my place tonight.'

Laura nods, but then looks over at David, 'Sure I won't be in your way?'

David shakes his head with a laugh. 'I'll go to bed with Cain tonight. He's company enough.'

'Is he gay too?' Laura asks bluntly.

'The dog? I don't know, I've never asked him.'

They all laugh. David takes the suitcase and heads for the exit. 'By the way, Laura, you'll have to put up with my car. It's probably going to be a bit of a tight squeeze.'

Cain's already fast asleep. David had spent the whole afternoon with him in the forest while Carmen had been at her parents', and later, when he'd picked Carmen up again, they had gone for another long walk in Raven Wood. They had coffee and cake in the Raven's Nest, and Cain was given the bowl of food that the restaurant's dog, a St Bernard, had turned his nose up at. 'Ours is so spoilt, he'll only eat rump steak and chicken breast!'

Laura is amazed at the sight of the giant dog. 'I can't see where he starts and where he finishes! I don't know where to sit. I can hardly lie down next to him. Where did you think I could put my bags?'

'Hang on a second.' Grabbing the bags, David opens the back door of the jeep, throwing the car-keys on to the driver's seat, carefully pushes one bag after another towards the front, between Cain and the side, then climbs in after them and kneels down by Cain without disturbing him. He still manages to keep the bags propped upright.

'Brilliant,' says Carmen. 'Who's driving?'

'You are. The keys are in the front, you just have to start it. On the top on the left you've got the light-switch, just pull it out, to the left you've got dipped and full headlights, and the indicator's on the right. And of course you know where Laura lives.'

'Fine, capitano.' Carmen is rearranging the seat and the mirror, and Laura climbs into the passenger seat.

'Nice car,' she says. 'Have you ever driven it to Africa?'

'No, not yet, but if you want we could think about it!'

'All three of us?' asks Laura.

'Four.' David points with his thumb at Cain, who is rhythmically twitching all four paws in his sleep. He's probably running through the afternoon walk again, scouring the forest for the deer.

'Four, of course,' Carmen says to Laura, 'unless Wilko comes too?'

'Hmm.' Laura pulls a face while Carmen slowly drives out of the car-park. 'Wilko didn't exactly live up to the demands he always makes on other people.'

Carmen looks at her uncomprehendingly.

'In other words, he's shown himself to be pretty shabby and pathetic.' Laura points at the road ahead. 'And now, if you'd please look at the road, I don't want to end my Brazilian holiday in the ditch, particularly seeing as I'd be at the bottom of it.' And she points at Cain. Enthusiastically chasing through his dream forest, he still hasn't noticed a thing.

Carmen and Laura sit facing one another in the Laguna. David has been heroic to the last, bringing the two women to the restaurant before saying goodbye. They have a pretty little table away from most of the other customers. The restaurant is nearly full, and the air is filled with the smell of pizza and cigarette smoke.

'Stay with us,' says Carmen, who thinks David is stupid to leave when he's still hungry. Laura also urges him to take the enormous calf out of the car and join them for a pizza. But David won't.

'You've got enough to talk about, and I don't like smoky places. Cain and I will go home and have a quiet drink with my neighbour. If I know him, he'll have something cooking anyway.'

He takes Carmen in his arms and kisses her on the mouth. 'I'll call you tomorrow,' he says.

'I'm at work tomorrow.'

'Then give me the number quickly.' He tears off a piece of paper napkin and takes a pencil stump out of his pocket.

Laura casts Carmen a glance that clearly expresses what she's thinking. What, he doesn't even know your telephone number? Carmen grins while she gives David the number.

'And your surname, darling,' he adds. He's noticed Laura's expression.

Carmen laughs. 'Sure! Say hi to Martin. Tell him I've fondled your belly. He'll know what I mean!'

'My God, so we got that far?' David grins, dodging Carmen before she can pinch him. 'Have a great time,' he says, briefly raising both hands to say goodbye before he leaves.

'Holy Christ, where did you find him? Pretty special!' Laura nods encouragingly at Carmen.

'Laura, if I could tell you everything that's happened over the last fortnight, we'd be here till the small hours.'

'No can do. I've got school tomorrow. Alarm at half past six. I just want to know how you met him. You don't get single guys like that running about all over the place.'

Carmen laughs. 'That's exactly what I said to myself. But don't laugh, he's single.'

'Was,' Laura corrects her. 'He *was* single.'

'That'd be great. One Laguna pizza with double cheese, and one lasagne, please, and half a litre of house red.'

'Do you want salad with that?' Enzo is serving them personally.

They both shake their heads. 'That would be too much,' says Carmen, and Laura pats her flat stomach.

'Don't make me laugh!' Carmen raises her eyebrows. 'Are you starting on the Laguna diet, or what?'

'Something like that,' Laura laughs over at Enzo, who is walking to the bar. Laura slips forward on her chair: 'Quick, get to the point. Tell me exactly where you can find heroes like that around here.'

'You're thinking of Siegfried and the Nibelungen, aren't you? You're not far off, you're not far off. But unlike Wagner's Siegfried, the leaf from the lime tree – the one that did Siegfried in – didn't fall on David's back, but on another sensitive spot.'

'Hmm? Explain.'

'Think about it. You're good at that.'

'Don't be so sarcastic, it doesn't suit you – ah, you mean, he's . . . he's got a problem? Or is he gay? He didn't seem that way. What's the catch?'

Enzo serves the wine, and Carmen and Laura clink glasses. They look each other in the eyes and exchange a grin. Laura would say the grin was dirty, though Carmen would prefer to describe it as complicit. Whatever, they grin at each other like two friends who have known each other inside out for years. They put their glasses down at the same time, and Laura reaches for Carmen's hand.

'It's good to have you back.' Carmen blows her a kiss.

'You can't be left on your own for a minute. Now tell me, honey-pie, what've you been up to?'

'Okay, listen. Laura I placed an ad. Peter was getting on my nerves, really badly, and here, in this very restaurant, I had what you might call an epiphany, and everything became crystal clear. I decided to create my own perfect relationship.'

'Aha!' Laura nods, 'I thought David looked freshly caught . . .'

'Just listen and stop being silly. David came later. So, we were talking about the ad.'

'Okay, you were looking for a man.'

'Yes, but not some sort of composite from the second-hand-parts warehouse. Someone whose parts were brand spanking new.'

'Christ almighty, could you stop talking in riddles?'

'I was looking for an impotent man.'

At first there's silence, then Laura shakes her head. 'You're bananas! What do you want with an impotent man? You of all people? Don't make me laugh!'

'Stop it. You're acting as if I'm some kind of man-eating insect. I'm fed up to the back teeth with all that standing-round-the-flagpole stuff, pre-sent *balls*, cock att-en-shun, all, and the obligatory twenty-one-gun salute right at the end. I'm fed up with it.'

'I can tell you are,' Laura says dryly. 'Here, slow down, have another drink, you're talking up a storm.'

'You see, once you start talking about it you're halfway to getting over it. I feel much better already!'

'What do you want to get over? The men talk, or the coercive way of thinking? Or what?'

'Just the stuff that bothers me personally. And since it's bothered me for years, and even more so lately, I'm ridding my life of all the things that annoy me.'

'So that means you don't want to sleep with any more men.'

'Exactly. I don't want to be pressured all the time.'

Laura picks up her glass and drinks. 'And David's part of the plan?'

'What do you mean, the plan? He's one of the impotent men who replied to my ad!'

'Interesting. So? Were there many?'

'Loads. You wouldn't believe it.' Carmen laughs and shakes her head.

'Unfortunately I gave all the letters away. But maybe I should get them back so that you can see what's been going on.'

'Thanks. I've just been through a disaster of my own, I don't need another one.'

Enzo serves their dinner. As if on cue, they reach across the table and grab food from the plate opposite.

'Wilko would go bananas. He's so namby-pamby, so well mannered, the snake.' Laura shakes her head and blows on the forkful of lasagne steaming in front of her mouth.

'So you're at loggerheads?'

'Hardly the phrase. I could kill him.'

Carmen is still sawing away at the little piece of pizza on Laura's plate. 'Honestly, Laura, you know, I've got nothing against Wilko. On the contrary, over time I really came to like him. But the first time I saw him I really wondered why you'd chosen him.'

'Let me give you a hand.' Laura cuts the piece off for her and holds it out on the side of her knife. 'Right,' she says. 'I was in love. The fun should have gone out of it the first time we slept together. It probably did. I just didn't notice because my brain was fuddled by emotion.'

'How come, what was up?' Carmen gnaws carefully at the corner of pizza.

'He came to bed in his underwear. Can you imagine? He didn't even take off his Y-fronts. Can you imagine what that looked like?'

'Did he leave his socks on too?'

'Right,' Laura laughs, 'no, he didn't. Instead he sweated, making everything wet. After three minutes of love-making he needed three bath-towels to dry off. And I didn't look or feel too great either.'

'Hmm.' Carmen has finally put the whole piece of pizza in her mouth, and is trying to locate some bits of lasagne that are cool enough to eat. 'You're right, it doesn't sound too good. How long did you put up with that?'

'Until I was sick of it. By then it was too late.'

'What do you mean, too late?'

Laura says nothing, just taps her belly gently.

Carmen lowers her fork and looks quizzically at Laura. 'You're not serious! You're having a baby?'

'Whether I'm having it, I don't know. I went to Brazil to make up my mind.'

'How come I don't know anything about this? Why didn't you tell me before?'

'You must forgive me, Carmen. I found out, I wanted to be on my own, I booked a last-minute flight, I was off. I even played with the idea of getting rid of it over there. No one would have been any the wiser. I would have told you later. But now, here we are again!'

Carmen stands up, walks over to Laura and crouches down beside her and gives her a hug. They press their heads together. Carmen puts a hand on Laura's belly and says, 'Now I see what you mean about putting on weight!'

Laura smiles.

'And now?' Carmen asks. 'How do you feel? You know that if you keep it I'll help you as much as I can.'

'I know. You're the only person I can really rely on.'

'Does your mother know?'

'I'll tell her tomorrow. I didn't talk to anyone about it before I went to Brazil.'

'And Wilko?'

'Since he revealed his true self, I've realised that he simply drew me into it. He'll relish his triumph. It wouldn't be his first child. He has plenty of experience in this grubby field.'

'How can you think that of him like that? He wanted to carry you around on a silver platter, or that's what he always told me!'

'Only as long as I stayed up there nicely and did as he

wanted. You have to acknowledge him as the Good Lord himself, with all life beneath him. And he doesn't only think that
way in his private life. I just made a mistake, like others before
me, that's all. He isn't really the serious businessman he makes
out he is, but a shabby, unprincipled con-man. Not to mention
a megalomaniac. Realisation hurts. But it's true! I really fell for
it and now I wonder how stupid I've really been. But I really
don't want an impotent man. So please don't go placing any
ads for me!' They laugh, and Carmen goes back to her chair.

'To think that there's a baby in there . . .' Carmen shakes her
head.

'An embryo, please. I'm in the fifth week, you can't really
call it a baby.'

'Thank you, teacher, that's quite right.' Carmen tries the
lasagne. 'Hmm, hot but tasty. I needed that. At least as a
teacher you're a public servant, so you've got a bit of health
insurance. So dear old Wilko won't be able to take you to
task.'

'He'll try, because his pride – based on what, one wonders – will be injured because I left him. Bet your life on it.'

'Spare me. I'm not betting on anything. But I am drinking
wine, with you, and if you decide to keep the child, my dear,
then that was your last glass of alcohol for the next nine
months.'

'Eight,' corrects Laura.

'Eight?' Carmen asks.

'I think. But they calculate these things in weeks and I only
ever calculate from one holiday to the next. But I know what
she's going to be called: Alina Olivia Carmen!'

'She?' Carmen grins.

'Of course. We have the power to eliminate men once and
for all. We just won't have any!'

They both burst out laughing, much too loudly for a
restaurant, but they don't care. They laugh themselves hoarse,
then they toast each other.

'Welcome to the club,' Carmen giggles.

'You can keep your impotent men,' Laura says and grins.

'And anyway, you haven't told me anything about David. I mean, it seems a real shame. How can a man like that be impotent?'

'A motorbike accident, Laura. Three years ago. He says he doesn't want to be impotent for ever, but he's gained something from the experience – character, tolerance, maturity. At least he regards women differently than before his accident.'

'I can imagine, given his looks. Was your hi for Martin and the bit about having his belly fondled something to do with his lively past?'

'Nothing gets past you, does it?'

'Not a thing. Maybe he's got a twin brother or a good-looking friend who just happens not to be impotent.'

'Martin wouldn't be much to your taste. There were better-looking guys among my replies – you'll see.' She takes a forkful and holds it out to Laura. 'Try this, it's not too hot now. It's terrific – much too good for the time of day!'

'What? Show me!' Laura points to Carmen's watch, and Carmen holds it out to her.

'Where have you left yours?'

'Only nine, is that possible?'

'It's usually right. Where's yours?'

'I wouldn't take a decent watch to Brazil. I might never see it again. I don't earn enough for that. As a mother-to-be I have to think of my child's inheritance.'

Carmen laughs. 'You seem to be getting into the part.' She puts the last forkful in her mouth and scratches a last bit of baked cheese crust out of the bowl.

'You bet. I have another idea. Why don't we settle the bill, go back to your place, drink a glass of mineral water in bed and talk for a bit longer before we go to sleep?'

'Sounds good to me. Call Enzo over if you catch his eye, Laura. And you're sure you've got everything for tomorrow morning? For school? It didn't look as though David had to carry all that much upstairs for you.'

'I never have much on Monday. I have to leave early and I get home early. That's where we differ from you insurance people. You set off late and get back late. So we could never get married, you and me. We'd never see each other.'

'The best arrangement for a marriage.'

'Can it be, my dear Carmen, that you're going through a spiteful period? There may be marriages that work, and partners who really love each other. Morning, noon and night.'

'I wouldn't argue with that. Not at first, anyway. But what do you do afterwards?'

'No idea. Invite Dr Ruth along and go out for a drink with her. Let's go.'

On Monday morning Carmen goes out of the office to see some customers. She draws up a life insurance policy, advises a company about legal protection and then goes back to the office in a good mood.

It's shortly after twelve. Britta is out at lunch, and there are six messages on her desk. Carmen flicks through them. Oliver, Stefan, Frederic, David, Felix and Peter, all asking her to ring back. That's not on. They can't paralyse her business. Men – taking over, as usual! She goes into the kitchenette and looks in the Thermos jug to see if there's any coffee left. There's a lukewarm drop at the bottom. Better than nothing. She pours herself a cup and goes back to the phone. She phones David first. She's been thinking about him all morning, and about Laura and her baby. Who'd have thought it?

'David Franck, hello.'

'Hey, David! Carmen. How are you?'

'Good to hear from you. I'm filled with longing. It's fizzing and hopping and leaping all through my body. It's a very weird sensation.'

'It sounds rather nice.'

'Depends whether or not I suffer alone. If you feel the same it's fantastic. That's true.'

'Well, I can't wait to see you again soon.'

'Fine, then why don't you come over!' His voice sounds hoarse.

'Sure. When?'

'What about this evening?'

'Yeah . . .' Carmen hesitates. She thinks of Laura. She can hardly invite her along too, but at the moment she really doesn't want to leave her alone.

'Is there a problem?' David has sensed her reticence. 'Is it Laura?'

'You're almost right. But it isn't just Laura. She's having a baby and she's feeling pretty delicate at the moment. She doesn't know whether to keep it or not.'

'Of course she should. You must talk to her. Doesn't the baby have a father?'

'What? Of course there's a father . . .'

'Yeah, but with you lot you never know, it could have come from the sperm bank.'

'Then the question of whether to keep it or not would never have arisen in the first place.'

'You're right there – bring her along.'

'Do you mind?'

'She's not going to move in, is she?'

Carmen laughs. 'You're a love. Shall we say seven at your place?'

'I look forward to it.'

'Shall we bring something?'

'Don't you dare. Just a good mood. And a bone for Cain.'

'Are you looking after him again?'

'I'm starting to get used to him. He was the perfect partner last night. He doesn't say anything, he doesn't want anything and he provides warmth in return. I must say . . .'

'I get you,' Carmen laughs. 'I'll have to make an effort. I'll let you do the talking this evening.'

'Or Laura. Perhaps we can help her.'

When Carmen puts the phone down she has a pleasant feeling. She doesn't want to ruin it by making any more calls. She has promised to see Frederic the next day, Oliver needs a definite no, Felix is still in the balance as she really doesn't feel like seeing him any more, and she has to return Stefan's call. Okay. She dials Stefan's number.

'Kaltenstein, hello.' He picks up after only one ring, as if he was waiting by the phone.

'Carmen here. Hi, Stefan.'

'Nice of you to call.' He sounds as though he's under pressure.

'Has something happened? To Elvira?' Elvira had assured her she was fine when she knocked on her door that morning. But you never know.

'Something has happened. Not to Elvira, but to me, Carmen. I didn't sleep a wink last night. Elvira's hints about my parents' accident – that would mean that I'd grown up with their murderers. It's so terrible. I feel completely rootless, the ground has been pulled from under my feet. I desperately need to talk to someone. Do you have time?'

Carmen groans inwardly. It's all coming at once. But she doesn't want to leave him dangling either.

'When, Stefan?'

'Right now would be great.'

'Oh, I can't, this afternoon I've got three meetings I set up ages ago – the clients probably want to sign, and I can hardly turn them down.'

'I'll make up the difference. And a consultation fee as well. As far as I'm concerned you can charge a therapist's hourly rate, it seems appropriate enough in the circumstances.'

He must be in a bad way.

'I wouldn't take it, Stefan. That would be even worse. Give me a call in half an hour and I'll see what I can do.'

It's really awkward. She's particularly unhappy about cancelling one of the clients. She's been working away at him until he's at the point of signing. She's about to pick up the phone when it rings.

'Lessing Law Associates speaking.'

It takes a moment to click with Carmen. Christ, that stupid, ignorant, what was his name, Herr Hermann.

'We never had a reply to our letter, so we just wanted to ask . . .'

'Hi, Herr Lessing. What letter? I never got a letter.'

'You should have got it over a week ago.'

'Did you use the old postcode?'

'Was that a joke? We weren't born yesterday.'

You're the joke, thinks Carmen, and I completely forgot that you used pincers to put your trousers on.

'I can't help you, Herr Lessing. My assistant is very reliable, and we haven't had a letter from you. What does it say?'

'That we think your suggestions are very sensible and that the contracts could be signed with a few small changes.'

'What sort of changes?' asks Carmen, thinking, aha, that's why he's telling me the letter was sent a week ago, so it's still within the time limit. Elegant Herr Lessing is trying to pull a fast one on me. So that's where the problem lies – right there, on his own desk.

'Nothing major. One contract can stay as it is, the sum on the second will have to be altered a bit, and we'll have to drop the third completely. When would you have time?'

'I'll have to check whether a cancellation and an alteration are possible, Herr Lessing. You've exceeded the cancellation period by two weeks.'

'Now, Frau Legg. If your mail isn't carefully processed . . .'

'That's enough, Herr Lessing. You and I both know what's what. I'll check what can still be done, and call you back today or tomorrow.'

That old trick, she shakes her head, putting down the phone. But still, two contracts, she wouldn't have thought old Hermann capable of it. She'll get a tin of caviar and a bottle of crémant for this evening. This calls for a celebration. She thinks of Frederic again. Oh God, how's she going to explain to him that she's really fallen in love? With someone else? She'd better not, she says to herself. There's plenty of time for that tomorrow. She picks up the phone just as Britta returns from lunch.

Britta is only at the bottom of the ladder towards becoming 143 a fully fledged insurance broker, but she's hard-working and resourceful. Why wouldn't she be successful? Could Britta take on this afternoon's meetings? They're only about signatures. And if Britta slipped up with anything she could probably sort it out.

Britta is enthusiastic, and thanks her over and over for her display of confidence. In the end Carmen feels guilty, as she's only really responding to an emergency. 'That's okay,' she says. 'Just be bold. You can do it. Best of luck!'

Carmen is driving up the road to Castle Kaltenstein. Her dinner with Stefan wasn't all that long ago. Last Thursday. It seems as though years have gone by since. All the things that have happened – how quickly things can change.

She almost drives past the turn-off. It looks different in daylight. She brakes and turns. The big cast-iron gate is skilfully wrought, and embellished with a magnificent gold shield. She is about to get out to ring the bell, but the gate opens by itself. She looks up to the camera. Blinded by the overcast sun, she can just see the red light.

Everything is very well looked after. The hedges are tidily trimmed, the roads seem to have been freshly swept, the avenue looks like a company of Prussia's finest soldiers: all the trees are the same height, the same distance apart, neat and well tended, interchangeable. Everything is so beautiful, so defect-free, that it's almost boring. Slowly she drives around the corner and sees the house, which is much bigger than she could tell at night and in the rain. It really is the size of a palace. On Thursday she couldn't see the gables and towers, or that the staff quarters were housed in a very imposing half-timbered building.

The dark blue Jaguar stands in front of the steps leading up to the main house. Carmen parks her car behind it. One of the butlers comes down the steps. Should she stay in the car until he opens the door? That's probably what's intended. But she feels a bit strange sitting there waiting, so she pretends to be looking for something in the glove compartment. Then the butler appears and the car door opens.

144   'Welcome to Castle Kaltenstein, madam.'

'Many thanks, that's very kind, Herr – can I know your name?'

'William, just William, madam. The baron is waiting.'

'Thank you very much, William.'

Carmen gets out and walks up the red carpet to the open door. Stefan comes out, and stands there waiting. He is pale, and to Carmen's surprise he is wearing jeans. She would never have expected to find him dressed so casually.

'I'm really pleased that you could come,' he says, giving her a firm handshake. 'Thank you.'

'I'm very pleased to be here,' says Carmen.

He smiles at her, his face even more austere than usual, his skin stretched like parchment over the bones of his face.

He walks ahead of her to the study, and then steps aside to let her go first. A cosy fire is burning in the fireplace, the *digestif* trolley has been wheeled close by, and on a table between the two leather sofas is a tray of canapés. Next to it is the silver-framed photograph of Hannes.

Carmen feels a little oppressed when she sits down on one of the sofas. Stefan sits opposite.

'Really, Carmen, thank you so much for coming so quickly. I feel helpless.'

William enters.

'What would you like to drink with the canapés, Carmen? Tea, wine, champagne?'

'Thanks, tea is an excellent idea.'

'With rum?' asks Stefan.

'Lovely,' nods Carmen.

William bows slightly. 'Very good, Herr Baron!'

A world of its own, thinks Carmen. Far from any reality, far, far away, in some book of fairy stories. Only for the moment Stefan doesn't look like the prince. He looks more like Cinderella.

'How can I help, Stefan?' asks Carmen. Stefan points to the canapés.

'Please, help yourself, Carmen. I had them made specially for you.'

'For me? And what about you?'

'I'm not hungry.'

'That's not right. You've got to eat something. I'll eat one of these for every one that you eat.'

'That's blackmail,' says Stefan, smiling weakly.

'The world is a bad place, Stefan.'

It is quiet. The logs crackle in the fireplace.

'You're right there. The worst thing is that my foster-parents died too soon. I can't ask them whether it was really as Elvira believes. And I can't ask them how they managed to build their own happiness on my parents' misfortune. The uncertainty is terrible. And what is even more terrible is that my feelings tell me that Elvira is right. That was what my family was like. My grandfather really was a patriarch, a ruler who abhorred disobedience. The clan could only be powerful if it held together. Anyone falling out of step was expelled. Yes, I can well imagine it. A Red in the family! If my father had been elected, it would have brought shame on all the Kaltensteins. My grandfather would not have been able to hold his head up high with his friends. I'm sure he tried everything within his power to make sure it didn't happen. And Hannes probably wouldn't be influenced, and clung to his convictions and fled . . .' Stefan sinks back. 'The idea is unbearable.'

William comes with the tea, serves it silently and disappears. Carmen stirs in a sugar cube. 'It might have been better if you'd never met Elvira. Then you wouldn't be having these doubts.'

'I don't know. It was going to happen sooner or later. Elvira will be able to tell me lots of things about my parents. It's just that – at the moment I couldn't bear it. But I simply had to talk to someone about it, or I was going to go mad.' Saying this, he gets to his feet, walks over to Carmen on the other side, sits down close beside her, puts his arm around her shoulders. At first Carmen doesn't know what to think. 'Stefan,' she begins, but hardly has Carmen spoken his name when he wraps his arms around her, sobbing dryly, and kisses her hard on the neck. 'Please help me, I can't go on. What am I to do?'

146

'Stefan, Stefan, please!'

As if she had pressed a hidden starting button, he hurls himself on to her with all his weight. Carmen slips sideways under his weight, into the corner of the sofa, and at the same time she tries to use her forearm to push away the face that is now hovering above her, big and open-mouthed, trying to cover her with kisses. Stefan is everywhere. Now she is forced to defend herself with both hands.

'Stefan, what are you doing?' Her voice is dark, she is half-buried beneath him. He clings to her as if he is drowning. She is still shifting somewhere between astonishment and revulsion, but slowly she begins to panic. He kisses her on the mouth, tries to force his tongue between her lips. She shakes her head indignantly.

'You want it, admit it, you're just being frosty because you think I can't get it up, but I'll show you, I'll show you,' he wheezes, trying to climb on top of her. Her left arm is forced beneath his right knee, and he is pressing her right hand into the leather. She can hardly move.

Carmen turns her head away. 'Stefan, for God's sake stop it, you're ruining everything!'

He tears at her clothes, gropes at her bosom under her pullover, and then tries to hoist her skirt up. 'You're playing with me because you think I can't do it! No one plays with me! No one plays with me, nobody!' He presses his knee between her thighs, she painfully feels his kneecap against her flesh, he's almost right on top of her now, painfully pressing his forearm down on her breasts while he tries to shove his hand up under her skirt. He groans, he sobs, 'I'm not impotent, I'm not impotent,' he rages like a beast.

'Stop it, this is madness! Stop it, Stefan!' Carmen has all her wits about her now. He's out of his mind, he can't see or hear anything, everything's bursting out of him and spilling out all over Carmen. Only sheer force will allow her to escape. Words are no use, they won't reach him. She arches her back and tries to sit up, but he's stronger and pushes her down again. 'Let me, let me,' he wheezes, 'I'll show you. I'm a man.

I'll show you.' And he bears down and tears at her body. Carmen manages to raise her knee and ram it with all her might into his genitals.

With a great yell he falls on his side, drops away from her and lies between the table and the sofa on the carpet. There he doubles up and weeps unrestrainedly.

Carmen flees behind the back of the couch, straightens her clothes and tries to think clearly. Everything is mixed-up in her head. How could that have happened? What got into him? Is he a psychopath? A schizophrenic? She waits there undecided for a minute, listening to him sobbing, and then slowly walks around the sofa. He is still lying on the floor, head down, his whole body racked with sobs. Carmen thinks. She really wants to make her getaway immediately. But if he's really sick, can she leave him here like a poor old thing? She stands there trying to make up her mind. Should she call his butler for help? But if William sees him like that, the baron will be finished once and for all. And for a moment she remembers those country-house murders with everyone under the same roof . . .

The loud sobbing has stopped, giving way to a quiet, steady weeping. Carmen looks at him suspiciously. She's ready to flee. Maybe he often has attacks like this, and if so what he needs is counselling. She remembers what he said about her therapist's fee, and it almost makes her laugh. You think you've escaped assaults by men once and for all, and all of a sudden you're out of the frying-pan and back into the fire. She'll send him a bill all right.

She leaves the room quietly, looks for William and asks him for paper and a pen. She thinks quickly, and writes, 'That's not what we bet, the stakes were too high. Go to a doctor!' She folds the letter in half and gives it to William.

'If you would please give this to Herr von Kaltenstein. At the moment he needs rest. He doesn't feel well and doesn't want to be disturbed for the next half hour.'

'Do you think we should call him a doctor?'

'I think that's something he should decide for himself. But look in on him later on, will you.'

'I will, madam!'

It isn't apparent in William's demeanour, but Carmen senses that he is worried. He walks Carmen to the car. He's bound to read the letter first and then make a bee-line for the room. But Carmen couldn't care less. When she looks up from the car to the house she sees Stefan's face, chalk-white, at the window. Let's get out of here, she thinks. She lowers the right-hand side window and calls to William, who is already standing back on the steps again. 'Please can you open the gate!'

If not, you've got another nice surprise ahead of you, thinks Carmen as she starts the car.

William turns to her, 'Very well, madam.' He smiles. Doesn't he look like Klaus Kinski from a distance? Doesn't he grin like that?

Now you're seeing ghosts, she says, and puts her foot down.

The gate is open when Carmen turns the corner into the avenue. She drives through it, holding her breath. And now? It's early in the afternoon. She should really drive to the office and sort out the contracts herself. But she doesn't want to breathe down Britta's neck – what would that look like? Apart from that she isn't in the right frame of mind to worry about life insurance. She'd rather go home. She urgently needs to speak to Elvira. But what should she tell her? Everything? Wouldn't she reproach herself for confronting Stefan with her suspicions? Her head whirls. How could it all have happened? What should she make of it? Does he have a personality dis-order, is he actually schizophrenic, is he simply at the end of his tether? She's no psychiatrist, but some things she can imagine. Probably everything came together at the same time – the long-suppressed anxieties about his potency and the truth about his past. Certainly, after Elvira's revelations he felt even more worthless than he had done when he only had his impotence to worry about. Should she have talked to him? 149

Should she have left him lying there like that? You and your stupid Good Samaritan act, she scolds herself. That was attempted rape, he was lousy, disgusting, repellent! You should have kicked him again for that! But she's not one hundred per cent sure. She's not furious with him, just sorry for him. Someone like that, who seems to have everything, and who is so miserable inside, you have to feel sorry for him.

She's reached her garage. She gets out to open the door. A cold November wind is blowing, and she shivers in her pullover and her short skirt. Her teeth chatter, but she knows it's not just the piercing cold. It comes from inside. She feels miserable and longs for a hot bath. And that's what she's going to allow herself right now. Hot water, relaxation and no more thoughts of Stefan. She parks the car in her narrow parking-space, throws her coat over her shoulders, picks up her briefcase and runs over to the house. The mailbox is empty, thank God, no more impotent men. She has quite enough already. Although you shouldn't be unfair, she says to herself, thinking of David and Frederic. A smile crosses her face, and she feels her good mood returning. There are crazy people everywhere, whether they're male or female, gay or lesbian, monogamous, polygamous, bisexual or impotent. So what. She can't become a hermit just because of that! And if she thinks about it, she's probably a bit loonie herself. Who in their right mind would go in search of an impotent man?

Carmen runs the bathwater. She takes off her clothes, snuggles up in her fluffy bathrobe and fetches the telephone so she can call Elvira and David when she's feeling steadier. She'll postpone Frederic for another while. She'll have to think about how to deal with that. She tests the temperature and is about to get in when there's a ring at the door. Hmm, who can that be? Shall I open up or not? She really doesn't feel like it. It's probably someone trying to convert her to some religion or other, or sell her lavatory brushes. She is so polite that she always finds it hard to get rid of them. The doorbell rings again. One long, two short. Oh, it's Laura.

Thank God! She runs, naked and barefoot, and presses the intercom, opens the door to her flat and darts back into the bathroom. And what if it isn't Laura, she thinks, half into the tub. Then there's nothing I can do, she says to herself as she slips in. Ah, that's good! She hears footsteps and the door closes. She holds her breath – what if it's Stefan? She thinks of the movie *Psycho*. She would have to think of that right now. But then Stefan isn't Anthony Perkins. Or let's hope not.

It's Laura. Carmen exhales slowly. You watch too much television, she says to herself as she smiles to Laura, 'Hey, babe!'

'What's up? You look spooked! Hi.' Laura bends over to Carmen and kisses her on both cheeks. 'Can I join you in the tub?'

'You think there's room?' asks Carmen dubiously. She once tried it with Peter because they thought it was going to be sexy, but her little tub was far from comfortable.

'Okay, just an idea. I'll make some tea, shall I?'

Carmen nods. She relaxes again. It's nice lying in the warm water, being spoilt. Laura comes back with two teacups and sits down on the edge of the tub.

'So? How are you?' asks Carmen.

'Pretty much the same as yesterday. How are you?'

'One step forward, or one back. Depending on how you look at it.'

'Okay.' Laura takes a little sip from her cup. 'What do you mean exactly?'

'Stefan!' Carmen pulls a face. 'I'm glad you're here. I don't know what to do.' She puts the cup down on the edge of the bath and blows the foam away from her face.

'Sorry, you're talking in riddles. What about Stefan?'

Carmen describes what happened that afternoon. Laura sits in silence listening to it all, and in the end she shakes her head: 'And you think impotent men don't have problems of their own. It makes me laugh.'

'Go ahead, laugh,' says Carmen, with a sulky undertone to her voice. 'It doesn't make it any better. What'll I do with Elvira? Can I tell her? She'll see me as the guilty party.'

'Why don't you introduce me to the old girl and I'll tell you if she's up for that kind of news or not.'

'That's a great idea!' Carmen sits up with a jolt, spattering the thick foam and sending the water splashing around the edge of the tub. 'And I've got an idea, too.'

'Yes, what?' Laura moves her cup to safety.

'I'm not going to tell you. But I'll show you in a minute. Just wait. I'm getting out.'

Ten minutes later they are making themselves cosy on Carmen's bed. Carmen is wrapped in her bathrobe, and is trying to find the most comfortable position on her stomach, while Laura sits cross-legged beside her. Between them is a photograph, Felix Hoffmann.

'You're not going to tell me he's impotent as well!'

'Of course he is, that's why he wrote to me! Here, read this!' and she hands Laura his letter.

'Had a lot of stress from work and girlfriend, so escaped into impotence . . . ssss,' Laura hisses through her teeth. 'Can you believe it! He's good-looking, this guy.'

She takes the photograph, holds it up to her eyes, then a bit further away. 'In fantastic shape. Have you taken a good look at this?' Glancing at Carmen. 'You reckon he can be cured?'

'No idea, Laura. I don't want someone who can be cured. Then it will start all over again.'

'Oh yeah, and what about David?'

Carmen hesitates a moment, then laughs. 'Good question. I don't really know. But in the end I don't think so. Because imagine, Laura, and this is fantastically interesting – you've got this guy and you're not always waiting to see how he's going to deal with trying to get you into bed.'

'But what if that's the exciting thing?' Laura frowns.

'Yeah, yeah,' says Carmen, 'at first, of course. Been through it a hundred times before. But what then? I want a partner, not someone who's constantly trying to get into my knickers.'

'It's happened.'

'What do you mean?' Carmen lays her head on one side.

'A blind man with a white stick could see it. You're in love.

Hopelessly in love with David, and now you're just trying to convince yourself without having to think about the fact that he can't get it up.'

'You're so cruel.'

'Maybe.'

They say nothing for a while. They look at each other indignantly, then laugh in unison, as if on command.

'Okay, Carmen, whatever. I think your David's very nice. I really like him. And if Wilko had been impotent at least this would never have happened.' And she runs her hand over her stomach.

Still lying on her belly, Carmen edges towards Laura and puts her ear to her stomach. 'I can't hear a thing.'

Laura laughs, 'You won't hear much till the fourth month.'

'Does that mean you're keeping it?' Carmen lies back down.

'I've given myself a week to make up my mind.'

'And if Wilko and you . . .'

Laura waves her hand, 'You can't rely on him. He'll try anything he can to deny he's the father.'

'It is him, though, isn't it?'

Laura looks Carmen straight in the eyes. 'I was so in love with him that it would be outrageous to suggest anything else. But if I've got his measure, he'll try to say that anyway.'

Carmen shakes her head. 'Sorry, I can still hardly believe your relationship went so badly wrong. I thought Wilko was completely different. That he was at least fair, and that he'd stand by his actions.'

'Me too, me too, Carmen, believe me. Let's leave it at that. Tell me about your idea.'

Carmen grins. Then she taps Laura on the chest. '*You* are going to meet Felix.'

'What?'

'Right, you're meeting him. You fancy him and, well, what can you lose by it?'

'But my name isn't Carmen Legg, it would be deception!'

'You can tell him you're my friend. Or you could just check him out.'

Laura taps her finger on the photograph. 'The things you come up with. Single pregnant woman marries impotent man. Nonetheless, it has a ring to it. I like it!'

'Okay. And tonight we've been invited to David's . . .'

There's a ring at the door. Carmen sits up. 'Who on earth can that be?' She thinks of Frederic. It's cosy here now, why should she open the door?

'Don't you want to go and find out?' asks Laura.

'Not really.'

There's a knock at the door. 'He's outside the flat.' Carmen jumps to her feet. She ties her bathrobe tighter and walks to the door.

'Hello?' she calls, without opening it.

'It's me,' comes the muffled answer. 'Elvira!'

'Elvira!' Carmen tears the door open. 'This is a surprise!'

'If Mohammed won't come to the mountain, the mountain must go to Mohammed.'

Carmen kisses her on both cheeks. 'Stop it, don't make me feel bad. I was going to introduce you to Laura some other time. But this is even better as it happens. Come on in!'

Laura emerges from the bedroom. The two women shake hands.

'Elvira, what would you like to drink? Tea, coffee, some wine?'

'Tea would be nice. Goes with the weather.' She sits down on the couch while Laura curls up on the chair and Carmen disappears into the kitchen.

'So how are you, Elvira? Can I call you Elvira? Carmen's told me so much about you.'

'She has? That's nice. All I know about you is that you're always flying around the world, and that you'd like to take your class with you.'

Laura brushes back her short black hair. She laughs. 'The flying classroom – like that children's book by Erich Kästner? That would be brilliant.'

Elvira nods.

'It's nice if someone leaves something behind when they

die. Kästner has the edge on us there. In people's minds he's immortal. Almost . . .' She looks at her hands and runs her fingers over some liver spots.

Carmen, who is just coming in with the tea, hears Laura's reply: 'If there are children, then perhaps something is always left behind . . .' Aha, she thinks, while she puts down the cups and fetches sugar and rum, so Laura's touched on the subject.

Elvira looks up, glances at Carmen; then back to Laura: 'I thought you would know all about it.' And, with another quick glance at Carmen, 'That's alright too.' Carmen lowers herself into an armchair as well. 'Well,' Elvira continues, 'over the past few days I've been giving Stefan a lot of thought. I shouldn't really have said anything to him. Or rather I should have seized him and taken him away back then. But of course that's crazy. I couldn't have abducted a baby. And where would I have taken him? What next? In those days a single woman with a baby was socially ostracised. Or treated like scum. I probably wouldn't have been able to work. What could I have offered him? What kind of world would he have grown up in? Not to mention what would have happened to me if they'd caught me.'

Carmen looks at Laura. Oh no, she thinks, Elvira doesn't know Laura's pregnant. 'Why didn't you tell the police what you knew?' Laura wants to know.

'The Kaltensteins had power. How could I turn their employees against them?'

'That's right,' says Carmen, backing her up. 'Some things would be a problem even today. Only views on single mothers have changed since those days. Now plenty of children are brought up by their mothers alone. Some out of wedlock, some after divorce. Of course, women always carry the can,' and with a sideways glance to Laura, 'but they do reap the benefits too.'

'You've said that before,' Laura grins, knowing very well what Carmen means.

'You talk as if you were a mother yourself. How do you know that? You're not pregnant, are you?' Elvira leans forward slightly.

'Ha!' Carmen laughs. 'That'd be funny. I haven't had a man for three weeks or more.'

'Well, Carmen, three weeks is nothing. Pregnancy lasts longer than that.'

'Carmen's not the one who's pregnant, Elvira, I am. I have a week to decide what to do.'

Carmen is astonished at Laura's openness. And Elvira stays silent for a moment. Then she says, 'What do you mean you have to decide? What's to decide? You're having a baby. That's a wonderful thing!'

'Of course.' Laura sips some tea, her brown eyes sparkling suspiciously. 'Of course it's beautiful. If you have a home to give the little creature. But I can't even provide a dad.'

'Advice might sound strange coming from me, given that I would have been at best a mother substitute. But I feel guilty that I didn't act, and take Anna's place. She didn't want to make a Kaltenstein out of Stefan. But you can't turn back time. What it must be like for a biological mother! I'd love to be in your shoes.'

'My situation isn't that easy.' Laura pulls up her legs and wraps her arms around them. 'What do you get after maternity leave? The state does nothing for you. No child-minders, no kindergartens, and if there are any they open and close at stupid times of day. A woman can't work sensibly and feed herself and her child.'

Elvira picks up her teacup, 'You don't get anywhere if you don't fight your own battles. That hasn't changed, at least.'

'But the battle is about to destroy Stefan,' says Carmen. 'If we're talking about such intimate things, I have to tell you, Elvira, that he's at the end of his tether. He's doing things he wouldn't dream of doing if he was compos mentis.'

Elvira blanches. 'Stefan? How come? What's happened?' Carmen tells her what happened that afternoon. Elvira shakes her head again, takes a sip of tea and slides anxiously back and forth on the sofa. Her dark blue dress rustles quietly. When Carmen has finished, she slowly puts her cup down. 'Now you see what can happen to someone who falls into the wrong hands. I wonder how I can help him – and I'm sorry, Carmen. That must have been a terrible experience for you.'

'I'm over it. But do give him a call and tell him you want to speak to him. That would probably be for the best,' Carmen suggests. 'He's not about to kill himself.'

Elvira can't help laughing. 'No, I'm not really afraid of that – but you're right, perhaps I really have to go on the offensive.'

Laura nods. 'That's what I think. The best thing would be for you to call him immediately.'

Carmen points to her telephone. 'You can do it from here if you like.'

Elvira shakes her head. 'Don't take it wrongly, but I'd rather do it from downstairs. I'm a creature of habit.'

The two women nod to her. 'If there's anything we can do to help, give us a call.'

Elvira rises slowly to her feet and walks to the door. Then she turns around again. 'I'll tell you what happens. Thanks very much.'

Hardly has Elvira closed the door behind her than Laura turns to Carmen and claps her hand on her thigh. 'Okay, baby, I'm in a more reckless frame of mind now. Let's call Felix.'

Carmen, who has been weaving her hair into a thick plait for the last few minutes, jumps up. 'Congratulations! We're on the attack again. I'll get his number.'

She runs into the bathroom, finds a hair elastic and grabs the letter on her way back. '73 117,' she calls to Laura.

Laura is dialling already. She waits for a moment and then speaks. 'Hi, it's about the Legg box number, is that Felix Hoffmann? It is? Brilliant!'

Carmen sits on the couch, draws up her legs and throws her bathrobe over them.

Laura switches the phone on to loudspeaker. It's a bit tinny, but the voice at the other end sounds nice.

'I'm glad you've finally got through, I didn't think you'd   157 make it. Particularly when you stood me up for brunch that time.'

Laura glances at Carmen and shrugs her shoulders. She doesn't know anything about what he suggested for Saturday.

It doesn't matter, Carmen thinks, she'll find a way out.

'I was sorry about that as well,' says Laura, pulling a face, 'but we can make up for it.'

'Why don't you suggest something?'

'Well, weekday brunches are out, unfortunately, I've got to work, but afternoons or evenings are fine!'

The astonished question 'You work half days?' makes Laura laugh. 'Almost, I'm a teacher.'

'Really?' Felix sounds surprised. 'But in the phone book it says you're an insurance broker.'

Laura glances at Carmen, but she doesn't give up. 'That's my friend's name. I used it as a pseudonym. My name isn't Legg, it's Rapp.'

'That's all very complicated, don't you think?'

'No – I could have got a colleague of mine to call you, and then we'd both be standing there like dummies. Hence the detour.'

Carmen is amazed. Unbelievable. How Laura can twist facts in a flash and make a new truth out of them – with a talent like that she should be in politics. But while she's been thinking she's missed the answer, she sees Laura looking at the ceiling and then at her. 'What is it?' she whispers.

Laura holds her hand over the phone. 'He's another teacher!' she whispers quietly, rolling her eyes.

'He can't be!' Carmen laughs.

'And now?' asks Laura.

'The meeting,' whispers Carmen.

Laura nods. 'I see, what do you teach?'

'Sport and English at the Fontane Gymnasium.'

'Impossible!' Laura explodes, 'and you were under such stress there that . . .'

He's going to put the phone down now, thinks Carmen, but

to her surprise he laughs. 'The stress was probably more from my girlfriend than the work, I admit. So, we both teach, well so what. You placed an ad, I replied, so why don't we meet up. Which school do you teach at?'

'The secondary school.'

'Well then, if we can't stand each other, at least we won't be constantly running into one another. I don't see a problem.'

'Neither do I.'

'How about tonight? Eight o'clock at Paletti's? Do you know it?' Laura looks at Carmen. 'In the town centre, near the old town hall,' she whispers.

'Fine,' says Laura.

'What do you look like?' She can hear his curiosity.

'Oh, I'll recognise you, Felix. I've got your photograph. But if you really want to know, to avoid any mistakes,' she hesitates, 'I'm four foot five, seventeen stone and four pounds and I have thin brown hair in a perm.'

There's a brief silence at the other end. Carmen bends double with suppressed laughter. Laura waits another three seconds, then giggles and says, 'No, don't worry, Felix. I'm five foot seven, eight stone, I have very short black hair and brown eyes, I'll be wearing black jeans and a black polo neck. You can't miss me.'

'I'd rather you were fat.'

Laura laughs. 'Wait till we've eaten – it happens of its own accord,' then she looks over at Carmen and draws a nine-months-pregnant belly in the air with her hand.

'Till tonight, then, I'm depending on you,' he says, and she answers 'Booked!'

Then she slowly puts the phone down. Carmen points a threatening forefinger. 'I thought you were coming to David's with me this evening. You'd rather see Felix?'

'No, of course not. But I think it's a good idea for you two to spend some time alone together. And it'll be fun with Felix. Just the thing for my damaged soul!'

'Well!' Carmen gets to her feet. 'Then I'll get changed. I haven't got that much time. I don't suppose you could ring Elvira, 31 357, and find out what's happened.'

Laura dials, and immediately puts the phone down: 'Engaged.'

'Is that a good or a bad sign?' Carmen picks up a coin from the table beside the candle, tosses it in the air and claps it down on the back of her hand. 'Good,' she says.

'What was it?' Laura asks, curious. 'Heads or tails?'

'Heads wins,' Carmen smiles and walks towards the bathroom. 'Can I get you something stronger to drink?' she asks.

'No, thanks, I'd like to keep a clear head. It's the first time I've had a date with a fellow teacher!'

The phone rings. 'Get it, would you?' Carmen calls from the bathroom.

She hears Laura answering. 'Legg household?' and then, 'It's Elvira, Carmen. She's going over to Stefan's. He's not doing so well. His car's picking her up in half an hour.'

'Great, I'm glad. Ask her if there's anything we can do for her – and, wait a second, Laura, ask her if we should drop by at midnight.' She hears Laura repeating everything and saying goodbye, and then she joins Carmen in the bathroom. 'Fine, apart from that bit at the end. Was that some sort of running joke?'

Carmen puts on some eyeliner, and turns around to Laura and winks at her. 'My first date with an impotent man. As arranged, she came up to my place at midnight to protect me from him.'

Laura laughs, and all of a sudden Carmen remembers Frederic. She still hasn't explained the new situation to him. But doing it on the phone seems cowardly. She'll have to call him later today.

Carmen parks in front of number 17. Now that it's dark outside and the house is brightly lit, it looks like a doll's house. She can see everything: an open-plan living-room over two floors with a steel staircase, sparse modern furnishings, a stainless steel kitchen and a study full of books, white rolls of paper and two drawing-boards in the middle. She doesn't even know what David does for a living, it occurs to her, but that day was so short, and so eventful. Did he really ring the forestry office? She'll have to ask him.

Carmen opens the garden gate. It doesn't squeak, although it looks as if it should. She slowly walks along the stone paving. It's arranged irregularly, and if you don't pay attention you step in the wet grass. The lighting is poor: a skinny little bulb on a skinny stem every thirty feet or so. It must be art, Carmen thinks, because it certainly doesn't do anything else. She's halfway there when the door opens and a giant shadow leaps out, straight at her. For a moment Carmen is terrified. She isn't sure Cain will recognise her. What if he decides she's a burglar and corners her?

'Hi, Cain, my old friend,' she calls to him, cautiously. Cain gives a short, hoarse bark and then dances around her, spraying dirt. Okay, thinks Carmen, so she's got clumps of earth on her heels and now she's had dirt sprayed in her face too. But strangely she's not bothered. So what? She can wash her coat, and some soap will deal with her face.

'Cain! Come here! Leave Carmen alone!'

Carmen's heart beats faster. David walks down the three steps and comes over to meet her.

'Welcome,' he says, and wraps his arms around her. 'Ah, that feels good.' He sniffs her hair and kisses her on the mouth. 'Come, my princess, don't twist your pretty little ankle,' and he picks her up in his arms. 'No, stop, David,' she says, but he's already carrying her to the door. Cain jumps ahead of them, barking. Only once they've crossed the threshold does he carefully put her down.

'You look fantastic!' David takes her coat and looks her up and down. Carmen hasn't loosened her plait, and it falls, full and red, to the left of her bosom. Her woollen dress, figure-hugging, cornflower blue, is decidedly sexy, but it looks loose and light. She's also wearing dark blue tights and high-heeled shoes that are a number of different tones of blue. 'We should go out so I could show you off,' David beams.

Carmen's delighted. 'Thank you, David, but you're looking good yourself!'

He's dressed in black from head to toe, but to match his green eyes he's wearing a green tie showing Albert Einstein bathing his feet in the sea under a big parasol. 'That's funny,' laughs Carmen. 'You would envy him, wouldn't you?'

David has had his hair cut. His blond mane has clearly been trimmed, but it still shows rebellious tendencies. His hair lies as though shaped by the wind and the waves, not by a brush and a hair-dryer. He looks outrageously handsome. And with his tanned complexion and his white teeth, it's almost too much for Carmen. She smiles to herself as one of her mother's sayings springs to mind: Handsome men never belong to one woman. Maybe this one does!

'Come in, Carmen, enter the bachelors' den. Martin has made such an effort – and so have I. Martin is the chef, and I'm the cellar-master.'

Carmen nods and walks in behind Cain, who runs purposefully into the living-room. There is a modern open fireplace in the middle of the room, and a long table has been laid out along the wall. The table-top is metal, and so are the chairs. Gaudy candles on long, thin metal candelabras provide a flickering light. Halogen bulbs, dimmed, hang down from the ceiling on long cables.

'Interesting,' says Carmen, and she means it. She mentally compares it to Stefan's dining-room. The difference could hardly be more striking. But where does she feel more at ease? Stefan's warm cherrywood room and matching parquet floor take a lot of beating. But if she's honest, she thinks this interior works brilliantly, although in the long run it would be too cold for her. I'm bourgeois, she admits to herself, I'm normal to the tips of my toes. Her passion for high-tech is limited to her stereo system. Everything here's high-tech. Fine.

'Do you like it?' asks David, who's been watching her.

'Yes,' says Carmen. 'It's extraordinary, because the style has been imposed so consistently. I don't see anything private or personal.'

'How do you mean?'

'You know, kitsch, personal souvenirs, old photographs, anything not quite right, anything that's just there.'

'Nothing's perfect here,' David laughs, 'really, absolutely nothing. It just looks that way in this light. I'll show you my bedroom later, that's where I keep all my personal stuff, if that reassures you. From the photograph of me sitting on my potty for the first time, to the photograph of Bruin, our first dog, to a picture of my first girlfriend when I was sixteen. She wore a brace on her teeth and had a big bum. But she was incredibly nice, and her kisses were fantastic. Particularly down below. Maybe that's why I'm so keen on metal!'

'Oh, spare me,' Carmen explodes, and she thinks, oh, no, not another nutter, he probably likes metal suspender belts.

David laughs and takes her in his arms. 'Don't worry, it's not a fetish. This is more Martin's doing. I like things a bit cosier myself, but I'll explain our arrangement to you later on. Look, he's left us something over there. We thought Laura was coming, that's why there's extra. He was going to come and join us himself, but when you rang and said Laura wasn't coming he decided not to disturb us.'

'Oh, that's sweet of him.' Carmen's touched. 'Does he get a bite to eat at least?'

'He had plenty earlier on – and anyway, it wouldn't do him any harm . . .'

They're standing in the kitchen. A pot of goulash is simmering away quietly on the stove, and yellow corkscrew pasta, fusilli, are keeping warm in a pot. A big bowl of mixed salad is on the kitchen table.

'You've gone to an incredible amount of trouble. I really hadn't expected it!'

David embraces her again. They kiss long and passionately. When he lets go of her again, Carmen thinks she can actually hear the blood rushing through her head.

'So, now we've worked up an appetite, let's eat,' says David, picking up a little steel pot. Carmen isn't sure whether

163

he's being sarcastic, or whether that's how David deals with impotence.

He pours goulash from the big pot into the little one, puts it and the pasta on to a tray and takes it into the living-room. Carmen brings the salad.

'Now,' David is standing by the table, 'where would you like to sit? With your back to the fire or the other way round?'

How things come round again, thinks Carmen. Nearly everything does . . .

'With my back to the fire, please!' Now she'll have the pleasure of looking at his face in the flickering flames. As Stefan did with her on Thursday.

'Great.' David puts the tray down, takes her plate and starts to serve. 'Stop, that's enough!' says Carmen, waving her hand.

'You're not going to give up at the first hurdle, are you? Martin's well known for his goulash, you really should tuck in.'

'It's not Martin's goulash I'm worried about, it's my waistline, David. What you've piled up on my plate would normally last me for two days.'

'No wonder you're so thin. You can leave the rest!'

On the table there's a carafe of red wine, and now he fills long-stemmed, full-bellied glasses.

'Cheers! To us!'

'Yes, to us!'

The glasses clink and Carmen and David gaze deep into each other's eyes as they drink.

'Excellent wine,' says Carmen, taking another sip.

'I hoped you would like it.' David smiles and puts the glass down. '*Bon appétit*, Carmen. It's so good that you're here. If I could say a magic word and swap you for Martin, I'd do it right away.'

'So what's your connection with Martin?' Carmen picks up her knife and fork.

'He's my half-brother, my father's illegitimate son. What you might call the product of an amorous caper. His mother's a very successful architect, and this is one of the houses she built years ago. And since Martin and I are almost the same age – my father was sensible enough to impregnate his mother when my mother was in her ninth month with me – we moved in together, after we both, coincidentally, started studying architecture. The way life pans out. Don't you think that's funny?'

'I don't know, really.' Carmen spears some pasta with her fork and then tries to spike a juicy piece of meat as well. 'I think funny things go on all the time. Wherever you look, the most incredible things are happening.'

'So what do you think?' David has his mouth full and picks up a napkin. 'Do you like it?'

'Excellent, David, thanks very much! It's really very good!' And it's true. The meat is tender, but highly spiced, and it's been cooked with a number of other ingredients. She's going to eat it and this delicious pasta until she keels over, she knows it. 'Goulash, particularly if it's as good as this, has the same effect on me as crisps. I don't eat it very often, but once I start I can't stop.'

'Very glad to hear it. Martin will be delighted as well!'

'Where is he now?'

'He's gone out with some friends, so you don't have to worry. He won't be back before midnight.'

'Does he have a steady girlfriend?'

'Boyfriend. He's homosexual.'

'Oh, stop.' Carmen shakes her head. 'This is crazy. For the last few days I've felt as if I'm living in a madhouse.'

'Do you mean me?' David has already had seconds and is now taking a third helping, when he stops for a moment and looks at her with concern on his face.

'No, I mean everything. But it's too complicated to explain. You don't know Elvira, you don't know Stefan, and you don't know Frederic. And tonight Laura's meeting Felix, another man who responded to my ad. She's practically stolen my date!'

'What?' David puts down the serving-spoon. 'You're sending a pregnant woman out with some madman? Are you off your head?'

'Stop, stop, Laura's only six weeks gone. This guy isn't going to lay a finger on her, and anyway they're going to Paletti's, all open and above board. There really isn't a problem.'

David chews and shakes his head. 'Paletti's? The mafia joint? You could have sent her to a brothel, at least she'd have made some money that way.'

Furious, Carmen takes a sip of wine but it goes down the wrong way, and she coughs, short of breath. David puts his fork aside, runs around the table and pats her on the back until she's breathing properly again. Then he runs two fingers down her plait to her left breast. He lingers for a moment on the tip of her breast, touching her nipple, which promptly responds. He's standing so close behind her that a shiver runs down Carmen's back. She feels his breath on the nape of her neck. He kisses her there. Hairs stand up on her arms and legs.

He bites her gently at the base of her neck and then goes back to his seat. 'Of course Martin's goulash is no match for that. But I won't tell him, he'd never understand.'

'Do you work with him?' Carmen briefly rubs her arms to rid herself of the feeling of excitement. Then she takes another helping as well.

'Six years ago we went independent, and since then we've been partners. Franck and Baumann.'

'Sounds good,' Carmen smiles.

'So who are all these people you've just been talking about? Friends? Relations? Lovers? Ex-lovers?'

Hmm, thinks Carmen, picking up her napkin and her glass. I wish I'd never mentioned them. How do I explain?

She starts with Elvira, telling a truncated version of the story of Elvira and Stefan but leaving out this afternoon's altercation. Anyway, she feels as if the business with Stefan happened decades ago. What will they be doing now? She glances at the clock. Gone ten. They'll be on the third course, if Stefan is up to eating.

'And Frederic?' David asks. He's been listening. Carmen tells the truth, describing how he came to the rescue when Elvira was lying on the floor in a faint. But she is careful to leave out what she and Frederic were doing immediately beforehand.

'And after Stefan and Frederic, now it's my turn,' David nods. Carmen's not sure whether his tone is amused or annoyed.

'It took you a long time to send your letter. I'd already had about ten letters by the time I got yours. I could hardly tell them, leave me alone, David'll be along in a minute.'

David laughs, 'We are a bit prickly, aren't we? Would you like some more? Or you could leave some room for pudding.'

'Pudding?' Carmen slowly shakes her head. 'Sorry. Salad was too much for me, the goulash was so good.'

'Martin will be pleased. Fine, then I'll show you my room.'

Cain, who has been lying quietly on his blanket all this time, opens an eye and gets to his feet.

'He thinks I'm going to bed.'

'Does he really always go with you?'

'Like I told you. And not only that, I assume he'd be very generous with you.'

Carmen shakes her head and laughs. 'Did you take it that seriously when I mentioned a dog in my letter?'

'I didn't,' says David, 'but he did.'

Cain is already walking to the hallway and the steep steel staircase. His claws make a screeching sound as he goes upstairs.

'Eech!' Carmen puts her hands over her ears. 'I'd put down some stair-carpet.'

'Martin's mother would be fatally insulted. She gave us the house on the grounds that it would be kept the way it was. She thinks if she rented it out they'd clutter it up with carpets, curtains and wallpaper.'

'She might be right.' Carmen follows Cain, who is heading straight for one of the frosted glass doors.

'Can you see into all the rooms?' Carmen asks. 'Even the bathroom and the toilet?'

'It's very practical – you can tell from a distance whether or not it's occupied.'

'Well, I don't know.' Carmen shakes her head. 'And the bedrooms? How can you live in a glass box, with people watching whatever you're doing from every direction?'

The corners of David's mouth turn up. 'That's something I never have to worry about.'

Carmen mentally claps a hand over her mouth. What has she said now. What a stupid thing to say. Cain stops by one of the glass doors and presses the handle down with his muzzle. Even the dog's watching me, Carmen thinks, but she doesn't say anything. David walks ahead, and a light comes on. Then he lets her walk before him. The room looks very cosy, quite unlike the others. It's modern, but it's much warmer, influenced more by light and colours. On one side is a big iron bed. The duvet cover, busy, bright and cheerful, softens the severity of the rest of the house. It's very homely. On the modern shelves there are all the personal effects – old books, photographs, collector's items – that Carmen missed downstairs. Opposite the bed is a powerful hi-fi system, with a widescreen television set sitting up above it. To its right is Le Corbusier's classic suite: the curved couch in steel and black leather, the strictly geometrical three-seater sofa and the matching rectangular chair. Between them a coffee table covered with magazines.

'I like it here.' Carmen stands on tiptoes and kisses David on the tip of his nose.

'Pleased to hear it.' His arms wrap tightly around her and she puts her head on his shoulder.

'We can stay up here if you want. I'll get our glasses and leave some food out for Martin so he can have something waiting for him when he gets home.'

Carmen nods and turns to go as well.

'And what are you up to?' asks David, followed by Cain, when he is almost at the door.

'I was going to give you a hand.'

'We don't do that in the Franck-Baumann residence, my dear. Just put your feet up and make yourself comfortable. I'll be back in a minute. Would you like a cognac or some other digestif?' Carmen finds herself being vaguely reminded of Castle Kaltenstein.

'No, thanks. I'm happy with my wine. I really don't want any more alcohol.'

David blows her a kiss and walks out. Carmen takes off her shoes and lies down on the bed. What a strange feeling. In the past, this would have been an unambiguous situation. But to keep her distance she would have had to sit in the chair. Now it doesn't matter. She doesn't even have to think about the consequences.

The television remote is beside the bed. She switches it on. It's the titles of the film *Baby Boom*, in which an American career woman inherits a baby, can't deal with it to start with, then loses her high-flying job because of the child, with high ideals buys a house in the country, is swindled by the estate agent, moves in, gets back into business as a producer of organic marmalade and can finally turn down all kinds of offers from her former company. The film's great, she's seen it before. Laura should see it too. Maybe she's at home already. Carmen looks around. There's a black phone beside the bed. She dials Laura's number, no reply. Her own number, answering-machine. Then the operator for the number of Paletti's. The door opens, and David comes back in with a tray. Two portions of ice cream garnished with fruit and hot chocolate sauce, the carafe of wine and the two glasses. Cain brushes dangerously past his arm.

'Sorry, David, but *Baby Boom*'s on, and I just wanted to tell Laura to watch it. Right now she'd love it!'

'Did you get through to her?' He puts the tray down on the coffee table.

'No, I didn't. She's not at home, she's not at my place, and I was just going to ask the operator for Paletti's number.'

David picks up the remote, presses in a few instructions and then walks back to his tray. 'That's sorted, my darling. Take the cassette with you when you go. Do you like eating ice cream in bed?'

'Thanks very much, you're brilliant. Actually I'm full, but ice cream always goes down nicely, doesn't it? If you don't mind, I'm happy where I am. It's so comfortable, and this widescreen television's incredible. It's like being in the cinema!'

David hands her a bowl, takes off his shoes and lies down on the other side. They eat their ice cream together, a couple of feet apart. Carmen moves across slightly, lies on her side and crosses her feet over his. She rubs back and forth a little and he looks at her with his spoon in his hand. 'I'd love to come and cuddle you, but I daren't. I don't want to promise anything that could make us feel unhappy later.'

'What could make us feel unhappy?' Carmen has found a stone in the cherry, and picks it carefully out of her mouth. David holds out his hand for the stone. He flashes his green eyes at her, and Carmen thinks, I don't need to ask any more questions. It's clear what he means. But why does she want to know? Why can't she let it rest? Their bones are snuggling up together. That's great. But just because their bodies can communicate to each other that doesn't mean they have to make love! Carmen notices an interesting phenomenon about herself: the more clearly apparent it is that she's the hunter not the prey, the more strongly she is drawn to him. It's interesting, she thinks. If he were physically intact, I'd have been on the defensive and probably furious with him because, like all the rest, he was controlled by his penis. But because he can't get it up I try to arouse him. The irony! She looks up and thinks she detects a familiar gleam in his eyes: pure pleasure. He quickly turns his head away and puts down his ice cream, then he slides nearer, turns to face her, puts his hand on her side and runs it along the curves of her body. From her hip downwards and then back up over her waist to the point where her breasts begin. He lingers there and lets his fingers wander back down again. Carmen starts stroking him too. Through the fine fabric of his shirt she feels his firm chest, the muscles on his belly. She runs the tips of her fingers up to his throat. As his head is on its side, the muscles and tendons are clearly visible.

'Do you play competitive sports?' she asks, running her hand over the muscles of his chest and down to the belt of his black jeans.

'I used to do the decathlon, but I was never really that good. And once I finished my studies I didn't have the time for intensive training. Anyway I was always too tired in the evenings. I still do a bit now and again, but really,' and he taps himself gently on his chest muscles, 'that's all that's left.'

'And very nice it is too,' says Carmen, running her lips gently over his body. Before she reaches the waistband of his trousers David brings her gently back up. 'Carmen.' He strokes her head and runs all five fingers through her hair. 'Please don't. You're causing some very strange feelings. It really isn't doing me any good. I know I'll suffer.'

She puts her head on his shoulder. 'I wouldn't want that. Of course I wouldn't. I just wanted you to feel some warmth, to give you a bit of my love. It's just that I feel so much for you. It's hard to express it.'

He delicately strokes her back. 'You want to sleep with me.'

'No,' she says resolutely, 'that's not what I want. I'm enjoying the fact that we can hold each other close without groping for each other's crotches!'

'You use some pretty direct language for a well-raised young woman.' He taps her head gently with his knuckles.

'Maybe over the years I've just forgotten how to soft-soap. Although at times like this I'm battling against my mother's upbringing. Always be polite, don't hurt anybody, be kind, always look for the good in people. I expect I'd politely tell a burglar he was using the wrong key by mistake. And by way of consolation I'd tell him it happens to everybody . . .'

David laughs and presses her to him.

'I think I've made a really good catch. And I'm really happy you're here.'

Carmen cuddles up to him and presses her face into the hollow of his neck, 'Me too, David. Me too.'

Carmen is lost in her thoughts. She is barely paying attention to Britta Berger, who has been telling how well everything went yesterday and is wanting to know if she'd done everything right. 'You were fantastic,' Carmen automatically concurs, 'I couldn't have done better myself.' Britta beams, coming out of her shell for the first time since she's been working with Carmen, talking excitedly, with all sorts of funny details, about how she closed all the deals. Carmen's astonished. She's never seen Britta like this before! So euphoric, so affable, so happy! It distracts her from her own thoughts. 'Just a moment,' she says eventually, interrupting the torrent of words with a laugh, 'I think this calls for a celebration!' She goes into the tiny side-room of the office and opens the fridge. There should be a little bottle of champagne there. And there it is. Carmen takes it out, fetches two champagne glasses from the shelf and walks with them to Britta's desk. 'So, let's drink to your achievement! You've taken an enormous step forward, congratulations!' She pops the cork and fills the glasses. Britta is overjoyed, and almost hurls herself at Carmen.

How easy it is to make people happy, Carmen thinks. She clinks glasses with Britta again and then goes back to her desk, getting there just as the phone starts ringing. Carmen picks it up, and hears Laura on the line.

'I desperately need to talk to you!'

'God almighty, what's happened?' Carmen nods to Britta, who raises her glass to her again in the distance, and then goes back to her desk.

'You could say that! Your "impotent" Felix tried his damnedest to use me as a cure.'

'Oh no, not again. Not really? How?'

'It's hard for me to tell you right now. I'm in the staff room. There's no one here at the moment, but walls have ears. I don't especially want to turn into gossip material.'

'My place tonight?' Carmen asks curtly.

'Great. I'll bring some mince and everything you need to make a nice bolognese. Have you got some spaghetti?'

'Yep!'

172   'Red wine?'

'Definitely!'

'Okay, great – about seven?'

'Perfect, Laura. I'll look forward to it – and I can't wait to hear about it.' She puts the phone down and glances at Britta. Of course she's been listening in.

'You can go early if you like, Frau Legg. I don't mind staying till six.'

One day Britta's going to be the boss and I'm going to be working for her, thinks Carmen. She dealt with those contracts so well yesterday that she'll now be setting her goals a bit higher. You never know! Oh, nonsense, she thinks then, pulling herself together, she's just nice and helpful, and that's all. She's not your classic career woman, waiting to elbow you out of your job. Or is she? She'll end up in charge of the whole client file. What if she sets up in competition? With copies of our documents?

'Many thanks for the offer, Britta,' she says in a friendly voice, 'but I've got things to do. I'll be here till six myself. But you can go early if you like. Go and celebrate with your boyfriend!'

'Oh, that's very kind of you!' Britta springs to her feet, quickly arranges her desk, switches off the computer, grabs her bag and is gone.

Carmen's completely astonished. Okay, I take it all back, Britta's completely harmless. But has she really got a boyfriend? Why shouldn't she? It's just that Carmen can't imagine it. What would he look like if he suited little, mousy Britta? Don't be so arrogant, your own history isn't exactly chock full of handsome men. She thinks briefly about various men from her past and laughs: that's enough. To work, Carmen, get something done.

Carmen has achieved more than she originally planned. She works late and sees Laura driving up just as she's closing the big garage door. Laura parks in one of the free spaces, jumps out of the car and hugs Carmen violently. They kiss each other on both cheeks and burst out laughing, as if on command.

'You dumped me in it.' Laura is helpless with laughter.

'Sorry about that,' says Carmen, 'but you wanted to give Felix a try. So, tell me what happened.'

Laura links arms with Carmen and the two of them go up the street to the house.

'Okay, at first he was really very nice. He's fantastic-looking, he told me about his sports, about his travels, and we laughed a lot. Then at some point he had too much to drink, and wouldn't stop talking. Okay, why not? He carried on till midnight about the first time it hadn't worked, exactly what it was like, what he had felt. You know,' Laura stops for a moment while Carmen opens the front door, 'you know how my mind works when that happens. I thought less about him and more about his girlfriend. But he didn't go into that. He didn't really give a damn about her feelings. Anyway that's what it sounded like to me . . .' They walk past the door to Elvira's flat. 'Have you heard anything from her?' Laura interrupts herself. Carmen shakes her head. 'Shall we ring her doorbell?' Laura presses the button. As always, her three-note bell sounds bright and friendly, but there's not a sound inside.

'Oh, my God!' Carmen groans.

'What if she isn't there?' asks Laura.

'She's always been there before. I bring her any shopping she needs from town.'

'Maybe the situation has changed.' Laura rings again, and Carmen knocks.

'Not a thing!' Carmen thinks for a moment. 'I've arranged that she should leave a message in my mail-box if she leaves the building.'

'So?' Laura looks at her. 'You haven't even looked.'

'I didn't want to interrupt you. Wait a second.' She puts down her briefcase and runs down the stairs two at a time. There's a little note, folded in four, in Carmen's mail-box. Carmen picks it up along with some other letters and dashes back upstairs.

'What have we here!' She leans against the doorframe
beside Laura, breathing rapidly.

'You could do with some exercise,' Laura says dryly, patting Carmen gently on the shoulder.

'See if you can fit it into my diary,' says Carmen, wrinkling her nose. 'For the past few weeks I've hardly had time to catch up on my sleep.'

'And now I'm back. Let's see what it says.'

'Very nice.' Carmen unfolds the letter and reads out loud:

Dear Carmen, dear Laura! Stefan and I talked about the past almost till breakfast time, and then I spent the night in one of his guest rooms. His butler is about to set off to fetch me the things I need from my bathroom, and drop off this little note so that you don't have to worry. Stefan is shattered, particularly by yesterday afternoon's events. So he wants to see a psychiatrist. Stefan's very ashamed about what he did, Carmen, and I'm afraid his condition isn't likely to improve while he's still tormenting himself with it. So I ask you in confidence to grant him some kind of absolution. I know it's a lot to ask, but I would be very grateful if you would give him a word of for-giveness,

lots of love – Elvira

'Hmm.' Carmen turns to Laura. 'What do you think?'

'He's killed her and written the letter himself.'

'Oh, stop it!' Carmen shivers. 'It's her writing. I know it from her shopping lists.'

'Then he's holding her prisoner and he dictated that to her.'

'I think you're a bit muddled, Laura. Why would he do that?' Carmen puts the letter with the others, picks up her briefcase and starts climbing the rest of the stairs to her flat.

Laura catches up with her. 'What do I know? Since I've been back I've slowly come to the understanding that any-thing's possible.'

Still walking, Carmen turns around. 'Sure, and your name isn't Laura, it's Rosemary, and that,' she says, pointing at Laura's belly, ' is Rosemary's Baby. Isn't it?'

'You're daft,' laughs Laura.

'All right, so are you.'

They're at the top of the stairs, and Carmen opens the door. 'What have you done with the stuff for our spaghetti, Laura? I can't see anything . . .'

'Sorry, I was too late. But you'll have got some garlic, so we can have spaghetti con aglio e olio.'

'Dear, dear, dear.' Carmen shakes her head with a laugh. 'You'll come to a bad end. Wait a minute, let me change into something more comfortable, and then I want to hear about Felix.'

'Can I mix myself a spritzer?'

'Make whatever you want.'

From the bathroom, Carmen hears the fridge door closing. 'How should I understand your generous offer,' she hears Laura calling from the kitchen.

'What do you mean?' Carmen hangs her trousers on a hanger, with her blouse and jacket over it, then carries them into the bedroom and grabs a pair of leggings and a thick sweatshirt.

Laura comes and leans against the frame of the bedroom door.

'You're no better then I am, darling, you're practically out of drink. Which is to say that there's half a bottle of white wine in there, but it's open and tastes like it's been that way for ages.'

'Hmm.' Carmen puts on some thick socks and looks up. 'The red wine isn't in the fridge, it's in the dining-room.'

'No it isn't,' grins Laura.

'What are you suggesting?' asks Carmen, sitting up.

'Let's go eat!'

'Oh, no! I've just changed. Let's get a take-away from the Laguna.'

'Perfect. Do you have their number?'

'It's in my address book beside the telephone. I'd like the vegetarian pizza with salami and double cheese. And two bottles of red wine. But tell him I'm not going to pay him any special take-away prices for the wine. Tell him to give us a bulk discount. And another discount for being regulars as well.'

'I expect you'll want him to pay us for eating it as well,' says Laura, on her way to the phone.

'Too right,' says Carmen. 'Tell him that, too.'

She sits down on the couch and waits for Laura to make the call, and then taps the cushion beside her with the palm of her hand.

'So, Laura my darling, now it's your turn. Finally, I want to know what your Felix got up to yesterday.'

'First of all, you can keep "your Felix" for a start. And secondly, you can keep all your other impotent men as well.'

Carmen laughs. 'So what went wrong?'

'I'll tell you.' She drops down on to the sofa beside Carmen and then leans slightly towards her. 'Okay, he told me the story of his disaster in all its awful details. At first I wasn't really mad about hearing it all, but later on it got more exciting – and why not, it was interesting for me to hear something like that. So, after his first sexual breakdown he made a number of efforts to get things going again. First he tried going manual, because he didn't want to make a fool of himself with his girlfriend any more. When that didn't work either he realised that this was exactly what his unconscious mind wanted. Remember, Carmen, he writes that he escaped into impotence and wanted to share the experience with someone. Sounds fine, but that's not the way I see it. Okay, once he'd worked out that it was the fault of his unconscious mind, he decided – typical teacher – to track down the cause. And where do you think he got by psychoanalysing himself? Where do you reckon?'

Carmen shrugs her shoulders. 'No idea. Where?'

'His mother, darling. Isn't that obvious?'

Carmen takes a deep breath. 'Of course, where else.'

'Exactly. So he had himself hypnotised to find his way back to his mother – and not only that, he wanted to get back inside!'

'Enough!' Carmen shivers.

'I'm telling you the honest truth. But the hypnosis went wrong. He tried it a number of times, he used up all the money he'd saved to travel around the world, but he still didn't get rid of his trauma.'

'Was he going to the right doctor? It could be a physical problem, and then he might have spared himself the whole hocus-pocus.'

'He was going to his GP at first, because he thought it was some kind of displaced flu or something, The doctor couldn't find anything.'

'Didn't he go to another doctor? A specialist?'

'No, a fortune-teller.'

Carmen laughs.

'Don't laugh, she told him he'd have to find his way back to his mother if he wanted to be cured.'

'So, the same thing as the hypnotist told him.'

Laura shakes her head. 'No, the same thing he'd convinced himself of in the course of his self-diagnosis. But he knew the hypnotist couldn't help.'

'And the fortune-teller told him what he wanted to hear. Of course. Why didn't he go to his mother and talk it all through with her? That might have been some real help. Don't you think? Not because she was the origin of his failure, or whatever – what nonsense – but because a mother probably feels more love for her child than anyone else in the world. Do you remember when your mother used to blow on your cuts and grazes when you were a child, and they stopped hurting just because you believed in your mother's power.'

Carmen has really got herself going. She should probably have met Felix. Maybe she could have helped him deal with his problem, as he had put it so nicely in his letter.

But Laura makes an impatient gesture and frowns. 'That occurred to me too, but it's not so easy. His mother's dead. How could he talk to her?'

'Oh, no!' Carmen, who has been sitting bolt upright for the

past few minutes, sinks back into the cushions. 'What a tale. And you listened to that for hours? Poor thing!'

'Well,' says Laura. 'It was all so grotesque I wanted to know everything. You don't switch off the TV just as things are getting exciting.'

Carmen brushes her hair back. 'But the guy sounds dangerous. Obsessive. What happened next?'

'Then they wanted to shut the restaurant. He'd had ten beers or so by then, I wasn't counting – although I think he'll be missing his PE lesson today – and he asked me if I thought it would be terrific to cure an impotent man. He said I would find it insanely satisfying.'

'Insane I can believe,' says Carmen dryly, 'but satisfying?'

Laura laughs. 'Yeah, pretty crafty. After all the celestial arts had failed, he turned to more earthly remedies. He went to a brothel. He wouldn't have to explain himself if nothing happened, he paid, he stayed anonymous and was able to save face.'

'And?' Carmen listens attentively.

'As usual, nothing happened. Absolutely nothing. He went through all the prostitutes, red-haired, brunette, black-haired, blonde, fat and thin, until he was skint and went back to the fortune-teller. And she told him, wait for it, the only one who could help him was someone who looked like his mother.'

'Oh, stop, it's too revolting.'

'Yes, and there's better to come. That's why he was so quiet for a moment when I described myself, do you remember? His mother was short and fat with brown curly hair.'

'Heavy stuff!'

'So he wanted to persuade me to sleep with him. At least he had a fantasy that I might be short and fat.'

'No!' Carmen snorts the word and sits back down again. 'It can't be! And what about you?'

'I paid and left.'

'What, you paid for that? For him to use you as a shrink? Send him a bill for a session of therapy.' She remembers Stefan.

Somehow, problems with impotent men don't get any smaller. On the contrary. They seem to get bigger and bigger. But thank God they're not all as deranged as this one. She thinks of David and Frederic. There are perversions everywhere. Impotence may just be a trigger.

'That'll be our pizza, I'll get it.' Laura goes to the door. After a few steps she stops and turns around again. 'And do you know the strangest thing? Not that he wanted to sleep with me in his mother's clothes, or the other way round, I can't remember exactly, because when I was leaving . . .'

'What?' Carmen gives a start, 'you didn't tell me anything about that!'

'I didn't want to spoil your appetite – I don't have the nerve to repeat any more of it, I've had it up to there – no the greatest thing was that the next morning I started to doubt whether he was really impotent, or whether it was all just a show to get a woman into bed to satisfy deranged fantasies!'

Carmen fetches plates, glasses and cutlery and, while she's quickly laying the table, she says, 'And he looks so cute and harmless. Once again it goes to show that you can never tell. I'm also surprised he was so open, you being a fellow teacher.'

Laura laughs. 'Okay, I was drawing him out, I do admit. And he was pretty drunk. But he intended to try it on with me from the start, I'm pretty sure of it. Maybe he'd worked out that the trick might work on me, what do I know? And then it went too far.'

She opens the door.

She finds herself face to face with a broad-shouldered man in a tattered leather jacket and washed-out jeans. He hesitates for a second, and runs his fingers through his black, unruly hair. 'Hello?' He narrows his blue eyes. 'Not how I remembered Carmen at all!'

Laura looks at him steadily, then takes a step back towards the living-room without taking her eyes off him. 'Carmen, could you come here a minute?'

'What is it?' They've probably brought the wrong pizza, or she hasn't enough money, Carmen thinks, forcing herself to get up from the sofa. At the living-room door she bursts out laughing. 'Frederic! How lovely!' She runs over to him and gives him a big hug. I'd totally forgotten about you, she thinks, and I meant to call you yesterday. Well, anyway, here you are, and now I'll have to tell you about David. Laura stands beside them, waiting. Carmen detaches herself from Frederic and takes Laura by the arm.

'This is Laura, my best friend, and this is Frederic, a good friend, a very good friend.' They shake hands.

The doorbell rings again.

'And that's the pizza,' says Laura, pressing the door-handle.

'Tell me where you've been!' Carmen pinches Frederic in the side.

'Where do you think, at my dear sister's, dreaming of you.' He takes off his heavy leather jacket and hangs it in the cupboard. Laura takes a close inspection. He's wearing a plain olive-green cotton T-shirt, with a round neck and no apparent seam. So it's either very cheap and from Taiwan or it's very expensive and with a designer label, also from Taiwan.

Carmen laughs. 'You old charmer, you're putting it on. You were happy to have a few days off, admit it!'

There is a knock at the door. Laura opens it with a lilty-mark note in her hand.

'Thanks,' says David, taking the note from her hand. 'What a nice welcome! Is there more where that came from?'

'David!' With a shriek Carmen throws her arms around him. 'What a surprise!'

'That's what I was going to say.' Frederic folds his arms.

Over Carmen's shoulder David looks at the assembled company. 'Evening, everyone.'

There is a ring at the door.

'That will be the pizza!' says Laura, pressing the buzzer.

Carmen detaches herself from David and turns around. Her eyes are beaming, and her feelings for David are obvious. She says to Frederic, 'This is David,' and to David, 'This is Frederic. I've told you about him.'

'Ah,' says Frederic, 'how nice! What have you told him?'   181

David holds out a hand to him, 'About your timely intervention with her neighbour. Elvira was lucky that you were
there.'

'That's so long ago I can hardly believe it happened.'

'Not even a week ago, Frederic,' laughs Carmen. 'It was last
Wednesday.'

'Quite a few things have happened since then.' Frederic
looks from Carmen to David, from David to Laura and back to
Carmen.

'When you're right, you're right,' Laura nods and opens
the flat door.

Enzo is standing at the door, balancing two pizza cartons,
with two bottles of red wine clamped under his arm.

'Great, the chef himself,' Carmen greets him.

'A party?' asks Enzo. 'Not much here for this many people!
Why don't you come over? It would be easier!'

'The party wasn't planned,' laughs Carmen happily, taking
Enzo by the arm. 'But won't you come in? Have a drink with
us.'

'Sorry, I came myself because I couldn't spare anyone, it's
chaos down there. And if it hadn't been you,' he gives Carmen
a melting glance, 'I'd have said no straightaway.'

'Oh, but that's so sweet,' says Carmen, delighted. 'But won't
you have just one little glass? A little sip?'

Enzo shakes his head sadly. 'I couldn't even bring you
another delivery. We're really in dire straits. Piero's off, his
wife is having a baby, and Luigi's sick. I really can't!'

'I'm sorry,' Carmen takes the pizzas from him, Laura the
two bottles.

'What do we owe you?' asks Laura, holding out the fifty-
mark note.

'Let's sort it out next time you come by.'

Carmen walks him to the door. 'Many, many thanks again,
Enzo, I won't forget it.'

'Don't worry,' he says with a wave, and a kindly smile
spreading over his round face. 'I was happy to do it for you,
mia bella. And a good evening to you all.' He rubs his hands

quickly on the big towel that he wears as an apron around his waist, waves to everyone, turns and leaves.

Now they're alone, four of them with two pizzas. Carmen becomes aware of the situation. How stupid, she should have put Frederic off, or at least warned him. She puts the two cartons on the table, Laura puts the two bottles down next to them, and goes into the kitchen to fetch a corkscrew. The two men stand side by side watching each other. They don't feel terribly at ease, you can not only feel it, you can see it as well. They don't know what to think about each other, so conversation is impossible. Laura casts a glance at Carmen. Carmen frowns briefly. There's nothing she can do. It's just unfortunate.

'Two pizzas for two people; I would suggest, Frederic, that you and I take Enzo's advice and eat in the Laguna.' Laura looks quizzically at Frederic.

'No, no, there's enough here for everyone. We can cut them in half, and I'm not feeling all that hungry anyway,' Carmen contradicts her quickly.

'But I am,' says Laura. 'Or do you think I'm going to share my pizza with you? Or David? Or Frederic? I want a pizza all to myself.'

'But they're your pizzas,' says David. 'It should be up to Frederic and me to sort out the extra ones, not you two!'

Frederic looks over at Laura. 'I think Laura's right. Why don't we have a cosy evening in the Laguna, Enzo can serve us and you two can see how you get on.' He takes Laura by the arm and guides her into the corridor. There he turns back to Carmen and David, who are standing there open-mouthed. 'If you need us, you know where we are!' He picks up his leather jacket, throws it over his arm and takes the next-best coat for Laura, and the door closes behind them.

'Oh, oh,' says David, frowning. 'That wasn't so good, was it?'

'It doesn't matter.' But Carmen has an uneasy feeling in her stomach. 'We'll sort it out.'

David wraps his arms around her. 'Don't I get a proper

welcome, then?' They kiss, in a close embrace. Then David suddenly detaches himself from her. '*Andiamo*, our pizzas are getting cold. That would be a shame. Is my favourite pizza in there?'

Carmen laughs: 'I don't even know what Laura ordered. I like the vegetarian with salami and double cheese.'

'Strictly vegetarian, then?' David grins and puts two equal halves on the plates. 'That way at least the other one'll stay hot longer. It looks like a quattro stagioni!'

Carmen nods. 'You're right, I often have that. What's your favourite?'

'Quattro formaggi. They're nearly too much for me.'

Carmen smiles at him tenderly and opens a bottle. 'I can't imagine anything being too much for you'

He looks at her seriously. 'You are.'

Embarrassed, Carmen says nothing.

David glances at the clock. 'Just before eight. Carmen, would you mind if I watch the news? There's just been a robbery at a big jeweller's shop in Frankfurt, did you hear about it?'

Carmen shakes her head. 'I haven't heard any news today. Why, what happened?'

'We built the building two years ago, and now the question is how the robbers managed to get through the security system at night. Either they knew it very well, or they had the plans. I had a visit from the police today.'

'What, because of a break-in?'

'Armed robbery, hostages taken and stolen goods totalling more than two million marks.'

Carmen puts the piece of pizza back on the plate and jumps to her feet. 'Then we'll have to go into the bedroom. I only ever watch TV in bed now – the news and late-night films.'

'No rush, we've got a couple of minutes.'

'Hang on a second, I've got a breakfast tray that you can fold out in bed, it's very handy.'

184 She darts into the kitchen and comes back, and while

David is putting plates and glasses on it she switches on the
television. They get there just as the news is beginning.

Carmen unfolds the short legs of the table, gesturing to
David to sit on the bed with his legs stretched out, and she sits
down close by him. With a combined effort they heave the
little table over their legs.

They both watch the news items with considerable excitement. Deaths in racial rioting in South Africa, an earthquake
and landslide in Japan, people injured in a mining disaster in
Lorraine, the Chancellor on an official visit to Washington.
And then: a siege in Frankfurt. Carmen takes a sip of wine.
Not much to see. Outside view of the shop, hypermodern
architecture. David makes things like that? Good for you!
she thinks, impulsively putting her hand on his, which lies
quietly beside his plate. The building has been cordoned off
from some distance away, and there are police cars, an ambulance and a huge number of journalists. The commentator
explains what has happened, while the camera records details
of the building. 'Three men are assumed to have forced their
way into the building overnight, surprising staff at the opening of business and threatening them with weapons. They
demanded that staff open the safes, tied up the sales staff and
cleared the shop. Running from the jeweller's shop, the three
were noticed by a passing patrol-car, whose occupants immediately stopped and tried to apprehend the gangsters. A
get-away car managed to pick up two of the perpetrators,
while the third was left behind. He took a passer-by hostage
with his gun, and retreated with her into the jeweller's shop.'
Now the reporter himself is seen on screen. 'He is now holding seven people hostage. The two other men have escaped
with some two million marks. In the meantime the owner,
who owns a number of other large jewellery shops, has been
informed. He is coming by private plane, with a view to nego-
tiating with the armed robber. A police psychologist has also
been called in. So far the armed robber has made no
demands – ah, I can see a police escort pulling up, that must
be Stefan von Kaltenstein, the owner. A question to . . .'

With a jerk the tray falls over, and everything pours over the bed covers. Carmen is suddenly kneeling up on the bed to get closer to the television. 'What was that?' she stammers. David looks at her in amazement, and quickly picks up bits of pizza and glasses. The red wine is already seeping in large patches into the covers. Carmen is oblivious of that. The reporter walks up to the column of cars. Out of the second car steps – Stefan!

A police officer shakes his hand and the camera team pushes forward. 'Herr von Kaltenstein, what do you plan to do to save the lives of the hostages?'

Stefan looks pale, but somehow imposing. He is impeccably dressed, his voice is quiet and deep, and he articulates precisely. 'We will do everything we can to not endanger the lives of the hostages, whatever the armed robber demands.'

'What offers will you make him?'

'So far, to my knowledge, he has made no demands.'

'Will you try to persuade him to release them?'

'That is a matter for the police psychologist, not for me. I can only do what is within my power.'

'What is within your power, Herr von Kaltenstein?' asks the reporter.

Stefan's face in close-up. His expression reveals nothing. 'Money. If I can save these people's lives with money, I will do so.'

The reporter is alone on screen again. 'We will come back in the course of this programme if there are any new developments. Back to the eight o'clock news.'

Another story follows, and Carmen falls back into the cushions. 'I'm going mad,' she says, and looks at David, who has brought everything into safety. 'That's incredible!'

David runs his hand gently over her hair. 'If I'd guessed you were going to get so excited . . .'

'It's no wonder I'm getting excited! Stefan involved in a hostage crisis and the owner of those jewellery shops . . .' She is completely breathless.

186   'I really don't understand.' David gets to his feet. 'Let's

put the duvet cover in the washing-machine, or you'll never get those stains out. And then you can tell me why you're getting so excited. I should really be the one who's getting excited . . .'

Carmen is so distracted that she hasn't even noticed the red-wine stains. 'What do you mean?' she asked, and slaps her forehead. 'How idiotic! Elvira's sitting in his castle right now, and being drawn into all this excitement – I'll have to call her!' She glances at David, who is looking at her uncomprehendingly. 'Sorry, you can't possibly understand. That was Stefan, the Stefan I told you about in connection with Elvira, my neighbour. Do you understand? Isn't the whole thing crazy?'

David drops back on to the bed. 'No, you're right. I know Kaltenstein, he was the ultimate authority when we were drawing up our plans and designs and carrying out the work. But you didn't tell me your Stefan was *the* Stefan!'

'I had no idea!' Carmen runs off, coming back with her address book and the phone.

'Well,' says David, 'Kaltenstein's a big fish, a very big fish. His ancestors made big money in South-West Africa with gemstones, especially diamonds, and in Brazil as well. I think he owns big jewellery shops in other countries too.'

Carmen is already dialling.

'William, is that you?' Her voice is high-pitched, and she clears her throat. 'No, I'm not from the press, I'm Carmen Legg, I've been a few times . . . oh, you know? That's great. Tell me, is Elvira Gohdes still with you, the old lady who . . . yes? She's gone to lie down? What? A doctor? Is it serious?'

She drums her fingers on her address book. William's detailed explanations are taking too long. 'Hang on, William, tell her Carmen's on her way. Yes, I'll sort everything out. Yes. And don't let anyone from the press in – oh, the baron's said that already . . . yes, I'm on my way.'

She slams the phone down. 'David, Elvira's ill, she's in bed and the doctor's on his way. I think I'd better go over there. Will you come?'

'Put the bedclothes in the washing-machine, two minutes won't make any difference.'

'How can you think of bedclothes at a time like this?'

'Because otherwise you'll have to throw them away, and you can't do that. And also maybe you should call Enzo and tell the others.'

'You do that. I'll pack a toothbrush just in case.'

She pulls some jeans on over her leggings, and fetches some warm winter shoes and a thick leather jacket. 'Okay, I'm ready. Have you got through to the others?'

David picks up his car keys. 'No, they had been there, but Enzo didn't have a table for them.'

'Never mind, we can call later from Stefan's.'

They run down the stairs together.

'Do you think Herr Kaltenstein will mind me coming with you?'

She hadn't even thought of that.

'Why not?' she asks rhetorically. After all, it's a pretty exceptional situation, it's about Elvira and a hostage situation, and he's hardly going to be getting back from Frankfurt tonight.

At the bottom of the stairs she pulls open the front door and stands in front of David's jeep, which gleams faintly under the streetlight.

'I suggest we take two cars.' David puts his arm around her. 'I'll stay as long as is necessary, to make sure that Elvira doesn't have to go to hospital or whatever, and then I'll come home. You'll probably want to stay until tomorrow.'

Emotionally, Carmen wants to refuse, but she knows it's really the best way.

'Fine,' she nods, and then wraps her arms around him, 'though I'd rather we stayed together.'

'Nice of you to say so, but this way will be better, believe me!' He gives her a loving kiss, and for the first time in ages Carmen feels the desire to sleep with a man. Maybe he could give her the strength and peace that she so needs, and which he exudes as though it were the most natural thing in the world. She extracts herself from his embrace, gives him a slightly crooked smile and then runs across the street to the garage. It seems to take forever. Carmen hopes Elvira's okay, and she mustn't miss the news. She steers the car up the slope, David is already standing ready to close the garage door. He's a dream, she thinks, so loving, so attentive and yet so masculine! She waits until he's climbed into his jeep and then sets off. Genesis is playing. Take that cassette out, I mustn't miss any news reports. It's half past eight, a while before the news. If anything crucial happens, the local radio station's bound to have a newsflash. Isn't it?

She drives fast, ahead of David. Now she's happy to be driving a functional, reliable BMW, and not some sort of novelty car. She looks at the car's clear outlines, listens to its noise, powerful yet contained. For some reason the car reassures her. Her nerves stop flapping, her heart beats rhythmically again, her blood is no longer concentrated in her head and has stopped rushing in her ears. She breathes in deeply and puts her foot down. In the rear-view mirror she sees that David is still close behind her. If there's a radar trap they're both done for.

By the castle gate she brakes hard. She nearly drove past it. David has trouble coming to a halt so suddenly behind her. Carmen turns in and jumps out of the car to ring the bell, but even today the big cast-iron gate opens, as if moved by some magic hand. What was she feeling yesterday when she drove out of here yesterday – can it have been yesterday – and in what state is she driving back today? Now she feels part of a whole. She isn't thinking about whether it's going to do Elvira or Stefan any good, or whether David might have certain reservations. As far as she's concerned it's all quite clear – she has to help, she's part of it!

Carmen drives straight up to the steps and leaves her car where the blue Jaguar was parked yesterday. David stops right behind her. They get out at the same time and walk up the stone steps. William comes towards them.

'I'm very glad to be able to greet you, madam, and you too, sir, of course.'

189

'This is David Franck, a good friend.'

'William nods to them both and walks ahead of them to the door. 'Is the doctor here? How is she? Is there any news from Frankfurt, William?'

He takes their jackets in the hall. Carmen has left her overnight bag in the car, thinking that it might make more sense to take Elvira home later. If not, she can grab the bag when she needs to.

David stands there and looks around. I must have gawped like that the first time I came here as well, Carmen smiles gently, feeling like the lady of the manor. How idiotic of her. Although she really does feel as if she's at home here.

'Unfortunately I don't have any news, madam, but Andrew is sitting by the television and has three radios tuned to different stations so that we don't miss anything. We're very concerned, as you may imagine. The old baron always made sure that the private and the professional remained firmly apart. And now the younger baron is exposed to the public gaze. We are very concerned, very concerned.'

'What are you afraid of?' asks Carmen.

'You see, the jewellery shops have never been publicly associated with the von Kaltensteins, and with good reason, ever since an abduction in the Kaltenstein household was foiled at the last moment. The von Kaltensteins didn't want to have to live in some kind of high-security establishment.' He walks ahead of them to the stairs. 'I'm sure you would like to look in on the patient first, if I may walk ahead of you. We had to cancel the doctor at her request. She says she's much better and has all the medicine she needs. She's glad you're coming.' And he nods gently towards Carmen. He's being incredibly outgoing today.

'Has she got a television in her room?' David wants do know.

'I'm afraid that would be too much for her.'

'On the contrary, William, truth is more reassuring than uncertainty!'

'You may be right.' He has reached the top of the stairs and walks over to a door thickly upholstered in green leather, and knocks on the wooden frame. 'I'll bring you a television straightaway. Would you like anything to drink? He looks at Carmen. After a faint 'Come in!' he opens the door and announces her arrival: 'A visit for you, madam, your friends!' Then he turns back to David. 'And you, sir? Some refreshment? A beer, perhaps?'

David nods. 'Many thanks, an excellent idea. Do you have any alcohol-free? I have to drive later.'

'Of course! And for the ladies?' He walks into the room ahead of Carmen. A wide antique four-poster takes up the whole of one wall. Elegant wooden spirals support the canopy, and lengths of fabric fall delicately from each corner to the floor. In the middle of the bed is a little face, Elvira, slowly emerging from big downy pillows.

'Elvira! The things you get up to. At least tell me you're all right.' Carmen charges past William, leans down and kisses her on both cheeks.

'Might I bring the ladies something to drink, and perhaps some snacks?' William is waiting politely by the door. Carmen looks over at him. What has he been through in his sixty years or so? Foiled abduction? She must talk to him about that later. 'I'll have a Campari and orange, please, and Elvira, what would you like?'

'I've got everything I need, thanks,' she says. 'I'm so spoilt here that I'm looking forward to tightening my belt again.'

William bows gently and leaves the room. Carmen laughs and puts her arms around Elvira. 'Look, Elvira, this is David. The one with the big card and the glass-cube villa, do you remember?'

'Of course. I may be a bit weak at the moment, but I haven't gone senile. What's up with Stefan? They're so keen to spare me any anxiety that they're driving me up the walls!'

'We're about to get a television, and the other butler, I know his name now, Andrew, is sitting downstairs listening to several radio programmes at the same time too. So we won't miss anything.'

'I hope not.' Elvira takes a deep breath and then looks over to David. 'So you're the secret letter-writer who knows his Rilke. Did you copy it out, or do you know it off by heart?'

David grins, walks over to her and, step by step, quotes the poem all the way through.

'Bravo!' nods Elvira at the end, and Carmen's blood runs hot and cold. 'Why did you cancel the doctor? Wouldn't it have been better . . .?'

Elvira interrupts her, 'I'm so wrapped up in cotton wool here that my old bones are in a state of rebellion, they're simply not used to it.' Carmen shakes her head, but Elvira anticipates what she's going to say. 'No, really, it's no cause for concern. I got worked up about what was happening in Frankfurt, that was all. My discussions with Stefan went very well, so it wasn't that. I knew I was feeling faint, and I took my medicine and immediately felt better. William's exaggerating.' She smiles faintly and pats the edge of the broad bed. 'Won't you come and sit down by me?' There is a tap at the door, and two young men come in with a television. How many people work here, Carmen wonders. More than you would expect at first glance, she thinks. I wonder if he has business insurance? Life insurance? Fire insurance? She shakes her head to rid herself of the thought. David helps them find the aerial and gets the television working. It's nearly nine o'clock.

'Is there a radio anywhere?' Carmen asks, looking around.

One of the young men points to a chest of drawers in the shadows. 'There should be one in there.'

And there is a portable radio.

David tunes in the station he wants. Just in time for the news. Frankfurt comes at the end, nothing seems to have changed. He's still sitting holed up in the shop with his seven hostages, and hasn't made any demands.

'Surely they can take out one man!' says Carmen, shaking her head.

'Who would do it, and more importantly, who would take responsibility?' David sits down on the bed beside Carmen.

'The government's crack team, of course, the GSG9! Why do we have such a highly trained taskforce if we only use it twice a year? When Dieter Degowski hijacked that bus a few years ago, those two passengers needn't have died if they'd had a crackshot standing by. And because of the cowardice of the state and wrangling over responsibility, two people, that Italian guy and the girl, had to die!' The two young men nod to her and go.

'Not all people see it that way, Carmen. For many people a bullet from a police revolver is worse than one from a terrorist's gun, even if the terrorists are firing on civilians. In Germany, criminals enjoy high status until you happen to be a victim yourself. Then everyone's shouting for the police at the top of their voice.'

'That other guy, the Red Army terrorist, what was his name, Wolfgang Grams, who was shot while he lay on the ground, he was another one,' adds Elvira. 'No one gave a thought to the GSG9 policeman he's supposed to have killed. It's paradoxical really. But they've got to give the man in the jeweller's shop a chance. There's been no bloodshed so far, after all.'

'Do we know that?' asks Carmen. 'So far no one in there has been able to say anything. It's all just supposition. They could all be dead in there!'

There's a knock at the door and William comes in with the trolley. In the middle is a huge dish of canapés, which evoke strange memories in Carmen. Next to it are their drinks.

'*Bon appétit*, and if you require anything else, please ring the bell or dial 9. I will be at your service all through the night.'

My God, thinks Carmen, at his age? What a job!

'That won't be necessary, William.' Carmen stands up to take her glass. 'Many thanks for your offer. We can take care of ourselves, so enjoy the evening off.'

It is as though Carmen has committed the greatest faux pas of her life. William's face darkens for a moment, then relaxes again. With a barely perceptible smile, he says, 'We have been in the service of the barons von Kaltenstein for three generations now, but the kitchen has always been our domain. I am sure your offer was a kind one, but things will not change. So, please ring the bell. Good night!'

He turns and goes. Carmen looks at David and makes a long face.

'It's obvious,' he says, 'you'd put him out of work. You can't just go blithely marching in taking away the very thing that he's done all his life, the thing he thinks is important and correct.'

Carmen shakes her head, as though in a trance. 'That wasn't what I meant, I just didn't want him to have to sit around on our behalf at his age.'

'He'll do that anyway. Whether you call him or not. He will be ready and waiting all night, particularly as long as we're in the house and Stefan hasn't got back.'

'Aha, you mean he's keeping an eye on us? To make sure we're not attacked? Or that we don't organise something ourselves?'

David hands Elvira a dish of slices of cheese and sausage, and Elvira puts three of them on a plate.

'I just assume he's protecting what he regards as sacred. And that's the past, the Kaltenstein family and the house. It's obvious.'

Carmen nods and helps herself to some canapés. She picks out some liver paté with pieces of mandarin, and cheese with grapes.

'I have to change the subject, Elvira, because I'm dying to know what really happened between you and Stefan.'

Elvira glances over at David, and Carmen tells her, 'David knows about you and Stefan.'

This is supposed to point out to Elvira that she hasn't told David about yesterday's assault by Stefan. Elvira puts another pillow behind her back to make herself more comfortable. 'Well, we've tried to work through the past. He wanted to know a lot about his parents, and I tried to bring Anna and Hannes to life for him. Anna, argumentative Anna, who went through the world wide-eyed and hating injustice. And

Hannes, who had found a real fighter in Anna and felt such strength in her that he couldn't deny his ideals. I just talked about the past.

'Was he very excited?'

'He's devastated. He sees his life as one great big lie, he's afraid he's a quite different person from who he thought he was for all those years. He's been bombarded with far too much, recently, and he's completely confused.'

Carmen reaches for Elvira's hand.

'Yes, and then we talked about his impotence. He's very troubled about it. Especially, I think,' she looks at Carmen, 'in connection with you.'

David hesitates for a moment, then he asks Carmen, 'Is he impotent too? Is he another of your candidates?'

Carmen swallows her little bit of paté, her throat dry. 'I thought I'd explained that when I told you about him.'

'That's right!' David clicks his finger close to her cheek. 'He's another potential rival.' And he kisses her full on the mouth.

'He *was*,' Carmen corrects him with an accusing look, 'and anyway – what's important is what we feel for each other. And I think that's a lot.'

'I'd be happy for both you!' Elvira leans forward to both of them. She puts her hand on David's arm, and he turns to face her so that she can look straight into his turquoise-coloured eyes. 'Carmen looks very happy, quite different from when I first met her. If that's down to you, then you've achieved a lot already!'

David smiles.

Carmen takes his hand and cuddles up to him. 'Now, don't listen, David! He's the perfect man for me, Elvira. David's everything I'd promised myself in a man who doesn't put sex at the forefront all the time and make everything else – harmony, joy, happiness – dependent on it. You can control most men according to how and how often you sleep with them. If you do it a lot, and imaginatively, they'll be at your feet, like puppets, following your every whim. If you follow your own needs and if you're not always willing, dissatisfaction follows. It starts with, "What's up with you?" and ends up with massive rows over the most trivial things. I think David and I can rule that out!' She glances over at him, then grins and says, 'I see, you're not listening. Okay, Elvira, to come to the point: David can't do it and he makes me happier than any potent man ever could. That is to say, perhaps men can only be like that if they've lost their potency. Then they put emphasis on other things, turning on their intelligence rather than being constantly pressured and influenced by their unreliable little companions!' She blows David a kiss. 'I hope I haven't said too much.'

David takes her in his arms. 'Unfortunately I didn't hear a thing, could you repeat all that again?' He hugs her and turns to Elvira. 'No, really, she's right. The most important gauge for a relationship, as far as a man's concerned, really is sex. I know it, from my own experience. A woman can be intelligent, interesting, she can possess a fantastic aura, she can be a terrific companion, understanding, independent, she can spoil a man in every area of life, tidy up after him and cook him the most amazing meals, but she'll still take second place to someone who will be constantly dragging him into bed, and who will do nothing more than that. How many men replace their first, brilliant wife with some bimbo, leaving everyone shaking their heads? Why? It's obvious. With the second one they're the greatest!'

'You don't seem to have a high opinion of your own sex,' Elvira observes dryly.

David has piled his plate full again, and takes a good sip from his glass. 'I'm slowly starting to see through the motions. Maybe it's easier for me because my impotence has taken me out of that witches' cauldron. Women don't have to pretend to me any more. Can I offer you some more canapés? Paté? Ham? Salmon? Cheese?'

'Lovely, one of each, please.' She hands him her plate and then leans back into her pillows. 'But I'm interested in how you see these things. Stefan sees it quite differently. He has a massive problem with it. For him, loss of potency amounts to loss of power. And I don't think it's just about women. After we spoke yesterday I sensed that men need their potency above all as a way to have power over each other.' Elvira shakes her head. 'I know it sounds strange, but I realised that these are very archaic feelings, and that you're losing something if you lose control of the pack. Which is to say, your rival's inevitably going to turn up, the females are inevitably going to run off with him, the impotent man – or the man who's not naturally quite up to it, whatever – will inevitably be the loser. And it's nothing to do with his intelligence, skill, quickness or strength. That's what I find so crazy, because I'd always thought that love between two people would sort everything else out, so that you wouldn't have to think about it any more. But it doesn't seem to be as simple as that.'

David laughs. 'Quite honestly, Elvira, impotence is no solution. When women like Carmen start looking for impotent men in order to form a solid relationship, then something's gone badly wrong. But in all likelihood men take their pride and joy much more seriously than women do.'

Carmen takes a sip from her glass. 'Of course they do. All this fuss, as if it was of any importance who had the thickest or the longest, it's really all about competition between men about women. Women themselves don't really care too much. What a man focuses on, thinking it's the most important thing for a woman, is the last thing on a woman's mind when she's thinking about men. Isn't that ironic? Isn't there a fundamental genetic flaw there somewhere?'

David laughs. 'I'm so lucky I don't have anything more to do with that. When I hear all this I almost thank my lucky stars. These guys you're describing must be appalling. And the worst thing is, I even think you may be right. Sexuality really does swamp other perceptions. But I'm interested to hear what women feel about it too. I'd always thought, and I'm not much different from Stefan in this, that you have to have something to offer a woman. Particularly in bed. And if, as people say, men today hold back and put the woman's satisfaction first, all that means for the man is a delayed orgasm. I admit it, we look at relationships through a zoom lens, you look at them with a wide-angle one. You see everything, we see one thing. I've never really thought about it that way before.'

'David, the news.' Carmen was hanging fascinated on his every word. A man who sees things the same way as she does. What a wonderful stroke of luck, what a fantastic combination. That ad was the best idea she's had in ages. But now she's glanced at her watch and given herself a start. They'd been talking so much she'd almost forgotten Stefan!

David picks up the remote and turns up the television. 'Another five minutes,' he says. Immediately there is a feeling of unease. Maybe that's the soil in which conversations like this flourish, Carmen reflects. When do people talk so openly to each other? Certainly not between the end of office hours and dinner.

Elvira excitedly grabs her hand. 'Let's hope it's all gone well. Let's hope no one was hurt. And all because of money, money, money! That was how things were in South-West Africa. The Kaltensteins were a dynasty, rich, powerful, arrogant. Because of their money they had more influence than anyone else. They practised politics down there, they practised politics up here. No one touched them. Only Hannes dared defy the family orders. That was why Anna loved him so much!' She slides back into the pillows and then concentrates, like Carmen and David, on the television.

The killings in South Africa are the main story once again. Then Carmen hears her heart beating when the announcer says they're going straight over to the siege in Frankfurt. Carmen intuitively reaches for Elvira and presses herself up against David. It can't be good news! It's the same reporter they had on the early evening news. The camera shows the building caught in harsh spotlights. Seven people are leaving the building, slowly, carefully, in the distance. A single person goes in. Slim, upright, resolute. Carmen can hardly listen for excitement: 'Once the negotiations became tougher and no outcome was in sight, the sole owner of the jeweller's shop, Stefan Kaltenstein, suggested that he be exchanged for the life of the seven hostages. The armed robber immediately accepted his offer, although the police had at first refused any such transaction. After lengthy consultations with Stefan von Kaltenstein, the security organisations responsible agreed, just a moment ago – and with distinct reservations – to this exchange. It is obvious now that the armed robber is going to demand a get-away car, and that he should have few problems in the company of the wealthy baron.' The first hostages come on screen, officials and Red Cross helpers cover them with blankets, and the press are kept at bay. The first news will come after serious questioning by the police. The reporter appears on the screen again, saying that he will report again as soon as he can, and hands back to the studio in Hamburg.

Elvira is as pale as a sheet. 'He'll kill him! As soon as he doesn't need him, he'll kill him. It's obvious. How could he do that? How can he put himself in danger like that?'

'I think he's very brave. I admire him,' David hands Elvira a glass of water. 'Do you need any medicine, Elvira? Can I get you something?'

Elvira slowly shakes her head. 'Crazy. The last time I saw him was as a babe in Anna's arms, and now I find him as a man, and I'm about to lose him again? Life can't be as unjust as that, it can't be so unfair.'

Carmen cuddles up to her. 'Nothing will happen to him, Elvira. He'll be fine. It would be pointless. He's only useful to them as long as he's alive.'

'Who has overall power of attorney? Do you know?' asks David suddenly.

Elvira looks at him in surprise. 'No, of course not. Why?'

'Because our man needs Stefan to make his escape, and if it works, he's going to demand money for his release. A lot of money. That much is obvious. But who's going to pay the ransom? The state? The *Land*? The city? Frankfurt's broke, and so is Hessen, and the government won't lift a finger. So all that remains is Stefan's money. And who has access to it?'

'No idea,' says Carmen. Elvira shakes her head as well. 'He'll have a financial administrator, I expect, I don't know . . .' She pulls up her knees and sits in the enormous bed like a little heap of misery. 'Why is he doing this? Do you think he has to prove something?'

'That might come into it,' says David. 'But it's probably something inside him. He's a strong, courageous man. Impotence on its own wouldn't drive a man to do something like that. David gets to his feet, walks to the phone and dials 9. Carmen watches him. It's so good that he's there. He sorts everything out so decisively.

'William,' she hears him say, 'did you see that? You did? Are you in contact with the police there? You're not? There's a news blackout? Even for relatives? . . . I see. And what about close friends?' He listens and then puts the phone down. 'Damn, we haven't a chance of getting any information. He has no direct relations. His wife left after their divorce and lives in Los Angeles. There were no children. And we can't put forward our family retainers here, legally they count for nothing whatsoever.'

David paces up and down. There must be a way, he thinks. Carmen watches him. 'David,' she says, suddenly having thought of something. 'Why don't we go to Frankfurt? I can't bear sitting around like this!'

'What good would that do us? The whole area around the building is closed off. We'd learn more by watching television. And if the armed robber does escape with Stefan, there's nothing we can do to help him.'

'But if he lets him go we'd be there! So he'd have something, psychologically, I mean,' says Carmen.

'He probably wouldn't be too delighted about me, and if he saw you, he'd start getting his hopes up, and you wouldn't be able to fulfil them. And Elvira? Do you want her to go for a long car journey in her state and then wait for ages in the crowds?'

'You're right, no. But we've got to do something!'

David goes back to the telephone and asks the operator for

the number of police headquarters in Frankfurt. He asks them for their press department. David cheekily introduces himself, saying 'Castle Kaltenstein', and asks for more detailed information about the Kaltenstein case, as he's worried about his uncle. It's no use, as Carmen can hear from his answers. '. . . Yes, I know there's a blackout, we're not going to pass anything on, it's just for our own reassurance. We're all terribly worried about Stefan, surely you can understand that!'

A few seconds, and then David holds his hand over the receiver. 'What's the phone number here, Elvira, quick?' Elvira tells him quietly, and David repeats at full volume.

'Okay, thank you, we're very glad, yes, thank you, goodbye!' Heaving a sigh, he puts the receiver down.

'We were lucky, I got through to a nice guy. He's going to see what can be done and call us back.'

'He'll check if the number was really Castle Kaltenstein,' says Carmen.

'That's what I think too,' says David, 'so it would have been pretty embarrassing not to know it.' He grins. 'Maybe that'll get us a bit further.'

'Shouldn't you tell them downstairs, David? So that William knows what's going on and puts the call through?'

'You're right, Elvira.'

'I'll go down.' Carmen stands up. 'It'll do me some good. Do you want anything else? Do you want me to bring anyth . . .' She meets David's gaze. 'Okay, I'm with you.' She runs over to him and wraps her arms around him and he presses her firmly to him, they stand there cheek to cheek for a moment. 'I'm glad I've found you, David. I can't imagine how I spent so long without you.'

She walks down the wide stairs, past the murals, and finds herself in the middle of the hall. Where to now? She knows the two doors leading off to the study and the dining-room. But what could be behind the others? And where's William? She should have rung down, it would have been easier. And now?

'William?' she calls nervously. No answer. 'William?' No reaction, nothing moves. She has to find him before the call comes in from police headquarters. If I press three times on the front doorbell he'll come – Carmen opens the heavy front door. The night is heavy, and it has started to rain. Lamps burn on either side of the double doors. They aren't particularly bright, but along with the light coming from the hall through the open door, it's enough. She looks around and examines the stone wall. No button, no bell-pull. Of course, people just don't come up to the front door of a castle like this and ring the doorbell. Then she hears the gravel crunching. She turns around and peers down the steps. But she can only just make out the two cars. She must have made a mistake. She's about to turn back to the front door, when she clearly makes out the silhouette of a person standing beside the car. The next moment a flashgun goes off, and another, and another. She stands there for a few seconds, completely blinded, and then runs in and closes the heavy door behind her. She leans against it from inside, her whole body trembling. William seems to have noticed something as well, because a door in the hall opens and out he comes, perfectly turned out even at this time of night.

'Can I help you, madam?'

'I'm glad you're there, William. Is it possible that some strangers are wandering about in the grounds? I was outside a moment ago and someone took my picture.'

'Hmm.' William frowns. 'Before he left for Frankfurt, the baron was worried that the tabloids would be crawling around the place. I will do everything that needs to be done. Is there anything else I can do for you?'

'Yes, we've just called police headquarters in Frankfurt to get special information about Stefan. We're expecting them to call back – could you put it through upstairs? I assume it's a test to see if we're really calling from here. We'll let you know if anything happens.'

'Very good.' William bows slightly, but then breathes out

with evident relief. 'That is good. I hope nothing happens to him. We're praying down here.'

The idea had never occurred to Carmen. She nods to him. 'Can we do anything about the journalists in the grounds?'

William stiffens again, as if he had never uttered a personal word. 'Very kind of you, but we're equipped for everything here. All it takes is a phone call.'

'Then I'll go back upstairs.'

Carmen runs up two steps at a time. Upstairs in the gallery she notices through one of the big windows that it suddenly seems to be daylight outside. She walks to the window and looks out. There are hidden spotlights everywhere. The whole grounds as far as Carmen can see are as bright as day. Men with Alsatian dogs emerge from the half-timbered building. Carmen is transfixed. It's like a thriller, she thinks. I should pinch myself to wake myself up. She watches for a little while, then a shiver runs down her spine. What if the man has already got into the castle? What if he's broken in through a window? What if he suddenly appears behind her? With a funny feeling in the pit of her stomach she looks along the dark corridor. Nothing. She goes quickly back to Elvira's room.

'What's been going on?' David points to the brightly-lit park.

'I just went outside for a moment and someone took my picture. Now some men have gone off to check the grounds.'

The phone rings. David picks it up.

'Nice of you to call back,' he says, and then nods a few times. 'Good,' he says finally. 'We're very grateful to you, goodbye, yes, thanks.' He slowly puts the phone down.

'What is it?' Elvira sits bolt upright in bed.

'They were making sure that our number was correct. We're now among the people to be informed if anything dramatic should occur – those were the words he used.'

'And for now?' Carmen tugs on the bell-pull for William.

'As we predicted. The gangster is demanding a two-engine turbo helicopter for a long-distance flight, and he wants two

million marks in used notes. The same amount that his colleagues managed to get away with. At the moment they're
organising everything. The helicopter and the money.'

'My God.' Elvira frowns. 'Since I met you, Carmen, my life
hasn't stood still for a minute!'

Carmen brushes her long, heavy hair back and twists it
into a bun. 'I'm sorry, there's nothing I can do about it, Elvira.
That's just the way things have turned out.' And, defiantly,
'But then through me you've found the son of your bosom
friend, you'd have to admit that, too.'

'It wasn't an accusation, Carmen.' Elvira raises a placatory
hand. 'It's just how it is, that's all.'

There is a knock at the door, and William enters. David
briefly tells him the current state of play.

'A helicopter for a long-distance flight?' William wonders
out loud. 'Where could he want to go?'

'Do you want to join us for a while?' says David, encour-
aging him to stay.

'It's very kind of you, but I would prefer to stay by the telephone. The men outside are in radio contact with Andrew,
who is keeping an eye on the cameras, and the whole thing
has to be coordinated. But if I can bring you up something to
drink, I would be happy to do so. I see your glasses are empty:
that is not how we do things in this house, and the baron
would certainly not be pleased.'

'In view of the circumstances, would you allow me to help
you? Then you could stay by the telephone, which is clearly
more important right now. And if you need a man to help
with anything, I'm more than willing.'

'So am I,' says Carmen.

William's face shows no emotion. 'I am very grateful for
your offer, Herr Franck. Would you like to come down with
me?' Carmen joins Elvira on the bed, while the two men go
out the door. 'Yet again,' she says, 'while we women sit here
going mad waiting.'

Elvira laughs and pats her hand. 'There is an art to waiting,
my darling. At thirty-five I couldn't do it either. But you're so

much in control, so much at ease with yourself, you should really be able to keep yourself in check.'

'Really? Is that how I come across?' says Carmen, astonished. 'Maybe when I'm at work, maybe to other people. But with you two, with David and you, I feel as if I'm a little girl. I really don't know how you think that.'

Elvira looks at her affectionately. 'I'd like to have a daughter like you. What's been missing in my life is a normal, happy relationship.'

'Me too.' Carmen points to the big bed. 'Do you mind if I lie down for a while? Just for a bit, on the covers?'

'Of course.' Elvira moves aside slightly, although given the size of the bed that isn't really necessary. 'Of course you can. But don't deceive yourself, Carmen, you're not going to have a normal relationship with David either. That's the product of your frustration with other men, and you shouldn't forget, perhaps, that not all men are the way you see them.'

'So what are they like?' Carmen stretches out on the bed, trying to find the most comfortable position.

'I think you provoke these reactions by looking like you do. You're very attractive, you're very open, you spare time for everyone – not everyone knows what to make of that.'

'How do you mean?'

'Well, what you see as harmless fun might be taken as a challenge by a man.'

'I haven't the faintest idea what you're talking about.'

Elvira sits up slightly and looks down at Carmen.

'You see, if a man uses all his chat-up lines on a little grey mouse, she won't see it as an annoying intrusion, she'll be delighted. Don't you see? Because what happens to you three times a day happens to her three times in a lifetime, if she's lucky – being desired by men!'

'You mean it's all down to my face and my bosom?' Carmen screws up her nose.

'And your manner, of course. You're prettier than average, you're intelligent, you have long hair, you have everything that drives a man wild. And because of the way you deal with men, the only thing they can come up with as a counterbalance is their potency. They don't pounce on you then and there, but something's happening in their minds and somehow they have to translate it into words. As they never would with a little grey mouse. Ask a woman who's forever being ignored by men – you'll see what she has to say. She won't understand a word of what you say about men.'

'Yes, but not all other women are little wallflowers. There are enough attractive women around. Look at Laura.'

'Laura's got the same problems as you.'

'She doesn't want an impotent man, she told me herself. I don't know why not though.'

'She sees men differently.'

'Hmm, you're giving us a fair amount of wisdom here. But maybe your theory's right in some way. I'll ask Britta Berger. She sprang to mind when you were talking about grey mice. It's true, I let her go home early recently, and told her to go and celebrate with her boyfriend, and I was astonished to learn that she had one. But maybe someone like Britta Berger meets a different sort of man from me. That's a possibility.'

'Or the same man behaves differently when he's with your Britta.'

Carmen laughs and falls back on to the covers. 'Whatever. I'm staying with David. I think I could love him, Elvira – if I don't already.'

'I'd be delighted, Carmen, I really would.' As Carmen cuddles up to Elvira, the door opens and David comes in balancing a tray of drinks.

'How William manages his job so well at his age is a mystery,' he says. 'There's a real art in getting up those stairs. I thought everything was going to topple over, and the tray's really very heavy!'

He puts it down, hands out the glasses and then pulls up a comfortable leather chair from a corner.

'I wonder how Stefan is?' Carmen thinks, taking a sip. 'I wonder if he has been tied up? What on earth could be on his mind?'

'He'll be frightened, just like any other person in his position.' David has placed the wide chair opposite the bed and sits down in it, takes his shoes off, then asks politely, 'May I?' and crosses his legs with Carmen. Then he raises the glass in a toast. 'Of course, we can try to wish him power with our thoughts. That's all we can do.'

'Do you believe in that kind of thing?' asks Carmen, fascinated.

'I certainly do. I think that man has powers he doesn't know about. Or at least most people don't know about. I include myself in that.' He points to the big fire on the other side of the bed.

'We could light a fire, it would be much cosier. It's not especially warm in here.'

'William asked me this afternoon, but I didn't want to put him to any trouble.' Elvira pulls up the covers.

'I'll see to it.' David puts down his glass and goes back out.

'He can't sit still,' Carmen smiles.

'No wonder, all this waiting would drive anyone mad – and he's an energetic man. He doesn't look as though he could bear sitting still for long.'

'It's true,' Carmen says thoughtfully, 'we've always spent our time moving about. If it comes to sitting or lying down, he gets twitchy.'

'Might the fact that he avoids resting have something to do with his problem? When you're always in motion, you don't have to think about it!'

'Do you think so?'

Midnight has long past and the fire in the grate has burned down by the time David picks up the phone again. They've been talking about everything under the sun for hours, but now, for all their excitement, they are tired. Why has no one called? Have they simply been forgotten, despite the assurance from the police?

'I don't know,' David says to bring their uncertainty to an end. 'Why don't I give them a call?'

And he is told that nothing will happen before morning, because the helicopter pilot has refused to fly in darkness. So they will have to wait until daybreak before any more decisions are made. Nothing is going to happen before eight o'clock.

'What'll we do now?' asks Carmen from under the covers, with a big yawn.

'First we'll have to tell William, so that he doesn't spend the whole night sitting nervously downstairs, and then I'll drive home and put my head down for a few hours. I have to be reasonably fit for some meetings tomorrow.'

'You're going?' A tousled Carmen appears from between the fat pillows.

'I can hardly spend the night here in the chair. I'd be absolutely whacked tomorrow.'

'I'll come too.'

'No, you stay here.' David picks up the telephone and tells William, and then holds his hand over the receiver. 'William has just offered me a guest room, and he's offered you one as well. Obviously that changes everything.'

'Why two? We can take one.'

'He's not to know that.'

'Then tell him.'

'Frau Legg is already very comfortable in Frau Gohdes's room, William. The bed is big enough, so one room will be quite sufficient.'

'Why did you say that?' asks Carmen when David puts the phone down.

'Because I don't want to hurt his feelings. It's more proper for him to offer us two rooms. He's coming up in a minute to show it to me, by the way.'

Thirty minutes later Carmen and David are lying in a bed the same size as Elvira's next-door. Carmen cuddles up to David. She was extremely tired, but now that she's so close to him she's wide awake again. David strokes her gently, and then starts to kiss her delicately all over. Carmen responds like never before. Her whole body trembles, her nerves are almost completely out of control. She slips from one orgasm into the next, her whole being an explosion of pleasure. When he finally lies beside her she's completely exhausted.

'That was wonderful, David.' She cuddles up to him and starts to stroke him, too.

'Please don't, Carmen,' he says.

'Why not?' she asks quietly. 'You spoil me so much. Can't I give you anything back? It's hardly fair.'

He turns away from her. 'Please don't make it more difficult than it is already.'

It gives Carmen a bitter aftertaste, but she doesn't ask any more questions. She would love to press herself against him, but now she doesn't even dare do that. How can she tell him that his impotence means nothing to her? He talks about it so clearly, so analytically, so why can't he stick by it? She wanted him like that, and she loves him the way he is. I'll have to talk to someone else about it, she thinks, ideally a psychiatrist. Maybe he'll be able to tell me how to help David.

It was on the breakfast news before David called police headquarters. The helicopter with the armed robber and his hostage, Stefan von Kaltenstein, set off for an unknown destination early in the morning. The cordon in front of the jeweller's building was widened so that the helicopter could land and set off unhindered. The pictures showed the masked criminal leaving the building behind Stefan, a gun to his neck, and disappearing into the helicopter that stood waiting for them. Elvira watched the programme from her bed and then told Carmen and David about it.

They had breakfast together as they watched television.

'So it's happened,' says Carmen dryly, and Elvira nods. 'Now we're going to be getting either some very good news or some very bad news. I'm prepared for anything.'

'I'll get William to tell you as soon as the press department calls. Maybe they'll stick to their promise to keep us informed about any changes.'

'Well, they haven't.' Carmen takes another sip of coffee and then pushes everything away.

They are sitting in the breakfast room, a bright room with flower-patterned wallpaper, matching curtains and tablecloth and a dark green carpet. Everything suggests sun and joy, except for their faces.

'We may as well go.' David puts his napkin down beside his plate and nods to the others. William comes in, helps Elvira up from the table and hands her her walking-stick. She feels better, she has told them that morning, and unlike yesterday she has a little colour in her cheeks.

'Thank you, that's very kind of you, William. You've been a great help.'

'Please, madam, it was the least I could do.'

Carmen also gets to her feet. 'What I wanted to ask you, William – what happened to that man who crept in and took my picture yesterday?'

'Our security men found the place where he climbed over the wall. We are assuming it was a reporter from the gutter press. We will discover which one, and the baron is sure to take legal measures.'

He says this firmly, as though there is not the slightest doubt that Stefan will emerge safely from all this unharmed.

Such fatalism won't reassure Carmen though. She slowly pushes her chair back to the table and then stands behind it. 'Why are you so sure everything's going to be okay?'

'The von Kaltensteins have never taken a back seat when things have got out of hand, and they have never suffered any harm as a consequence. He would only be the second Kaltenstein after Hannes, the present baron's father, to die in an unnatural manner. The young man crashed on a flight with his wife. We are certain that Baron Stefan will be back with us tomorrow.'

'I wish I had your faith,' says Elvira quietly.

William helps Elvira and Carmen into the BMW and loads their stuff into the boot, and David is already starting his engine. The sun flashes through the trees, there is dense morning mist on the meadows, and the occasional leaf has blown into the drive and the narrow road.

'There'll soon be an army out there wielding brooms and shovels,' Carmen says ironically as she starts the car, 'so that everything's neat and tidy when Stefan lands in front of the castle in his helicopter with his kidnapper. I assume William has made provision for tea and biscuits.'

Elvira gives her a sidelong look but doesn't say anything.

Back home, Carmen takes Elvira upstairs and is about to help her to bed.

'That's enough now.' Elvira pulls the door to the bedroom closed. 'I can't lie in bed day and night, I'd go mad. I'm going to settle in front of the television now, and if William calls I'll inform you and David immediately. And now you make sure you get to the office, it's nearly nine o'clock.'

'Okay, Mummy, straightaway. Aye, aye, I'm on my way!'

Elvira threatens her jokingly with the flat of her hand, Carmen slips out of the door and runs upstairs.

There are nine messages on her answering-machine. How dreadful, she's got to listen to all of them. With any luck there won't be anything important. She switches it on, pen and note-pad to the ready. Three from Laura and Frederic last night. She should have expected that, they hadn't had a clue what was going on. Then another one, after the late news. Aha, now they've heard something, but they only suspect that there might be a connection. They spent that much time together, that's interesting, thinks Carmen. So where were they? They didn't say in any of their messages. They certainly weren't in the Laguna. Then two hang-ups, and Oliver in New York describing what she's missing. As far as she's concerned Oliver might as well be in another world. He's coming back on Wednesday and would be very glad if she could pick him up from the airport. 'Then you could save yourself the taxi fare,' she says out loud, while counting impatiently. 'Number seven, another two to go, get on with it!' A client twice asking her to call him back. She jots down the number and goes into the bedroom and changes quickly.

211

Carmen is back in her car just in time for the nine o'clock news. I'm just living from one news programme to the next, the way Laura lives from holiday to holiday, she thinks as her car stops at the lights. Perpetrator and victim are off in their helicopter, she knows that, and nothing more is reported. There's probably another news blackout, they can't be in the air all this time. Maybe Elvira knows more. She'll call her from the office.

Britta Berger is already there, punctual as ever. When she sees her, Carmen remembers Elvira's theory about the grey mouse. She'll pursue the matter further today. Britta has already made coffee and brought in some croissants. Today of all days, when Carmen has had breakfast. But she's pleased anyway, and she pretends to be incredibly hungry. And why not, if a small gesture can make people happy? Then she calls Elvira. William hasn't rung yet. Good, says Carmen, she can reach her at the office for the rest of the day.

Britta Berger is sorting out the post and drinking her coffee at the same time. It's a good time for a conversation.

'Britta, can I ask you something personal?' A shame to start in such a stilted way, but too late, she's said it now.

'Go on,' Britta says looking up in surprise.

'Are you and your boyfriend serious? Or are you even engaged? I know so little about you, and I think that's really a shame. After all, we spend so much time together every day.'

Careful, she says to herself at the same time, don't let things become too familiar or this will be happening all the time, even when you don't want it to.

Britta hesitates for a moment, and then she says, with a calm, radiant smile spreading across her face, making her really pretty for a moment, 'Yes, I think I've met somebody. And I even think he's starting to reciprocate my feelings.' She falls silent for a second as though she's startled herself, and then goes on. 'You know, Frau Legg, if you don't mind me saying this – it isn't as easy for me as it is for you. If I'd had a man like your Peter, I'd never have let him go – but of course it's easy for you . . .'

Carmen puts her coffee cup down. 'Why, I don't understand, why wouldn't you have got rid of Peter?'

'Because he loved you. It's the most beautiful thing in the world, to be loved by a man. And he obviously did love you, at least it always looked that way when he picked you up. And the number of times he called you every day. You must have been very happy.'

That was exactly what always got on Carmen's nerves. Couldn't he leave her in peace for a few hours? Did he always have to be there, on the end of the line . . .

Now she's a bit embarrassed. How can she explain what she thinks?

Britta picks up where she left off. 'But of course I understand that it's easier to kick a man if you have dozens of them at your feet . . .' She stops, shocked. 'I'm sorry, I didn't mean it to come out like that!'

'Is that how you see me?' Carmen throws back her long hair. 'Be honest now. Is that how it seems to you?'

Britta hesitates. 'Yes,' she says slowly, 'yes, it is. I mean, so many decent men come here, phone you, collect you and shower you with flowers. None of them has ever so much as noticed me. Don't you see? They haven't even registered I'm there, that there's someone else in the room. And sometimes that hurts me, because it makes me think the world is unfair. Not because I envy you those men, Frau Legg, no, not that at all.' She sits there, blushing to the tips of her ears. 'No, please don't think that. But you see, you have so many men around you, fighting over you, and for years I've been fighting for one man, and I'm dreading the day that he finds another, more beautiful woman and then I'll be worthless.'

'Oh goodness, Britta.' Carmen is moved. 'You mustn't say that. You're a very sweet, intelligent young woman, you're very perceptive and I'm sure you have many qualities that I can't even dream of. So why should you be so afraid of rejection?'

'Because none of it counts for anything if a prettier woman comes along.'

She's probably right, thinks Carmen. The world really is unjust.

'But you're pretty.'

'I'm not exactly ugly, okay, but I'm not exactly pretty either. I'm just there. I'm unostentatious, and I get on with things, and that's that.'

Why does my car spring to mind? Carmen shakes her head. 'That isn't true, Britta, the man you're with is a man to be envied.'

'Fine, but what if he doesn't know that? A man like that thinks that the man who has *you* is a man to be envied. And he'd get everything from a woman like me. And nothing at all from one like you. But you're still more interesting.'

'But women like you tend to get married.'

Britta utters a short laugh, a laugh of resignation that Carmen finds strangely moving. 'Yes, because women like you don't want to get married, Frau Legg. You'd be stupid – what would be the point? You can make yourself a nice life until you're sure you've found the right man. And even when you're a bit older, there'll always be a man there who's happy to find you.'

'It's not like that,' says Carmen. 'Men don't necessarily want to marry women like me. They'd rather have women with their feet on the ground than airy-fairy women like me.'

'Perhaps,' Britta concedes. 'But what you call women with their feet on the ground, women like me, are good wives because they play along with everything because they're grateful with what fate has dished out, but if their husband can get a prettier woman into bed he's hardly going to say no.'

'Oh Britta, don't be so cynical. Why should a man stray if he's got you? It would be idiotic.'

Britta laughs quietly. 'Men are like children, they like playing games. Even I know that.'

Carmen smiles at Britta. 'At any rate I hope that your boyfriend knows what he's got. And if you sense that he doesn't, send him over to me. I would guess that once he's got to know me properly he'll really value women like you again.'

Now Britta really laughs. 'Nice of you to say so. But it's too risky. He might get addicted, and then I'd be left empty-handed.'

Carmen frowns. 'I don't think so. Once he's out of withdrawal he'll be glad he can see clearly again. I'd bet on it.'

They smile at each other like fellow conspirators, and then go back to work. Carmen's head is buzzing. What sort of life am I leading, she wonders. Do I only ever skim the surface, am I forever dancing somewhere between heaven and earth in some airy-fairy, celestial realm? Nonsense, she tells herself. You have both feet on the ground, just like Britta. The difference being that your feet are that bit daintier, and your life is therefore that bit easier. Or not. That's the question – is it easier to angle for a man, or try and fight him off? It would be interesting to slip into the shell of this little grey mouse for a few days. Carmen picks up her cup and takes a sip of cold coffee. I could take a holiday from myself and spend a week in sackcloth and ashes, tie my hair up in a bun, no make-up, dungarees. But the idea doesn't even make her laugh. No, it's not her world – and you can just imagine the kind of dung-arees-and-muesli man who would go for her. Would he take off his walking boots in bed? Now she grins. I'll stay the way I am. What's the point, I've got used to myself over thirty-five years, why should I change everything now? And I'll keep my impotent man, because it's a kind of freedom, a kind of revolt. I don't want your common-or-garden uptight German con-formist male who'll give me five kids and sweat and wheeze on top of me, I want a man for life, someone who'll give me something more than a couple of his own spermatozoa.

She looks over at Britta. She already seems to be immersed in her work again. Pull yourself together, Carmen says to her-self. What must it look like, you sitting there staring into space. She takes out her diary and glances covertly at her assistant again. Good, she's going through the post and looks as if she's concentrating very hard, but her thoughts are bound to be somewhere else. Funny that life always works at extremes, she thinks. Some people have nothing, some have everything. And she thinks of Stefan. Just then the phone rings. Telepathy, she thinks and picks up the receiver. But it isn't Elvira, it's Laura.

'It's break and I wanted to know if you were still alive. We got really worried, especially when it dawned on us that Stefan the hostage is your Stefan. Where have you been?'

'In the castle,' says Carmen curtly, because she doesn't want Britta to know too much. 'But you can talk. You disappeared without trace. You weren't in the Laguna, anyway.'

Laura laughs. 'That's right, we were at Frederic's house. I spent half the night talking to him and his sister. She's fantastic, Carmen. I really liked her – you've really got to meet her.' And without a pause, 'What's happening with Stefan? Do you have any news? Did he get out alive?'

'I'm afraid I don't know. But they're supposed to be keeping the castle informed, and Elvira's going to call me and David. Whether it works is another question. At the moment I would guess they've got other things to deal with.'

'Are you taking a break for lunch?'

'I don't dare leave the phone.' Carmen draws a little man on her note-pad.

'I'm free till three. Should I bring over a pizza, or would you rather go to Elvira's? Then I could bring three pizzas.'

'Pizza,' groans Carmen, 'does it have to be pizza? I'm seeing pizzas in my sleep!' The matchstick man is joined by a matchstick woman, with long hair. They are holding hands.

'Not necessarily. I could bring you a salad from McDonald's, there's one just around the corner.'

'Even better,' says Carmen, although she really doesn't feel like one. But it's probably because she's just eaten a croissant and isn't hungry. Now the couple on the note-pad are surrounded by a big heart.

'Let's meet at Elvira's. It'll do her good. But I can't do more than an hour today.'

'That's fine. I don't have to be back at work till three, and I could do some shopping for Elvira, or hoover, or whatever.'

'You?' Carmen snorts into the phone.

'Oh bugger you,' snaps Laura, and then, in a friendlier voice, 'Okay, see you in a minute.'

Carmen slowly puts the phone back down and grins. It's funny, she loves Laura as if she were her twin sister. Can you have such feelings for other women? That's how it must have been for Elvira and Anna. Under her little drawing she scribbles David and Carmen, tears off the sheet, looks at it and puts it in her drawer.

Laura's already there when Carmen arrives at Elvira's. She's set the table nicely, taken the salad out of its plastic containers and draped it skilfully over the onion-pattern plates, making it look like something from a high-class delicatessen.

'Where's the champagne?' asks Carmen, putting down a baguette. 'Can I make a contribution? Fresh from the bakers on the corner. Elvira,' and she wraps her arms around the old lady, who is just coming out of the kitchen with a bottle of red wine and three glasses, 'how are you?'

'Stop, stop, let me put these things down,' she laughs at Carmen's impulsiveness, then pulls a worried face. 'Physically I'm fine, psychologically I don't know. I'm somewhere in mid-air. Particularly because I can't understand why we're not hearing anything. He can't go flying around for five hours. He must have landed somewhere ages ago.'

'They won't give anything out because the robber's mates are still at large,' guesses Laura. 'Maybe they're afraid they could all meet up and then flee together, possibly with the helicopter and with Stefan as a hostage. There'll be some reason why we haven't heard anything.'

'Quarter to one,' Carmen says looking at the big grandfather clock. 'Elvira, could you turn the radio up a bit so that we don't miss anything?'

'Don't move, Elvira, I'll do it.' Laura stands up, walks to the radio on the chest of drawers and then turns back towards the table. 'It's as old as Carmen and me. A real vintage radio, with valves that have to warm up and a little wire showing where you are on the dial, isn't that right?'

217

Carmen grins. 'Which is to say that it's a really fashionable item again!'

'Just like us,' Laura nods and sits back down at the table.

'That's what you say. So where did you spend the night, you fashionable little item, you?' Carmen tweaks at her nose.

Laura stretches her head back and shivers. 'I told you, at Frederic's parents' place, with him and Clara, his sister. What a woman!'

Elvira looks up from her salad, which she's been reflectively picking at, and Carmen casts a brief, searching glance at her friend. Laura keeps a straight face for a moment, then bursts out laughing. 'Okay, okay. Yes, I fancy him. And what can I do about the fact that he's one of your impotent guys? And just so as you know and don't think I'm joining you in your droopfest, I'd rather he wasn't. We could have had quite a lot of fun last night!'

'I believe you,' grins Carmen with her mouth full. 'So you only had a bit of fun instead then?'

'Silly question, of course!' Laura raises one eyebrow, pours herself some mineral water and picks up her glass.

'Did he prove to you that he was impotent?'

'What gives you that idea?'

'He just might have.' Carmen raises her glass to her, Elvira joins them and they take a sip together.

Laura is the first to put her glass down. 'Nonsense. How can you prove something like that? We sat up half the night eating and drinking, and at about five I lay down on the sofa and went to sleep. At six I had to get up again. But anyway. I can think of a few other ways I'd rather have spent that hour. Then perhaps I wouldn't have been so tired at school today.'

'I seem to be the only woman round here who's off her head!' says Carmen, striking her forehead with the palm of her hand.

'No, I am too!' Laura nods.

'Yeah?'

'Yes, I've fallen in love with an impotent man. There's got to be something bonkers about that.'

Elvira emerges from her thoughts and listens to the two of them with a quiet smile playing about her lips. 'Well, if that's all it is . . . I'm no stranger to it!'

'No, it's not all. This impotent guy's going to be a father!'

'What? How?' Carmen looks at Elvira, who shrugs her shoulders helplessly. 'I don't understand! He can't be!'

'So what's going on exactly?' asks Carmen, and then leaps in the air, sending her chair flying. 'Laura, you're keeping your baby!' She runs around the table and throws her arms around her friend. 'That's the best news for ages! Oh, you're making me so happy! That's fantastic, fantastic!'

They rub their heads together. Elvira has stood up now, and kisses her on the cheek. 'My very best wishes, Laura. I wished with all my heart for you to make this choice. I'm here to help you whenever you need me. A baby needs a granny too!'

Laura stands up, moved. She smiles at Elvira, her eyes beaming. 'Many thanks, Elvira, that's very kind of you!'

Carmen sits back down and glances at the clock. Another five minutes before the news, so there's time enough to ask. Now she wants to know: 'And what was all that talk about Frederic being the father? You're not going to tell me that in that one night, while you were eating and drinking and spending an hour sleeping on the sofa, he developed paternal feelings and is now assuming paternity? I mean, I know Frederic's very spontaneous and is capable of many things, but that would be practically crazy!'

Laura picks up a fork of egg and ham, and patiently wraps it in a lettuce leaf. 'No, I didn't mean quite that seriously. But we spent the whole night talking about the subject, that much is true. In fact it was Clara and not Frederic who suddenly asked why I didn't move in with them. The house is far too big for the two of them anyway – that's true, by the way, it's a massive great bunker over three floors – and it sounded like a brilliant solution. Instead of paying rent somewhere, I could pay them a peppercorn rent and keep the rest for the child. Clara is a graphic artist and does a lot of work at home, Frederic's still studying, and with my irregular school hours it would be ideal. The child would be looked after around the clock. And, you won't believe it, I had the sense that they were both really looking forward to it, and it wasn't just a spur-of-the-moment suggestion. And can I tell you something else, Carmen, since I've noticed how much other people, yourselves included, are looking forward to the child, I've started to like the idea myself. I'm still a bit worried about the future, and I'm not quite as thrilled as you are, but it's getting better by the day. And I think I'm really going to love the little creature,' she pauses for a second, 'as long as he isn't too much like his father. Then I'd find myself looking at a miniature edition of Wilko, and that would be like a prison sentence!'

'Nonsense.' Carmen raps her knuckle on the table-top. 'She won't look like Wilko, your Alina Olivia Carmen. She'll be a spirited, vivacious specimen of womanhood, just like her mum.'

Laura grins and holds her hand on her belly. 'Anyway, allow me to welcome you to the world, little human. I'm going to make you official now. And I'm going to tell people at school.'

'Hang on, shh!' Elvira puts a finger to her lips.

The lunchtime television news. Once again, they are reporting only that the helicopter flew off to an unknown destination this morning, that air traffic control has been informed about the siege, and that otherwise there is a news blackout for security reasons.

Elvira sighs, the three women look at each other in worried silence. Then the phone rings. It's David, wanting to know if William has called. No, Elvira is close to tears. Carmen and Laura look at each other. 'We'll have to take more care of her,' Laura whispers. 'I can tell you the rest about Frederic and Clara another time!'

Carmen nods.

Elvira hands her the phone. 'Here, Carmen, David would like to speak to you.'

'David! I really miss you.'

'Me too, Carmen, me too. I just wanted to say that I've got a bit of a handle on this story. It turns out that it wasn't

anyone from my company who was involved, but a former
employee of Stefan's company.'

'That's reassuring. Good news at last!'

'Why, have you got bad news?'

'Well, so far, nothing at all as far as Stefan's concerned. It's
so painful and nerve-racking.'

'Give William a call. And if he doesn't know anything – or,
even better, I'll call him myself. If that doesn't yield anything, I'll
give police headquarters a call. I know my way around now.'

'That's a good idea, David, we'd be really grateful.'

She puts the phone down. 'So, David's going to ask the
police again.'

Elvira has sat down on the couch, her hands folded in her
lap. She says, 'That's good. Your David is a fine man, Carmen.
One of the best. You should look after him.'

Now Elvira's starting too, Carmen thinks. Britta was
enough for one day, thanks very much. Is she given to devouring men, or tearing them limb from limb? You'd almost think
so! She sits down next to Elvira and affectionately takes her
hands in hers. 'I plan to keep him, Elvira. I like him very
much as well,' she says, looking her in the eye. 'And not only
that, I like him an awful, awful lot. And if I was rather more
steady in these matters, I'd even tell you I loved him!'

Elvira closes her eyes and nods. Laura drops into one of the
armchairs and grins cheekily. 'Well bravo. Here we sit, little
babes in the wood, with men who are practically bursting
with power and dynamism, and we're having platonic
relationships. You should have told me that before I went to
Brazil. I'd have laughed myself sick.'

Elvira sighs.

'Are we getting on your nerves, Elvira?' asks Carmen, concerned. 'Would you rather we talked about something else?
It's just that if I have to think about Stefan all the time I'll go
mad. All we can do is wait. Then your thoughts start going
round in circles.'

'I'd rather you distracted me a bit. What will be will be,
whether you brood or you don't.'

221

She looks at Laura. 'Now I've got a question for you. Isn't it all going a bit too fast? Until recently I had the impression that Frederic was in love with Carmen, and now all of a sudden he wants you and baby to move into his house? I don't quite get it.'

Laura jumps to her feet. 'I've got to go and get my glass first. Would you like yours?'

'Yes, while you're about it, and maybe we can drink a toast if David has good news.'

'Do you think he will?' Elvira looks at her inquiringly.

'I do,' says Carmen, 'and so do you, Elvira, if you're honest.'

Elvira looks into the distance and nods quietly. 'If things don't work out, at least he'll be with his parents.' She takes the wine glass that Laura hands her, and sips from it.

'Well, Laura, don't leave us in limbo, what really happened?'

Laura pulls up her legs in her armchair and slides back and forth until she has made herself comfortable.

'Okay, I don't really know how to explain it, because Frederic was wild about you,' she says blinking her eyes at Carmen. 'That is to say, I assume he still is. But I saw him yesterday and I thought, it's him or nobody. He's an exact match for me. His behaviour, the casual way he has, his clothes, I just love it all, it suits me, it's brilliant!' She clicks her fingers. 'And when he worked out what was happening with David, his illusions crumbled as well. He was very hurt yesterday, you'd better believe it.' Carmen doesn't know why, but the sentence gives her a flicker of satisfaction. She picks up her glass. 'But then I set about rebuilding his illusions,' Laura continues, 'but in a slightly different way, obviously. And honestly, when is a man more receptive if not when he's been hurt? I think that when he agreed with his sister, when he agreed to the idea of our all living together, he thought it was brilliant. Maybe not because it's me, maybe he'd rather be sharing with you, okay, things like that don't change from one day to the next, but I promise you, I'll sort it out. I like him, and I'm going to keep him!'

'It sounds like a cattle market.' Elvira shakes her head. 'I don't think I've heard anything like it in all my eighty years. Do you always share out your men like this?'

'No, in the past our taste has always been very different.'

Carmen looks at the clock. Why doesn't David call, it's been ages and she's got to get back to the office.

'That's not true,' says Laura, raising a threatening finger. 'There was a fling, and another one was your boyfriend and my cousin.'

'Doesn't matter,' Carmen insists. 'That's how it was.'

The phone rings. Elvira stands up to get it.

'Do you think David's found anything out?' Laura sits up, Elvira picks up the receiver and answers, Carmen holds her breath with excitement.

Elvira turns around, her hand trembling, Carmen leaps to her feet, runs over to her and supports her, with Laura bringing up the rear.

'What is it, for heaven's sake, what's happening?' Carmen fears the worst, and thinks her heart is going to stop beating. Laura supports Elvira and guides her to the couch, while Carmen takes the phone.

'David, David, what is it? Elvira's close to collapse here!'

'I'm sorry, I didn't mean that to happen. But you must know: Stefan's free, he's alive and uninjured. They're flying the helicopter back now. A GSG9 man was hidden on board, and the pilot was another, and when the moment was right they overpowered the hostage-taker. The hostage-taker was injured, which will doubtless provoke outrage in the press, so they're still not letting any news out. Apart from anything, it's because the police are afraid the two criminals who are still at large might carry out some act of violence. They want to catch the others before they let out any official information. The hostage-taker has been handed over to the police, and Stefan will fly back to Castle Kaltenstein, all top secret, of course. The helicopter will stay there for a while until the whole thing's blown over. Stefan's going to be having police protection in his house. The press officer told me because he

223

thought that as a family member I'd have to make preparations. Then I passed it all on to William, which is why it took
a while to get back to you.'

'Thank God. Thank God, David. I can't tell you how happy
I am. A great weight has been lifted from my heart. You know
what, I'm going to take this afternoon off. Are you free?'

'Sorry, we can't see each other until this evening. I've got to
keep working, I have two meetings and deadlines to keep.
Give my love to Elvira. I'd love to see you this evening.'

'Do you know when Stefan's going to arrive?' Carmen hops
from one foot to the other – now it's all over, her bladder is
suddenly making its presence felt.

'At about seven.'

'In six hours. Why's it taking so long?' She watches Laura
help Elvira lie down on the couch, and then fetch her a glass
of water for her medicine.

'I assume they want to hide their traces and land in darkness. The grounds are big enough. I can't think of any other
reason.'

Carmen makes a kissing sound into the telephone. 'We'll
drink to it, David, I'll tell you that. We'll have a drink for
you. You've done a fantastic job!'

'It wasn't much of an achievement. The achievement was
all Stefan's. But please don't plan anything too extravagant by
way of a welcome. A big heart-shaped firework display might
be rather conspicuous!'

'Honey,' Carmen laughs affectionately, 'nobody but you is
going to get red hearts from me, believe that once and for all.
For some reason I feel connected to Stefan, maybe because
of the business with Elvira. But it has nothing to do with
love.'

'And what about us? Does that have anything to do with
love?' His voice sounds muted, as though he isn't alone.

'About us I don't know. As far as I'm concerned, absolutely!'

Now it was out in the open. God almighty, Carmen, you
didn't really say that?

224   'Me too,' says David soberly and resolutely.

'In that case nothing can go wrong,' says Carmen emphatically.

'Possibly not,' he answers.

'Ditherer!'

'Big kisses – and hi from Martin, he's standing right behind me.'

That's what she had thought. 'Hi to him, kisses to you!'

She gets slowly to her feet, but stays by the phone a moment. And afterwards I'll find myself a shrink and give him a call, she thinks. It's not on, him kissing me all over and then turning away the minute I touch him. There must be some way to make him stop it. She'd like to stroke him, to spoil him as he spoils her. She just can't understand why he shrinks from her touch. She turns around.

'Raise your glasses, girls, Stefan's unharmed, he's free, he's on his way home!' For a moment she thinks of her cheeky little outburst this morning, about tea and biscuits at the ready just in case his helicopter swept in. If she'd known how right she was! She grins at the idea.

'Just a second, I'll go upstairs, I still have a bottle of champagne in the fridge. Let's have it now! Put the water and that old red wine away, Laura, we're about to savour the pearl of the grape!'

'How poetic,' laughs Laura, putting the wine glasses away and swapping them for champagne glasses. Elvira is lying there quietly with her eyes shut. Carmen feels an urge to embrace her. She kisses her on the cheek. 'Isn't that brilliant, Elvira? Isn't life incredible? Tell me, how do you feel? Happy? Are you okay?'

Elvira reaches for her hand. 'I secretly felt responsible to Anna, and now I'm delighted that nothing happened to him!' She exhales heavily. 'I'm four stone lighter!'

'Great, I'll dash upstairs.'

'What do you think, Carmen, shall we eat the rest of the salad?' Laura points dubiously at the half-full plates. Then they look at each other, pull faces and shake their heads. Okay then. Laura starts clearing the table.

225

Carmen fetches the bottle of champagne from the fridge and then looks quickly in the phone book. Where would you find a psychiatrist? Under P? Psychological Advisory Service of the Protestant Church; Advice on Questions of Religion, Youth, Marriage and Life. What does the Church know about impotent men? And then there's the Psychological Advisory Service, Regional Branch. Civil servants as psychologists? She can't imagine it. No, she'd rather pay a decent price for an hour and feel she was on neutral ground. Psychotherapeutic Practice – Axel Deisroth – Psychotherapist, all Public Medical Insurance Accepted. What? Can she sort out David's impotence problem on the health service? Hardly, because she has private insurance and David, being self-employed, probably does too. Underneath there is a State-examined Practitioner practising Family and Couples Therapy and Hypnotherapy. Isabella Prodan, a woman, she'd prefer that. But hypnosis? She immediately thinks of Felix. But he hadn't seen a psychotherapist else they'd have kept him in. He would have seen some kind of charlatan. So, why not. She writes down the number and calls it. The receptionist wants to know what the problem is. Carmen describes the case, and is offered a date in December. 'Sorry,' she says, 'I need a quick consultation. I don't want to cure my boyfriend of his impotence, just his fear of physical contact. You must understand, I have nothing at all against his impotence. Quite the contrary, I like it.'

'One moment,' the receptionist interrupts, 'I'll just put you through to Dr Prodan herself.' A deep contralto woman's voice answers. Carmen describes the case again.

'Interesting,' says the psychotherapist finally, 'I could fit you in on Friday lunchtime. We'd normally be closed, but if it's that urgent . . .'

Carmen thanks her, writes down the address and goes downstairs.

'Where have you been?' says Laura.

'Sorry, I've just arranged a meeting with a psychotherapist.'

'What? You? Why?'

'For David. He's terrified of physical contact and I want to find a way of getting him accustomed to my hands and my body.'

'Thrilling,' Laura grins, 'I'll come with you. Can you call her again and tell her we're coming together?'

'Why?'

'Because I want to find a way to get Frederic up and running again.'

'That's not on.' Carmen taps her forehead gently and prepares to open the bottle.

'And why not, Mrs Know-All? We can try!'

'Here's the number.' Carmen gives her the piece of paper out of her pocket. 'Call her yourself.'

At that moment the cork pops out, unleashing a flood of champagne.

'Elvira, will you have a glass?'

Elvira opens her eyes. They immediately fill with tears.

'You're so sweet,' she says, 'and I'm a tearful old woman!' Carmen carefully fills the glasses. 'Don't talk that way, Elvira! How would you like to be at the castle when Stefan gets there? Shall I try and arrange it somehow?'

'I don't know if he'd like that.'

'Why not? As some sort of mother substitute? Of course he'd like that. He's got to have a welcome. He has to be told how important it is to us all that he's still alive. Otherwise he might think it didn't matter whether he lived or not. And that's not the way things are. You'll be speaking for us all if you're there to tell him how anxious we've all been on his behalf. Of course you'll do that! I'll just tell William.'

Carmen raises her glass, and they clink glasses.

'If you think so.'

A quiet smile spreads across her features.

'Of course.' Laura sits down beside her on the couch. 'Of course you'll do that. It'll do you good, and it'll do him good as well. And us. Everybody!'

Carmen grins at her. 'It takes you a whole sheet of A4 paper to express a single idea. That's one thing that's never going to change!' And to Elvira, by way of explanation: 'She's always been like that. In German she once managed to get a whole two points for a twelve-page essay. You have to convert that into pages and then into words!' Carmen grins. 'That's probably why she became a teacher, to get her own back.'

'Really? On who?' asks Laura.

'On the wrinkly old teachers who made our lives hell, and who are now, slowly but surely, being sidelined to make way for a young, dynamic generation.'

'Sidelined indeed – stop talking like a management consultant! All that happens is that you go into well-earned retirement and take things easy. That's what we've all been working towards for years!'

'Right,' Carmen grins, 'I can see that's what you've been doing.'

'I'm still amazed that you weren't thrown out of school!'

'Me too, Laura darling, me too!' She gives her a big kiss and is about to fill the glasses. Laura pulls hers away and reaches for the mineral water. Carmen nods to her, 'To Alina! But now, Elvira, let's think about how we can get you to the castle without attracting anybody's attention. We could still do it – any later and they'll have closed the place up. Do you want us to pack something for you?'

Elvira sits up slowly and runs her hand over her hair. 'Don't pack anything, but could you help me with my hair?'

Carmen looks at her snow-white, slightly permed hair. 'What do you mean?'

'Just tidy it up a little. I'll wash it quickly, and you can dry and comb it. I can't do it very well on my own. I'd like to look a little pretty.'

Carmen and Laura glance at each other. It hadn't even occurred to them that someone might think about their appearance at that age.

'Of course.' Carmen taps her chest. 'I'll help you wash, and Laura can dry.'

Elvira is already on her feet. 'No, I can wash it on my own. I'll just have a quick shower. Then you can help.'

She takes another sip from the long-stemmed champagne

glass. 'To Stefan,' she says with a smile, and goes to the bathroom.

'Fine. Okay then, I'll give Britta the afternoon off, and we
can get a crash phone lesson from dear Otto, my hairdresser,
and hear what he has to say.'

'Wouldn't you rather phone Vidal Sassoon?'

'What do you mean phone him? Let's get him over!'

Laura laughs. 'This is going to be fun, Carmen. Particularly
because you've got to do it all on your own. I've got games
from three o'clock onwards, as you know!'

Carmen is already dialling her number to tell Britta, but she
slams down the phone.

'Don't go.'

'I can't do that.'

'You're not well.'

'I was fine this morning.'

'You're having a baby.'

Laura hesitates. 'That's true, of course.'

'Well then,' smiles Carmen. 'Here's your chance to drop
the bombshell.'

Laura hesitates again. 'Not now.'

'Your baby isn't going to like bouncing around in the gym
too much, either.'

'What nonsense, it's just an embryo.'

'All the worse. How much room do you think the poor
little creature has in the womb? It'll be flying around from one
end to the other like a ping-pong ball . . .'

'Oh, stop it. You were never exactly top of the class in
biology.'

'Maybe not, but I've read up on my people-watching. You
can tell from the tip of your nose, for example, that you're
wondering whether all this hopping around could really
damage your baby!'

'Well,' Laura admits, 'I really don't want to lose it.'

'How times change,' Carmen grins cheekily.

'Give me your number. Tomorrow you're going to the
gynaecologist and having an ultrasound while I go to the   229

therapist. We must see what the little thing looks like, so we can watch it develop from now on.'

'Let me call.' Laura takes the phone out of Carmen's hand and puts it to her ear. 'And then we can meet in a café like two hysterical women who have nothing in their heads but their doctors' appointments.'

'Well,' says Carmen, 'that's exactly how it is. Doctors' appointments and impotent men. That's all you really need from life.'

'And maybe a drop or two of champagne?' Carmen affectionately rumples Laura's hair.

'You maybe. But not for Alina!'

When she reaches the high hedge and the wall, Carmen eases her foot off the accelerator. This time she's ready for the sharp turning to Castle Kaltenstein. 'Imposing,' murmurs Laura in the back seat, when they pull up in front of the cast-iron gate. Beside her, Elvira is excitedly pressing her bag into her lap. In her dark blue coat and matching suit with white lace collar, Elvira really looks like the first lady. Carmen and Laura have brushed and blow-dried her hair, so that it lies elegantly back from her face, and applied some light make-up.

'Can I really go in like this?' Elvira asked dubiously before the door closed behind her.

'You look wonderful,' Laura reassured her, leading her down the steps.

Carmen is about to get out to ring the bell when the gate opens, as before, of its own accord.

'Goodness!' Laura is impressed.

'I'd love to know how the security system works here.' Carmen gestures across the park with a sweep of her hand. 'It's all under surveillance, but you don't see a thing.'

'You mean they can see us now?'

'Certainly can,' nods Carmen. 'They've probably got cameras installed in the trees, and from this point on they'll be keeping an even sharper eye on us.'

The drive to the castle is already full of cars. Carmen drives past them all and up to the steps. All she wants to do is drop Elvira off.

William comes down the steps towards them. Carmen gets out of the car.

'How delightful that you could come, madam. The baron has already called to assure us that he is fine, and he has also asked after you. He is delighted to learn that you will be waiting for him.'

Carmen is uncertain. Who is he referring to? Elvira alone, or Carmen, or both?

'I intended to leave right away, William,' says Carmen, pointing to Laura in the back seat.

'Oh, no.' William's voice sounds hurt. 'You couldn't do that at the house of Kaltenstein. Please bring your friend in, at least for a cup of tea, the baron would be distraught if I simply let you drive away.'

Carmen bends down to look into the car at Laura. Laura shrugs her shoulders. 'Why not? Some tea would be really nice and Elvira won't be left by herself.'

Carmen nods to William. 'Fine, we'd be delighted to accept your kind invitation.' William bows, and helps Elvira up the steps to the front door.

Laura gets out and winks at Carmen. 'Since you've been here your language has changed completely. Have you noticed?'

Carmen closes the car door behind Laura, and they walk up the steps side by side. 'It happens automatically when you're talking to William. And why not, it's nice to be polite in your dealings with people.'

Laura grins. 'Most courteous, madam, most exquisitely courteous.'

Carmen nudges her in the ribs. 'Okay, yob. Drink your tea like a good girl and keep your gob shut.'

William is waiting for them upstairs by the door, and Carmen and Laura walk past him into the hall to join Elvira. Laura stops, astonished, by the murals. 'It's all so obvious,' she

says to Carmen, 'my great-grandfather clearly made a poor
career choice somewhere along the line. He must have committed some dreadful blunder. Shame I can't ask him.'

'Would you follow me, please?' William walks ahead of
them into the study, which Carmen enters with mixed feelings. The fire is burning in the hearth. The little table
between the two sofas is set for tea. Hannes is back in his
place, and beside him the photograph of Anna. What a
shame that Stefan lost his head like that, she thinks. It's left
a bitter aftertaste. She deliberately sits on the other couch,
with a view of the door. Laura drops down beside her, and
Elvira sits down opposite. William quickly goes out to get tea
and biscuits.

'This is the life.' Laura runs her hand gently over the
nubbly leather of the sofa. 'Only the very best!'

'You always wanted to meet Stefan,' says Carmen, 'you
might like him . . .'

'Lovely things always have conditions attached,' Laura
groans, sadly shaking her head.

Carmen laughs. Elvira looks across to the wall with the
photographs.

'What did you actually talk about on that evening you
spent together, Elvira? Just about the past, or about the future
as well?' Carmen lights the candle that stands on the table in
a plain silver candlestick.

Elvira looks away from the photographs. 'About the past,
just the past. We tried to work through what had happened
back then – I've already described that to you. And then we
talked about our lives for a while . . .' Elvira stops. William
has silently wheeled in a trolley, and is serving tea and biscuits. He puts a small silver bell on the table in case they
require his services further, and he disappears.

Carmen balances three heaped spoons of sugar from the
little silver bowl into her cup. 'He must have talked to you
about his impotence – he hasn't discussed it with me.'

'What a surprise.' Laura looks at her as though she's taken
leave of her senses. 'There is a difference! He sees you as a

woman he desires, Elvira as a woman he can talk to, pour his heart out to. Isn't that obvious?'

'Hmm.' Carmen cautiously takes a sip of tea from her thin porcelain cup. 'Be that as it may, I know that he's been impotent for five years, but I don't know why. Is it physical? Psychological?'

'Goodness,' Elvira says and nibbles on her biscuit, 'I really didn't ask. What sort of a subject would that be over a cup of tea?'

'One like any other,' Carmen answers defiantly. 'And we've got time to talk about it now. We could talk about the weather if you'd rather!'

'Okay.' With a sigh Elvira puts her biscuit back on the plate and leans forward to be a little closer to the others. 'I don't know if it's physical or psychological. He'd rather it was physical than psychological, because he doesn't believe in mental healing. Or at least that's what he told me. Well, whatever, he says it started when he got married. One day it just stopped working.'

'Aha, so his marriage was to blame. It was his wife's fault. Couldn't really have been anything else.' Carmen pulls a face.

'Give her a chance!' Laura shakes her head. 'Let Elvira finish her story.'

'Carmen isn't so far wrong. He really did think it was his wife's fault. At the age of forty she suddenly felt she'd missed out on lots of things in life, she felt unfulfilled and went into the fashion business. She became a partner with Linda Green, and Linda Green – the name means nothing to me – suddenly became highly successful with its avant garde fashion. So the well-to-do lady of the manor became a businesswoman. And she was making really good money too.'

'Brilliant,' Carmen interrupts, 'that's exactly what I'm trying to do all the time.'

'Oh, come on', says Laura. 'Who's going to make money if you don't?' She strikes the bolster with the palm of her hand.

'You could give it a try yourself,' says Carmen. 'So then what happened?'

'So then all of a sudden that was that. The woman was no longer his wife, and everything ceased to function. At first he laughed, then he tried other women, and then at some point he gave up completely.'

'You say he's never been to a doctor or a psychotherapist?'

'No, he sued for divorce, and that was the end of it.'

'A crusty old bachelor.' Laura looks at Carmen. 'Could you live with something like that?'

'I think it's his upbringing.' Carmen nods to Elvira. 'You should have taken him. His relations have turned him into a twisted person, don't you think? So many codes of honour, so many constraints, being oppressed all the time – it's hardly a wonder a woman turns away from that.'

'And if he breaks down and does something crazy, that's hardly so surprising either.'

Laura pat's Carmen's thigh.

'Perhaps he should see a doctor,' says Carmen thoughtfully. 'Couldn't you persuade him, Elvira? Oh, William, hello.'

'Telephone for you, madam.' He remains standing some distance away.

'For me?' Carmen jumps to her feet.

'If you please.'

Carmen follows him through an unfamiliar door. Behind it is a study with big, heavy furniture, dark wood on the walls and the ceilings, old prints and shelves full of books. A study right out of an English stately home, Carmen thinks.

'The baron wished to speak to you undisturbed. This is his telephone.' William points to the big desk, covered with papers. 'We will transfer the call immediately. Could I ask you please to pick it up when it rings?' He nods his head slightly in her direction and quickly withdraws. The phone rings immediately. Everything is perfectly organised here, she thinks as she picks up the receiver.

'Hello, Stefan?'

'I'm glad you're there, Carmen, I wanted to talk to you alone before I arrive. I'm about to get back into the helicopter, and I'll be there in about an hour. But before then I want to know what I can expect when I get there.'

'Yes,' Carmen hesitates, what does he mean? 'I can't see

what preparations are going on outside, it's all secret, but there are lots of cars there . . .'

'That's not what I wanted to know, I know the people there will be doing their job properly – what interests me is what's on your mind.'

Carmen plays with the heavy glass ashtray beside the telephone. 'I think everyone's very happy you're coming back. We were terribly worried about you.'

'What do you think yourself?'

Carmen takes a deep breath. 'I have erased what happened from my memory, Stefan, if that's what you mean.' She takes a silver picture frame facing the chair behind the desk, and turns it to face herself. 'That is to say that I have no aversion towards you. On the other hand, I'm no longer interested in an intimate relationship, if that's what you wanted to know. That's all over. But I am interested in friendship, if that's enough for you.'

There is a brief silence on the other end. Then she hears his voice, changed and harsh. 'No, it isn't enough for me, Carmen. I'm sorry that it's come to this, and I do apologise with all my heart for that . . . undesirable incident. I seem to have lost control of my senses, and for that I cannot forgive myself. But the idea of meeting you again without the chance of our having a future, that would be rather too much for me today, Carmen. So could I ask you to leave the house before my arrival? I should like to be alone.'

Carmen swallows hard. She's being thrown out, and it's never happened to her before.

'Is Elvira there too?'

Carmen nods, and then forces out a dry 'Yes'.

'Good, please welcome her to Castle Kaltenstein in my name, she is free to stay. I hope you are not insulted.'

'No, no, that's all fine, Stefan. I'll tell her.' Her tone has changed as well, she notices that she's suddenly switched into business mode.

'Fine, then goodbye, Carmen.'

'Bye, Stefan!' She slowly puts the phone down.

235

She turns the photograph on the desk right round to face her.

It shows a pretty, very smart woman of about forty. She is standing by a Mercedes convertible, with the castle in the background. Under it, in curly feminine handwriting, it says, 'I love you!' It's the same motif endlessly repeated, Carmen thinks, the same lie that the world's in order. That's a woman who got herself out of an impossible position.

'Well done you,' she nods to the picture, turns it round again and walks from the room.

'So, Elvira, Stefan's very pleased that you're here.' She pauses, while she walks through the main study to the couch. 'But he'd rather not see me.'

'That's impossible, after all you've been through over the past few hours! After all you've suffered!' Laura's expression is incredulous, and Elvira is looking at Carmen as though she's joking.

'No, that's the way it is, he's just made it very clear to me. Very clear. He doesn't want me to be at the castle when he gets back.'

Elvira shakes her head. 'I don't understand, why ever not?'

'He wanted to know what I felt about him, and I told him I saw him as a friend but nothing more than that, and he said he'd rather be alone, that is, alone with you, Elvira.'

'What can I say . . .' Elvira gets to her feet and walks slowly over to the photographs.

'Nothing, Elvira, you're staying here, that much is obvious.' Carmen follows her, stands beside her in front of Anna's photograph and puts an arm around her shoulder. 'He is Anna's son.'

'He needs a shrink,' says Laura from the couch.

'He certainly hasn't had an easy time of it. The only thing that mattered in this family was being hard, even to oneself, being aware of one's status and having a certain drive. He has his parents' blood, but it's the result of his upbringing – difficult as it is for me to grasp. But please understand that if I were to go now, it would change nothing. He would become even more eccentric, even more narrow-minded.'

'Obviously you must stay to welcome him.' Carmen presses Elvira to her. 'I'm all in favour of that. I just mean he needs help. He's ill.'

'I don't know if he's actually ill. He's a highly intelligent man, a man with leadership and charisma,' says Elvira.

'Geniuses often are. The two things aren't mutually exclusive – you can be highly intelligent in your mind and your job, and yet not have a clue about relationships. He needs help, and soon.'

'Ask your psychiatrist tomorrow,' says Laura.

'Precisely,' answers Carmen, 'I'll do that for sure.'

'It's a very odd situation,' says Carmen when they are driving back down the avenue away from the castle. 'I was really worried about him – I don't understand why he's reacting so oddly. Does he really expect me to shout "Here I am" and hurl myself at him?'

The gate opens silently before them. On either side security personnel stand with walkie-talkies, and the castle is screened off by guards. Stefan is expected to land in about thirty minutes, the professionals are preparing to welcome him, and guard him for the next few hours.

'What are your plans for this evening?' Laura turns around to watch the gate closing automatically behind them.

'What I was going to do anyway, spend the evening with David. And what about you?'

'I'm going home. There might be a message there.'

'You mean from Frederic? Carmen gives her a sidelong glance.

'That would be nice,' Laura says. They both look silently out of the window. 'The effect of potency on the psyche – it's almost impossible for a woman to grasp.' Laura looks at Carmen. 'Can you imagine a whole man, average five foot eleven, being so completely dependent on those three to seven inches? I just can't get my head round it. Isn't that idiotic?'

'Am I hearing you right? You've always been pretty keen on those seven inches!'

'Only because I hadn't really given them much thought. If something's in good working order you don't think about it that much. And now I can see there's a whole philosophy attached – what am I saying, philosophy – there's a world attached. A whole world. Your world can crumble because of a little bit of flesh. It's all wildly out of proportion.'

'It's true,' says Carmen dryly, 'particularly since every little impotent man has great antecedents. Dwight Eisenhower was impotent, yet he managed to lead America to victory in the Second World War. Pu Yi was impotent, and he was the last emperor of China. He had to marry five wives, and not one of them could give him an erection. Louis XVI couldn't get it up even before he cast eyes on the guillotine, and even the great anarchist Mikhail Bakunin, scourge of the aristocracy, was a flop in the sack.'

'Heavens!' Laura pats her thigh. 'But somehow I don't think it's such a big deal for Frederic. At least I don't have a sense that he sees impotence as a real problem. Or perhaps he's just putting it on. What do you think?'

Carmen turns into the street leading to her flat. 'It's hard to tell with Frederic. He's a good actor and he's still young. I think he doesn't mind so much because he reckons it's going to come back. He doesn't like to force things, so he's going to let it come back to him. The same way as he lives his life, I would say.' She stops right by Laura's car. 'Do you want come up, or are you going to go straight back home?'

'What are you going to do up there?'

'Just get my messages and pack an overnight bag – you never know!'

'At least we don't have to worry about AIDS.' Laura's face is a mixture of irony and self-pity. Carmen gives her a farewell kiss on the cheek. 'You see, when you look for the positive things in life, everything gets much easier. You're going in the right direction, sweetheart.' Laura gives her a nudge in the ribs, wrinkles her nose and gets out of the car.

David has left three messages, and she calls him back immediately. At first they can't decide who should go to whose, and then David decides he could do with a change of scenery. It's been an annoying day, and tomorrow isn't going to be any better. Should he bring something? Carmen isn't sure what she's got in the house, she has to have a quick look. 'Don't worry,' says David. He's setting off already, and he says he'll just pick up some chicken and red wine from the take-away on the corner. That'll do fine.

Carmen dashes around the flat like a whirlwind, clearing up, washing the basin and the fittings in the bathroom, putting on fresh make-up, getting the breakfast table ready on the bed. And the doorbell rings.

He stands in the door, blond and green-eyed, fresh colour in his cheeks. He looks so good that Carmen wishes she was with him on the beach. She sees dunes and lapping seawater, she feels the warm wind of a summer evening on her skin. He takes her in his arms and kisses her, she breathes in his aroma, the merest hint of after-shave, a masculine smell. She wishes she could stand there for ever. She presses herself tightly to him.

She knows how he will react, and realises it's happening when he pushes her from him, affectionately but resolutely, and looks at her. 'You look fantastic, I could eat you up, Carmen. What it must be like to love you.'

'You can love me.'

'You know exactly what I mean.'

'And you know I'm happy the way things are. I don't need that little thing to be happy with you. I don't want it. I need you whole, just the way you are!'

She embraces him again, he picks her up and carries her inside. He closes the door with his foot and carries her into the bedroom. He puts her down gently and then slowly starts to open her blouse. Carmen squirms. On the one hand she's terribly aroused, on the other she's bothered by the situation. She's going to be naked in front of him, and he hasn't even taken off his suede jacket.

The game would have a definite erotic charm if David wasn't so serious about it. Why won't he let her touch him? She starts running her hands up his thighs. His legs feel hard and muscular under his jeans. The sound of her fingernails on the coarse material gives Carmen goose-bumps. David seems to react as well. For a moment Carmen sees a gleam in his eye, sees him drawing spontaneously towards her. 'Oh Green-eyes,' she sighs, plunging her hand into his thick blond hair and pulling him gently down towards her. He is almost lying on top of her, his heavy torso touching her naked skin, pressing gently on her bosom. Her nipples respond immediately, and Carmen feels them pushing excitedly up through her dark red bra. David bends down towards her and touches them gently with his lips, plays with them, teases them through the light fabric. Carmen moans with desire, she presses herself to him, grabs him by both shoulders and presses her body to his, enfolds him with all her strength. He slides away from her slightly so that only his torso remains in contact with her. Carmen immediately notices his detachment, feels his passion growing weaker, the violent excitement fading to nothing. She lets the waves slowly die away, puts her arms lightly around him and runs her hand through his hair. 'Why don't you just let yourself go? Why can't I be with you? I just want to feel you, press you to me, that's all. Won't you get undressed?'

He presses her head to his and whispers in her ear, 'I can't, Carmen, really I can't.'

'We could take a shower together. Or a bath.' She tries to find a way to make him less nervous of her.

'Please don't torment yourself,' he says, lying close beside her.

'I don't want to torment you. I just want us to have a normal time together, I want you to know that I want you just as you are. You don't need to hide from me. Look, I'm not hiding from you!'

She stands up, stands in front of him on the bed, her blouse unbuttoned. He stays where he is, and turns slightly on to his side.

'Look, I have nothing to hide from you!' She opens the remaining buttons of the blouse, takes it off and hurls it across the room, then she unhooks her bra, her full breasts floating freely, opens the zip of her tight skirt, lets it fall on the bed and kicks it away, and then, with some acrobatic balancing exercises on the wobbly bed, she takes off her tights and, finally, her panties. She crumples them all into a ball and hurls them into a corner. She stands over him, completely naked.

'Look,' she says, 'my breasts are too big and not as firm as they were, my appendix scar is ugly, I've got stretch marks on my bum from the pill, and the rest of me is imperfect as well. If you take a good look, you can see. So why should you be any different? If you can love me as I am, I can love you too.'

David kneels silently and wraps his arms around her thighs, pressing his head against her belly, against her sex. He stays there for a moment, then lifts her in the air and falls back on to the bed with her. He wraps his arms around her, strokes her back down to the cheeks of her bottom and back up again. Then he turns her gently so that she's lying beside him. Carmen waits quietly, open to any reaction.

'You're a wonderful woman, Carmen.' David takes off his jacket, his shirt and his socks, but keeps his jeans on. Then he kisses her on the shoulders, on the breastbone, on the tips of her breasts. 'But maybe my accident left more scars than you think. It isn't a question of stretch marks that you can hardly see, or a tiny little appendix scar – you wild creature. The damage goes deeper than that. And I think it's fantastic the way you use everything you've got. But I can't just run away from my own shadow.' He kisses her navel, and then looks up at her. 'A scarred, limp penis – I can hardly bear the sight of it myself. Why should you?'

At first Carmen says nothing. She runs her forefinger carefully over the contours of his face. 'How can I get it across to you that it means nothing to me, on the contrary. In the past I've only ever seen erect penises, chasing after me. Can't you see how I think it's nice that it's different once in a while . . .'

David comes up to her, kisses her on both eyelids and then on the mouth. Carmen returns his kiss, long, calm, full of warmth and love.

'Will you give me some time?' he asks quietly.

'All the time in the world,' Carmen smiles at him affectionately. He covers her with kisses again, from top to bottom, Carmen closes her eyes, breathes in his aroma and listens to her body. As in the castle the previous night, she feels her nerves responding to every touch, her whole body surging, twitching, uncontrollable. Finally, when he is lying in her lap, not just exploring her hidden parts but kissing and touching them as deliberately as if he intimately knew all of Carmen's desires, she clutches the bed-head behind her with both hands. She arches her back, so precisely is he able to reach and stimulate her very depths. No man has ever empathised so strongly with her. And she's baffled as to how a man can begin to do it. How can he know so precisely what does her good, exactly where that spot is, and how long and how strong the stimulus can be? She's always imagined that making love with a woman could be like that: a partner who doesn't just squash you and pump away at you, but who arouses you thoughtfully, carefully in that very familiar way. But she's never managed to take that step, taking a woman as a lover – and here comes David, fulfilling all her dreams of lesbian love.

She dissolves, and soon she isn't thinking anything at all.

When David is lying stretched out beside her, she cuddles up to him, to his warm, muscular chest with its patch of light blond hair. He gently reaches for the duvet and pulls it over her. Carmen sighs with contentment. 'This sounds trashy, it sounds like a romantic cliché, but you're incredible. I've never experienced anything like that with anyone else. I don't know if it was impotence that made you like that, but if it was, you've won. You've won all the prizes. No other man could do that!'

David smiles and presses his face into the curve of her neck. 'I think the thing that really matters between two people is whether or not they can smell each other. And you smell so good that I could eat you up. I just like the taste of you, that's all.' He gently bites her neck, laughs and sits up. 'I've forgotten something.'

'What?' asks Carmen excitedly, pulling up the covers. Since her body has returned to its normal temperature, she realises that in all the excitement she's forgotten to turn up the heating. It isn't especially warm.'

'Our chicken and red wine are sitting patiently out on the landing, waiting for someone to come and collect them.'

Carmen laughs. 'Oh, great. Let's celebrate. I'll get plates and glasses, and we can make ourselves really comfortable!'

'Stay where you are, I'll do it. It's all in the kitchen cupboard, isn't it?'

'And see if there isn't a bottle of crémant in the fridge, I really feel like some. And bring the champagne glasses, not the cheap ones and – oh, I'll come myself.'

'Stay where you are and find us something nice to watch on TV. And don't let's miss the news. Can we manage that?' When Carmen nods he picks up the little folding breakfast table and vanishes.

Carmen hears cupboards opening and closing, then the ping of the microwave, and almost immediately David is back. He has decorated the little breakfast table beautifully: on a big white napkin stand two full champagne glasses, a burning candle and two big soup plates – at this distance Carmen can't tell what's in them. David unfolds the little legs, puts the table carefully down over Carmen, liberates himself from his jeans and slips under the cover in his dark blue silk boxer shorts. 'Chicken with lemon and coriander!'

'Ooh, it smells good!' Carmen holds her nose over it and then looks at him incredulously. 'And you conjured this up as quickly as that?'

David laughs and kisses her firmly. 'No, you fool, Martin did it at home. I just picked up the chicken, tossed it in with the rest of the ingredients and bunged it in the microwave – and immediately I'm a hero.'

'You're amazing!' They clink glasses, then reach for their spoons. 'And it tastes fantastic!' After they have enjoyed their food in silence for a while, she suddenly looks at him with a sceptical look. 'I hope you aren't just a dream!'

He laughs heartily. 'All my past partners called me a nightmare. I must be doing something wrong with you.'

By the time the news comes on everything has been cleared away. Carmen and David are sitting close together, happy and content. They have put the pillows behind their backs and pulled the covers up to their bellies and are peeling satsumas on the duvet cover. They are the first satsumas that Carmen has eaten this autumn, and she's slowly starting to feel that it's the run-up to Christmas. The smell of the peel reminds her of her childhood, when her mum put peel on the stove and that sweet, familiar smell filled the house.

David nudges her, although he doesn't need to. Stefan and the hostage exchange are now the second item. Carmen and David haven't heard any news all day, or they would have known. The two other men were caught late that evening, trying to get into Holland in a silver Audi. They were wearing wigs and carrying false passports, which immediately attracted attention. The customs officials had grown suspicious when they noticed that the colour of the paper was slightly different. If they'd travelled with their own papers, in all likelihood nothing would have happened, because with their stocking masks no one had been able to give a description of them. They had been quickly overpowered, putting up little serious resistance despite having guns under their seats. There was not a trace of their booty.

David grins. 'Nearly the perfect robbery. Clean, no one dead or injured apart from the kidnapper himself, and a bag of swag that no one's ever going to see again.'

Carmen pinches his arm with excitement. The next shot shows Stefan in his park beside the helicopter. The camera has deliberately kept away from the castle. He is being interviewed by an attractive woman reporter. How he feels, how he plans to get hold of his money again, and what effect the incident will have on security systems in his jewellery shops. Stefan, as composed and aristocratic as ever, stresses that he is happy at the way things have turned out, that the jewellery is a trivial matter compared to a human life, that even the best security system is worthless if people abuse the trust that has been placed in them. You might as well leave the doors wide open, and in his case the most effective thing was traditional security methods, men and dogs. Dogs at least were, he hoped, incorruptible.

'A witty man,' laughs Carmen and shakes her head. 'Oh, I'm glad everything sorted itself out. Specially for Elvira. She was really suffering.'

'I was surprised you didn't stay to welcome him back . . .' David narrows his eyes at her.

'I just wanted to be with you,' Carmen answers, hesitates for a moment and then gives free rein to her disappointment at Stefan's reaction. 'I just wanted to help him, to be there if he needed someone. That's all, no ulterior motives.'

David affectionately puts his arm around her shoulders and presses her to him. 'I think that may be your dilemma. You're always wanting to help other people. Think about yourself for once. You don't owe anything to anyone in the whole world!'

'Okay,' says Carmen slowly, 'but it's just in me. Our mother brought us up like that, and at times like this I always hear her talking about her childhood: even if they had nothing at all, her mother would always boil up some bread soup for a beggar, because he had even less than they did. And in the wider sense I'm the same. I don't distribute bread soup to the poor, but I always try to give something of myself. Strength, courage, positive thinking, energy – I don't know, it's just something I have.'

David takes her in both arms and slips with her under the covers. 'Stay the way you are, my girl, stay the way you are.'

Wrapped in a close embrace they go to sleep together.

Friday morning, nearly the weekend. Carmen is in a wonderful mood. She's bought croissants for herself and Britta, and she's also bought each of them a little chocolate Santa Claus and a big box of chocolates. Britta quickly makes some coffee, childishly delighted by her considerate gesture, and tells her that she's incredibly happy with her boyfriend. Yesterday he brought her flowers, and now she's wondering whether she should get him a little present. But what do you give a man? Indeed, what do you give a man, Carmen wonders. Does he use a particular after-shave? He does? What about some shower gel to go with it? Britta is delighted, yes, that's a good idea. I could give David a little surprise as well, Carmen thinks. But what? She doesn't even know what after-shave he uses, and she hasn't showered with him yet either. Oh, life is tough, but this afternoon should sort out a few things, or so she hopes.

'Psychotherapy, Isabella Prodan.' One plaque among many others. She has arrived at the clinic, having imagined an old art nouveau house with rose bushes and abandoned children's swings. And it's this big functional block. Well, anyway. Carmen gets into the lift and presses the button for the third floor. A long corridor with three doors. Urologist, gynaecologist, psychotherapist. Sensible, thinks Carmen, failing to suppress a grin. If your urologist can't help you, you can just pop two doors down the corridor and lie down on the couch . . .

The plaque on the door is as plain and functional as the whole atmosphere of the place. She rings the bell. No response. Carmen looks at her watch. Ten past twelve. Lunchtime. That's what they'd arranged. Or has the doctor forgotten? Perhaps she didn't write it down. She rings again, a longer ring this time. Impertinently long and importunate, in accordance with her mood. Not a soul.

Now Carmen feels a bit miserable. She had been so looking forward to this meeting, she was so excited about it. And now? She rings again and rummages in her handbag for some paper and a biro. She's got a big till receipt and that's all. Okay, she turns it over and writes on the back: 'Turned up at 12.10, unfortunately nobody here, please call back . . .' Then the lift arrives. Rapid footsteps on high heels approach, and Carmen turns around. A tall, slim woman with a dark brown pageboy haircut is coming towards her. In a tight woollen suit her body looks surprisingly sexy, and she's clutching a paper bag. Carmen guesses she is in her mid-forties.

'Frau Legg? I'm sorry, I'm Isabella Prodan. I just nipped out to get us something to eat. Afternoons are long, and otherwise I find my stomach starts to rumble after three o'clock.' She gives Carmen a wide smile. Her teeth are brilliant, she's generally dazzling. Carmen doesn't know what she had imagined a psychotherapist would be like, but it wasn't like this, she's sure of that. The two women shake hands, Isabella Prodan opens the door and lets Carmen go in first. Here too, in the hall, Carmen feels as though she's at the dentist's. A little reception desk, sober and white, some pictures on the wall, doors with inscriptions. Isabella Prodan walks ahead to the one without an inscription. She opens it and they both walk in. Carmen is disappointed. No sign of the classic red psychotherapist's couch. A modern desk with a glass top, and in the corner a brightly coloured couch made up of separate sections, arranged around a little low table. Isabella walks over to it, puts down her bag, gestures to Carmen to sit on the couch, then walks quickly over to a bright, narrow cupboard, and fetches glasses, two plates and cutlery. Then she slides, ladylike, into one of the armchairs and unpacks the bag: a bottle of multivitamin juice, four little plastic bowls containing various gourmet salads, a round, medium-sized camembert, a whole Italian salami and a small baguette, and a bunch of fat and fruity grapes. Isabella takes the lids off the salads, puts the cheese and salami on a round wooden board along with a sharp knife and says encouragingly to Carmen: 'Do start. I assume you'll be skipping lunch today too.'

'But I can't . . .' I can't simply have lunch at the expense of a woman I don't know from Adam, she thinks, but the doctor interrupts her. 'I'll add it to your bill, and then that'll be that.'

Carmen laughs. It's liberating, and her initial inhibitions have vanished.

'Okay then,' she says and helps herself.

'Why didn't your boyfriend come with you?' asks Isabella, pouring out the juice.

'I didn't want him to know . . .'

'It's unusual for the girlfriend of an impotent partner to come to the practice. It's usually the person who needs the treatment . . .'

'Sure,' Carmen breaks herself a piece of bread. 'But our situation is different. You see, I'm fed up with men making passes at me all the time. You think you're happy with a man, and you soon find out it all depends on what goes on in bed. If lots goes on then it's good, if not so much goes on then you've got problems. So I placed an ad looking for a clear-headed impotent man.'

'Interesting.' Isabella puts a piece of cheese and a grape in her mouth at the same time.

'Yes, and I got a few replies. Some of them I didn't even answer, but passed them on to another woman who'd asked for the impotent men I rejected.' Isabella looks up briefly but doesn't interrupt Carmen. 'And then there were a few nutters, but three were really remarkable. One of them is completely at ease with his impotence, he doesn't get specially upset . . .'

'How old is he?'

Carmen thinks for a moment. How old was Frederic? 'Twenty-eight,' she says. That's right, twenty-eight.

'Okay, then he hasn't got too much to worry about. At that age potency can go overnight, and come back overnight just as easily.'

Carmen nods and cuts herself a big piece of salami. 'That's what I thought. The next one was Baron Stefan von Kaltenstein, who's just been in the news because he agreed to be a hostage . . .'

'Yes, I know the case. An extraordinary man. You say he's impotent as well?' Isabella puts another grape in her mouth and bursts it between her front teeth.

'Yes, and I now believe that's the source of all his peculiar
reactions – some pretty odd things have happened. He's really

the only one who needs urgent help. But I don't know if he would come of his own volition. Elvira, a friend of ours, said he thought he was ready to see a psychiatrist, but I almost believe that she may have changed her mind since. The best thing would be for me to send Elvira to you, so that you might be able to find a way to help him.'

'Not a bad idea!'

Carmen looks at her watch. 'Oh, no, it's half past one and I haven't even started to tell you about the thing that really concerns me, which is David.'

'My receptionist comes back from lunch at two, but the first patient doesn't get here until two thirty. As long as you've got time we can go on sitting here.'

Carmen wonders. What's she got in her diary today, is there anyone booked for two? 'If I could just make a quick call I'd have a better idea.'

'Then I'll make us a coffee. Sit where you are and I'll get the phone.'

Britta takes a quick look in Carmen's diary. She has a meeting with a client, but not until three.

'It's fine,' she says to Isabella, who is just coming back in with a jug of water, opening the cupboard, fiddling with water, coffee and filter-bags and switching on a coffee machine.

'That way I'm my own master,' she smiles to Carmen, taking out two cups, saucers and a sugar bowl and carrying them over to the table. 'In the case of men Stefan Kaltenstein's age, impotence is a much more difficult matter than it is for the young man you were talking about a minute ago. There can be many reasons. Physical or psychological, sometimes the two factors merge. But even if the disorder is purely physical, its consequences always rebound on the psyche. You mustn't forget that a man sets great store by his sexuality. For a man, an erection equals power, ability, perfection, the justification and the proof of life.'

She stands by the coffee machine again, takes cream from a fridge and waits for the coffee. Carmen has been listening from the couch, and says, 'I can imagine! So are these disorders widespread? I was amazed that so many people replied.'

'It's estimated at ten per cent.'

'Ten per cent? That would be,' Carmen calculates quickly, 'dum da dum . . . three million men. Is that possible? Surely that's too many . . .'

'That's about right.' Isabella carries the coffee jug to the table and pours them a cup each.

'And what do they do with all their impotence? I mean, why do we never hear anything about it?'

'Oh, it's started attracting attention. Once you think about it, you'll start noticing it. The major magazines have carried reports about it, the National Institute of Health in America had a conference in Bethesda, Maryland, new impotence centres are being set up all across the United States, they've got them in Sao Paulo and even in Shanghai. And there are specialist journals and global conferences with up to 150 papers on erectile dysfunction.'

'No!' Carmen is speechless. 'I can't believe that. And what are they doing about it? Can you get replacement parts, or whatever?'

Isabella laughs heartily. 'That's exactly what men imagine when their bits stop working. They go to the doctor wanting a non-psychological, technical and mechanical treatment – they want a hard-on and that's that. Most patients assume some kind of physical disorder, because if that's the case they imagine it can be cured by some sort of medication. So that covers hormonal disorders, the ageing process, diseases of the bladder, genital changes, injuries or accidents.'

Aha, accidents, thinks Carmen.

'These men are mostly frightened of psychological things,' Isabella goes on, pouring the steaming coffee, 'they can't imagine what it could mean. Is there something wrong with them? Some of them think the diagnosis is outrageous. And if you ask them to bring their partner along to their next appointment, they often get furious. No, it's nothing to do with their partners, and anyway everything's fine at home. That's the way it is.'

Carmen grins. 'Funny. I was just reading by chance something about famous men like Eisenhower and Louis XVI, who were impotent as well, and I jotted down a phrase because I thought it was so good: "Tormented by rheumatism and impotence, they can't accept that what was formerly supple is now stiff, and what was formerly stiff is supple."'

Isabella smiles. 'What is clear is that for the man affected, impotence is a serious blow to his personal pride, and this seems to apply particularly to your Baron von Kaltenstein.'

'I would like to bring him to your practice,' Carmen cautiously takes a sip from the hot coffee and then lowers her head, 'but, as I've said, I don't think it's going to be that easy to get him to come. How long would a course of treatment be, and what would it cost?'

Isabella pours cream into her coffee. 'I've got patients who come for three to four years, four hours a week. An hour is 150 marks.'

Carmen chokes. 'What? One hundred and fifty marks an hour?' She happens to glance at her watch. Two o'clock. Right, things are going on outside, voices, laughter, the beeping of a computer.

'Don't worry,' Isabella reassures her. 'I didn't put you in my diary as a case for treatment, this was a general consultation. And if I get Stefan von Kaltenstein as a patient thanks to you, then that will be a bonus.'

'I don't know,' replies Carmen, who immediately feels compelled to help. 'I mean, we might be able to get to him through Elvira . . .'

'Do try, do try. But that has nothing to do with your problem . . .'

'Yes,' Carmen swallows. 'Could you quickly tell me the likelihood of curing impotence? I mean purely physical impotence, caused by an accident, for example.'

Isabella is sitting opposite her with her long legs crossed, her long, slender hands wrapped around her coffee cup as though she is drinking from her hollowed hands. Then she leans forward, keeping the cup in the same position. 'There is the semi-rigid prosthesis, that's two partially pliable plastic rods that are implanted in the erectile tissue of the member. Then there's erectile tissue self-injection therapy, where the men inject a vasodilatory substance into the erectile tissue so that minutes later the penis is erect, remaining like that for about eighty minutes. Then there's the vacuum suction pump – air out, blood in – a pretty unstable affair, and the hydraulic prosthesis, a handpump is implanted in the scrotum and a fluid container behind the pubic bone, the patient pumps it up whenever he needs to, and then there are testosterone injections, controversial but greatly in demand, and . . .'

Carmen waves a dismissive hand. 'Stop right there, Dr Prodan, it all sounds revolting. No one would do that of their own free will. Ten per cent of men, you say, and they're all trying to cure themselves in one way or another? That's . . . why don't they accept that that's just the way things are?'

'Because women like yourself, in search of impotent men, are pretty rare.'

Carmen shakes her head. 'Doesn't it tend to be the men themselves who think that way? I think of rhinoceros horn powder, what an awful business that is. Making a species extinct just because it's supposed to restore your potency, a miracle cure.'

'That's why it's such big business. German sex shops do hundreds of millions of marks' worth of business in cures for potency. And they're not going to let that slip through their fingers. Where money is concerned, animal protection takes second place.' Isabella drinks from the hollow of her hand again.

'And psychotherapists?' Carmen tilts her chin cheekily.

Isabella laughs. 'We take ourselves very seriously, and think that we're fundamentally in a different category from pleasure drops and rhinoceros horn.'

'And what's your success rate? Are there statistics available?'

'We estimate it at about seventy per cent.'

Carmen leans back in her couch. 'Honestly, I'm glad I'm a woman.'

'I believe you. But I'm still not quite sure what it is you want. You seem to have a Sleeping Beauty syndrome . . .'

'Oh?' Carmen leans forward again. 'What would that be?'

'Usually attractive women who don't want sexual contact with any of their admirers, and wait for the Prince Charming of their dreams.'

'Hmm.' Carmen shakes her head. 'That certainly doesn't apply to my past. I had plenty of sexual contact with my admirers, but—' she grins. 'Prince Charming never showed up.'

'But he's here now . . .' Isabella uncrosses her long legs and puts the coffee cup back on the table.

'Yes,' says Carmen slowly, 'but the problem is that he's so anxious about physical contact that I'm even nervous about brushing against his jeans. He turns away immediately, he creeps back into his little shell. He caresses and indulges me to a fantastic degree. I hadn't imagined a man could do that. But I'm not allowed to touch him below the waist. He won't even take a shower or a bath with me!'

'There seems to be some powerful kind of irritation involved here. What happened? How old is your friend?'

'Thirty-four, a year younger than me. And he had a serious motorcycle accident. He says he wasn't castrated, just badly scarred. And he says he can hardly bear to look at it himself, so how can he expect me to?'

'Hmm.' Isabella runs her hand through her hair. 'Have you talked to him about it? Have you told him you don't care what it looks like?'

'I've used all my powers of persuasion on him. I've even taken all my clothes off and stood naked in front of him so that he can see I'm not perfect either.'

Isabella laughs. 'A good exercise. You're very inventive, I'll say that for you. And did it do any good?'

253

'Sadly, no. He said he needed time.'

'How long have you known him?'

'Since Sunday.'

'Which Sunday?'

'Last Sunday.'

Isabella laughs again. 'I think you should probably give him a bit more time. You're trying to understand his most delicate spot. For him it's probably like taking your clothes off after a serious operation and not being able to feel your body any more. I think that's the best way of seeing it. He needs security, he needs to know you're serious, he needs to build up confidence in you.'

Carmen nods. 'Yes, I can see it when you put it like that. I don't want to force things, either. But the fact that he always turns away, that he moves out of my way if I even touch him around there with my leg accidentally, of course it worries me and it makes me sad.'

'Sure. But in your case I'm interested in something quite different.' Isabella's brown eyes are fixed on Carmen's face.

'In my case?' Carmen asks. 'What is it?'

'Another question – what does he look like, this David? Is he erotic, handsome, does he have a fantastic, masculine body? Is he what you're after? Is he your dream man?'

Carmen's facial expression changes immediately, she feels her eyes growing moist, feels an incredible emotion pulling and tearing at her. Instinctively she puts her hand on her heart.

'It's something indescribable,' she says enthusiastically. 'He's tall, he has light blond hair and green, no, turquoise-coloured eyes. When he looks at me I sometimes think it can't be so, that he can't exist. At first I even suspected him of wearing coloured contact lenses. But he doesn't. And the way he looks, his eyes go deep inside you. And he's so sweet. He replied to my ad with a wonderful enormous card and a poem by Rilke. And he spoils me whenever he can. He's my dream man, that much is true. Yes, he's real, and I even think I love him. Although I've never been too sure about that feeling. But with him I am. Yes, I really think I love him. With all my heart. Just the way he is.'

'So,' Isabella interrupts, 'are you really quite sure, the way he is? Or are you hoping, secretly perhaps, that once you get your hand on his penis it'll stand to attention again? Don't you think that desire, however small, however hidden, however repressed, might lurk somewhere in your mind?'

Carmen clicks her fingers and thinks of the fantasy she had the previous evening when he greeted her at the door. She can see the dunes, the water, she can feel him coming inside her. And she thinks about what Laura suspected at the very first. Yes, Isabella is right. It's out in the open.

'Now it's me on the couch!' she says, changing her position slightly. 'If I pay you a fee, it'll be justified, because you're right. But it's because of David that I'm suddenly thinking this way. I still feel that way about other men, I'd rather have them impotent. But where David's concerned, I don't want to want it, because it would hurt David terribly if he knew what you know. It isn't fair to him. I don't want to mess him around just so that he can sleep with me. It would be extremely selfish of me, and mean, because he's forever spoiling me, and gets nothing in return. I just don't know how to help him. Not to make him potent all of a sudden, but just for him to allow me a place in our love.'

Isabella stands up, walks to her desk and looks quickly in her diary. 'If it's just about getting close to him, time will sort that one out. He'll learn to accept you and your love. He will open up to you very slowly, one bit at a time. It could take a month, it could take a year. I don't know how his mind works, I don't know the level of psychological injury after that accident.'

Carmen nods silently.

'But if it's a matter of you sticking to what you've just learned, to what you really want, then you'll have to find a way of getting him to a doctor. First of all I can offer you a consultation with me. We can find out whether it's purely physical, and whether he has to get to a doctor . . .'

'You've got one just around the corner,' interrupts Carmen, 'how practical.'

Isabella nods. 'He's a pretty good doctor, although I know it looks like a fiddle on this floor.' Okay, you're ahead of me, thinks Carmen. 'Or,' Isabella goes on, 'we can find out whether it's chiefly a psychological problem. Then I can help. Of course you can take him somewhere else, I'm just making you an offer.'

'Why should I?' Carmen gets to her feet too, putting her hands behind her waist and leans backwards slightly. 'I'm very happy here, Dr Prodan. But I'd like to say one thing, which is that if you find out that it isn't a psychological problem but a physical one, I don't want anything to do with those tubes and rods and pumps you mentioned. I'd really prefer not to bother with them, just as I planned originally, and then he'll never need to know that I've got this ulterior motive. Is that agreed? Can I depend on you?' Carmen walks over to Isabella and holds out a hand. 'That is, unless he wants medical treatment as a solution.' She hesitates before shaking hands. 'That would be something else again, but I hope he'd talk to me about it first. And I'd advise him against those mechanical devices or injections or whatever they are. He's so valuable to me the way he is. And there's really no point going mad over a few inches of erectile tissue.'

'Fine.' Isabella shakes the hand she offers. 'I know that my diary is full, but I'd like to do something for you. I'll ask my receptionist to move one of my appointments. My girls are very resourceful and diplomatic. I'm sure something will occur to them. We will be in touch with you right away. And if all is well, we will meet again next Monday lunchtime, but this time with David.'

Carmen nods to her. 'If I can manage it. I still have to persuade him that it's okay to visit a therapist. How would you want it to go?'

'I'd want him to tell his story.'

'Like you did with me?'

'Exactly the same.'

They shake hands. Carmen turns around and goes. She barely registers anything: neither the receptionists nor the lift nor the street nor her journey. It's as if she is in a trance, thinking about how Isabella managed to get out of her something she hadn't even admitted to herself.

She has a busy afternoon. Carmen forgets Isabella and their conversation, and after her three o'clock meeting she has three other appointments outside the office. By the time she gets back to work to collect her papers it's just before eight. There are a number of messages on her desk, three of them private: David, Laura and Elvira. She'll sort them out at home. She longs for a hot bath, and wants to think in peace for a while. About herself, about her feelings, about David, about the future. She is turning off the desk lamp above her desk, when there's a knock on the glass front door.

It's Laura. She is gesticulating wildly and laughing. Carmen opens up. 'Ciao, bella!' They kiss each other on both cheeks. Laura's skin feels fresh and cold, like the cold, wet night falling over the roofs outside.

'Brrr, bring the cold in, why don't you,' says Carmen and shivers.

'Oh, stop complaining,' Laura chaffs, 'you can't have been out of the cold yourself for long. When I drove past half an hour ago the place was in darkness.'

Carmen laughs: 'Perhaps, but I was under such pressure that I didn't even notice. Whatever, now I'm going right home for a nice long bath.'

'Oh, don't. I just wanted to have a chat, go out to eat or something. You can't just disappear like that.'

Carmen gets her coat and puts it on, collects her bag and her car-keys. 'You can come with me, if you like.'

'What's up with David?'

'I'm supposed to call him back. But I'll do it from home.'

'I wouldn't want to get in the way . . .'

'I'll let you know if you're in the way . . .'

The two women smile at each other and hug.

'Okay. My place.'

257

Carmen's surprised. She hasn't been driving particularly fast, but she seems to have lost Laura on the way. The bath is nearly full when Laura rings downstairs. Carmen stands by the door in her bathrobe. Laura comes running up, two steps at a time, swinging a paper bag. 'I don't know what your plans are this evening, but having a bite to eat isn't such a bad idea,' she calls, completely out of breath.

'You're a sweetie.' Carmen glances at the writing on the bag. 'Pizza?' she asks suspiciously?

Laura laughs. 'You'd love that, wouldn't you? No, Indian. I stopped off at the Namaskar.'

'Brilliant! I fancy something good and hot.'

'So?' Laura closes the door behind her and follows her friend into the bathroom. 'What's up with you? Change of heart?'

Carmen sighs. 'If only I knew.'

Laura points to the bag. 'Hang on, let me put that in the kitchen, back in a second. Do you want something to drink?'

'Champagne!' Carmen slides carefully into the hot bath water.

'Is that some kind of joke?'

'Yes. Have a look and see if there's some prosecco in the fridge. Or some crémant. That's what I feel like.'

'You feel like a lot of things today, don't you?'

Carmen immerses herself completely and then blows a hole through the bubbles. Laura comes back with a champagne glass in one hand, a glass of orange juice in the other.

'What's up with you . . .' Then Carmen splashes out of the water, nearly spilling it on to the floor. 'You've been to the doctor's, of course, what does it look like? Have you got a photograph?'

Laura nods, a grin spreads across her whole face and she takes a black and white polaroid out of the back pocket of her jeans.

'Are you off your head? In your trouser pocket? It should be in an album.' She reaches for it impulsively, then pulls her hand back. 'Hang on, my hands are wet, just hold it out for me.'

Carmen curiously studies the black and white blobs in the picture. 'I can't make anything out.'

Laura grins. 'There!' she says with the proud voice of an Olympic champion. 'You can see it quite clearly.' She points to a blurred, longish thing. 'And the best thing is, Carmen, I heard her heart beating. Imagine, there's a second heart beating in my belly, isn't that incredible? I've been completely over the moon since I heard that bump-bump-bump. From my child – can you imagine?'

'I'm so happy for you, Laura, I'm really happy. Next time, can I come along? Is it allowed? I'd like to have a listen!'

Laura puts the picture back in her trouser pocket and sits down on the edge of the bathtub.

'Please, Laura, take the picture out. It's the first photograph of your baby. You can't just . . .'

Laura nods, runs out and comes right back in again.

'So tell me, how were things with Old Mother Shrink? Did she give you any tips for unwrinkling David?'

'Unwrinkling is good.' Carmen sinks into the foam until it comes up to the tip of her nose, then slowly re-emerges. There is foam on her face and in the long hair floating around her. 'That's what I wanted to think about this evening.'

'Then tell me, what did she say?'

Carmen opens her eyes and stares at the ceiling. Then she takes a deep breath and looks Laura in the eye. 'Don't laugh. She told me that I wanted David not impotent, but potent. She analysed *me* rather than what I'd told her about David. And she probably did that the whole time!'

Laura laughs now. 'Sorry, Carmen, but it's too ironic. You wanted an impotent man, and you've got the impotent man of your dreams and now you want to turn him into a potent superman. Precisely what you couldn't stand. And I, who always set greater store by men's potency than by the rest of the stuff like profession, education, upbringing, I'm starting to feel great without sex. Since this afternoon I've begun to feel that my body is manufacturing a baby, and that I'd probably think of it as an invasion, a disturbance . . .'

'Should I give you the address of my therapist?' Carmen jokes. 'Pregnant women are supposed to be really keen on sex.'

'That must be what our grandmothers said. It was the only time you could really let go without being worried you might have a baby. Something other than your usual simple fare. But I've never exactly gone without – and now I'm having a break.'

'With Frederic?'

'Yes, he came by yesterday and – really Carmen, we complement each other really well. I feel incredibly at ease with him. But what about you? Was Old Mother Shrink right?'

'Stop calling her Old Mother Shrink, she's not like that at all. She's an attractive, alert woman called Isabella.'

'Okay, then, Isabella – so what's up? Are you going off in a different direction?'

'I'm not quite sure myself – but . . .' The doorbell rings, one long, two short.

'Oh God, who could that be?'

'Did you call David back?'

'No, I was going to do that from the bath . . .'

'Well, then he'll be thinking that he might as well drop by . . . Hang on, stay where you are, I'll open it.'

Laura is about to run out the door, and Carmen holds her back.

'Laura, what with Frederic and everything, have you done any research into potency restorers?'

'What? No!'

'Not technical or mechanical, just, you know, medicines or whatever . . .'

Standing in the doorway, Laura looks at her and raises her eyebrows. 'You mean like powders that you mix in their dinner and so on, have I understood you correctly? Secretly?'

Carmen nods faintly. There's another ring at the door.

'Hmm,' says Laura and walks to the door of the flat. She presses the buzzer and waits. It is David, and he follows Laura into the bathroom, kissing Carmen tenderly by way of greeting. Laura stands in the door watching them. David is wearing a thick white pullover, a polo neck with a zip-fastener that he now pulls open. The very sound of it reverberates through Carmen. It's a good thing she's sitting in the water, and that he can't sense her arousal through the bubbles. Despite the warm water, gooseflesh runs along her back. Ah, if he'd only unzip his trousers like that too, clamber into the tub and make love to her. She'd go wild, she can feel it. Carmen darling, Isabella's right, she thinks soberly all of a sudden. I want to have him. It's probably because he keeps me at such a distance, it turns me on. Totally, completely and unbelievably powerfully. She dips below the water. When she comes back up she sees David and Laura walking out the door together.

'Hey, what's going on?' she calls after them.

'Don't worry,' Laura grins cheekily. 'We're just going to cook and lay the table so that everything's ready when Cleopatra emerges from her ass's milk.'

'That's a good idea.' Carmen reaches for the shampoo to wash her hair. Three minutes later Laura's back again. 'Some odd guy just called, says his name's Oliver, and he couldn't work out why you didn't answer the phone, he just said that your decision not to fly out with him was very wise because before he flew back he met the woman of his life, a Chinese woman who – can you believe it – was all woman and knew what it meant to be at a man's side all the time and he was going to bring her back to live with him . . . Does that make any sense? And he wouldn't let me speak, he just said that I – you – should think about how foolish I'd been, and then he put the phone down.'

Carmen rubs shampoo out of her eyes. 'A screwball. Of course he needs an Asian woman. She'll tend to his jade-stick when it's dangling all the way to China . . .'

'Ooh, you're awful.' Laura shivers.

'It's true though,' Carmen, says, annoyed. 'It makes my blood boil, hearing that kind of thing. Someone who knows what it means to be a woman – of course, he needs a slave rather than a partner. And now he's found this poor creature who probably thinks she's made the catch of a lifetime . . .'

'Telephone,' calls David from the living-room. 'Carmen, shall I get it?'

'If you would!' she answers and stands up. 'I'll just rinse this foam off in the shower and I'll be right there.'

'It's Elvira, she's staying in the castle tonight, we're not to worry about her, she's fine.'

'That's good news for once.' Laura pulls the shower curtain shut in front of Carmen and goes back out to David.

Laura's Indian food is really incredibly hot, but Carmen's thoughts are miles away. She is looking at David and imagining a future for them both. Chiefly because as far as David and Laura are concerned there seems to be only one topic of conversation: Olivia, Laura's daughter-to-be. 'Do you think the spices are too hot for her?' she asks David, and they are immediately immersed in a crazy discussion about what you can, may and should expect embryos to be able to do. David is so wrapped up in the subject, so apparently fanatical, that Carmen is spurred on in her quiet reflections. This guy clearly wants a baby. So she'll be doing him a favour if she starts going in search of some sort of magic potion tomorrow. There must be some kind of remedy that's stronger than that stupid motorcycle accident.

She listens to the other two for a few minutes. They're actually talking about sexual intercourse. Whether it's likely to affect the baby or not. That's funny, Carmen thinks, but bites back any comments of her own on the subject. Here's a man who can't father a child, sitting beside a woman who's with a man she isn't going to sleep with, talking seriously about a subject that remains intractably abstract for them both.

'You're so quiet,' David says to her suddenly. 'Are you okay?'

'Yes, sure, I'm fine. I was just listening, that's all.'

'Have you ever thought about children?' David asks her.

Touchy subject. If she says yes, it may hurt him because he can't fulfil her desire. If she says no, she'll seem cold and selfish, and anyway it wouldn't be true.

'I think all women after the age of thirty think about children. I've just put it out of my mind because the
circumstances have never been right.'

'And would they be right now?' David looks at her with a
curious expression, and Carmen thinks, what is this, where's
this going? 'If I got pregnant it would be a disaster. I'm independent – I rely on myself. I don't know how I'd manage.'

David reaches over the table for her hand. 'Aren't there two
of us?'

She smiles, completely confused. Does he want to bring up
somebody else's child as well? 'I'm glad you see it that way. It
makes me feel secure, but a baby isn't just for Christmas, so to
speak, it's a lifelong responsibility.'

'Yes,' Laura says. 'Nice though. Imagine yourself all alone in
your old age. There's no one who belongs to you, who talks to
you from time to time, wouldn't that be terrible?'

'Terrible.' Carmen says.

She really does think it's terrible. But she finds the subject
just as terrible, because she can't change things. She doesn't
want to give up her job, on the contrary, she's on the way up
and she doesn't want to stop at this point in her career. And
she's with a man who's impotent and whom she has known
for far too short a time to know if he's really the man she
could share such responsibility with. So everything argues
against the idea of a baby, and anyway the whole idea's ridiculous, because whatever else happens, David isn't capable of
fathering a child. And that's the end of that.

Laura seems to sense Carmen's impatience, and says goodbye. Carmen takes her to the door of the flat and, when she
gets back, sits down on David's lap, straddling him. 'Why are
you suddenly talking about children? Is that what you
want?'

'Not so much what I want, because it's impossible. It's my
dream. But maybe you dream just as strongly of things you
can't have.'

Carmen presses her face to his. 'Is it absolutely certain that
your condition won't change? Over time, perhaps?'

David presses her firmly to him with both arms. 'I thought you wanted an impotent man!' His voice sounds rough, his lips are right by her ear.

'I want you!' They press themselves to each other and kiss lingeringly. Then he picks her up and carries her into the bedroom. Once again he spoils her, from head to foot, he kisses and strokes her, but today, once again, he won't let Carmen get too close to him. She racks her brains. How can she get him to drop his guard?

'My impotence must really be getting on your nerves,' he says suddenly, just before he goes to sleep. She has cuddled up against him and is lying safely in his arms. She feels very much at ease, but now she gives a start. Don't say anything out of place. Just don't spoil anything with some stupid remark.

'No, I love you the way I love you,' she whispers in his ear, rubbing her cheek gently against his stubble.

'That's all I wanted to hear,' he says quietly, tenderly, sleepily.

I'm going to have to be very careful about this, Carmen thinks and kisses him on the cheek. If he knew what I had planned, he'd be deeply hurt. And I don't want to lose him, even if he stays impotent until the day he dies.

It's the first weekend she's been able to spend relaxing with David. They linger over their breakfast until early afternoon, read the paper, chat, and finally, happy, content and tired, they go back to bed for a cuddle. It's one o'clock in the afternoon, there's a milky autumn sun shining outside and the weather is surprisingly good. Carmen draws the curtains. 'I don't want to see it right now!'

David laughs. 'Later on we can go and get Cain. He's probably missing me terribly right now, and we can go for a bit of a scamper. I know a wonderful forest path that's very picturesque at this time of year.'

Carmen jumps on to the bed and rolls from one side to the

other with David. 'I know the path very well, you just want to see if that guy's still up in his shoot.'

'No, I want to eat you up in the forest.'

Carmen laughs, lies on top of him and drums on his chest with her fists. 'I won't let you!'

'Yes you will, I'm going to nibble off a bit of your ear, then your belly-button, then I'm going to bite off your little toe.'

'Oh, how dreadful!' Carmen rolls off David.

'Tomorrow we're celebrating our one-week anniversary. Should I cook something nice? Then I have to go shopping. I'm a bit short of time. Would you rather we went out to eat?'

'Before or after coffee with your parents?'

'Oh, you're horrible!'

She hurls herself on top of him again, playfully bites his neck. He holds her tight, but then suddenly sits up. Carmen slips to one side.

'I'm sorry,' he says, 'but I can't bear getting too close. Don't be sad, it'll sort itself out.'

'It doesn't matter,' whispers Carmen, pushing him gently back. 'We've got time, all the time in the world.' She smiles. At that moment there's a ring on the doorbell.

'Who could that be?' Carmen wonders. Peter wouldn't be so cheeky and . . . 'I'm not going to get it'.

'What if it's something important?'

'The most important thing is lying here beside me.'

'You've said that before!' The bell rings again.

'Shall I go?' David looks at Carmen. Not a bad idea, Carmen thinks, because then any unwelcome guests will be confronted with the situation, and politely turn away. She nods. David gets to his feet, puts on a pair of jeans over his tight boxer shorts, pulls on a T-shirt and leaves the bedroom. Carmen listens curiously. It can't be Laura, as she called that morning to say that she and Frederic were going around the baby shops with his sister. Just to see what they were going to need, where there were nice things and how expensive it was going to be. Maybe she cancelled the shopping trip when she saw the prices, and changed her mind? No, that wouldn't be like Laura. Once she starts something she sees it through. Now she hears a voice. It's Elvira! Carmen leaps out of bed, fishes for a sweatshirt and a pair of jeans and runs barefoot from the room.

Elvira is standing in the living-room, balancing a baking-tray wrapped in aluminium foil on both forearms.

'Greetings from Stefan, and he'd like to apologise for his behaviour.'

She looks a little strange standing there, Elvira in her smart suit, quite the lady of the manor and no longer the nice old woman from the first floor. Carmen overcomes her slight feeling of distance from her, walks over and kisses her on the cheek. 'Sweet of you to come, Elvira.'

Elvira sighs. David takes the baking-tray from her and puts it on the table. 'I've felt bad about you two . . .'

'Oh heavens, why? Sit down!' Carmen lifts a corner of the aluminium foil. 'Fresh plum cake, that's fantastic! I'll just make us some coffee.'

David waves the idea aside. 'You sit down with Elvira. I'll do it.' And goes into the kitchen.

'A really fine man.' Elvira nods to Carmen, and the old familiarity gradually reasserts itself. Then she sits down carefully in the armchair and lies back until she's sitting deeply and comfortably in it. 'When I think of all the things I have to be grateful to you for, Carmen, I don't know how I can ever thank you enough.'

'Nonsense, what do you have to thank me for? That's complete rubbish. I discovered by chance that you have the same photographs on the wall, and that's all.'

'But also for the hours you spent with me. Not just you and Frederic the time I collapsed, I owe you my life for that, but you and David in the castle too. I don't know how I'd have survived that night without you. And I've told Stefan about it all. And he's very sorry he reacted how he did.'

'Really? Why, all of a sudden? In the phone call the day he got back he gave the impression of being serious about what he said.'

Carmen draws her legs up beside her.

'And he probably was at that point in time. I think you unleashed a lot of things inside him. There were a lot of things inside him that were in turmoil and you unleashed them all.'

'Really? How do you mean?'

David comes back in, puts cups and plates on the table, takes the aluminium foil off the tray and slices up the cake. Carmen watches his skilful movements, and so does Elvira.

'He's built an invisible armour around himself, and he feels at ease in it. That's how I see it. And yesterday evening we spent a long time talking about it, and I think I'm right. He wouldn't let anyone get close to him, because he was afraid of being hurt. And so he stayed inside the little case that he's made for himself, without disappointments, without emotions, but also without joy.'

Carmen leans forward. 'And you're saying I triggered something off? Without meaning to?'

Elvira nods slowly, and her dark eyes come to rest on Carmen.

Carmen leans further forward, glancing over to see if David is out of range, and then says quietly to Elvira, 'Elvira, I went to see a psychotherapist yesterday. About David. I'm telling you this in confidence. But I talked briefly about Stefan as well, and she said she'd like to meet him. Perhaps she can help him. Or you could go and see her first. She might be able to give you a few tips for him.'

Elvira nods. 'Thanks for the offer. But I think he's already started his own psychotherapy.'

'What do you mean?'

'Well, that reporter who interviewed him when he got home seems to have fallen in love with him. And I think that's doing him good.'

'Ah.' Carmen nods and drops back into her old position. 'The one with the short blonde hair. I know, I saw her. Well,' Carmen can't help asking, 'does she know he's impotent?'

'I don't know, but I think so. We sat up together all night

and talked about everything under the sun, and the atmosphere was very relaxed, very easy and cosy. But I think she knows.'

Carmen thinks about it. So people are as interchangeable as that. A little while ago she was the woman of his dreams, he poured out his feelings to her, he pounced on her and then he never wanted to see her again, and now another woman is effortlessly taking her place, harvesting the fruits that she so strenuously sowed. So much for the dream of being lady of the manor. Don't get yourself in a twist, you silly creature, she says to herself, it's exactly what you wanted. And now you're in a huff just because one of your impotent men has found someone else!'

David comes back with the coffee jug.

'So, what's up?' he asks, pouring the coffee.

'Stefan's got a new girlfriend, that reporter we saw on the news – do you remember? Attractive, with a cheeky short blonde haircut.'

David nods. 'Yes, I know the one, she was very good-looking. No wonder Stefan hung on to her.'

Don't you start, thinks Carmen.

'Yes, and he'd like to invite you both to dinner,' Elvira says and smiles.

Oh God! Carmen doesn't feel pleased, just revolted. Is she supposed to sit at the same table with a woman who's playing lady of the manor? And with Stefan, about whom she has pretty unpleasant memories? She looks at David. David looks back. 'Whatever you like, Carmen. Fine by me, but you don't have to.'

'Yes, Elvira, that's sweet, and tell him many thanks for the invitation, but really, it's too soon. I need a little time, too. And if I did come I'd rather Laura and Frederic came along as well so that it was all a bit more fun, you know?'

Elvira nods and picks up her coffee cup. 'I understand, Carmen. And Stefan will too.'

'And how's he dealing with his history? I mean, what is he
feeling now about what his family did to him?'

Elvira takes a sip and thoughtfully puts the cup back down. 'He's working on it. And in that respect I'd be really grateful for your help.'

Carmen raises her eyebrows briefly to warn Elvira. She isn't going to start talking about her psychotherapist, is she? But Elvira continues, 'If you've got an evening free, Carmen, we could talk about it in detail.'

Carmen nods and puts a slice of pie on her plate. She's still full from breakfast, but she liked the look of it anyway. 'So you're going to move into the castle with him?'

Elvira nods. 'Stefan mentioned the idea this morning at breakfast. He thought that with my disability and my poor health, I'd be better off in the castle. But it's all going a bit too fast for me. I like it there, but I want to keep my flat here. At least to begin with. So that I'd be more independent.'

'Great,' says Carmen delightedly, making Elvira laugh spontaneously. 'But I am pleased. What would I do here without you?'

'You've got me,' David interrupts with a hurt expression. Carmen blows him a kiss and laughs.

And Elvira says dryly, 'You're a man. It's not the same.'

For the first time in ages, Carmen had been able to enjoy a cosy breakfast on a normal Monday morning. David got up early, bought fresh rolls and butter and jam and laid the table while Carmen was still in the bath. Then they sat together and Carmen enjoyed such a blissful sense of companionship that she felt quite peculiar.

Now in the car she is able to think about the weekend. It was wonderful, just as she imagined spending time with a partner she loved. On Saturday afternoon, after Elvira had gone downstairs for her afternoon nap, they had gone to get Cain and then spent three hours or so tramping through the countryside, stopping off at a magical country inn on the way back. Carmen was almost spontaneously tempted to spend the night in one of the cosy rustic rooms, but without clean underwear and a toothbrush she figured it might be a bit difficult. 'Next weekend,' said David by way of consolation. It was the first time that Cain had spent the night at Carmen's, and it was Cain who woke them from their sleep on Sunday morning when he urgently needed to be taken out for a walk. At first Carmen was irritated, but once David was awake as well they laughed and made the best of it, and put on jeans and thick jackets and took him into the country. David had carefully chosen their destination, because after an hour's walk they ended up at another country inn, this time for a hearty country breakfast. The autumn sun was warm, and they were able to enjoy the morning sitting on a sheltered veranda. A little later eight horses were allowed out into the adjoining field, and Carmen watched, fascinated, as two very young foals jumped, bucked and frolicked over the meadow, fooling around with each other, then darting back to their mothers. This is how I'd like to live, she thought, and she immediately laughed at herself. Such nonsense. Fields and meadows, you can cope with that in your time off, but not in real life.

'Do you like horses?' David had asked her.

'I love nature as such – particularly horses. What girls – and women – don't?'

David had smiled, and when Carmen finally leaned back contentedly, the landlord had come over and said everything was hitched up. So Cain's full bladder that Sunday morning led to a ride in a horsedrawn carriage which made her feel almost like a little girl again. The horses trotted along the forest path in time, with Cain jumping along beside them, and David had his arm around her. She breathed in the scented air, listened to the clatter of hooves and felt immeasurably happy.

Carmen smiles. She notices, because she's stopped at a red light, and the driver of a car in the next lane is smiling back at her. She hadn't been smiling at him, but Carmen is so filled with happy memories that she nods back. Then the lights change, she turns her car and is alone with her thoughts again. David didn't come to the obligatory Sunday afternoon coffee with her parents yesterday either, but he was at her door on the dot of eight to take her out for dinner. And for their one-week anniversary he took her out to a three-star restaurant that she knew only from hearsay.

I'm having a great time, she says to herself as she drives to the parking-space in front of her office. There's a car parked there already, despite the big sign saying it's a private space reserved for her registration number. Okay, no need to get annoyed. She drives a street further down and finds an empty space. With a parking meter. So she'll have to move her car later on once the other person has left her space. She parks and gets out. The weather has got worse again, and a cold wind smelling of snow hisses around the corners. Carmen has put on a cashmere polo neck, jeans and thick shoes. Now she slips into her thick leather jacket and zips it up. Okay, it's not too far. She walks quickly, burrowing both hands into her deep pockets, and then she feels that strangely oppressive feeling that comes over her when she's in bed with David. Not that she wouldn't enjoy his caresses, but the way he reacts to her approaches gives her a funny feeling. She feels like a child, as she did when her mother would tell her off because of something naughty she'd done. Rejection, dismissal, restraint – it was all very painful. And she can't deal with it now, either. Especially when she hoped David would slowly open up to her. But last night it was all quite clear: it wasn't going to happen, he kept moving further and further away from her. And Sunday night could have been made for a new chapter in their relationship. The dinner and the wines had been wonderful, David had ordered a taxi so that they could enjoy everything to the full, they had joked and laughed, and were in love up to their ears. And then, once they got home, it was like a cold shower. He held her at a distance as though he had the plague from the waist down. I've got to call Isabella, she thinks as she reaches her office door, stopping briefly to think about something else. From outside the room looks very cosy. Britta is there already, she has switched on the desk lamps and is in the side-room making coffee. At least the little door is open. Carmen takes in the effect. From the street, the office consists of a glass façade, so that anyone passing by

can see the whole room. Despite the filing cabinets and computers, it exudes an inviting atmosphere. It is probably down
to the little details like pictures, flowers, a few ornaments
and the designer carpet. Carmen is happy. That's how it
should be – a place you're happy to come into. She walks in,
and Britta comes towards her with the full jug of coffee.

'Good morning, Frau Legg. Laura's called twice, she says it's
important but she wouldn't leave a message. She's going to call
back in a minute.'

'Good morning, Britta, thanks!' Carmen takes off her
jacket. It is complicated and troublesome for Laura to phone
from school, so if she has called her a few times already something must be up. 'And she didn't say anything else?' she asks,
just to check.

'Nothing, just that it's important.'

Carmen hangs up her jacket, pours herself a mug of coffee
and switches on her computer. Well, nothing to do but wait.

She digs up some client details that need working on, but
she can't concentrate. She looks at the clock a few times. Nine
thirty. Laura's next break won't be until ten. Or has anything
changed in the meantime? What could have happened? She
can't have had a miscarriage, can she? The idea sends her
nerves spinning. Should she call Frederic? He's sure to know.
But there's no point alarming him before . . . The phone rings.
Finally. 'I'll get it,' she says quickly to Britta, who is going
through the mail, and picks it up. Hope it's Laura!

'Legg Insurance, good morning.'

'At last. You were late this morning.'

'I know, Laura, someone was in my parking-space and I
had to find another one – tell me, what's up?'

'Your mother is ill, you've got to call her immediately, she
couldn't get through to you.'

'What's up . . .'

Laura adds quietly, 'It's not true, I just said it for the benefit
of my nosy colleagues around the corner. Have you got today's
paper in front of you? I'll just read it out to you quickly, listen:
Problems with potency, question mark, remedies from

grandmother's kitchen. How to get your man back into action. Maria Heitzer, phone number 3 96 66, full stop. Isn't that amazing? You've got to call her straightaway.'

Carmen doesn't know whether to laugh or not. 'Well Laura, that sounds a bit . . . a bit gruesome, really. Black magic, goat's blood and abracadabra.' She's said too much now, Britta is listening.

'Just don't get so worked up, you old warhorse, you're not going to . . . or you might. Go on, give her a call, you've nothing to lose.'

'Thanks, when you're right, you're right. Okay, Laura, it's sweet of you. When am I going to see you?'

'I'll call you, ciao, Carmen, got to get back,' and she adds loudly, 'and wish your mother a full recovery from me, do you hear, and that doctor's number is 3 96 66. He's strongly recommended, ciao!'

Ping, the receiver falls back on its cradle, and Carmen sits there with her head in her hand. Magic potions? She sees last night's situation in her mind's eye and hears Isabella saying, 'You want him potent.' So why not? It might be a way. Should she ask Isabella first? No. Why should she. Wasn't her practice going to call to arrange an appointment? But David was supposed to come along to that too, and she hasn't uttered a word about therapy to him. Maybe it's better to keep everything quiet. Whatever, she can't phone the witch lady while Britta's there. That would be the last straw. So she's got to get rid of Britta on some pretext or other, either that or dash to a phone box herself. Carmen glances over to Britta. She's going through the paper for announcements of deaths and births. She can hardly take the paper off her now, and she doesn't need to, because she's jotted down the number and the name.

'Have you had breakfast today, Britta?'

Britta holds her forefinger over the paper and looks up: 'Yes, thanks, I had a good breakfast with my boyfriend. Why do you ask?'

'I'd have asked you to go and get some croissants,' Carmen smiles to her.

273

'I'll get some for you if you're hungry!'

'No, I can't ask you to do that, I can always go and get them myself.'

'No, no, I'm happy to.'

Slavery, thinks Carmen, like in colonial times. 'No, no,' she says resolutely and gets to her feet. 'I'll do it myself. Would you like anything else, Britta? Some cake for this afternoon?'

Britta shakes her head and pats her belly. 'Now I have a boyfriend I eat too much anyway.'

'So everything's okay? Congratulations. Is it all okay?'

Britta beams. 'It's wonderful!'

It's true, Carmen thinks, you can see. She looks much prettier and more relaxed than she did before. And next to her I probably look like a wizened old crone. 'I'm really happy for you, Britta.' She goes and gets her jacket, and as she's leaving she sees that Britta is fighting back tears of emotion. I'm so preoccupied with myself that I only ever notice half of what's going on, she thinks. I'm a terribly selfish woman. Outside the man is getting into the car that's blocking her parking-space.

You don't get away that easily, thinks Carmen as she walks over. 'It would be nice if you would give a thought to your fellow human beings in future,' she says to the man of about fifty who is just about to close the door of his Mercedes.

He looks at her, irritated. 'Why do you say that? Are you collecting for something?'

Carmen can't help laughing. 'Yeah, I'm collecting excuses. You're in my parking-space. So what's yours?'

He looks at the wall in front of him. A white sign announces that this is a private parking space. 'Oh,' he says, genuinely surprised. 'I'm very sorry, I didn't see it, I was in such a hurry. I'll pay more attention in future.'

Carmen points to the door of her office. 'If you want to take out some insurance with me you can park here, for free. Is that a reasonable offer?'

He looks at her, with a rather spongy face, a big nose and bushy eyebrows, and laughs. 'That's a reasonable offer. I'll

come back to you on it?'

Carmen nods to him and walks on. Her mood has improved considerably already. Let's see what comes out of her call to Maria Heitzer!

There's a phone box on the corner. One of those unfortunate public affairs whose only major function is to be the object of wanton destruction. Carmen doesn't even bother opening the door. What she can see from outside is enough. A tattered phone book, wires where the receiver used to be, shattered panes of glass and, to top it all, a pile of human excrement in the middle of the footpath. Repelled, Carmen sets back off towards the town centre. What kind of people would do that, she wonders. What's going on in their minds? She walks faster, holding the collar of her jacket closed. It's really cold. The first snow must be coming. She walks for a good ten minutes before she sees the next phone box. By now she's near the main post office. If she'd known that she'd have sent Britta to the baker's. At least it's just around the corner.

She's in luck. The phone box may smell of old smoke, but otherwise it's intact. She puts in some money and then, with numb and excited fingers, she dials 3 96 66. She is greeted by an answering-machine. She can't have the woman calling her back at home. What if David was standing next to her? And it's not so good in the office, either. So her long walk has been in vain. She's about the slam the phone down, but decides to leave a message. 'Hello, Frau Heitzer, my name is Carmen Legg, I'm sorry not to have reached you, because if you called back . . .' Click, someone picks up the phone at the other end. So Frau Heitzer prefers to hear who's calling first. Interesting.

'Hello, Maria Heitzer speaking, Frau Legg, I'm sorry, but I get so many unspeakable phone calls that I have to filter them through the answering-machine.'

'Really? Because of potency problems? That's fascinating.'

'Yes, most people misunderstand, unfortunately, and want to be cured straightaway. By me! And you know, Frau Legg, that's not quite what I have in mind.'

Carmen laughs. 'Yes, I do understand. But it's quite a weird advertisement, Frau Heitzer, you must admit.'

'Okay, but there is a demand for it, I see that every day. What can I do for you?'

'Well, my problem is my boyfriend's impotence. He's suffered from it since a motorcycle accident three years ago, and I'm not sure now whether it's psychological, you know what I mean, or if it's physical. He's so determined to keep himself covered up below the waist that it may have had an effect on him – do you see what I mean?'

She opens the door to the phone box. The cold that floods in is still more agreeable than the smell.

'You mean he's repressing his urge, and that's why he can't do it?'

'That's what I don't know. The worst thing is that he won't let me anywhere near him, and I can't tell exactly what's up. I've tried to stop him being afraid of contact, but I simply can't. I've been to a psychotherapist already, but now I've started hoping there might be some other way . . .'

There is a pause, Maria Heitzer is clearly thinking. 'You know, I could sell you all sorts of things, but the case seems more complicated than that. I'll tell you honestly, if he's been seriously injured, my little remedies aren't going to do anything for him. They're really just for tired men who want to perk themselves up a bit.'

Carmen is disappointed, but she doesn't want to give up quite so easily. 'Couldn't we try anyway?'

'Of course you can try. And I'm happy to advise you. You'd have to drop by. And a consultation costs one hundred marks, I'll have to tell you that straightaway.'

'That's fine. When? And where are you?'

'Number 7 Marktstrasse, whenever you like.'

'That's no distance away. I'm in a phone box by the post office.' Carmen thinks quickly. She hasn't looked in her diary this morning. Had she arranged any meetings?

'Would you have time right now, Frau Heitzer? That is to say, I'd have to call my office first, and then I'd be able to tell you.'

'That's fine. I'll put the phone down now, and speak to you later.'

Britta, as kind as ever, quickly runs through her appointments and then tells her it isn't a problem. Klaus Wiedemann from the regional office is coming in the afternoon, but not until three. That old windbag, thinks Carmen. She phones Maria Heitzer and sets off. She feels a bit funny, like a child entering a fairy-tale land. She thinks of Hansel and Gretel. She's probably about to meet a witch for the first time in her life. On the phone she sounded quite normal, with a bright, alert voice, not croaking, not hoarse. But there must be young, pretty witches as well. She'll have red hair and freckles. Masses of freckles. Carmen grins at herself and almost misses number 7. The narrow house is part of a mediaeval terrace of about twenty houses painted ochre, madder and dark red. An arcade runs along it, sheltering the doors and shops beneath. On either side of number 7 a pharmacy and a baker have put out their displays. A broad flight of stone steps runs along the whole line of houses, connecting the arcade and the street. Carmen has only ever driven past the mediaeval terrace, but close up it looks very picturesque, almost a little Italian with its bright colours, Carmen thinks, walking up the wide steps to the door. A number of names, with Heitzer at the top in gothic script. Okay, thinks Carmen. She probably reads tarot cards and palms as well.

She rings the bell. Nothing happens. Then she notices that the door is ajar. She opens it. There is a dark hallway behind it, full of bicycles, tricycles and children's toys, and a narrow flight of stairs leads upwards. She goes in. There is a smell of dust, old beeswax and yesterday's leek soup. Heitzer was the name at the very top, suggesting that she lived in the attic. Carmen walks up floor after floor. On the fourth floor the door is open, and a woman of about forty-five, with a dark brown pony tail, is waiting for her. She is slim, wearing jeans and a loose oatmeal-coloured polo neck. Carmen shakes her hand, and likes the woman immediately.

'Do come in.' Maria Heitzer steps to one side and lets

Carmen walk in past her. Carmen is surprised. She had imagined a dark old flat, but she's standing in a bright loft studio
with a light parquet floor, and enormous room divided up
with a number of screens, sparsely but tastefully furnished, a
mixture of modern designer furniture and antiques.

'I like this,' says Carmen spontaneously. She likes it better
than her own flat. There's something free about it, she can
sense a hint of nonconformity, a disregard for bourgeois
norms. 'I'm glad,' says Maria, pointing to a big old wooden
table slightly to one side under one of the big studio windows.
It must be fantastic in winter when the snowflakes are practically falling on your head, Carmen thinks, and sits down
carefully on one of the narrow cherrywood chairs.

Maria sits down opposite her. The two women look at each
other in silence for a moment. Maria's narrow, not particularly
striking face, is dominated by slanted green eyes, which fas-
cinate Carmen.

'You've got real cat's eyes.'

'Do they disturb you?'

'On the contrary, I think they're very attractive. They're
extremely interesting eyes. They give you a, a . . .' Carmen
looks for the right word, thinks for a moment and then gets
the words out. 'They're how I would imagine a witch's eyes.'

Maria doesn't seem the slightest bit surprised, she smiles
gently revealing a row of even teeth. 'We always recognise
each other.'

Carmen doesn't say anything. Her blood rushes. What did
she say? We recognise each other? We witches recognise each
other? Goodness! She feels awkward all of a sudden. What
has she got herself into? Or is it true?

Maria has been waiting, saying nothing, just watching.

'I admit it, you've disconcerted me rather. I've never seen
myself as a witch before.'

'I'm surprised. Don't you ever think about yourself?'

Carmen's mouth is dry. A weird situation. Of course she
thinks about herself. Or doesn't she? 'I've always thought I
278 knew myself quite well.'

The green glimmer in the eyes opposite intensifies. 'You've always got what you wanted. You play with people, you try to bend them the way you want them. And it usually works. Where do you think that comes from? It's not just your pretty face! Or have you always thought it was?'

'I always thought I was lucky.'

'Typical woman,' laughs Maria. 'A man always explains his success by saying that he's simply better than other people, a woman always says she's just been lucky!' She changes the tone of her voice and speaks insistently. 'You aren't just lucky. Luck comes into it, but luck seeks its own way and finds the right people. Don't you see that? You have power, you are strong, you impose your will on other people. Maybe you don't notice it yourself, but that's how it is, that's how it works. Your inner power shows you the way. Not fate, not luck!'

Carmen feels very small. She can't feel any inner power at all at the moment. She's tiny, insecure, inconspicuous. 'If the world works as you say it does, then you're superior to me, I can certainly feel that!'

'This is where I live. What you feel is my aura. I'm the strong one here, or at least you feel that because this is my cave. Outside things would be different. Completely different if we were at your place.'

Carmen isn't convinced. The woman exudes something that she can sense almost physically, and which gets stronger the longer they spend sitting opposite each other.

'Can I ask you something about the subject at hand? What kind of remedies do you use, and how did you find them?'

Maria laughs. 'Our grandmothers weren't stupid. In many respects they were cleverer than we are. They had to rely on nature, because that was all there was. Nowadays we tend to turn to chemicals. Most people have lost their feeling for natural powers. Almost a hundred years ago my great-great-grandmother got hold of a book about the forces of nature, particularly in the sexual sphere. In those days women were particularly concerned with contraception, of course. But I suspect that if I'm correctly interpreting the underlined passages and the passages marked with a cross, I think my great-great-grandmother was more concerned with something else.' She laughs again. 'I suspect my great-great-grandfather was a bit of a sleepy character.'

'And you're going to give me something like that now?'

'I'll familiarise you with everything. Just a moment,' she stands up. 'Would you like something to drink? Water? Tea?'

'I'd love some tea, if it isn't any trouble.'

Maria, as she walks off, turns around again. 'That sentence doesn't suit you. Of course it's some trouble. But normally you wouldn't be interested in that. Am I right?'

Carmen nods. Yes, she's right. Why did she say it? She doesn't know. She only knows she finds this woman slightly weird.

A few moments later Maria comes back with a file and an old leather-bound book.

'Okay, this contains everything that may be able to help you.' She looks intensely at Carmen. 'This may perhaps be able to help you, assuming that your boyfriend has not suffered severe physical injury.'

Carmen nods. Maria goes on. 'Okay, this isn't just from Grandma's herb garden, there are also things that I can make for you, or things that you can buy in the shops. Some of them are pretty expensive.' She glances up, and her moss-green eyes fix on Carmen again.

'Yes,' Carmen hesitates, 'I haven't really thought about this. Can you give me an example?'

A kettle whistles somewhere. 'Hang on a second.' Maria jumps to her feet and comes back with a teapot. 'It'll have to draw for a moment,' she says, and fetches two cups and saucers of the finest porcelain. She puts a matching bowl filled with brown sugar next to them on the table.

'Okay.' She sits down again. 'Fine, a root of red ginseng, the Koreans have a state monopoly on it incidentally, will cost 1,000 dollars, you'll get grated deer penis from China for 1,500 dollars. Let's not even speak of powdered rhinoceros horn, not just because it's so expensive but because the rhinoceros is on the brink of extinction.'

Carmen nods. 'I wouldn't even think of rhinoceros, the idea of grated deer penis is revolting, and the ginseng's too expensive. Is there anything else?'

'Not as strong but effective nonetheless, according to popular wisdom, are pollen and oats, the unsaturated fatty acids in cod liver oil are supposed to thin the blood so that it flows more easily into the penis, and if you don't trust any of those, any sex shop will sell you Oriental Love Bonbons for twenty-two marks!'

Carmen shakes her head. 'I don't like any of those so much. It sounds too . . . too normal. I'd rather have some kind of mysterious potion that I can prepare, cook in his food or put under his pillow, something that's going to work every time!'

'Every time?' Maria laughs and shakes her head. 'Well, let's see.' She opens her book and leans back. 'I'll tell you what our great-great-grandmothers knew: *Coriander multiplies unchaste semen. Cress stimulates sexual desire. Watercress seed causes lust and immodesty.* And of flax it says: *Mixed with honey and pepper and enjoyed as a cake, it rouses the passions of love – and helps the cold man back into the saddle.*'

Carmen laughs and asks, 'Flax? What is that exactly?'

'Linseed, as in linseed oil? It's a thin-stemmed plant with pods.' She looks up. 'Will you pour us some more? Otherwise it'll get too bitter.'

While Carmen looks after the teapot, Maria goes on reading, '*Valerian, strewn in men's beds, excites the senses, oil of nutmeg applied to the penis stimulates venery . . .*'

'Venery?' Carmen interrupts again.

'Sexual intercourse,' Maria explains and goes on, '*Pepper puts the man back in the saddle, with the woman down below.*'

'You mean with him on top and her underneath?' Carmen wants to know.

'Supposedly males and females only ever had intercourse in the missionary position. I don't believe it, because even cavemen had different models.'

281

Carmen laughs. 'Sorry, I interrupted you.'

'*Anis rouses to conjugal acts. Mugwort placed under the bed brings unchaste desire. Galangal root* – pay attention now! – *if eaten or placed on the genitals, means intercourse twelve times in a row!*'

'What's that root called again?' Carmen stops mid-pour.

'Galangal,' Maria repeats.

'I'll have to remember that. Sounds good. What else is there?'

'*In the harems of Constantinople, hemp is given to weak men. But be careful, if used to excess it has the opposite effect.*'

Carmen grins. 'We've got the opposite effect already . . .' and sips at her tea.

Maria takes a sip as well and then continues. '*Hildegard of Bingen writes that after taking fenugreek, a healthy man will be consumed with lusty desire. Herb Paris has a power that strengthens the member in venery. Ginger is also good, as a root it helps against weakness of the sexual organs.*'

'It all sounds great! A friend of mine used to swear by radishes. Are they any good?'

Maria laughs and shuts the book. 'Wind can cause erections. Beans, onions and leek have the same effect. Add a couple of beers and a clove of garlic, and off you go!'

'Okay for you, perhaps,' Carmen shivers. 'I don't much fancy erections caused by flatulence. Were any of the remedies you mentioned really dependable? Would they work in normal circumstances?'

'That's what some of my customers claim. But of course I don't know if it's faith or if it's really the herb. There are more powerful things. Many people swear by a potion of powdered cantharides, also known as Spanish fly. The Spanish fly is a beetle, and a pretty dangerous one at that – 0.6 grams is enough to cause poisoning, 2–3 grams are fatal. If you want to risk it, there are pills with traces of cantharides, called *pillules galantes.*

'Hmm.' Carmen leans back. 'I'm not sure. I don't really want to poison him. Isn't there some harmless remedy that works? Couldn't I boil him up some kind of broth?'

'Thessalonian women swear by wild orchid root. They boil them up in hot goat's milk – but do you think your friend would drink that of his own accord?'

Carmen shakes her head.

'Then yohimbine might be the best thing for him. It's extracted from the bark of the yohimbi tree, and the natives of West Africa have known it to be a powerful aphrodisiac for a very long time.'

'I see, and how does it work, this yo . . . yohim . . .'

'Yohimbi,' says Maria helpfully. 'It has hormonal effects on certain messengers in the stimulants to the nervous system, and it also stimulates the sympathetic nervous system.'

'I see, and what does that mean?'

'It encourages the flow of blood to the pelvic area, particularly to the penis.'

Carmen smiles, relaxed. 'That sounds good. I like that one. How can I get hold of yohimbine?'

'Yohimbine is available in various dosages, and for some of them you need a prescription. But your psychotherapist might be able to help you there. Or you could try it in a weaker form.'

'Can you get hold of that for me?'

Maria hesitates briefly, then looks at her watch. 'It depends, when do you need it for?'

'Tonight.'

'You're in a hurry!'

Carmen nods and looks at Maria with her head tilted to one side. 'I just want to know. And I can't wait. And I'd also like some of that herb that you scatter under the bed. What was that one?'

'Valerian.'

'Yeah, that one. Can I get it in the health food shop? And that other plant, the one you put in cakes?'

'Flax?'

'Exactly.'

'I don't think you can get that here.'

'Can you get hold of it?'

283

'Of course. That's the service on offer. The only thing I don't know is whether I'll be able to do it at such short notice.'

'The main thing is that you know where to get it. The rest will happen of its own accord. Okay, listen. I'll cook him up a proper three-course dinner. He can have a cress soup as a starter, you can get cress anywhere, that's not a problem. Then he has a main course with – what?'

'I'd suggest asparagus. Asparagus with hollandaise sauce, heavily spiced with lovage. It's another aphrodisiac. And boiled potatoes.'

'Fine. It's just – where am I going to get asparagus at this time of year?'

'I'll get it for you. It'll cost you, though.'

'That's okay. And then a flax cake for dessert. Or what would you suggest?'

Maria pours another cup of tea, and her smile makes her eyes even more feline.

'I'd take some cinnamon ice cream, cinnamon's excellent, and I'd put a mixture of honey, flax, crushed galangal, crushed ginger and chopped almonds on top it. Then you could garnish it with a few bits of stem ginger. It looks good and tastes fantastic. I've tried it myself!'

'Really?' Carmen opens her eyes wide. 'And? Did it work?'

Maria laughs. 'Unbeatable!'

'Okay, and then valerian, and – what was the other thing for under the bed?'

'Mugwort.'

'Exactly, and you put that under the bed and under the pillow. And in the meantime he gets a little dose of yo . . . you know the thing I mean, yohimbine, yeah? What do you think?'

'He'll either keel over, or his cock will hit the ceiling!'

'Well, at least I'll know. That's fantastic of you, Frau Heitzer. You've been a great help. Can you do all that for this evening?'

'It's going to be tight. I'll have to make a lot of phone calls and drive a few miles before I've got everything.'

'Don't worry about the cost, if you've got everything by this evening I'll add a hundred-mark note to whatever it is.'

'And if my magic arts are insufficient?'

'That's the risk I have to take.'

'Okay, agreed. But I'll have to get started right now!'

Carmen gets to her feet. 'I've got to get back too. When can I drop by again?'

'About seven?'

Maria Heitzer walks Carmen to the door. Carmen thinks of something else. 'And to drink? What works?'

'Almond milk.'

'Doesn't go so well with the meal!'

Maria laughs. 'Take some champagne. That goes with everything and will boost the effect!'

Carmen dances her way down the dark stairs. She is in thoroughly high spirits, and wants to get down to cooking straightaway. She hopes she can get it all done on her own. On the bottom step she trips over something and loses her balance. She tries to support herself on the wall, slips down the rough plasterwork on her right hand and lands heavily on her knees. A skateboard crashes to the floor next to her. In her euphoria she hadn't noticed the thing by the stair. 'Oof.' Carmen gets up slowly and sits back on the bottom step. Her right hand is grazed, and her left wrist hurts. Her knees are okay, and her trousers are unscathed. Okay, that was the first cold shower on the way to bliss, she thinks, getting slowly to her feet. She walks to the front door and opens it. She studies the palm of her hand in daylight. Then she carefully moves her left hand. It really hurts. How is she going to prepare all those roots and herbs if she can't move her hand properly? She'll have to ask Laura. Laura's better at cooking anyway. She's studied it, apart from anything else. Okay, then, she'll sort everything out somehow or other. She wraps the thick jacket around her, folds her arms across her chest and sets off. It's cold, really cold. She has cold ears and a cold nose, and briefly wonders if she should take a taxi. Then she rejects the idea. The fresh air will do her good, clear her head. And she needs a clear head now. What did she say? A hundred-mark note as a bonus? She must be off her head. Throwing her hard-earned money at some alchemist. Who knows what herbs Maria used in her tea. She'd never have thought of anything like that if she'd been sober. My God, a whole love-menu for David, if he only knew! A *menu surprise*, a *menu à la Aphrodite*. Laura will laugh herself hoarse. And maybe Elvira can copy it for Stefan and his new reporter girlfriend. Maybe she should copyright the recipe. The percentages alone would make her a millionairess, given the potential demand. If you consider that one man in ten is supposed to have potency problems, given three million men and a price of – let's say – ten marks per recipe . . . She calculates and thinks some more, and calculates, and by the time she's reached her office she's sure she's going to publish an encyclopaedia. Only after she's tried out the recipe herself, of course. But if she's going to try everything . . . she'll have to start coming up with some antidotes. Gingerbread is supposed to make men sleepy, she remembers that from her mother. At Christmas she always used to say that dad couldn't get enough of it. On the other hand, she thinks, German Christmas cakes must be the purest aphrodisiacs. Coriander, cloves, almonds, cinnamon, honey, pepper – they're all in there! She smiles to herself and opens the door to her office. A client is sitting with Britta. When he turns around Carmen recognises him. It's the Mercedes driver from earlier.

'What a surprise,' says Carmen, holding out a hand.

'Yes, I had a little time, and you caught me at the right moment this morning. I was just coming from my lawyer. I'm planning some personal and professional changes, and I would welcome your advice. And your colleague has been a great help to me for the past hour. I'm already a great deal better informed.'

'That's excellent!' Carmen looks out the window. 'Where's your car? We agreed that you could park your car in my space if you came to the office.' He grins, his dense eyebrows practically colliding. 'I didn't want to push things!' Carmen nods to him and hangs up her jacket.

'If there are any questions, Britta, I'd be happy to help.'

'Thanks, everything's fine so far.'

Carmen sits down at her desk. There are three Post-it notes in Britta's tidy handwriting.

10.10: David called;
10:30: 2nd call from David;
11.00: Call from David. Please call back.
Peter called. Will call again.
Psychotherapeutic practice rang: appointment
tomorrow, Tuesday, 12.00.

Carmen glances over at Britta, who nods to her. Carmen is grateful for her discretion.

As soon as they are alone again, Carmen picks up the phone. David answers immediately. 'I'm sorry I disturbed Britta so often, but I had to speak to you!'

'You did? Why? Has something happened?' Carmen involuntarily holds her breath.

'Yes, I have this indescribable longing for you! It's driving me out of my mind!'

'Really!' She takes a deep breath. 'That's fantastic. That tallies exactly with what I was going to say. I'd like to cook us something nice for dinner. Would you like that?'

'You can cook?'

Carmen laughs. 'I could try to for you, or would you rather I didn't?'

'Of course I'd be honoured, but I'm equally happy to bring something along.'

'Don't say that, not when I'm going to so much trouble!'

'You're right. I'd be delighted. Shall we say about nine? I can't make it earlier than that.'

'That's fine. Till then!' She blows a kiss down the telephone and then hangs up. With any luck Maria Heitzer will have everything ready in time. It would be a disaster if half of it wasn't there! She carefully feels her wrist. Moves her hand in a circle and from top to bottom. Better already. Should she ring Laura anyway . . .? She thinks about her menu again.

Cress soup. No idea, never cooked it. She'll have to get hold of a recipe. Potatoes aren't a problem, neither is asparagus. She can buy cinnamon ice cream, she'll cobble together the sauce somehow, she can get all the ingredients. She still has to get champagne and candles, lest her plan should falter in the light of day. Could Britta . . .?

'Britta, are you a good cook?'

Britta looks up in astonishment, but lately little that Carmen does surprises her. She nods. Of course, Carmen could have assumed as much.

'Have you ever cooked cress soup? Would you happen to have a recipe for it?'

Britta nods and smiles. 'Yes, we love it, we eat it a lot.' Listen to that, thinks Carmen. 'It's very simple. For two people, take . . .'

Carmen picks up a pen and note-pad. 'Slowly, please!'

'. . . two tomatoes, an onion, one and a half tablespoons of flour, a pint and a half of beef or chicken stock, a stock cube will do if you don't have any fresh, two bunches of cress and cream or crème fraiche, about a mug full. And then the yolk of an egg, cayenne pepper, salt and nutmeg. And a bit of white wine if you like.'

'It sounds good. And how do I cook it?' Carmen sits with her pen to the ready.

'Okay, I put the tomatoes in boiling water, then pour cold water over them, skin them and cut them into little pieces. And take the core out, of course.'

'Of course!' agrees Carmen, underlining it twice.

'Then finely chop the onions and brown them in the butter until they're transparent. Dust them with the flour and let them sweat briefly – don't forget to stir them. Then add the beef stock and let it boil for a few minutes, but don't let it get too hot – yes, and then keep aside a few leaves of the cress as a garnish and purée the rest with the hand-blender and add. Do you have a mixer?'

'Yes.' Her Christmas present from her mother last year, which everyone thought was so terribly funny.

'And then stir in the crème fraiche or cream. Season to taste with cayenne pepper and salt, and finally whisk in the egg yolk. But you've got to be careful the soup doesn't boil. When you serve, add the diced tomatoes to the soup bowls, which should have been warmed in advance, pour the soup over them and garnish with the rest of the cress. Simple!'

'Simple!' repeats Carmen. 'It sounds very complicated for such a simple little soup.'

Britta laughs. 'But it's worth it. It tastes fantastic.'

She really seems to know something about it, Carmen thinks, and asks, 'What did Peter want, by the way?'

'He didn't leave a message. But he's going to call later.'

Okay, thinks Carmen, I'd better not go near the phone or the door this evening. That would be a real laugh, if he burst in when the soup was being seasoned. Now I'll call Isabella and confirm the appointment. With any luck, by tomorrow lunchtime I'll have persuaded David to go of his own free will. If everything goes according to plan it should all work like a dream, like clockwork!

Carmen puts five hundred marks on Maria's wooden table, and leaves carrying a basket full of vegetables and herbs. One hundred marks consultation, one hundred marks as a bonus, one hundred marks for the one hundred miles she drove and two hundred marks for the magical ingredients. If Isabella sends me a bill as well I'm skint, thinks Carmen, as she carefully walks down the wooden steps. She presses the little old-fashioned light-switch on every floor. She isn't going to take a tumble this time, that much she's sure of. There's nothing in her way. She emerges safe and sound and runs down the damp stone steps to her car, which is parked on a double-yellow line. Her leather soles slip on the pavement but this time she is just able to catch herself. Her heart skips a beat. This place is under a spell!

Once she's at home, Carmen feverishly unpacks her booty. She hasn't much time, it's already half past seven. So,

champagne into the freezer, peel the asparagus and get everything ready for cooking, mix the sauce for the cinnamon ice
cream, put on the soup and quickly lay the table, whip into
the bathroom, shower, put on some sexy underwear, little
black number over the top, open the door, greet, eat, frenzied
passion, into bed.

Everything is clear and ordered in her head. All that's missing is the execution.

For the asparagus she uses the potato-peeler, and that
doesn't take long. She'd almost forgotten the potatoes
themselves. She peels the potatoes too, and that takes more
time than she'd expected. She needs another big cooking pot.
Okay, the roots. Maria has pulverised them already, thank
God, she would have had no idea how to grind them down in
such a short time. She empties all the little labelled bags into
a bowl. At first it's an indefinable, unappetising little pile.
Carmen pours the honey over it. It flows stubbornly out of
the jar and covers everything. Then she takes a fork and
slowly folds the honey into the mixture, until she has a solid,
resistant mass. She tries some on the end of her fork. It tastes
mostly of honey. You can taste the almonds and the ginger a
little, but they're not overwhelming. Is there a way of pepping
it up somehow? A shot of cognac? But maybe cognac's the
antidote. She could quickly call Maria, but five hundred
marks is enough for one day. Who knows what a phone consultation is going to cost. And the mixture is going to be fine
with the ice cream. Now the hollandaise sauce. She bought it
ready-made from the delicatessen, so it won't take long. And
so to the soup.

She looks at the clock. Nearly half eight. Time's flying. So
where's the recipe? She runs to her handbag. In her haste she
can't find it, and furiously empties out her whole bag. It isn't
there. Is it in her trouser pocket? She feels all her pockets. No.
Left it in the office? Probably. Can she call Britta? Hardly. Too
time-consuming. And she might be at her boyfriend's. And
she doesn't have a phone number for him. Come on, my girl,
you wrote it down, so concentrate. She looks in her shopping

bag. The ingredients will remind her. Look, there it is, the missing piece of paper. Of course, it makes sense, she used it when she was shopping. Okay. Off we go. I'll have to be careful with the cress, not cook it for too long else it'll lose all its active ingredients, and that would never do. Carmen juggles feverishly with pots and bowls, and at twenty to nine she runs out to lay the table.

Around the big white plates and in the middle of the table she puts brightly woven garlands of flowers, set off excellently on the black lacquered table-top. She lays cutlery for the three courses, arranges two silver candlesticks, lights the tall candles, puts two white cloth napkins in unusual napkin rings made of china flowers, to match the garlands. Now the champagne glasses, gently, gently, mind they don't break, and then she runs into the bathroom, throws her trousers and pullover and underwear into the washing basket, get them away, out of sight, showers at top speed, wraps a bath-towel loosely around herself and puts on a little evening make-up. Not too much, but enough to suggest a celebration.

Three minutes to nine. If he rings the doorbell now it's going to be terrible. Her hold-ups don't want to go on over her damp legs, she pulls and twists – and immediately a ladder runs from her knee to her heel. Carmen is close to tears, and pulls the stocking down. Now? Has she got another pair? Stockings fly one by one out of her stocking drawer until she's found a replacement pair. This time she calms her feverish fingers. Slowly, slowly, you'll do more harm than good – finally, they fit. Now the black lace body. She reflects that this evening's dinner, with champagne and all the ingredients, cost more than this exquisite piece of lingerie, which she thought about for a week before buying – she shakes her head to herself. Carmen, Carmen, you're round the bend. Never mind! She takes the stockings which are now spread wildly across the floor and indiscriminately stuffs them back into the drawer. Now the dress, the zip gets caught over her shoulderblades, it would have to be the one place that you can't reach on your own, ah – got it, now the high-heeled shoes, back into the bathroom, perfume, hair brushed until the red sparks fly, relaxed smile on the face, and back into the kitchen. Hope the asparagus won't have cooked for too long and the potatoes won't be falling to pieces. And hope he's on time, or the cress soup will be ruined.

There's a ring at the door. For a fraction of a second her heart stops, then her face reddens. She's sure to have forgotten something important, everything's sure to go wrong – she presses the buzzer, opens the door a crack and stands behind it. The light on the stairs goes on, she hears his footsteps, light, quick, masculine. Her pulse hammers, the blood rushes in her ears. Why is she so excited? He's the one that's supposed to be! Him, not her! That Maria's a witch. Somehow everything's the wrong way round. She's worked up to fever pitch even before the soup. The door is pushed open slightly, and Carmen steps forward. David is standing in front of her in a black cape, with a smoking jacket underneath, a white silk scarf around his neck, a top hat on his head and he is carrying nine long-stemmed roses.

'A shame we haven't known each other for longer,' he says by way of greeting. 'One for every day! You look ravishing, Carmen, wonderful!' He kisses her over the flowers.

Carmen laughs: 'You don't look so bad yourself! It really suits you! Come in!'

David twinkles his eyes at her and walks past her. Now that he's moving, she can see the red silk lining. Carmen looks at him, he looks like Dracula, really he does, and it gives him a weird and attractive quality. His blond hair and angular features in the shade of his top hat, really, the whole outfit suits him. With a flourish he takes off his cape and hangs it in the wardrobe, and puts his top hat on the little chest of drawers in the corridor.

'I wanted to bring a violinist, but I thought it might bother you.' He smiles and takes her in his arms. He's right there, thinks Carmen. Has he guessed? His hand slides down her back to her bottom and back up again.

They gently rub noses, then Carmen detaches herself from

him and walks on ahead. 'If the count would like to come in, the housemaid will serve dinner!'

David stops in the doorway. The table is solemnly lit, and Carmen has dimmed the other lamps. Alexis Weissenberg is playing Frédéric Chopin, and the piano concerto matches the mood. 'Carmen, what are you doing, you're casting a spell over me,' he says with a shake of his head.

'Just wait,' Carmen laughs. 'But first I'd be grateful if you'd open the bottle. No, don't come into the kitchen. Just sit down. I'll bring the bottle and two bowls of soup.' And bread, she thinks as she goes out, damn, I've forgotten the baguettes! But she has thought of ice-cubes. The kitchen is in total chaos. Carmen takes the bottle out of the freezer, puts it in the silver ice bucket and tips the ice-cubes over it. She carries everything in quickly, dashes back to her soup, which is on a gentle flame and is still trying to climb over the edge of the pot. Carmen pours soup into the two prepared bowls, garnishes them and then carefully carries them out. Let the game begin, round one, she thinks. And at the same time she remembers that she was going to scatter mugwort and valerian under the bed and under his pillow. But she didn't see the herbs anywhere – could they have been in those light brown paper bags? Did she inadvertently put them in the dessert?

David is looking at her expectantly, and Carmen imagines that in her short, tight dress, with her high heels and loose, full-bodied hair, the effect she creates must be pretty alluring. 'You look almost impossibly beautiful,' David says, and Carmen thinks, if he's so fascinated by my appearance I could have managed without all this fuss and greeted him with a pizza instead.

'I'm glad,' she says and puts the plate down.

'Now I'm excited,' smiles David, waiting until she's sat down.

'Me too,' she says from her bottom of her heart and watches him carefully dip his spoon in it.

'Ah, cress soup! I love this!'

293

Ah, thinks Carmen, and what about the effect? Should I have served him some radish?

The soup is delicate and creamy. Heavens, Carmen is astonished herself. How on earth did she manage that? Maybe she's a talented cook and she just didn't know? They raise their glasses and look at each other.

'I'd like it to stay like this for ever.' The candle-light flickers over David's face and he looks at her intensely.

'Me too,' says Carmen, secretly crossing her fingers. It's going to get better, David, much better, she silently begs, and then she remembers the two herbs she meant to put in the bed. She'll have to look and find them, and get them into the bedroom in time!

'You won't believe it, but Stefan's company called me today. They want to build another jeweller's shop, and we're in the running to do it. It's promising. I have a sense that Stefan's looking after us. Do you think that could be possible?'

Carmen looks up in surprise. 'What makes you think that?'

'Someone else called today, on the recommendation of Baron von Kaltenstein, he said. Serious business, a new bank. Stefan Kaltenstein had recommended us because we had experience of high-security buildings, and security and modern architecture can go well together.'

Carmen lowers her spoon. 'Oh, David, that would be wonderful. I'm so happy for you. For us. Stefan will be recommending you because he thinks you're good. But if you really want to know I could ask Elvira. But not today,' she smiles at him, and pouts her lips into a kiss.

David reaches across the table for her hand. 'Okay, if we get the commission, let me take you to the Caribbean over New Year, or the Maldives, or heli-skiing in Canada or to the Hospiz at St Christoph on the Arlberg in Austria – or whatever you like.'

'Oh yes, that would be great. Let's do that anyway, even without Stefan's commission. Maybe not quite that extreme, but two weeks away somewhere, okay?'

David nods with a smile. She feels such warmth for him, as

he sits so elegantly opposite her, that she almost wants to run around the table to embrace him. How can you be so madly in love with someone after such a short time? Two weeks ago she didn't even know David. Now she can't imagine being without him.

'What was that about the Arlberg? I've only ever been skiing in Switzerland, and on the Arlberg I only know Zürs and Lech. What was that you said about a Hospiz?'

David pushes the empty soup bowl away from him and leans back. 'Yes, the Arlberg Hospiz goes back over six hundred years. It's now a wonderful, very comfortable first-class hotel in St Christoph, and it's also the seat of the Brotherhood of St Christopher. Have you heard of it?'

Carmen shakes her head. 'Would you like some more soup?' Is it having an effect? It certainly is for her. She's completely swept away. Or could that be the champagne?

'Love some!' Carmen takes his plate, sweeps out and pours in the rest from the soup-pot. At the same time she looks in the basket for mugwort and valerian. There it is, in that brown bag at the bottom. She opens it quickly and checks it. Good. On the way to the bedroom she serves David the soup. 'I'll be right back, carry on eating, and then tell me about that brotherhood. The only fraternities I know are the Lions and the Rotary Club.'

She stops by the bed. How's it supposed to work if she scatters it under the bed? The mattress is far too far from the floor. Were beds different in the past? No, they weren't right on the floor, were they? So it must be okay. So – and now, which side? He's always slept on the left. She empties the bag under the left-hand side, scatters the herbs with her fingers and grabs a handful to place under the pillow. Then she hides the bag away, puts on a bit more lipstick in the bathroom and walks back to the table.

'It's really excellent. Did you cook it yourself, or did you buy it?'

'Fresh herbs, my darling, all fresh! Do you like it?'

The soup bowls are both empty, and she carries them into

the kitchen. 'I'll be right back, I'm just taking care of our main course.'

'What are we having?'

'Asparagus with hollandaise sauce with lovage and boiled potatoes.'

'Goodness, asparagus at this time of year? That's amazing. Is it fresh too?'

'Of course,' she calls from the kitchen.

'Where did you get it?'

'Connections, my darling, connections. Are you ready for the second course? The asparagus is just about ready!'

'Lovely.'

Carmen puts it on a plate with the boiled potatoes, and pours the sauce into a gravy-boat. Then she carries it all carefully in on a tray.

'Let me help you.' David stands up.

'Don't you dare, stay where you are.'

She puts it down in front of him, fills her own plate and sits down again.

'To the cook.' David raises his glass.

To Maria, thinks Carmen and clinks glasses. It tastes just as good as it would in a restaurant. Really good. Carmen is delighted that everything is working out so well.

'So what's the story about this brotherhood?'

'Well, it was founded more than six hundred years ago up in the mountains, when Heinrich Findelkind, a foundling – as his name suggests – from Kempten built the first shelter on the Arlberg Pass. Today the brotherhood supports, among others, mountain farmers and families in need. For example, when eighteen workers were killed in a rock-fall during the building of the Arlberg road tunnel, the brotherhood supported the sixty-four children they left behind. They received financial support until they were ready to support themselves.'

'Quite a sensible brotherhood, then. Just for men? Just for Austrians?'

'On the contrary. It has members of the aristocracy from all around the world, including Queen Beatrix of the Netherlands and her husband Prince Klaus and her son Konstantin, Princess Juliana of the Netherlands and Prince Bernhard, King Harald and Queen Sonja of Norway, Prince Hans-Adam and Princess Marie-Aglae of Liechtenstein, and, from Japan, Prince Mikasa Tomohito. And also people like you and me.'

'Heavens above, the things you know. Are you a member?'

'Not yet, but I'm interested, and if we really do go skiing there, I'll be able to join. And so can you, if you like.' Carmen is pleased to see him pouring more sauce on his asparagus. 'Your asparagus is excellent, darling, and the sauce tastes somehow, I don't know – different. How did you make it?'

'I just pepped it up with a few herbs.'

'Great. You must give me the recipe for Martin!'

Carmen laughs. Gay Martin, he would have a surprise. 'Just wait for the dessert, it's the best bit.'

'Is that you then?' His eyes flash and he runs his hands through his blond hair.

'If you like,' says Carmen flirtatiously.

David laughs.

When Carmen carries in her cinnamon ice cream with its concocted honey sauce, she is really exited. She put the yohimbine pill in a piece of ginger in the middle of David's cinnamon ice cream. Don't get the bowls mixed up, whatever you do. She puts hers down first and then sits down with David's bowl on his lap. 'Mouth open, eyes closed, taste!' She runs the dessert spoon lightly over the cinnamon ice cream and then puts the prepared piece of ginger on the top.

'Will you be cross with me if I don't like ginger?' David looks at her and the spoon.

Oh how ridiculous!

'Just one, please, just try it. You won't taste the ginger in the sauce. You can put the other two pieces aside. But I've gone to so much trouble!'

'Just because it's you, and because I have complete trust in your culinary arts . . .' He closes his eyes and opens his

mouth. Carmen takes a deep breath and puts the spoon carefully in. He chews and swallows and then looks at her. 'It
tastes really quite lovely with the cinnamon ice cream.'

'Try the sauce!'

She mixes the ice cream and the sauce together. 'Mouth
open, my darling!'

He rolls his eyes with pleasure. 'Mmm, that's delicious.
Fantastic. A mixture of summer heat and Christmas bells. It
tastes a bit like those little cakes we have at Christmas. You'll
have to give Martin the recipe for these too.'

Carmen grins and kisses him. 'I'll have to get back to my
seat, my ice cream's melting!'

She hardly has any sauce on her ice cream, a bit, for the
taste, but David should be starting to reap the benefit. Is he
changing yet? Is anything happening? They talk about everything under the sun, about Stefan, his abduction and his new
girlfriend. In the meantime she brings him a second bowl of
ice cream, and then she asks about Rilke.

'What made you think of Rilke? Why did you take so much
trouble with that incredible card? Imagine if I had been a
quite different woman. Then it would all have been for nothing. Imagine if you'd met someone quite different!'

'Well, the crucial thing was that you were looking for an
impotent man, and I was able to supply one of those, and then
of course I knew it would be you. I imagined that incredible
figure, that full hair, the slim, beautiful legs, that wicked
smile, the radiance of your eyes – of course I wanted to go
walking with you in the autumn. And the winter. And the
summer. And the spring. Year after year!'

'As you said. But your card really bowled me over.
Particularly because Rilke is my favourite poet. Do you know
his "Love-Song"?

'How shall I hold my soul, that it may not
be touching yours? How shall I lift it then
above you to where other things are waiting?
Ah, gladly would I lodge it, all-forgot,

with some lost thing the dark is isolating
on some remote and silent spot that, when
your depths vibrate, is not itself vibrating.
You and me – all that lights upon us, though,
Brings us together like a fiddle-bow
Drawing *one* voice from two strings it glides along.
Across what instrument have we been spanned?
And what violinist holds us in his hand?'

'O sweetest song.' Carmen completes the poem. They look
at each other in silence.

'I really think that two people have sought and found each
other here,' David says quietly after a while.

Carmen gets to her feet and walks around the table. She sits
on his lap and wraps her arms around his neck.

'Would you mind if I took off my jacket?'

'Be my guest!'

Carmen gets to her feet, as does David, who drapes his
jacket neatly over a chair, taking the opportunity to fill the
two champagne glasses. He holds Carmen's out to her. They
stand facing each other, the white of his shirt standing out
against his brown skin, his green tie gleaming. Carmen can
hardly restrain herself. She wants to throw him on the floor
here and now and hurl herself at him. This stuff's working on
me, damn it, rather than him, she thinks. Completely the
wrong way round! They clink glasses and drink, and then
David puts the two glasses back down. He takes her gently in
his arms and kisses her, running one hand along her body,
down to her bottom and back up again, slowly, arousing.
Carmen can hardly bear it. She presses herself against him.
But she doesn't feel anything. Don't get excited, she warns
herself, or he'll go into retreat again. Give yourself some time,
don't expect too much from him. At the same time she thinks,
if it doesn't work today, it's never going to! He nibbles at her
earlobe and then starts to unzip her dress. She feels his hand
on her back. Her body is on fire. The dress falls to the floor
with a quiet rustle, and now she is standing in front of him in

her black lace body, her black hold-up stockings and her high-heeled shoes. He kisses her on the mouth, then on the neck, then he falls slowly to his knees before her, moving his face over her breasts until his head rests in her lap. She feels him gently opening the poppers of her lace body with one hand. She is almost fainting with desire.

'The bedroom, David, please,' she whispers. He rises to his feet, takes her in his arms, carries her to her bed and lies down beside her. She starts undressing him. Loosens his tie, unbuttons his shirt. He takes off his shoes and socks and then turns to face her. He is lying on the wrong side, damn it, thinks Carmen. He should be on the other side of the bed. Otherwise those herbs are going to work on me rather than him. She kisses him, he passionately responds, and then she rolls over him to the other side.

Did she feel something there? Can it be possible? No, he's reacting exactly as he always does. If he suddenly had something in his trousers he'd be over the moon . . . So he couldn't. Not yet. It may yet come! At any rate, he's all over her as never before. He's almost whipping her into a frenzy, and he seems to be not far away himself. They roll around on the bed, she clings to him, he is almost brutal in his physical declarations of love. Carmen moans, she wants him now, and it's driving her mad that there isn't even a twitch, that he doesn't finally remove his trousers and take her there and then.

This mixture of expectation and disappointment is driving her completely crazy. Why isn't that valerian working? He's lying right on top of it! It must work! David seems to be going utterly wild, but it isn't having any effect on his manhood. It's probably having an effect on his head, on his nervous system, on whatever. It would drive you mad! Then he abruptly leaps to his feet and dashes to the toilet.

The door closes, and Carmen sits up. What's up now? Is he ill? She looks around. What does it look like here? There's green stuff all over the crumpled sheet. Where has that come from? She looks over at David's pillow. One of them has moved it in the throes of passion, and scattered the herbs all over the bed. Carmen panics. She tries to pick them all up, but she's far too slow, so she pulls the sheet away, balls it up with its valerian and mugwort and stuffs it in the washing basket, along with the jeans and the cashmere pullover. She is about to put on a fresh sheet when she hears the toilet door opening again. David comes in, stands in the doorway for a moment, looks at her with an impenetrable expression and then goes back into the bathroom. 'I'm sorry, I suddenly felt ill. I've got to brush my teeth. And perhaps I should really take a shower at the same time.'

Fine, thinks Carmen, so that's how the evening goes. He's puking up all that lovely dinner I cooked him. Impossible. She'll have something to say to Maria. But it's funny, why does she feel so good? Maybe it wasn't the food, but that pill. Was the dosage too high? What was that she said – toxic effects after 0.6 grams, death after 2 or 3? He's not going to die on me! She runs into the bathroom, where David is scrubbing away at his teeth. 'Sorry, David, I'm really sorry. Is it bad? Is it better? Is there anything I can do for you? Make you some tea or something?'

He really does look pale.

'My whole body's in revolt. I feel as if I've been plugged in to the mains. I don't know what's wrong with me. I'll just have a shower and then come to bed.'

'It can't be the food,' Carmen says, trying to justify herself, 'I feel fine.'

'Something must have gone down the wrong way. Maybe it was just too much honey. I don't know. Don't worry about it, the meal was fantastic, and you're a dream. And I'm feeling better already.'

On the way back to her room it occurs to Carmen that the yohimbine pill has nothing whatsoever to do with Spanish fly. Reassured, she smooths down the bed, takes another sip of champagne, takes off the rest of her clothes and lies down. When David comes back to the room they cuddle up together, but Carmen knows: she's going to have to come to terms with it, and the psychotherapist won't be able to do a thing. David

is impotent and he's going to stay that way, and no magic
potions or mind games are going to do anything about it.

By breakfast time, Carmen has rethought everything. She's
not going to cancel Isabella. She's just going to ask David if
he'll come with her. And if he refuses she'll just leave it. Then
it just doesn't matter. She is just beheading her boiled egg and
wondering how she should introduce the topic, when the
phone rings. Carmen gets to her feet and looks around for it.
Ah, it's on the table by the couch. Carmen walks slowly back
to the breakfast table with it. Typical, Laura's going to want to
know how it all went. Carmen notified Laura and Elvira of
her plans yesterday, and she told them both that she didn't
want to be disturbed under any circumstances. And now, of
course, Laura will be bursting with curiosity.

'Ah, Laura, how lovely. What's up?'

'You're one to talk!'

'That's true, but if you like I can come and pick you up . . .'

'What, where? Where are you going to pick me up?'

'Well, yes, no, maybe he'll come along as well, I could ask
him. When will you be there?' She sits down and looks at
David with a smile.

'Are you off your head? What are you talking about? I . . .'

'Yes, twelve would be fine. Isabella what . . .? Yes, and
where . . .? Great, I'll find it. It's no distance!'

'Could you explain what . . .'

'Terrific, Laura, that's great, see you at twelve, bye!' Carmen
hangs up and looks radiantly over at David. 'Hi from Laura.
Do you think you could disappear for two hours this afternoon? Yes?'

David shrugs his shoulders. 'Of course, why not? What is
it?'

'Laura's got an appointment with a psychotherapist and
she'd like us to pick her up.'

'What does she want with a therapist?'

'She has a few things to get off her chest, and maybe she
hopes that this Isabella or whatever her name is might be
able to help her.'

'I've no time for all that therapy nonsense.' That's what she was afraid of. 'But if it helps Laura, what do you need me there for? Wouldn't you rather speak woman to woman?'

'Oh, no,' says Carmen insistently. 'She asked specially for you. It's bound to do her good if we come together.'

'Okay. It makes no difference to me. I'll pick you up at the office just before twelve, okay?'

Carmen beams. She's over the first hurdle. Now she'll have to figure out how to get David on to Isabella's couch.

Carmen has hardly got to the office when Laura calls again. 'Tell me . . .'

'Okay,' Carmen interrupts her. 'I've somehow got to get David to see Isabella. And you can help me there, good friend that you are – aren't you?'

'After a beginning like that I can hardly go back, and anyway I've been wanting to examine my state of mind for a long time now. Particularly since an impotent man's going to be the father of my baby.' She laughs.

'Aren't you in the staff room?'

'No, I don't have to get back until this afternoon, I thought you'd worked that one out by now.'

'Oh, that works brilliantly.'

'Now, tell me what's up. I thought you'd lost your marbles this morning.'

Carmen looks over at Britta, who is rinsing crockery in the side-room. She won't hear everything. She turns around to face the window so that she can hear even less.

'Thanks for calling this morning, honestly. Perfect timing! At first I thought, typical, you can't contain your curiosity, but then I hit on this ploy of getting David to Isabella's this afternoon. You managed that brilliantly!'

'I did? Well, thanks. At least I've managed to do something. So, I'm listening, fire away.'

'It would be nice if you could be at Isabella's at about midday. I'll tell you what you need to know. You just wait for us in her room, and we'll join you. And you'll briefly outline your problem with Frederic's impotence, and Isabella will say there's a chance of a cure if Frederic would come to her office. And then I'll add a sentence . . .'

'This is turning into a bit of a farce.'

'Perhaps, but he's never going to go there of his own accord, I'm sure of it. So we'll have to introduce it almost in passing, and suddenly he'll be the focus of attention. And you can slope off!'

'Thanks, very kind of you. You should go into politics.'

Carmen laughs. 'So is that a date?'

'It's a date.'

Their timing is perfect, Britta is just coming back. But now she has to tell Isabella as well, and she also wants to call Maria. She promised she would do that. So she has to get rid of Britta. She's full to bursting, but she still asks if Britta would like to carry out the kind offer she made yesterday and dart out to the baker's.

'Croissants?' asks Britta kindly, as if she feels sorry for Carmen. Britta is bound to be having a full breakfast with her boyfriend every morning, and has everything in her kitchen, Carmen thinks scornfully for a moment before calling herself to order. Things are hard enough for Britta without somebody secretly making fun of her for it.

Carmen lets David find the address and the floor of the building. Isabella Prodan agreed with her suggestion, not immediately because she thought it dishonest, but finally as the last chance of helping David. Carmen briefly told her about her evening of love, and Isabella laughed heartily. Maybe she should give the recipe to the appropriate clients in future, she said.

Carmen rings the bell. David is wearing his black leather jacket with black jeans and a turquoise sweatshirt that perfectly matches his eyes. He is simply to die for, Carmen thinks, giving him a quick kiss.

He hugs her with a smile. 'I've never visited a therapist,' he says, and Carmen is about to say, 'this one's very nice,' but she manages to bite back the words at the last minute. The door opens, and Isabella is standing in front of them. David is clearly surprised. Once again, she's wearing a tight-fitting dress and elegantly applied make-up, very well-groomed, as though she had sprung from the cover of *Vogue*. David detaches himself from Carmen and introduces himself and Carmen. 'We're here to collect Laura Rapp.'

'Great, if you'd like to come in. We're just having a cup of coffee, perhaps I could offer you one too?'

'Thanks very much, that's very kind,' says Carmen quickly, before David can refuse. But he doesn't look as if he's about to. Isabella has turned away, and is walking towards her study. David is walking after her as though magnetically attracted. He wouldn't, thinks Carmen suspiciously, and falling behind. What if he falls in love with Isabella? Then she shakes her head. Nonsense. Isabella will have some wonderful boyfriend or husband, and what would a woman like that want with an impotent man anyway? She could cure him, her little devil whispers to her, but she's already standing in the room behind David. Laura is sitting on the couch exactly where she sat on Friday, and Isabella also asks Carmen and David to take a seat. Carmen sits beside Laura, David beside Isabella, who quickly gets two cups and then sits down gracefully. Her dark brown pageboy has a silken mahogany sheen, her face is flawless, she exudes the confidence of a successful woman. Through and through. You can practically smell it.

Carmen studies David. A funny feeling comes over her when she sees how he seems to be fascinated with Isabella's appearance. Laura seems to notice it as well. She glances at Carmen. Carmen shrugs her shoulders discreetly. That would be the final straw. She drags David along to a psychotherapist and immediately loses him to her. And then Isabella might make him potent again. That would be the absolute final straw. But David is practically rigid, studying Isabella as if he'd just encountered something incredible.

Isabella is busily making conversation without paying

David the slightest attention, giving Laura a number of buzz-words to which she doesn't react. Before she can say anything about herself and Frederic, David sits forward on his chair, moves closer to Isabella and looks her full in the face: 'Forgive me for asking, Frau Prodan, but do you happen to know a Regina Richter?'

'Regina?' Isabella looks at him in astonishment. 'She's my sister.'

'Ah,' David leans back, 'I thought I was seeing a ghost. The similarity was too incredible. Now it's obvious, of course. You've got married, so you've changed your name – but it's a funny coincidence all the same!'

Carmen and Laura look at each other. Now Isabella is interested too. 'How do you know my sister?'

'We went out with each other for a year.' He looks over at Carmen. 'I'm sorry, my dear, we haven't talked about anything like this.'

'Ah,' Isabella laughs, 'then you're – of course – David! Your surname meant nothing to me, but she told me lots about you, my little sister. You made a big impression on her.'

'Oh, really?' He looks over at Carmen again, and now it's clear that the subject's getting unpleasant for him. He probably wishes he'd never asked the question. 'But I don't think she was all that keen at the end. At least she was the one who insisted we split up.'

'Yes, and I know why. Because you were hyperactive day and night, weren't you? You finally drove her so crazy that I told her that you should split up.'

What? Carmen blushes. He wanted it day and night? That's what he told her. That was before his motorcycle accident. He did say that he was rather annoying to women. There's a short pause, and then David says quietly, 'But I'm not like that any more. I've stopped all that since my motorcycle accident, I've learned a thing or too. Recently I've learned a lot. Particularly thanks to Carmen.' He gives her a smile full of affection, and a warm feeling floods through Carmen. So everything's okay. How wonderful. He wasn't

responding to Isabella's attractiveness, just her resemblance
to his ex-girlfriend. Isn't life wonderful? Carmen snuggles
comfortably into her corner of the sofa.

'When did you have your accident?'

'Three years ago,' says Carmen automatically, thinking,
now everything's been set in motion. He knows her sister so
he's going to trust her and agree to a course of therapy. She's
done it!

'Three years ago?' says Isabella, looking at David.

He nods. 'Exactly. I seriously injured my legs and, unfortunately, my genitals as well. I met Carmen,' he glances over
at Carmen, 'can I tell her?' Carmen nods. 'I met Carmen,' he
says to Isabella, 'because I read a personal ad in which a
woman was looking for an impotent man. And since I quali-
fied I replied. And it was a great idea. We're very happy
together.'

Carmen nods from her corner.

Laura, who hasn't said a word so far, asks, 'Should I go?'

'No, stay for a bit,' says David, 'you know the story.'

'I'd like it,' Isabella says in a way that is at once emphatic,
full of authority and control and also at the same time kindly,
'if the two ladies would leave the room for a moment. Would
you mind?' She looks first at Carmen, then at Laura.

'No, no.' Carmen gets hastily to her feet, too hastily, she
thinks suddenly, with any luck David won't notice, maybe I
should have asked why, but she's happy that things are in
motion. So let's get out. Laura seems to feel much the same
thing, and they're at the door in a flash.

'Phew,' says Laura, leaning against the wall. 'Boy, was I
happy when you turned up, I thought she was going to turn
me inside out. I was in there with her for a quarter of an hour
and now she knows everything. The baby, Frederic, the father
of the child, the situation – do you think she's going to send
me a bill?'

'She's sure to send me one.'

Carmen leans against the receptionist's counter. As always
at this time of day, Isabella's colleagues are on their break.

'Do you think it's going okay in there?' she asks.

'Why shouldn't it? The conditions look good. She knows him from her sister's stories – he must have been a bit of a ladies' man, your David – and she knows about the motorcycle accident too. Didn't your menu work? You haven't told me a thing about it. Or about your visit to that herbal witch. All you said was that I couldn't call you. That's really uplifting, I can tell you.'

She runs her ten fingers through her short black hair, presses one foot against the wall and pushes the lower part of her body forward. Boots, Diesel jeans and a big jacket – Laura as she lives and breathes. Carmen just can't imagine Laura with a fat belly. She has a completely boyish figure, straight down from top to bottom, no problems with her figure. Will her belly be able to expand enough to hold a baby?'

'Hey, what's up? Are you dreaming?' asks Laura.

'I was just wondering what you're going to look like with a big belly.'

Laura shakes her head. 'You'll see that anyway. Just tell me what happened!'

Carmen describes the previous day in slow motion, and has just got to the prepared piece of ginger when the door to Isabella's study bursts open.

David charges out, hoists a puzzled Carmen into the air and pushes her down the corridor. Laura stands there completely dumbfounded, and Isabella has come running after him laughing. Carmen can't understand what's got into him, she can hardly stand upright and she's getting dizzy.

'David, David,' she cries, and he throws her over his shoulders, grabs Laura by the arm in passing, pulls her along and says, 'You've got to listen to this. It's the joke of the century. The millennium! It's just unbelievable!'

He drops Carmen down on the couch, hurls himself down beside her and motions to Laura to come and sit in an armchair.

'Isabella, you tell it!'

They're talking as if they'd known each other for ages, Carmen says to herself in astonishment. What could that mean?

'Okay . . .' but Isabella breaks off immediately. 'I'm sorry, but it's the sort of story that needs an accompaniment. Just a moment!' She walks over to her tall, narrow designer cupboard, opens it and then goes to the fridge, coming back with a bottle of champagne and four glasses.

'This is going on my bill,' she says to Carmen with a laugh.

Carmen hasn't the faintest idea what's going on. David opens the bottle and pours the champagne, and Isabella sits down with a smile all over her face.

'What's up?' asks Carmen.

'Just a moment.' Isabella raises her glass and they all clink glasses. 'To David's potency,' she toasts. Fine by me, thinks Carmen and drinks. Then she puts her glass down. What now? She looks expectantly at Isabella, and then at David, who erupts, 'Don't you understand?'

Carmen shakes her head. What's to understand? We're drinking to David's potency. Well, she was doing that for the whole of yesterday evening.

Laura is the first to understand. She crashes her glass down. 'David isn't impotent at all, is he?'

'What?' Carmen looks at David, who is sitting next to her with a grin all over his face. 'It's impossible? Why not? Of course you're impotent! You have been the whole time! How come you're not all of a sudden? It's fantastic!' She shakes her head. 'I don't understand. What's up? David?'

He hurls himself at her, so that she tips over and lies underneath him. He kisses her, embraces her firmly and then sits back up with her, without letting her so much as an inch away from him.

'Ow,' says Carmen, 'you're hurting me – and could somebody please explain . . .'

'Okay,' Isabella says and sips from her glass, raising it to David and Carmen and putting it back down. 'The solution to the riddle is quite simple, Carmen. You were looking for an impotent man, so David played an impotent man. At first just because he wanted to see you again, and then so that he wouldn't lose you!'

'What? What's up? You're not impotent at all? You never were?'

David shakes his head. 'No, and I hope you'll forgive me, but it was the only thing I could do. I couldn't escape from that vicious circle. Isabella only just told me that you were desperately trying to make me potent. And I could have laughed myself sick, you can understand that!'

'No.' Carmen slides a little way away from him. 'Sorry, but I don't understand at all. You replied to my ad, like everyone else. How did you know that I . . .'

'Shall I go?' Laura slips out of her chair a little way.

'Stay where you are,' says Carmen. 'Okay, I've got to know. I don't know what I feel now, whether I should be pleased, or whether I feel I've been deceived, or how or what, because it's all much too crazy. You replied to my ad!'

'You sat with that clown in the Café Mohren listening to his gobbledegook. And I was listening. And at first I couldn't work it out. Only when you had left did I notice the paper with the ad marked with a red cross. And then everything fell into place.'

'In the Café Mohren,' Carmen nods slowly. 'You were the one sitting alone. That's why I had that funny feeling by the door . . . and then you acted out that stupid part for me? Don't you think that's cruel?'

'I wanted to see you again, that was all. And I wasn't playing a part, it was all real as far as I was concerned. And then there was the fact that I really was rethinking my behaviour towards women. And I thought a bit of impotence couldn't do me any harm, it might solve the problem. So it wasn't deceitful.'

Carmen sits bolt upright beside him. 'And then?'

'The first time I met you I fell in love with you. And it got worse and worse. And then there was no turning back. And whenever I asked you if my impotence was so important to you, you always said it was. So what was I to do?'

Now Carmen bursts out laughing for the first time. 'I said it was because I didn't want to hurt you!'

'You even said it was the last time we were in bed together, when I was almost ready, in the face of reason, to put my cards on the table. I asked you if my impotence didn't really get on your nerves, do you remember?' Carmen nods. 'And you answered: "No, I love you!" So what was I to do? I was afraid of losing you the minute you discovered that I constantly had an . . .' he glances at Isabella, 'well, an erection!'

Carmen wraps her arms around him. 'So that was the reason for all that palaver, with you darting away whenever I tried to get close to you!'

'I couldn't really put a spell on it or tie it down with a bandage. All I could do was hide it, preferably in jeans, or keep you away from it. It's obvious!'

'And last night?'

'I still haven't worked it out. But something got to me and I thought I was going to burst. I couldn't bear it, so I had to take my leave for a moment in order to go and relieve myself. And that wasn't much use either, and neither was the cold shower. If you remember, I went to sleep on my stomach. That is, I didn't get to sleep. Yesterday it was worse than it has been for ages. I almost think it was worse than it's ever been!'

All three women laugh heartily. 'Haven't you told him?' Carmen asks Isabella. She shakes her head and laughs so hard that little tears form in the corners of her eyes. 'Maybe you'll do the whole thing again some time, Carmen – successfully, this time!' And Laura shakes with laughter as well.

Now it's David who glances irritably from one to the other. 'One thing isn't clear to me,' Carmen says to Isabella. 'How did you find out that David was potent?'

'Easy. His story about the motorcycle accident couldn't be true from the time point of view. He couldn't have become impotent three years ago, because he was still going out with my sister two years ago – and he was certainly potent then!'

David grins guiltily, then reaches affectionately for Carmen's head with both hands, and asks her, face to face, 'Is it so terrible that I'm not impotent? Can we try again? I wouldn't like to lose you. I'd like to keep you. For ever. And if you don't want to sleep with me I'll leave you alone. And anyway there are other things we can do.'

Carmen throws her arms around his neck and whispers in his ear, 'Shall we go home?'

She smells his sharp after-shave and feels his rough cheek, and he presses her firmly to him. 'Your place or mine?'

She laughs. 'Mine!'

'So, shall we play hooky this afternoon?' He nibbles at her ear.

'I reckon we've a lot of catching up to do. And on the way home let's get some Christmas cake. The baker's should have them by now.'

'What for?'

'I'll tell you later, my darling, you'll see!'